BALLAD OF THE FALLEN GODS BOOK 1

FALLING STAR

RYAN EDWARD JONES

Mosaic Night Publishing LLC

801 White Sands Blvd #1082

Alamogordo, NM 88310

Ryan.E.Jones@MosaicNightPublishing.com

Mosaic Night Publishing is an imprint of Mosaic Night Publishing LLC. Visit our website at www.mosaicnightpublishing.com.

Cover art and design by Book Cover Station

Interior Map Illustrations by Alec M

Hardback ISBN 979-8-9905899-0-2

Paperback ISBN 979-8-9905899-1-9

Ebook ISBN 979-8-9905899-2-6

First Edition May 2024

About the Author

Ryan Edward Jones graduated from Georgia Southern University with his Bachelors of Arts in Studio Art. While in his undergraduate study, Ryan became a member of the most honorable Sigma Lambda Beta International Fraternity Incorporated. The brotherhood, which focuses on cultural awareness and diversity opened him up to a new world of possibilities. It's through these possibilities that Ryan became determined to continue his pursuit of creative nirvana.

In his pursuit, Ryan's journey led him to Full Sail University, where he entered their Masters of Fine Arts program in Creative Writing. After some time his pursuit lead him down another path that he did not know would expand his search for creative nirvana. He enlisted and became a proud service member and veteran in The United States Air Force. Be swept away to worlds of Science Fiction and Fantasy, as you experience the captivating and enduring stories of his work. Ryan has traversed many paths and countless years in his pursuit. For not all who wander are lost, just yet.

Dylian kingdom
ASTILE
Fae Commonwealth
ELENDRA
The Dawn Sea
Western Arctic Wastes
The Evening Star Sea
Cape of Auron
Renata Republic
LAROUNGE
Nimh Theocracy
UMBARAH
Umbar Sultanate
ORIANA

Zenith Imperium
...PIRE
The Night Sea
Eastern Arctic Wastes
Free Cities
PORT SORENA
HOENHEIM
The Morning Star Sea
...SONKIN Tribal Lands
...BAD

Houtende
Eisenfeld
Vinsler
Basaw
Turgrave Steppe
Kirachow
NIMH
THEOCRACY
LAROUNGE
Poimiers
Shattered Marshes
Nocturne
Nalran
Kor'Jarin
Kor'nal
Riogo
Ovala
Ri'Jar
UMBAR
SULTANATE
UMBARAH
Ramah
Stonecrest
Cape of Auron
Aurontil
HOENHEIM
SB Ferry
Railhall
Propert
Southern Cross
RENATA
REPUBLIC
Waldensteig
Gulf of Twilight
Ermouklcio
Ialpagou
Chionnis
Lasinde
DRAKOBAD
DRAGONKIN
TRIBAL LANDS
TALIAN
The Southern Continent

PROLOGUE

On the storm-filled night the soldiers attacked the village on the edge of the Outnora Forest. A thunderous storm raging outside concealed the approaching footsteps. A cohort of soldiers was making their way through the cobblestone streets of the village. The soldiers were clad; in dark Behemoth leather studded gambeson, trousers, and boots. Orichalcum cuirass, pauldrons, greaves, and vibrances where layered on top.

They wore a long black cloak, lined with a purple inlay. Carrying with them a halberd or mace in hand, sword, and dagger at their waist. Atop their heads ornate Orichalcum half-helms covered them from the nose up. The bottom of their faces below covered with a Daemon mouth mouthguard.

These men were no ordinary company of soldiers. They were the elite soldiers of the Zenith Imperium, the Arcanum Praetorian. There was no sign or warning that the soldiers where coming. As serious threats were never apart of daily life in a village on the outer fringes of the Zenith Imperium. That stormy night proved to be a fatal lesson for the village. The people who had called it their home for many generations would never forget. What happened next would haunt the young boy and shape the man that he would become.

"Break off and search the residences. Find the mother and child, take out any who resist. Bring them to me and let no escape." The dark cloaked figure atop a mighty warhorse commanded.

"Yes, Lord Commander." The soldiers replied in unison.

In pairs of four, the cohort of Zenith Imperium soldiers broke off. They made their way down the streets to the doors of several different houses. The boy's house was the final house that the soldier's would assault. One by one, the soldiers began their assault as they struck each of the seven house doors. With a forceful impact that blew the doors apart.

Screams echoed throughout the village. The sound of clashing swords and armored footsteps sprang into action. The soldiers struck fast as they struck down any they found inside the houses, be they man, woman, or child. They were not there to capture the villagers. This was an execution. The elimination of dissidents against the authority of the imperium.

The door to the boy's room opened as his mother came rushing in with a traveler's pack and short sword in hand. Quickly closing the door behind her. A faint bluish glow began emanating from it. She set down the items beside the wall and woke the boy from his sleep. He was still half a sleep, when the items his mother brought came into focus.

He noticed the weary look in his mother's deep aquamarine eyes. They were the same color as his. Though his mother had auburn hair, his was of a white-silvery color, just like that of his late father.

"Mo...Mother, what is with that look in your eyes."

"There isn't much time. I need you to grab the traveler's pack and short sword I placed against the wall and climb out of your window."

"What is going on?"

"You must hurry and do as I say. There isn't much time left before they come, and by then I fear it may be too late." His mother responded in a calm but stern voice.

He didn't know what he should do. Should he do as his mother instructed, or should he press her for answers. That decision would be made for him. That moment a thunderous crash came from downstairs. The front door exploded apart into their home.

"We are out of time, hurry and do as I have asked of you, my dear loving son. Know that I will always love you."

He got up and grabbed the items his mother had set aside for him, making his way over the window. He grabbed hold of the ledge and jumped out his window, landing on the top of the roof below his bedroom window. Rain was pouring down onto him, as the storm continued to rage on. Slowly making his way towards the edge of the roof and climbing down the side of his house. When he got to the ground, he stopped and looked back up to his window. where he saw his mother crash through, her body bloodied and bruised flying through the air.

Run, was the last thing the boy could hear his mother say, just before her body struck the ground with a hard impact. Pushed by her last words, he turned and ran as fast as his feet could take him. He ran towards the deep shrouded growth of the Outnora Forest. His mind was a blank haze as he focused on getting away from his house and the village, he had called home for 13 years. He didn't know what was going on or why his mother had to die.

 He knew that he would do whatever it took to survive and find the answers to his questions. There was no going back and nothing for him to do but keep moving. one foot in front of the other and not look back, never looking back.

CHAPTER I
BELLAMY LEONE

5 *years later.*

It was a warm midsummer's day. There was a gentle breeze flowing through the trees and tall grass of the Torgrave Steppe. Off in the distance was a small herd of Torgrave Elk grazing on the lush tall and fertile grass of the steppe. Unaware of the cold piercing aquamarine eyes patiently watching their moves. He Reached into the dark leather quiver strapped along his back.

Bellamy grabbed an arrow and notched the recurve bow in his opposite hand. Rising from his kneeling position, he drew the arrow back and took aim of his target in the distance. The Torgrave Elk was a massive and swift creature, making it a rather difficult animal to hunt.

He had been following the tracks of this specific herd for a few days now. He would have to finish up soon, if he was hoping to get paid for the job. These types of jobs tend to be time sensitive and more difficult to complete. The pay was well worth it, if you had the skills to handle it. Bellamy knew that he had the skills to complete the job this time around and was going to get his proper share.

Aiming for the small area along the elk's neck below its jaw, Bellamy shot his arrow. The arrow left his bow and flew in a swift and fluid motion when it struck its target head-on.

One by one the small herd of Torgrave Elk let out a pained groan. collapsing to the ground, as five other arrows struck their targets an instant later.

"Alright, let's get the elk bound up and placed into the wagon. Good job on today's hunt." The loud commanding voice of the captain said to the others positioned around Bellamy.

"Nice shot, kid. Your training seems to have been paying off. Though, there is always room for improvement."

"I told you before, don't call me a kid Raine."

"True, but the way I see it, you are like a kid compared to me my friend. Or have you forgotten I am older than I appear, one of the many blessings of my kin." Raine responded with a sly smile, that women seemed to find charming.

Raine Rollo was a half Human and half Demi-Human, of the Wolf-Beastmen variety. He was tall with the athletic slender muscular build characteristic of his kind. With brown eyes, blackish grey fur ears and tail. There was a tribal band tattoo that ran down the side of his neck to his left upper forearm. Though Bellamy knew better than to be fooled by that smile.

Raine was an interesting sort of character to behold. He would come off as charming and charismatic with that smile of his to any woman that caught his eye. But beneath that mask was contempt and a sleeping rage, bottled away deep inside.

Bellamy had seen this side of Raine, in the early days. When he had first joined the company in the trade-city of Aurontil, in the Renata Republic. They had returned to the city after finishing up a job, and was enjoying at a local tavern. Then some drunk patrons spilled their drinks on him. At first, Raine collected himself. He calmly told the drunkards to apologize and watch where they were going.

This didn't happen and the drunkards pushed him aside and walked out of the tavern. That would most likely have been the end of it. but the drunkards were harassing one of the tavern maidens outside. Raine walked out and confronted them.

"It is one thing to spill your drinks on me and then brush me off. That I could've let go and considered it a drunken mistake. What I will not forgive is your brazen actions against this young tavern maiden, you have been harassing."

"This doesn't concern the likes of you. Now, if you don't mind the young maiden and I were having a conversation here, so piss off you lousy half-bred mutt."

That was one mistake that would cost them. For in that instant Raine jolted forward and struck the drunk brute square in the gut. He staggered backwards as he clenched at his stomach catching his breathe.

"Get him!" The drunk brute screamed through a strained voice.

The four other men with the drunken brute, rushed towards Raine and began attacking him. They swung at him from many directions. Each of the blows blocked or parried off to the side by Raine quick reflexes. For each blow that missed him, he struck back with a blow as fierce as the last. The brutes had no chance of matching Raine's skill and athleticism.

They hoped to overpower him with their numbers. One of the brutes managed to grab ahold of Raine from behind, a towering bulky half-giant brute. He squeezed Raine in a tight constricting embrace and raised him up off the ground.

Raine arched his head forward. He pushed back, headbutting the brute square in the face. Then kicking in his knees. The towering brute collapsed backwards and Raine broke free from his embrace. The other brutes stared, turned from him, and ran away in panic. One stayed behind, the brute that had started the whole confrontation. Pulling out a dagger from his side, he charged towards Raine while his back was turned away.

Raine summersaulted over the brute. He grabbed hold of his hand, and plunged the dagger into the attacker's gut.

The brute collapsed to the ground and died in a pool of blood. Raine walked over to the tavern maiden escorting her back inside. To collect her thoughts and move on from the terrible ordeal. That was the first time Bellamy had seen the skill and contempt that lied beneath the mask of Raine's smile.

Bellamy and Raine headed over to the Torgrave Elks, they killed. They began the process of binding them up, to transport them back to the city. Once the elk were bound, the members of the party assisted in carrying the elk to the wagon to be loaded on, one at a time. It was before midday when the party finished loading up the wagon. After retrieving their arrows from the downed elks.

 Bellamy hopped onto the front of the wagon to drive the horses. Raine and two others hopped into the back of the wagon. The captain and his vice-captain followed along the wagon on their own horses.

"Bellamy, we will head back to Aurontil by the northern road and eastern path. Take shifts and switch out amongst yourselves, we will not be stopping on the way back." The vice-captain advised.

"Yes, ma'am. We will do as you advised vice-captain Mira."

The trip back to Aurontil took only a day and a half, by traveling the northern road and eastern path. Bellamy was sleeping in the back of the wagon. He awakened as the wagon was coming down the path and he saw the sight of the trade city below. Situated in a secluded valley surrounded by towering cliffs on the edge of the Cape of Auron laid the city of Aurontil. It was a major trading hub.

Often the first-place people would come to, on their way to the center of the Renata Republic. For this reason, Aurontil was known as "the Gateway to the South". Making it the ideal place to find whatever it was that you might be searching for. Be it coin, commerce, or anything between.

After passing through the outer gates of the city. The party made their way to the Market Town District to head a Merchant's guild shop to turn in their haul. They collected their reward. The captain gave each member of his party their share for the job. He went off on his own, along with the vice-captain and one other.

The job had proved to be a lucrative one indeed. As after the shares were split, Bellamy was able to walk away with 2 Gold Dragon and 10 Silver Stag Renatan Notes. The only ones still waiting outside the Merchant's guild shop was Bellamy, Raine, and one of the newer members of the company Na'naya.

Na'naya Adina was a twenty-six-year-old Human female from one of the ancient desert tribes in the Umbar Desert, a part of the domain of the Umbar Sultanate. She was tall with a slender athletic build, with a beige-mocha skin tone common amongst her people. She had scarlet eyes, and long flowing deep auburn hair. She wore three jeweled braids woven in-between. This had been the fifth job she took, since joining the company a half year ago. She was respected and well-liked by the members of the company.

 She had proved herself to be a smart and capable travel companion. Generally even tempered, Na'naya has a bit of an appetite for booze. She could be somewhat unorthodox when deep in the wells of her booze. Bellamy, Raine, and Na'naya had become close friends over the course of their jobs together, becoming a close nit trio.

"So, what are your plans for today, now that the job is done?" Na'naya asked.

"I don't have any plans today. So, I will see where the day leads." Raine replied.

"There was something I wanted to check on, so I'll make my way to Messenger's Hollow in the Shipyards District. I might be able to find something out there, if what they say about the place is true." Bellamy responded.

Raine and Na'naya looked at one another with a subtle look of concern on their faces. Though, they knew Bellamy well enough. To know that he would find a way to go anyway if they tried to convince him otherwise. So, they decided on the obvious course of action instead.

"Alright, then its settled. We will go with you to Messenger's Hollow as well." They said in unison.

"Thank you, guys, I appreciate the company."

"It's no problem at all. Besides, someone must keep a watch on you and make sure you stay out of trouble."

"And I for one, don't want to be the one to explain to the captain and vice-captain why I wasn't there to watch out for you." Raine interjected.

The three of them set out and made their way through the crowded streets of the Market Town District. Passed the shops of stalls of vendors from all over the Renata Republic and lands beyond. As they went down the streets and got closer to the Shipyards District. there was fewer shops, more warehouses, and shipyards around the docks closest to the Cape of Auron. This part of Aurontil was where most of the travelers would first arrive when coming to the city by way of the ocean.

 It was crowded during different times throughout the day. Today was one of the quieter days. So there weren't many people around as the group made their way to western side of the docks. On the western side of the docks, towards the outer edge of the Guardian cliffs that encompassed the cape was a staircase leading down to a landing below. A solitary building was at its center and built into part of the lower cliffside. This was the infamous and renowned tavern known as Messenger's Hollow.

Bellamy walked up the steps and down the arched tunnel leading the front entrance of Messenger's Hollow. He was closely followed by Raine and Na'naya behind him. The door to the hollow was a massive oak and metal studded door. Bellamy raised his hand and knocked with three short consecutive knocks. An eye slit in the center of the door opened and a set of bold hazel eyes looked out upon the trio.

"What do you want. This is a private establishment, and no entry is permitted without a pass or a member's mark." A solemn grizzled voice responded.

"Me and my companions are here to speak with Madame Rhea."

"Haha…ha. Run along kid, no one speaks to the Madame without a direct invitation from the mistress herself."

Bellamy reached into his coat pocket and pulled out a small note of parchment with a wax seal affixed to it. He lifted it up to show the man behind the eye slit for him to see. The man carefully looked over the seal affixed to the parchment and closed the eye slit moments later.

"Let's go Bellamy, it doesn't look like he is going to let us in. We will just have to figure something else out instead." Na'naya replied.

"It would seem so. Alright let's leave." Bellamy responded.

Just then as the trio was turning to leave, the massive oak and metal studded doors of the Messenger's Hollow swung open. Standing to the left and right of them were two Demi-Humans twins of the Half-Giant variety. They were Muscular and bulky figures of immense stature. Long nightshade dreadlocks and matching goatees. They were the bouncers of Messenger's Hollow and Madame Rhea's personal bodyguards. Each one an exceptional warrior. The one closest to the trio on the left was Knox, and to the right his twin brother Locke.

The trio preceded through the threshold and made their way into the tavern/ brothel and gambling den that was Messenger's Hollow. The building was split into three floors, with the bottom level being the tavern and the casino areas. The second floor being the rooms for patrons to sample the women or men that sell their bodies here. Last was the third floor. The third floor was the offices and private residence of the mistress of Messenger's Hollow Madame Rhea.

Publicly, her reputation was that of an innovative and talented businesswoman. who has ties on both sides of the law if you are to believe the whispers of common travelers and merchants. Privately, she was known through select circles by her reputation. Throughout the Renata Republic and other nations as a key information broker. Able to acquire any information a client needed, for the right price of course.

The first floor was packed with various groups of people, from different social classes and races. Sitting at the bar counter, the scattered tables, and booths, or at the different game tables along the backside of the floor. There were also courtesans walking around amongst them. Flirting, and chatting with the patrons, trying to convince them to go upstairs with them and sample what they had to offer. A lively and soothing melody was encompassing the area, being played by a group of bards on a stage to the left of where Raine was standing.

"So, what now Bellamy? Now that we managed to get inside."

"I guess, we just enjoy ourselves and wait until we are granted an audience with the Madame, Na'naya." Bellamy responded.

"Sounds like a plan. If you don't mind me, I am going to head over to the bar and get myself something to drink." Raine replied.

"Just be on your best behavior, Raine. I don't want something to happen, or you get us kicked out before we are even able to talk to Madame Rhea."

Raine smiled at Bellamy and just waved his hand towards him.

"I don't know what you are talking about, but whatever I get you loud and clear. Well, I'm off you two."

Raine left the side of Bellamy and Na'naya making his way over to the bar. Bellamy and Na'naya looked at each other and just smiled back to one another.

"We just got paid for completing a job, and I am feeling lucky. I think I'm going to make my way over to the gaming tables and try to improve my funds. See yeah, Bellamy" Na'naya replied with a coy smile as she walked away and headed to the gaming tables in the back.

[*Well, okay then. I guess I'll just go and enjoy the music for a little while.*] Bellamy thought to himself. Bellamy made his way through the group of tables. He found an empty booth in the corner across from the stage and took a seat. A serving girl had stopped by the booth and took his order for a tankard of mead and a bowl of soup with bread. No more than fifteen minutes later the serving girl returned with Bellamy's order, and he paid her for the meal. The mead was a local brew found all over the republic. the soup and bread was a specialty dish, normally found in the artic regions of the Zenith Imperium.

The poles of this world were inverse. The northern and southern areas were warm and tropical areas. While the eastern and western areas were cold and artic. Then the regions in-between would tend be a mixture of warm and cold depending upon the season. Bellamy was a bit surprised when he saw that item on the menu.

 As it was normally found in the imperium rarely if ever, found a following outside its domain. This occurring on part because of the imperium's aggressive and expansion tendencies. Often conflicting with other nations that don't agree with its philosophy. It had been a few years since the last time Bellamy was able to eat this soup and bread. The taste filled him with a sense of nostalgia and sadness. as the soup reminded Bellamy of the one his mother used to make for them. Comforting them on the cold winter nights that would hit his village.

"Greetings, darling. Can I offer you another drink, or perhaps the lovely pleasure of my company." A voice calm and silky asked.

Bellamy returning to his senses, looked up at the figure who had spoken to him. The Demi-Human woman was of the Djinn Variety. Her skin was a bluish grey, with accents of green, that matched her emerald eye. There was a fine ornate eye band that covered her right eye, that wrapped around her forehead like a scarf. Long flowing white-blonde hair ran down her head to the small of her back.

She was a slender beauty who had an hourglass figure. With a buxom chest to her round ass. Her well-toned legs protruding from the slit in her long flowing elegant purple silk dress.

CHAPTER 2

"Pardon me. I was lost in thought for a moment there. I appreciate your kindness, but I'm afraid I will have to decline your offer." Bellamy replied.

"Uh. What a pity. I guess I'll be on my way then. Until the next time, do take care Bellamy."

A surprised look of recognition came across Bellamy's face. He didn't recall ever telling the woman standing next to him, his name. She turned to walk away, but before she did, she leaned over till her lips were right next to Bellamy's ear. Whispering into it with a gentle and alluring voice.

"Follow me if you please, the Madame is ready to meet you upstairs in her office."

Then she turned and started walking towards the staircase leading to the upper floors. Bellamy got up from the booth and placed his money down on the table for his meal and followed behind the woman. They made their way up the carved staircase to second floor above. Walking down the hallways past the different pleasure rooms available to the paying patrons. Bellamy followed his guide. They made their way through the decorative halls of artwork and statues aligning the walls of the upper floors of Messenger's Hollow. Taking in the views of grandeur and mystery that made the place a true exotic wonder to be hold.

The brief sounds of heated passion were echoing off the walls and being mixed in with the sounds of the actions on the floor below. After passing through another hallway, they came upon another staircase. This one rounded and more ornate than the one they had used to get to the second floor. At the top of the staircase was an open landing that split off into two different directions. A pair of finely carved Inkheartwood doors, flanked by Artic Werecat statues on each side.

The woman pushed open the doors and walked inside the room laying beyond. Inside the room was tall Eldarwood bookcases, lined with books, scrolls, parchments, and other small objects. There was a plush couch with a coffee table and three chairs by its side. An antique desk with a tall, cushioned chair behind them towards the back center of the room.

Though, the sight that caught Bellamy's attention, was the massive window along the backwall taking up most of it. Each pane was connected through an interweaving metallic frame of precious metal. Creating the cascading effect of a blooming flower. From the window the expansive view of the cape of Auron and the surrounding city could be seen. As if it were a masterpiece painted by a legendary master. The woman walked over to the desk and picked up an ivory and rosewood inlaid smoking pipe laying on the desk. She made her way to the couch, lighting the pipe and taking a seat.

"Please, have a seat Bellamy. Afterall, you came all this way to see me, and we have somethings to discuss."

Bellamy understood at once that the one he had come to see, was none other than the woman who had led him to the office, Madame Rhea herself. He walked over and took a seat in one of the chairs across from where Madame Rhea was seated.

"So, tell me Bellamy, what is it that you have come here to ask of me today? One thing though, do be honest with me. It's in the best interest of your friends downstairs and yourself...that you don't lie to me or try to deceive me. I have ways of finding the truth." Madame Rhea responded in a lighthearted yet threatingly calm and cold tone.

Bellamy paused and took a deep breath, organizing his thoughts. He contemplated how he would respond to her. Madame Rhea inhaled from her pipe and exhaled a puff of white cloudy smoke, as she waited for Bellamy's reply.

"I have thought about it over the years and realized that I have more questions than I have answers. It has puzzled me on what would be the right course of action to take and how might I get the answers I'm looking for. Then awhile back I heard whispers and tales of an information broker, who could practically find out any information that you could hope to find. I knew then that this person might be able to assist me in my search for answers. Which eventually lead me here to you, by the letter you sent me a week ago."

Madame Rhea didn't say a word. She just looked at Bellamy with a deep gaze of her emerald eye and took another puff of her pipe. Bellamy looked back to her, ready to say something else, when she raised her hand in a wait one moment motion. He held back from asking his question.

"Alright. There was no lies or deceit in your words. I will hear out what you have to say and decide from there if I will offer my services to you or send you on your way, Bellamy."

"Thank you for hearing my request, Madame Rhea. I appreciate the consideration in the matter."

"Don't thank me just yet, I haven't agreed to help you and if I do, know that nothing comes without an equal exchange. So, I will be expecting something from you as well of equal value in return." Madame Rhea interjected.

Bellamy was willing to do whatever it took. Whatever she asked of him in return to get the answers he had been searching for all these years.

"Six years ago, in my village on the edge of the Outnora Forest in the Zenith Imperium, my mother and six other families in the village were murdered by soldiers from the imperium. They weren't no ordinary group of soldiers either; they were knights of the Arcanum Praetorian. Elite soldiers and the personal protectors of the emperor and the imperial royal family."

"That is a very interesting tale you have there. Interesting indeed. I wonder...." Madame Rhea paused thinking to herself.

"...Well, no matter for the time being. Go ahead and continue with your request, Bellamy."

"I know it may come off as simple and straight forward. But it might prove to be difficult if not impossible, given the time that has passed. I would like you to investigate the incident. See if you could find out any information on why it happened. For what reason was it deemed necessary to kill my mother and the others. I would have been killed as well if it wasn't for my mother and the time, she gave me to escape." Bellamy finished.

Madame Rhea picked up a small bell resting on the coffee table and gave it a rang. A few moments later a servant walked into the office carrying a tray with tea and small cakes. She placed the tray on the coffee table and turned to exit the office, closing the doors behind her. Madame Rhea set down her pipe, laying it on the table in a stand and grabbed a slice of one on the small desert cakes. Looking at the desert cakes on the tray, Bellamy reached over and grabbed a slice of one as well.

He took a bite of the crumble and berry cake that was on his plate, the delicious taste enthralling his senses. Bellamy had eaten desert cake a couple of time before. But he had never had the opportunity to taste one as sweet and delectable as the one he was eating now. It was a pastry that would normally only be found amongst the upper-class and nobility. Or in a place like this that had patrons of various means and stature.

"It's delicious, isn't it? My personal chef who makes them used to be a skilled culinary master from the Free Cities and now works for me."

"Yes, it was certainly unlike any desert cake I have ever tasted before."

"I thought over your request Bellamy and will take on the job for you. Like I told you earlier you will have to do something in exchange for me as well..." Madame Rhea paused before continuing.

"If you choose not to then are business here is done. You can go about looking for other ways to get your answers. though I can guarantee that no one else will be able to do what I can do. So, will you do what I ask of you, or will you walk away?"

Bellamy finished up his desert cake and placed the plate back onto the tray. He took a sip of the warm herbal tea in front of him before giving Madame Rhea his response.

"What is the job that you would have me do for you, in exchange for you fulfilling my request?"

"Very well. Listen closely and pay attention as I rarely repeat myself. Head south to the republic's capital of Hoenheim and meet up with one of my informants there. He is serving as an aide for one of the senators in the Renatan Parliament. He has an important parcel, and I want you to go and retrieve it for me. Bring it back here and the job will be considered fulfilled."

Bellamy had an uneasy feeling about the job, he had done courier jobs before. This one yet seemed different and wasn't as straight forward as it was looking to be. He had told Madame Rhea that he would do whatever she asked of him. He wasn't about to back out now that he was getting a step closer to the answers he was seeking.

"One question first, if you don't mind me asking."

"I don't mind. Go ahead and ask your question."

"If the job you are asking for is a simple delivery job, why didn't you just have one of your subordinates do the job for you instead?"

Madame Rhea's emerald colored eye glinted with a shine. She leaned back on the couch and a gave Bellamy a teasing smile.

"I'm impressed. You are a clever young man, that's a good thing. Means I've found the right person for the job. I have received word that there are other parties that are interested in my parcel and want to get it before I can. So, I need a more subtle approach in acquiring it first. Someone clever and with the skills to handle the job. That's where you come in Bellamy. I have heard about your reputation working for the Falling Star Mercenary Company. I have been keeping an eye on you."

"Well, that explains the invitation you sent me. So, you already knew that I was looking for information. That the best chance I had of ever getting it would be to seek you out. I was already a piece in your game, and I didn't even realize it." Bellamy replied coldly.

Madame Rhea just stayed there looking at the cold look he gave her back. not of anger but one of disappointment in himself. For not realizing that he never really had the choice of backing out from the job, even if it seemed like an option.

"You may enter now." Madame Rhea commanded in an alluring yet authoritative voice.

The doors to the office sung open and a Demi-Human woman of the Half-Giant variety stepped into the office. She was tall with a certain wild beauty to her, with the athletic muscular build common amongst her kind. With medium length brunette hair that was parted in a mohawk on the right-side and braids on the left. Her eyes were a light-chestnut color, and she had a mighty Warhammer strapped to her back. Resting over her fur cloak and barbarian leather cuirass inlaid with crisscrossed straps and buckles. Thick formfitting tights covered her well-toned legs and fur topped leather boots with metal toe plates adorned her feet.

"This is Inara Novik; she will be joining your group as a guide and bodyguard. Her talents are top rank, she should prove to be a valuable team member. If you need any information or advice about the job, feel free to ask her, as she is one of my best and trusted agents."

"If that is you command my mistress then it will be done." Inara replied.

"Good, then our business here in concluded for the time being. I suggest you prepare your things and be ready to leave within the next two days. It is not a time sensitive matter but do be diligent in your time. Inara will show you back out and will be waiting for the rest of you to join her at the Eastern Gate. Good day, Bellamy." Madame Rhea finished speaking and moved from the couch over to her chair behind the antique desk. Focusing on some scrolls she had spread out.

Inara turned towards the doors and gestured for Bellamy to follow her. He got up from his chair followed her out of the office, and back down the rounded staircase he had first come up. As they were walking down the halls back toward the main staircase. Bellamy noticed that Inara walked in a deliberate and purposeful manner. With sleek and elegant movements not so common with her kind.

There was no wasted or unnecessary movement in her steps, a sign that she was indeed a skilled warrior. Honed through actual experiences and not mere practice. When they made it back downstairs Bellamy looked around to see if he could spot his friends. He found Na'naya was just finishing up at one of the gambling tables in the back and making her way towards him. Raine was still at the bar flirting with one of the bartenders, when he noticed Bellamy at the bottom of the staircase. He told the bartender that his friends were waiting for him, so he paid his tab and gave her a wink and a smile.

"Until next time, lovely maiden. I look forward to our next encounter."

The bartender blushed a light rose color across her freckled cheeks, as Raine made his way back to his friends. With the trio back together, they made their way and left Messenger's Hollow, and the Shipyards District behind them.

CHAPTER 3

T he Falling Star Mercenary Company's Guild Hall was in the Northwest of the Market Town District. A few blocks down from the gates leading into the Upper Wards and the Avenues Districts beyond. The guild hall was a two-story building with a stable to the right of it, a storage warehouse to the left, and training grounds behind it. The bottom floor was the great gathering hall, kitchen, pantry, library, armory, and command offices. Upstairs was the shared living quarters for the company members, and the private quarters for the Captain and Vice-Captain. Though, members of the company were free to live in other lodgings if they so choose to, for some the guild hall proved to be their best option.

Bellamy had called this place home since he first joined the mercenary company and found that the guild hall had a charm to it. One he would have missed had he found a place somewhere in the city to live. After telling Raine and Na'naya about his conversation with Madame Rhea and the job he had agreed to complete for her. He then made his way to the captain's office to inform him that he would be leaving for some time. Bellamy knocked on the oak door to the captain's office.

"Come in." The captain's stern voice commanded from inside.

Bellamy opened the oak door and made his way into the captain's office. The captain's office was sparsely decorated. A round table and chairs surrounding it at the center of the room. a couple of bookcases along the walls, and a small fireplace off in the back corner. The captain along with the vice-captain were sitting at the round table looking over some parchments and having a discussion. They noticed Bellamy walk in and gestured for him to take a seat at the table with them. Bellamy walked over and took a seat at the round table.

The captain of the Falling Star Mercenary Company was a tall, muscular middle-aged Human male in his early 40s. He had long shaggy midnight black hair that he wore in a ponytail, with a matching goatee that was tied in a braid. His eyes were a pale blue, like a mist covered ocean, made cold through years of experience in battle and three scars across his right cheek. They were wounds from the claws of a mighty werebear, the captain had slain in his youth.

"What do you want to talk about, Bellamy?"

"I wanted to let you know that Raine, Na'naya, and I are going to be leaving for some time. I was given a job in exchange for some information that I've been searching for over the last few years." Bellamy replied.

"As you know when you joined my mercenary company, I told you that members are free to come and go as they wish, if they do not hinder or bring harm to the company. Losing one skilled member for a time is no problem and easily handled, but to lose three at one time can put us in a bit of a bind. So, I'm going to need more information from you, if you plan on taking them with you as well."

The Falling Star Mercenary Company prided itself on being loyal to their clients. Upholding their clients and members confidentiality above repose. It was one of the reasons that drew Bellamy to seek employment with them. They didn't dig unto each other's personal life's or past if they didn't have a reason to. Of course, as members become close or like family, they would find out things about their companions over time. Bellamy never had a reason for not telling the captain or vice-captain about his past over the years. But knew he would have to tell them now if he was going the get permission for the others to come with him.

Bellamy recounted his story, told them about going to see Madame Rhea at the Messenger's Hollow, and that he had agreed to complete a job for her.

"I see why you would like Raine and Na'naya to go with you on your journey, Bellamy. You have picked an interesting and powerful figure to go into business with. From what I have heard over the years, it is best that you do not end up on her bad side, for you might not come out of it intact."

The captain of the Falling Star Mercenary Company clasped his hands together. He sat back in his chair as he thought over Bellamy's request. Vice-Captain Mira looked over at the captain, who gave her a nodding glance, before she shifted her attention over to Bellamy. She had watched him with a mentor's gaze over the past few years. Getting a better understanding of his character and skills. Taking that into consideration she paused for a moment before asking Bellamy her question.

"Before the captain gives you his answer. I would like to know what is driving this desire of yours to find answers to questions. That might cause you more heartache and trouble then you could imagine?"

The question caught Bellamy by surprise. He didn't think the vice-captain cared that much about his wellbeing. They were not the closest of members in the mercenary company. He had interacted with the vice-captain, from training and completing jobs a few times over the years. He never socialized with her on a personal basis. He felt that she thought of him like a child seeking their older sibling's attention. It seemed to Bellamy that what he had thought was not the case. As the vice-captain cared about those who were apart of the mercenary company as family.

"I have thought about that for some time. I have wondered if this is what I want given that there is no guarantee it will turn out in my favor. With that in mind that I must see this through to the end no matter the outcome. if I want to keep moving forward and with no regrets in my decisions. This is a journey that I need to go on, so that I may grow into a better and more complete version of myself."

"If that is how you feel, then you have my permission to go. I will let Raine and Na'naya go with you if that is what they want to do. You three are welcomed to come back and join us again at any time. With that you may take your leave, as we have other matters to discuss." The captain responded.

"Take care Bellamy and make sure you watch each other's back out there. There is more than one type of danger in this world, you would be best to keep that in mind." The vice-captain warned.

"Thank you, sir, ma'am."

Bellamy rose from his chair around the round table leaving the captain's office. He made his way upstairs to his shared room, to gathering his things for the journey ahead. He had packed his traveler's pack with the usual items he would take on jobs that would last a month or longer. Along with some specialty items that he had procured from past jobs, that might prove to be useful in a pinch. Bellamy did not doubt his physical skills, athletic ability, or weaponry mastery, it was his ability to use *The Arts* or lack of.

Unlike the other races of the world, *The Arts* didn't come easy and wasn't common for most Humans. Though some who show potential can learn it, if trained properly by a teacher. There are tales of people who have learned *The Arts* without proper teaching. But that can be very dangerous and unpredictable, even costing the person their life.

When he joined the mercenary company, Bellamy was hoping that maybe one of the members might be able to teach him or that he might come across a teacher in his travels. The ones in the company who know *The Arts* couldn't help him. As their abilities were tied to their specific races or not atoned in alignment with Bellamy's mana. As for his search during his travels the ones he came across who could use it, where not willing or keen to teach their secrets to an outsider. For it was clear to Bellamy that those with the ability to use *The Arts* did what they must to keep what power or advantage they had for their own purposes.

Rather than take the chance and be betrayed by the very person they taught. Not all felt this way. There were places and teachers willing to pass on their skills to those, they deemed worthy or devout in their faith to their specific religion.

To make up for his lack of skill in *The Arts*, Bellamy honed his skills elsewhere. He utilized magic-imbued items to cover the disadvantage. These items proved to be useful. The only downside was that most are only a single-use and the ones that are multi-use are not easy to come by or cheap. He was hoping that perhaps going on this job would give him the opportunity to find someone who would be able to finally teach him *The Arts.*

Bellamy believed he had the potential and ability to learn *The Arts.* He recalled, vaguely that the night his mother came and woke him, that his bedroom door had a faint glow surrounding it that was never there before. He figured that his mother must have used *The Arts* on it. Though he wondered why she never told him or showed that she possessed such ability.

It was just another question that he was searching for the answer for. This one driving his desire and curiosity to learn *The Arts* for himself. He thought that maybe Inara might be able to help him out or know of someone who can, considering that she was in the service of Madame Rhea herself. After making sure everything was packed. Bellamy went over to his bed and laid down staring up at the ceiling, slowly drifting off into sleep.

The first rays of light emerged over the tall guardian cliffs that surrounded the cape and city, making their way along the docks, over the walls, and down the streets. Filling the city with light as the new day dawned on the sleeping city and the residents starting to rise. Bellamy had gotten up, changed, gathered his gear, and made his way downstairs to the main hall. Raine and Na'naya where already sitting at a table eating when Bellamy came and joined them.

"Good morning, Bellamy. Nice of you to join us, we grabbed you some porridge and fruit."

"Thank you, Na'naya. So, I take it the captain has told you, that he has given permission for you both to go with me on my job."

"That he did and I'm glad I didn't have to step in and convince him. That would have been an unnecessary headache, Bellamy.

Do keep that in mind the next time you try to involve us in your little escapades." Raine said with a sly smile.

The trio talked and enjoyed themselves as they sat at the table finishing up their breakfast. Gathering their packs, they left the Falling Star Mercenary Company's guild hall. They headed down through the streets of the city to the eastern gate. Just as Madame Rhea had told him Inara was leaning up against the wall of the eastern gate. when the trio came walking through. She was waiting to meet up with them.

"Raine and Na'naya, this is Inara. She will be acting as a guide and bodyguard on this job. She was personally recommended by Madame Rhea and as such is a very skilled warrior. I'm sure she will be of help to us."

"Nice to meet you, Inara. I am Na'naya."

"The name is Raine. It is a pleasure to meet you, Inara."

Inara nodded her head to both in return.

"I see. Well, I look forward to working with this band of misfits. We will take the eastern road for three days until we reach the town of Stonecrest. there we will catch the regional train that will takes us to the republic's capital of Hoenheim. So, with that lets be off shall we."

CHAPTER 4

The first day of travel for the group had been calm and quiet. The eastern road was a well-traveled trading road, with caravans and travelers traveling along it during the peak seasons of the year. When merchants would come to Aurontil for the Winter and Summer Solstice festivals. Since it was the in-between seasons, the road was nowhere near a packed with travels. So the group encountered no one just the scenery and their thoughts to keep them company.

This was peaceful, as the countryside of the Renata Republic was a mixture of rolling hills, open plains, flowing Riverlands, and vast forest outside of the scattered cities and towns. Something the republic had, that no other nation did, was the vast and expansive regional railway. It snaked through the heart of the republic connecting the inner cities and towns together. Making it possible to travel between locations separated by many miles. Providing an economic boom to the republic's commerce industry.

The regional railway was a marvel to be hold. It wasn't available for all to use as the price for a ticket wasn't affordable to most. Making it more of a luxury or special gift for those who would save up to experience it. For this reason, most common folks would stick to the traditional means of traveling. From walking, wagons, by mounts, and or by sea.

Without taking a train the journey to the capital would have taken them three to four months. If they walked or managed to get some mounts or a wagon. The creation of the regional railway helped to shorten travel times and grow the prosperity of the republic. For all the time that Bellamy has lived in the republic and travelled around, this would be his first time to the capital and riding the regional railway train.

The group had been keeping a steady pace as they travelled along the eastern road through the vistas of the countryside. Still the road was not paved in areas along the route to the town of Stonecrest. Some of the areas where no more than dirt paths. Theses paths would wear on the toughest of traveler's feet, if travelled on for long extended periods of time. Na'naya was one such traveler experiencing soreness in the bottom of her feet. She stopped and leaned her back against a tall oak tree, to relieve her feet of the soreness she felt throughout.

"We should take a moment to rest for a bit, my feet are sore from all the walking we have been doing. I won't be able to go on if we keep pushing the way we are. It will do everyone some good to take a breath and rest for a bit. Don't you think."

"I agree with Na'naya. I think that we are still making good time to Stonecrest and can afford to take a little break. So, would you mind telling Inara to ease up her pace, so we don't get burned out Bellamy?" Raine jokingly mused.

Raine and Na'naya booth looked at Bellamy with gleaming innocent pouting eyes. Like sad puppies begging for a treat from their master.

"I get it already. So, stop trying to manipulate me with those looks because you're not fooling anyone. I know you guys too well to fall for that."

Bellamy put his pack on the ground next to Raine's, who had decided to join Na'naya on the oak tree. Resting on one of its lower hanging branches. He walked past the tree to the edge of the path along the tree line leading to a split in the road, with paths going south and east in direction. Inara was looking at the signpost in the center of the two diverging paths. The signpost had the following message attached to it. It read:

[Attention travelers,

Due to increased activity in the region, it is advised that extra precaution be taken while traveling along the Eastern and Western roads to any of the cities or towns in the interior of the Renata Republic. Renatan Expeditionary Legion units have been dispatched to track and handle the situations. Seek alternate routes to destinations within the affected area. It is advised, or except full responsibility for your livelihood should you choose to proceed otherwise. Unfortunately, aide cannot and will not be able to assist you should you need help at this time. On behalf of the Renata Republic, we thank you for your cooperation and understanding in these matters.

The Renatan Parliament]

The arrow on the signpost pointing down the south path was inscribed with *To Stonecrest*. While the one pointing towards the east path was inscribed with *To Summermore Brook Ferry*. Bellamy could see from the look in Inara's eyes that something was bothering her. He stood by and waited before he spoke to her, not wanting to disturb her thoughts.

"Is the message on the signpost giving you second thoughts on our best options to take on our path to Hoenheim, Inara?"

"I was thinking on that when you walked up Bellamy. I take it the others sent you over to ask me about taking a break and slowing down my pace some. Well, there is no need to ask anymore, as now we have a more pressing decision to make. Come let's go and join them and I will explain the situation at hand, so that we can make the decision as a group."

Bellamy and Inara walked back over to where the others were resting and sat down beside them. Inara told the others about the message on the signpost first before explaining what that would mean for them going forward.

"So, to start with we have two options available to us as of now. The first being that we continue down the south path towards Stonecrest and catch the regional railway train there. The second option being that we take the east path to the Summermore Brook Ferry. Take the ferry down the river to Summermore and catch a train for Hoenheim there."

"I understand what you're saying Inara. What exactly is the reasoning and difference between the two options, if in the end we are still catching a train to Hoenheim?" Na'naya inquired.

"The main difference is that the second option will add about one more day to our current time. Then shorten our travel time to Hoenheim. That and it should be less dangerous than the two days we still have before we reach Stonecrest. With the increased encounters in the region, I feel that if we can avoid any uncertain dangers on our journey, it will keep us in better shape for when the need arises."

"I can see the value in that option, Inara. But may I ask you something first about it?"

"Go ahead Raine."

Raine jumped down for the oak branch he was resting on. He sat down next to her before continuing with his question.

"Are you suggesting this option because you feel that in our current condition, we wouldn't be able to handle the risk involved with the first option. Or is it that you don't trust us to make sound judgement calls depending on the situations. I hope you haven't forgotten that each of us are skilled mercenaries that shouldn't be taken lightly. We have completed many jobs, some more than others but none the less capable."

A cold grin showed on Inara's face, brought on by what Raine had said to her.

"Tch...I know well what you three are capable of, as it is you who doesn't know what it is I am capable of. But that aside, if we were to take the first option, we would no doubt reach Stonecrest, but we would be exhausted and possibly wounded from the ordeal. Option two is a means of avoiding the unnecessary headache option one is most certainly going to be."

"Hahaha...Ah...Ha." Raine laughed heartily.

"Alright, option two is fine with me. What do you say Na'naya and Bellamy."

"If option two means avoiding unnecessary headaches, then I'm all for it." Na'naya Replied.

It seemed to Bellamy that everyone had already made their decision. They were set on pursuing the second option. He figured it would turn out this way once Inara explained the situation to them. There was no harm in taking the least dangerous path. Especially since they had just set out and there was no telling what might be ahead of them. So going with the majority's choice this time around wouldn't hurt. Especially if it saved them some time on their journey to Hoenheim and back.

"I agree with you all, that option two is the best one for us to go with."

"Continue to rest up and then we will set out for the Summermore Brook Ferry. I will take the first watch, Then Na'naya, followed by Raine and finally Bellamy. We will leave first thing in the morning."

The next morning when the sun raised the group was wide wake. Packing up their things to head onward down the east path to the ferry. Following behind Inara the others proceed along the twisting narrow path through the rolling hillside down into the lowlands and the Summermore Brook beyond. It was late in the afternoon when Inara pointed her hand at a structure coming up in the distance, sitting at the edge of the river. The structure was a medium sized trading outpost. There was open walled overhang seating area, with a small dock along the backside. At the end of the dock was the riverboat they had traveled to catch, The Summermore Brook Ferry.

"We should head inside and see about purchasing some tickets for the ferry. I'll go and talk to ferryman; you guys can go and sit on the benches."

Inara left and made her way to the ticket counter to speak with the ferryman. Bellamy and the others walked over to a bench and sat down. The seating area was crowded with many groups of people waiting to catch a ride on the ferry. There were travelling merchants from the border towns and cities of the republic, with merchandise. Associates from the Nimh Theocracy and Na'naya's Home of the Umbar Sultanate.

Their clothing, hairstyles and finery giving away that they were not local citizens of the Renata Republic. Trappers and Huntsmen from the frozen wilds of the far eastern and western regions. Bringing with them furs of mighty artic beasts and their meat. All well preserved for travel, so that they can sell it for a major profit.

Pilgrims making their journey through the lands as they prepare for the holy festival of the Mother's Moon. Which celebrated the goddess of creation herself, the Night Mother. Along with normal families and travelers making their way to different destinations along the way to the capital. Bellamy looked out into the tranquil waters of the river in front of him and was quietly lost in thought. Raine and Na'naya's conversation was fleeting words on the wind, as they didn't seem to reach Bellamy's ears.

"Bellamy. Bellamy. Hey, Bellamy!"

Bellamy jolted from his thoughts.

"Huh. What was that all about, Raine?"

"Welcome back. I was talking to you, and you didn't seem to notice. You were kind of zoned out there man. What's on your mind?"

"I don't know exactly. I feel a bit uneasy for some reason, but I can't seem to figure out why. You know what I'm talking about right?"

Raine lifted his hand over Bellamy's head and patted him on top, that sly smile of his showing on his face.

"It's alright to feel that way, it means that your instincts are sharpening and developing better. With our line of work, it is crucial that you understand that being alert even when in a relaxed environment will save your life and keep you prepared in case of the unexpected. After all, above any job, our livelihood comes first and foremost. Remember to balance your head and your heart when acting, they will guide you on the proper path." Raine responded sagely.

"Thanks, I will keep your words in mind."

"No problem kid, ha. That's what friends are for."

"Dammit Raine. I told you to stop calling me that."

CHAPTER 5

I nara returned and handed everyone their ticket for the ferry. The horn sounded as the loading bridge was settled and the passengers made their way onto the Summermore Brook Ferry, one by one. The ferryman collected the tickets from the passengers as they stepped aboard, making sure that everyone was accounted for. When the last passenger was aboard, the ferryman called out to the crew and the loading bridge was raised, the horn sounded again. The Alchemic engines started. Greyish black smoke billowed from the smoke stakes and the paddle wheels on the back began rotating, propelling the riverboat away from the dock. Picking up speed the riverboat set out on its course down the long river of the Summermore Brook.

There were three sets of bunkbeds in the cabin, that Bellamy and Raine where staying in. There were only three other roommates sharing their cabin, as the bottom bunk of the last one was empty. The girls had been given a cabin all to themselves. Bellamy would have preferred that the group stayed together. The girl's cabin was right down the other hallway across from them. He didn't doubt that they would be able to take care of themselves. They shouldn't expect any problems over the next day and a half of travel on the river, he hoped.

It was late at night, and everyone was sleeping off the booze and food they had at dinner. Raine was sound asleep in the bunk above Bellamy. He was moving restlessly caught up in some drunken dream. Bellamy opened his eyes unable to fall asleep, so he got dressed and made his way up to the observation deck above. A cool breeze flowed through the air and the night sky glittered with the light of the ancient stars. The subtle sounds of the engines running and the paddle wheels rotating through the water echoed in the quietness of the night.

At the other end of the observation deck, Bellamy noticed that there was someone else out here with him enjoying the cool breeze of the night sky. As he walked over towards the person, he saw that it was none other than Inara, looking off into the distance of the shadowed river. Inara was looking out into the darkness away from Bellamy when she spoke.

"What brings you out here this late at night, Bellamy? Couldn't sleep?"

"How did you know it was me and not someone else coming up behind you?" Bellamy asked curiously.

"I sensed no ill intention coming from you and I know the presence of your mana, along with that of the others. Let's say it's a special mana detection skill that I have. One that I value and wouldn't give up for anything in this world."

Bellamy was impressed by her skill. The fact that she had such a skill that was not easily come by other Artist, users of *The Arts.* He had heard of the various degrees of this skill that Artist would be able to have control over. One aspect or another of it, but to find someone who could use it so precisely was another thing entirely. It must have taken her years and intense training to hone the skill the way Inara had.

"Raine was moving around in his sleep, no thanks to the alcohol he consumed. I had a sense of unease bothering me, that was affecting my sleep. So, I figured I would come up to the observation deck and clear my mind. What brought you here?"

"Nothing in particular, I enjoy gazing at the night sky. It provides me with a sense of calmness and serenity, being closer to the presence of the Night Mother. The goddess of all creation. [*May her starry tears guide us and be our light. For she is the beginning and the everlasting endless night.*] Divine mother watch over us and guide us through the night."

"I'm surprised, I didn't take you for a follower of the Nox Pathos. You don't come off as the type, but I know better than to make assumptions without all the details. So, I apologize if that came as rude or insensitive."

Inara turned and gave a small smile to Bellamy.

"There is no need to apologize, as I can understand how you might get that impression. I am a follower, but I tend to keep my faith more closed off to others, than expressed. As I have done things that are not aligned with the general teachings of the Nox Pathos. But feel that the Night Mother would understand my transgressions and forgive me or not. That is what faith is after all. A willingness to except and believe in something unexplainable or beyond our comprehension." Inara responded kindly.

Bellamy stood there next to Inara and smiled back. He had got to see a different side to the Half-Giant warrior, one he was glad to have experienced. For warriors, especially Half-Giants were not known to be open or expressive in their emotions on subjects of personal matters to them. To people they barely knew. Though Inara was starting to trust them more and opening to them as their journey progressed.

Bellamy and Inara stayed on the observation deck for a little while longer. Gazing off into the night sky and shadowed river. It was quiet, when a sudden whooshing sound pierced the quietness. Followed by the sound of multiple metallic clanks making contact throughout the riverboat. Grappling hooks latched onto the rails of the riverboat and from the shadows of the river seven longboats emerged. As the longboats got closer, the raiders aboard climbed up the ropes attached to the grappling hooks and boarded the riverboat. The lookout above sounded the alarm, alerting the crew and passengers.

"Raiders! Raiders have boarded the ship. All hands prepare to repel the attackers!" The lookout shouted in haste.

"We need to hurry and regroup with the others." Bellamy told Inara.

Bellamy and Inara made their way from the observation deck and sprinted down the hall to their cabins to get the others. The cries of passengers and the sounds of weapons clashing back and forth erupted over the riverboat. as the raiders engaged the passengers and crew. Four raiders spotted Bellamy as he was turning down the hall to head to his cabin and came charging towards him. The raiders were lightly armored with leathered strapped and buckled gambesons, leather bracers on their forearms, and earthen colored cloaks draped over their shoulders. Each raider carrying a sword in their hand and a battle-axe at their side. One of the raiders also had a small buckler shield on him.

Bellamy reached down to draw his sword from its sheath, but his hand passed through air. His sword and sheath were not at his side. He had remembered that he had left them in the cabin by his bunk.

["*Damn! That's the last time I leave without my sword in hand. Well, this might cause a bit of a problem. Nothing to do now but improvise.*"] Bellamy thought to himself.

The first raider reached Bellamy. He swung his sword towards him, Bellamy jumped backed dodging the slash by mere inches. He went in for another strike. This time with two consecutive slashes, one to his right and the other towards his left. Bellamy maneuvered his body to the side parrying the slash to his right with his metal bracers. Pivoting his foot, Bellamy ducked down and elbowed the raider in the gut as his second slash passed to the left. The raider fell to his knees dropping his sword.

Bellamy grabbed the sword and thrust it through the raider's back. Pulling the sword from the raider's back, he took up a guard position as two of the three remaining raiders came up upon him, while the other one stayed back. The hallway was not wide enough for all four of them to have ample room to engage. Metallic clanks sounded as the opponent's clashed their swords against each other's blades, blocking and parrying strikes. The raiders were gaining the upper hand on Bellamy. As each blow was moving his position backwards.

Drawing closer to the wall at his back, Bellamy lounged using the momentum of his foot. He pressed against the wall like a loaded spring. His body flung forward towards the two raiders. Blocking their strikes as his body impacted them, causing them slam into the floor hard. The sudden crash of the group, caught the last raider off guard.

Not noticing the cabin door opening behind him and the figure emerging from within. Raine unsheathed one of his twin

Rondel Daggers; each bearing an Alchemic steel blade on an intricate rounded leather hilt with dancing nymphs etched onto the leather. With a swift fluid motion, he stabbed the unaware raider straight in the neck.

The raider made gargled sounds choking. As he tried to franticly put pressure on his wound, before falling to the ground lifeless. Raising to his feet, Bellamy turned away from the two raiders on the ground facing Raine. Raine lowered his arm to the side and grabbed a sheathed short sword. Leaning against the door and tossed it in air towards Bellamy's direction.

"Here. Catch, you forgot this!"

Bellamy leaped up, grabbed his short sword from mid-air and unsheathed it. The blade was fine crafted Elven Steel with runic glyphs inscribed in the center, with a black woven leather hilt. With two quick downward strikes, Bellamy pierced the raider's hearts ending their lives.

"Thanks. Though it took you long enough to act Raine."

"I figured you didn't need my help with a couple of river raiders and would wait until the time was right to strike. Perhaps, I misjudged your skill and should have stepped in sooner?"

Bellamy shook his head.

"No... No...Your judgment was sound; I was a little inconvenienced is all. I should have had my blade with me from the beginning. It is a problem that I won't let happen again."

Raine looked around the hallway to see if there was any more raiders or passengers in the immediate area. The sounds of the fights and screams earlier had seemed to be dying down. Only an eerie quietness seemed to be all that remained.

"Where are the girls, Bellamy?"

"Inara was with me on the observation deck, and we split up on the way back to our cabins. She should be with Na'naya now, making their way here."

The girls came rushing down the hall with the packs in tow. Bellamy and Raine retrieved their packs from their cabin. There was Tendrils of smoke raising up from the cracks in the floors. A sudden heat engulfed the area all around.

"Come we must leave and get off the boat. The river raiders have started a fire on one of the decks below and its starting to spread all over." Inara addressed the group with concern.

"Damn them. What in the Seven Hells were they thinking? There is nothing to be gained from this ceaseless destruction. No bounty, no rewards, no treasures, nothing at all." Na'naya Protested angrily.

The fire engulfed the river boat. The remaining passengers jumped from the balconies and decks into the cold dark waters of the river below. The group had reached the western shore, cold and drenched from their swim. A massive swirling explosion resounded in the air as the riverboat's engines exploded. Debris from the riverboat shot off in many directions. The last remnants of the hull sank down into the dark depths of the Summermore River.

"We need to start a fire, so we can dry ourselves off and regroup."

"No problem, I got that covered."

Na'naya collected some twigs and driftwood she found along the lakeshore. She placed them in the center of a makeshift stone pit she erected. Kneeling over the kindle she took out flint from her pack. She struck it on an arrowhead, creating sparks to light the fire. With the fire burning the group gathered around to take in the warmth, resting and drying off their tired bodies.

They sat around the burning fire lost in their thoughts. They contemplated the events that had befallen them on the riverboat. Watching each other with tired gazes. Waiting to see who would make the first move and break the silence the group had found themselves embraced in.

"So where exactly are we now, and how much longer will it take us to reach the trading town of Summermore?" Na'naya inquired, the first to break the silence.

Inara reached into her pack, pulled out a rolled-up parchment map and Wayfinder compass. She unrolled the map, placed it in front of her and looked it over before responding back.

"According to the readings from the compass, and matching it with the map, I would say that we are about ten miles Southwest of Summermore."

Inara pointed out their location on the map, so that the others could get a grasp of the current situation. They had ended up in an unfortunate place because of the attack on the riverboat. leaving fewer options available for how to continue forward to Hoenheim. Following the path along the river down to Summermore would take them longer now that they were on foot. The river twisted and turned for miles in either direction before straightening up before the town.

By bypassing the river and heading south through the lowlands until they reached the Fractured Peaks. Making their way to Hoen's Highway: the mountain road that went directly to Hoenheim, was now an option available to them. The last option was to head back up the river and make their way back towards Stonecrest. To catch the regional railway train there. Presented with the choices they had to decide which would be best for them to proceed with. As like it or not their trek was going to take them more time.

"I think I might have a general idea about how you are feeling. The choice you would most likely want to make but hear me out. We should take the second of the three choices and make our way to Hoen's Highway." Bellamy suggested with earnest.

"Bellamy, just because this option has become available to us now, I don't think you fully understand what it would require of us."

"Na'naya, I know what it is I am asking of all of you and myself to do. But the other options will take too much time away from us. We have already lost quite a bit thanks to these incidents. So perhaps a more direct approach will be beneficial to us, even if slightly more dangerous."

Na'naya looked at her friend with concern in her eyes, feeling that Bellamy wasn't listening to what she was trying to tell him.

"Raine. Inara. One of you try to get him to understand that the second option is going to be more difficult and dangerous than he seems to realize. Because he doesn't want to listen to me."

"She's right you know. It won't be as easy as you think it is Bellamy. But with that being said, I do think that pursuing the second option would be the best choice for us. I don't want it being said that Raine was a coward who tried to avoid adventure. Who only took the easy way out of difficult situations. My honor will not allow it of me."

"Sorry Na'naya, but I'm going to have to agree with them this time around. We have already been setback enough. Knowing my mistress, it is best that we take a more direct route when circumstances present themselves, no matter the difficulty a part of them."

Reluctantly Na'naya accepted.

CHAPTER 6

W ith the rise of the new day's sun and the last shadows of the cold night fading away, the group set out leaving the river shore behind them. It was already midday when they reached the lowlands. Off in the distance beyond was the long and expansive silhouette of the Fractured Peaks. The crossing through the lowlands to the mountains would take them over another half a day to reach the base. The lowlands were an area of wide-open grassy plains.

Rolling hills, scattered rock formations and the occasional small grouping of trees and shrubs. Daemons where common in these types of areas. Preferring to make their territory away from densely populated areas.

The group didn't have to concern themselves with the Daemons found in the lowlands. As they were more on the smaller and on the herbivore side of the ecosystem. Larger more predatory Daemons had wider territorial areas. So they tended to be fewer and far between another. Still, it was prudent to keep watch as there was no certainty that the group wouldn't run into one.

In this regard the area played in their favor. They didn't have to worry about being ambushed. Because if something came after them, they would be able to spot it from a decent distance away.

A sudden sensation caused Raine's ears to twitch, and he stopped in his tracks. First observing the surrounding area within his line of sight. he walked over to a small rock formation and jumped up onto one of the taller boulders in the formation. Inara raised her hand and signaled the others to stop. She watched Raine close his eyes and tilt his head in one direction and then another.

"What is it that you hear Raine?"

"The sound is faint, still a little off in the distance. But there is something coming in our direction. It is not Human or Demi-Human, that I am sure of. There is a heavy weight behind the footsteps, though its movements are steady and quick. A Daemon is coming, a massive and powerful one."

"It appears we may have ended up in the hunting grounds of a Daemon, that has caught our scent. We must flee, or we must fight, there is no other option for us." Inara responded with quick wit and determination in her voice.

"We have travelled so far already and the last thing I want is to be watching my back the rest of the way to Hoenheim. I say we fight."

"I agree with Na'naya. Let's make our stand and take care of this Daemon." Bellamy responded back.

"Alright." Raine and Inara replied together.

Raine still perched atop the boulder, drew his twin rondel daggers from their sheaths on the side of his hips. Reaching with her left-hand Inara grabbed her mighty Warhammer strapped to her back. The handle was four feet long carved from an ancient Eldarwood tree, wrapped in tough Oliphant hide leather straps. At the top was a heavy Uru Metal wide bodied sledgehammer head, with an anvil styled spike on the fore-end of the shaft. The Warhammer was crafted with exquisite balance, allowing Inara to wield it single or double-handed in battle.

Bellamy took up a position atop another boulder off to the side of the one Raine was perched on. He had taken out his recurve bow and quiver from his pack, equipping them to use. His Elven Steel short sword still sheathed around his waist, should he need to change tactics. He notched an arrow and pointed it off in the direction Raine and the others were looking. Na'naya took up a position off to the left side of Inara.

She reached down to her side and grabbed the four-sectioned Mithril Bo staff hanging from her waist. With a subtle flicking motion, the separate sections of the Bo staff came together as one solid staff. Five feet eleven inches long and with a two-inch-wide diameter. It was a unique and rare weapon that took exceptional skill to wield properly. One that was not native to the southern continent.

 Na'naya had told Bellamy once that she had inherited it from her master, a warrior monk from a country to the far east. Before he had passed from the Dreaming Sickness Plague. He had found her orphaned and alone in one of the desert villages on his travels. So, he took her in and raised her like his very own daughter.

"Raine is there any sight of the Daemon yet?"

Raine focused his hearing and his far sight, peering off into the distance.

"I see the Daemon. It is coming this way. You all should be able to see it momentarily. Prepare yourselves, we are going to be dealing with a Tiger-Bear Behemoth. They are powerful and dangerous apex predators. Do not take this battle lightly, if you value your life." Raine cautioned.

"Has anyone here ever fought a Tiger-Bear Behemoth before. This will be my first time dealing with such a beast." Bellamy asked.

The others looked at one another and shook their heads at Bellamy's question.

"I have not had the opportunity personally to fight such a Daemon. My older twin brothers have told me that they hunted one before on an expedition with Madame Rhea. A few years back before I joined her service."

"Did they offer up any advice on how to handle the Daemon, Inara?"

"Stay focused and present in the battle. The Daemon is giant but quick with its movements and strikes. That its susceptible to elemental *Arts* skills. Though it is still a tough Daemon to bring down, even with *The Arts*."

"Prepare yourselves. It's coming."

One hundred yards away from the group just coming over the rise of a distant hill. The mighty Tiger-Bear Behemoth came into view for all to see. It was six feet tall while in its natural hunched position. When it stood up on its hind legs the behemoth reached eight feet. From head to toe, its massive bulky body was covered in ragged Brown Gray fur with Black stripes crossing along the back, legs, and arms.

 The behemoth's head was more bearlike with feline features; with pointed ears, rounded maw with sharp fangs, and slanted eyes that were a bright piercing orange. The behemoth was hunched over walking on all fours. Using its massive muscular arms and hind legs to move around. Five two-foot-long sharp claws protruded from the behemoth's paws. A long feline tail swished and swayed back and forth, as it moved to the rhythm of the beast's mighty steps.

Spotting its prey, the Tiger-Bear Behemoth picked up speed and charged towards the awaiting group a deadly bloodlust in its gaze. Opening its maw it gave a horrifying and deep roar that echoed throughout the lowlands, bringing a chill down everyone's spine.

In firm and steady motions, Bellamy notched and let loose three arrows towards the charging behemoth. One of the arrows grazed the side of the behemoth's upper right forearm, deflected off as it shifted its weight to the left of the flying arrow. Though quick to react to the oncoming arrows. The other two struck home, hitting the charging behemoth in the mid and lower sides along its back. The behemoth snarled in annoyance from the impact of the two arrows, bearing its fangs at the person responsible for causing it pain. The Tiger-Bear Behemoth lounged forward swiping its massive paw towards Inara and Na'naya, causing to two to jump and sidestep out of the way of the strike.

Quickly sending another strike towards Bellamy and Raine, as it turned and shifted its body from the previous striking lounge. Raine backflipped off the boulder and gave a quick double slash with his daggers at the behemoth's arms. Creating a x-shaped wound in the process, before rolling out of the way of another strike from the behemoth's opposite arm. In that instant Bellamy jumped over to another boulder and notched another arrow. The arrow striking the behemoth's back.

It thrashed around in pain, kicking its hind legs into the boulders around it. The impact causing the boulders to crumble and fall to the ground, along with Bellamy who lost his footing. Bellamy hit the ground hard, shaken by the fall. His recurve bow had flown from his hands. It was crushed beneath the weight of rubble from the collapsing boulders. Na'naya rushed over and helped him back up onto his feet. Bellamy threw his quiver with the few remaining arrows he had to the ground and drawing his Elven short sword and tomahawk into his hands.

"Are you alright, Bellamy?"

"I will be soon, Na'naya. That fall just took the wind out of me."

"It looks like you and Raine managed to piss off the Behemoth. I don't think it's going to let us go and be on our way now."

"Yeah, that was never going to happen."

While Na'naya was helping Bellamy up off the ground, Raine and Inara had been busy distracting the behemoth. Inara blocked and dodged blows from the behemoth's mighty strikes. She looked for openings to strike at it. Raine made shallow cuts and slashes along the behemoth's body. He wove his way around, watchful of its unexpected and sudden movements. Enraged the behemoth stood up on its hind legs, reaching its full height of eight feet. It reeled back its arm and in a mighty downward slash knocked backed both Raine and Inara a few feet.

Slowly letting the air fill their lungs and exhaling it out in steady breaths, the group tried to ease the fatigue in their bodies from the straining battle. Bruised, battered, and a bit bloody they knew something had to be done soon. If they had any hope of overcoming the behemoth. Though they managed to inflict considerable damage upon the behemoth. It showed very little sign of giving in.

Blow, after staggering and timed blow, the fight continued dauntingly on. Bellamy and Na'naya joining in with the others, dodging strikes and attacking back trying to land a fatal blow that would bring the behemoth down.

"Guys can you buy me some time, I think I might have a way to bring the behemoth down. Though, we will only get one shot at it, as I won't have the energy for another spell."

"I didn't know that you could use spells, Inara." Bellamy replied.

"It is not a specialty of mine, so I don't use them in battle very often. Unless the circumstances call for such action, as it takes time to invoke and is taxing on the caster's body."

"We got you covered. Do what you need to do and cast your spell."

The others moved forward to cover Inara, striking at the behemoth to draw its attention away from her. Inara stepped behind the others and began casting her spell.

["*All knowing and powerful Mother beyond. Imbue in my hammer your divine power, so that I may smite the threat before me. In your name I offer you my essence as proof of my devotion and love for your blessing.*"]She chanted in a voice with a melodic quality.

The air swirled around her body and enveloped her Warhammer. Charged ethereal energy sparking and glowing with bright blue light, became visible as the spell started to take effect. It created a manifestation of a small maelstrom, as howling winds and torrential rains were imbued into the Uru

Metal wide-bodied sledgehammer head of Inara's Warhammer. Inara spun the Warhammer around and around, building up momentum for her strike. The behemoth once again raised up to its hind legs, ready to make another tremendous strike.

"Back away from the behemoth now!" Inara commanded.

The others backed away as they heard her words. Inara pivoted and charged forward. She jumped into the air. With a downward overhead blow, she struck the behemoth in the chest with her Warhammer. A loud thunderclap and concussive explosion echoed throughout the area, as the blow impacted on her target's chest. When the smoke from the impact cleared, the behemoth laid sprawled on the ground lifeless. Inara stood next to it leaning on her Warhammer for support. Tiring exhaustion aching throughout her body, as she tried to keep her balance and stand.

"That was amazing, Inara. I have never actually seen *Battle Arts* casted before." Bellamy said with excitement.

"Great job."

"We were able to defeat the behemoth and come out on top because of you, and your spell. Thank you."

"It was because of your help and buying me the time I needed to cast the spell, that we were able to win the fight. We should rest here and harvest what we can from the behemoth for the time being. I am exhausted and won't be of any help until I recover my energy."

The others agreed with Inara. They went about setting up camp and harvesting resources from the behemoth's corpse. The parts they retrieved from the corpse would provide them with an excellent bounty and material for supplies or gear. Bellamy went to where he had fallen off the boulder. He retrieved his discarded quiver and broken recurve bow.

It had been shattered into five pieces of various lengths that would take time and new material to repair it. So he gathered the pieces up and placed them in his pack. He headed back over to others, who were checking over their gear and bandaging up their wounds from the battle.

Unbuckling the straps on the side of his light-leathered and armored plated cuirass, Bellamy took it off in struggling motions. He sat it down beside his aching body. He unbuttoned his worn patterned tunic and grabbed the small container of herbal ointment from his pack. With care and a gentle touch, he applied the ointment to the bruises and cuts that marked his chest and arms. Each one a reminder of the battles he fought and the lessons he learned from them.

Though most would heal and fade away with time, there were some deep scars that would not completely fade once healed. It was those ones that Bellamy had endured his toughest lessons. That one shouldn't be so reckless with their life and that nothing is ever promised but must be earned.

CHAPTER 7

T he sun was overhead. Off its highest morning peak when the group reached the base of the Fractured Peaks. The start of Hoen's Highway. They would still have to travel a couple of miles into the mountains before they come upon the formal highway pass, through the mountains. The extra weight the group now carried with them, made the hike along the rocky trails leading to the highway a bit more cumbersome for some, than others.

Inara had regained most of her strength. But her movements were still a little sluggish compared to how she was before. *The Arts* have a taxing cost on the caster, that is equal to the number and power of the spells being cast.

So, in turn the more spells cast or the more powerful a spell is, the higher the strain on the *Artist* afterwards. That is why it is important to be trained. As it is not only a physical strain on the *Artist's* body but a mental and spiritual strain as well. Capable of consuming the *Artist*. If they are not prepared and skilled enough to handle the mana energy involved.

For these reasons those who can use *The Arts* use it strategically and sparingly when in combat against Daemons or enemies in battle. To compensate for this, magical items and "Pseudo-Alchemic" technology is used for common everyday life and or occasional military matters.

Raine had received some minor cuts and bruises from the fight. But nothing that appeared too serious for him to recover from. Beastmen vitality has strong natural healing attributes that, help them recover from wounds inflicted on them. If they aren't major or in critical areas of their bodies. Na'naya seemed to be in good shape, other than a bruised leg and exhaustion.

She had proved herself to be a strong and skilled mercenary. Handling herself against a strong Daemon for as long as she did and not get seriously wounded. That was a testament to her skills. Even Bellamy was impressed with his skills and experience during the fight. He was glad to see that his continuous training was starting to show results. Fights of that caliber had always been difficult and challenging for him. Still he kept pushing forward because he knew he had to live on.

"We should see the formal pass of Hoen's Highway coming up, around the bend. From there the path will be smoother and easier to travel."

"I can't wait to stay at an inn again and have a proper bed to sleep on. That and a nice hot bath to soak my tired body in. You boys don't understand or appreciate the effect a warm bath does for the body and mind. I'm sure Inara would agree with me."

"Oh...I've never been one to care about such things, but I do enjoy them when given the opportunity. I'm more at home in the wilds and nature at heart, than the confines of a town or city. So, I tend to travel quite often for my mistress."

Bellamy had heard that the Demi-Human races were traditionally more nomadic in their nature. Preferring to travel with the seasons from one location to another. Though over the centuries, Humans had caused their nomadic ways to dwindle.

As Human nations grew and expanded into different lands, impacting the Demi-Human's territories in the process. With these expansions came conflicts. That lead to strenuous tensions between the Humans and Demi-Humans over the years. Through agreements and treaties signed by the different leaders to create a newer peace amongst them. Though young and not without its difficulties.

For not all races of Demi-Humans are forgiving and trusting of getting along with Humans. They have watched them over the years. Seeing how they interact with their own kind, for the better and the worst. This has caused them to take an isolationist approach. Keeping to themselves and rarely interacting with them if they had too.

For their lives are much longer than the fragile lifespan of a mere human. Outside of their homelands or bigger commerce locations, you wouldn't interact or see some of the more secluded of Demi-Human races. Some of the other races traveled outside of their territories. By exploring, trading, hunting, and fighting on more frequent occasions, but still only interacted on a passing basis.

"There it is. We made it to the beginning of Hoen's Highway. That stone archway, lined by the two obelisks to the sides is the start of the formal mountain road to Hoenheim." Inara addressed.

Carved into the side of the mountain was an ancient obsidian and jade lined archway, reaching twenty feet high by eight feet wide. Depicted on the face of the stones that made up the archway, were scenes of the history of the region and the raise of the city of Hoenheim to capital of the Renata Republic. Quartz obelisks flanked the left and right of the archway. The ground was paved with a cobblestone road starting from the outside of the archway. Twisting, and turning as it snaked on through the mountains.

Bellamy and Na'naya marveled at the archway as they walked through. Admiring the craftmanship of the sculpted stone and vividness of the scenes depicted on each one.

Raine and Inara glanced over the art of the archway, as they made their way and proceeded along Hoen's Highway.

"Inara, do you know how long it will take us to reach the city, now that we've made it to the highway?"

"We should reach the city in about five to six hours. Other than the twists and turns of the highway, it is a straight shot to the city. As we get closer to the city proper there will be lamppost spread out along the path, to light our way."

"that's good to know. Considering it will be nightfall by the time we reach the city, and traveling at night can be dangerous." Na'naya replied in a playful fashion.

The walk along the cobblestones of the highway path, was a welcomed distraction for the group. Who had been traversing the different terrain of the countryside over the days since they left Aurontil. The calmness of the highway had given Bellamy the chance to comprehend and process the events that have befallen his group so far. On their journey to reach Hoenheim. They had gone through some difficult challenges to reach the highway from: ridding a riverboat down river.

To fighting raiders who attacked the boat. Then swimming to shore to escape the fire, and even battling a Daemon in the lowlands. Bellamy thought on how the challenges he had faced where handled and if he could have done something to change their outcomes. Each was a lesson to be learned from.

An experience for his skills to refine and grow more beneficial to the wellbeing of his group.

As they continued down the twist and turns of the highway pass, the empty road started filling with travelers making their way to the capital. Passing the first of the three checkpoint gates on the highway. The lamppost signaling the way to the city started to appear. Indicating that they had passed the midway point of the highway. The highway was lined with wagons and carts carrying goods and people riding along.

Traders and travelers on horseback to more exotic mounts, were traversing the highway. As well along slide people traveling on foot, all heading in the same direction of Hoenheim. Hoen's highway was safeguarded for travelers who choose to take this route to the city. By the three checkpoint gates and the guards stationed at them. To even the lamppost spaced along the pass.

For the stones in the lamppost besides offering a light source. They also emanated a mana field that repelled low level Daemons away from the highway pass. On the rare occasions where they didn't work against a stronger Daemons. Then guards or expeditionary forces would take care of any threat to the travelers. Hoen's highway was designed this way for traveling from the early days of the republic.

When the city was first founded, as it was one of the only safe ways to reach the city before the establishment of the regional railway. Since then, the railway had been the preferred method of travel to the capital. By those who could afford it or lived in regions north of the city. The sun was starting to set as twilight was enveloping the Fractured Peaks and the lamppost began to light up. As the group made their way through the second checkpoint gate.

"According to the guard at the gate, we are around four miles to the final checkpoint gate and the city of Hoenheim beyond."

"We should reach the city before the eighth hour of night. Then we can find some rooms at an inn and rest for the night. In the morning we can figure out our next steps from there."

"Sounds, like a solid plan Bellamy. Heavens know I could use a decent night's sleep and a warm bath to relax my wary body." Na'naya said agreeably.

Raine and Inara nodded their approval. Even though they didn't want to agree with what Na'naya was saying. As she tended to act a bit childish when she knew she was right about something. They had been traveling long and were not about to indulge her childish antics this time.

"Bellamy, when we get to the city, we can head to the Songbird Inn. It's an inn that is run by an old friend of Madame Rhea. I'm sure they will be able to provide us with suitable lodging for our stay in the city, until our job is completed."

"Alright then continue leading the way Inara and we will follow your lead. This will be my first time to the republic's capital. We have worked many jobs with the mercenary company. But our business has never brought us to Hoenheim."

"This will mark my third time visiting the capital. The other times I was escorting my mistress. Along with my twin brothers to handle some business negotiations and disagreements."

Bellamy could tell by the tone of her voice and the look in her eyes, that Inara had great affection for Madame Rhea and her twin brothers. He thought about asking her more about them. But decided another time would be better. He didn't want to wander too far off his goals for taking the job in the first place.

As close as they may have been getting on this journey, Bellamy didn't know if Inara's loyalties would stay aligned with his as the situations changed, and they had to adapt. Whether she would stay with the group or put her mistress's interest ahead of their own, if called upon to do so he couldn't say for certain.

Bellamy only knew he had no reason not to trust her. She had guided and aided them so far without concern. So he let that inkling be washed away to the back of his consciousness.

"There it is the last checkpoint gate, down the road. When we cross the gate to the path behind it and make our way to the top of the hill, we should be able to see the city of Hoenheim on the Highland plateau beyond."

Crossing through the last checkpoint gate the group followed the pass up the hill. Stopping at the overlook and see what laid off in the distance. Past the cold low clouds of the autumn night, resting upon the plateau the outer walls of the city stood strong. Formed from mighty ancient stone quarried from the mine caverns deep below. The glowing lights of the six districts illuminated the buildings of Hoenheim.

Giving the city a bright luminous and shadowed appearance of a beacon in a sea of blackness. The brightest of the lights coming from the great glassed dome of the central railway train station hub located in The Merchant's District towards the center of the city.

CHAPTER 8

In the densely populated area of the city, at the center of the six districts that made up Hoenheim was the Merchant's District. This was the district that many travelers coming into the city would come to first. As it was its economic center. Filled with a variety of shops from every day mundane to more mysterious and exotic ones. The central railway train station hub was located here.

Along with inns, taverns, brothels, and other places of a more questionable nature. Though beautiful and prosperous to the eyes of most outsiders and citizens. It is said it takes a keen look to see the true machinations of the elegant struggle for expanding influence that lies below the surface. Hoenheim is a city of many wonders and intrigues, but it is also a place of many secrets.

Four blocks down from the central railway train station hub along one of the city's many labyrinthine streets, the group arrived at their destination the Songbird Inn. The inn was a tall three-story building made of a combination of stone, wood with metal fastenings and a shingled terracotta roof. A small bell let out a melodic ring when the front door was opened, and the group proceeded inside. On the main floor was the common area with a fireplace towards the back wall and the staircase leading up to the floors above. The check-in/out counter with a bookcase behind it holding room keys, books and packages, and a small dining room with the kitchen beyond.

Inara walked up to the check-in counter to speak with the innkeeper standing behind it. She was writing in a ledger on the counter when she set her quill down and looked up at Inara.

The innkeeper was an older Human woman who had a slender yet buxom bodice with brunette hair that had streaks of sliver, and pale blue eyes. When she spoke, there was a hint of an accent in her speech. It was common amongst the barbarian tribes of the cold wilds of the eastern regions.

"It's been a while since I last saw you, Inara. What brings you back to Hoenheim and my establishment?"

"Isolde. My companions and I need some rooms for a few weeks at most. Madame Rhea sent us here to complete a job for her and she gave me this letter to give to you."

Inara pulled out a sealed envelope from her pouch and handed it to Isolde. She grabbed a letter opener and opened the letter reading it over. A small smile peering on her lips. As she glanced over at the companions standing behind Inara waiting.

"I see your mistress hasn't changed one bit over these years, and here I am getting older as the flow of time presses on. Oh well, best not to dwell on the past too much or your life will pass you by."

Isolde turned towards the bookcase and grabbed two room keys from the hooks. Placing them on the counter in front of Inara.

"Your rooms are located on the second floor down the hallway to the left. On the opposite side at the other end are the women's and men's bathing rooms. Breakfast and dinner will be provided daily. At the end of every week your bill for the rooms will be due. If you need any help, feel free to ask and I will do my best to help. One last thing, there is a curfew in the city, no one is allowed to be out past the second hour of the new day."

"Thank you, Isolde. We are grateful for the hospitality and information."

Inara grabbed the room keys and handed one over to Bellamy. They left the counter and made their way upstairs to their rooms. Inside the room, there was two double beds, a closet and wardrobe. A small square table with chairs, and a night-stand between the two beds with a lamp sitting on top. Bellamy set his pack down and took the bed closest to the window. Raine had set his pack down. Taking off his boots and plopped down onto the bed, burying his head into the cotton pillow. He closed his eyes and drifted off into sleep.

Bellamy looked out the window. Staring off into the lights and relative quietness of the city outside. He would see about finding a shop to get his bow fixed in the morning and then figure out their next moves about the job. The so-called easy part was done, they had made it to the city, now they had to move on to the next and meet up with their contact. Bellamy took off his boots and followed suit with Raine, laying down and finally going to bed for the night.

His body was exhausted, and he was more tired than he thought. As he fell asleep the moment his head hit the cotton pillow.

The scent of lavender filled the room coming from an incense lamp burning on the small square table. Bellamy and Raine woke up from their long night's sleep refreshed and relaxed when the scent hit their noses. The two of them looked at each other with a confused look in their eyes.

"Bellamy, I don't remember there being an incense lamp on that table, when we came into the room last night. Did I miss something, or did you place it there?"

"No. there was no incense lamp there last night. I'm as surprised as you are, especially considering I didn't hear the door open, or anyone come in. Did you not sense anything Raine?"

Raine tapped the top of his head with two fingers rhythmically as he pondered the question.

"I must have been more exhausted than I realized if someone was able to enter the room without me sensing them. I do not appreciate being caught off guard like that. I cannot let something like this happen again, my pride won't allow it."

"Let's change and go see if the girls know anything about it, Raine."

The two of them got ready and went to speak with the girls. They tried their room first, but they were not there. So they headed downstairs and found them in the common area, sitting at a table by the fireplace. Raine and Bellamy sat down across from the girls. They were chatting over bowls of oatmeal covered with mixed fruits slices, nuts and berries, and glasses of fresh squeezed juice.

"Good morning, you two. We got some breakfast for us to eat, try it out. Isolde happens to be a fine cook. So, dig in and enjoy."

"Good morning to you two as well."

Bellamy grabbed a bowl and joined the others in eating the breakfast provided to them. After finishing up his food and taking a drink of his juice. He sat back and asked the girls about the incense burner in their room.

"Huh. Well, I can tell you that it wasn't me or Inara, who put the incense burner in your room. We happened to wake up to the scent of lavender in our room as well."

"It must have been the innkeeper then. Though, I am still bothered and rather impressed that she was able to do that without any of us realizing it." Raine surmised.

They turned their heads looking over at the innkeeper standing behind the counter, who smiled and waved back at them all . They smiled back at her and turned back around, returning to their conversation at hand.

"That aside, what is the plan for today and going forward with our job?"

"We will need to send a message to the senator's assistant and inform him that we are in the city now. Then wait for him to give us a response and a meeting time to meet him. Other than that, there isn't much for us to do but wait. If there is anything you want to do in the city, you should use the time we have and do it."

Raine took a sip from his cup of fresh squeezed juice before speaking on the matter.

"Do you have a general idea on how long it might take for the senator's assistant to send his response to us?"

"I would say no later than the end of the week at the earliest. The senators are busy people daily. As such their assistants are also busy taking care of the administrative and personal work for them."

"With that in mind, enjoy your day my friends and I will see you all later this evening. I feel like partaking in what this city has to offer and enjoying some of its delicacies." Raine said with that cunning and charming smile of his.

He got up from the table, making his way to the front door and headed out into the city. Na'naya and Bellamy looked on in amusement. As they knew their friend was off to most likely cause trouble for some innocent tavern maidens, mature affluent ladies, or seductive brothel harlots. Raine was reliable in combat, a capable friend. But easily predictable when it came to spending his free time in a city or town and the women who inhabit it. They did not fault him for his more philandering habits, as they felt there must be some reason behind them.

One that Raine would one day speak to his friends about. But they would not press the matter if he didn't want to speak about it and would be contempt being there for their friend.

"What are you going to do Na'naya, with your free time?"

"I've heard that there are some interesting sights to see here in Hoenheim. I think I will do a little sightseeing and take in the sights around the city. What about you, Bellamy?"

"I plan to head to a weapon's shop and have them repair my bow. Though afterwards I will explore the city as well, since it is my first time here. How about you, Inara?"

Inara sat tapping her fingers on the table as she thought about her plans and what she wanted to do with her free time.

"There are a couple of things I need to do while we are here in the city. If you don't mind the company I can take you to a weapon's shop for your bow, Bellamy."

"That would be great, and I appreciate the offer. Thank you, Inara."

With their plans set, the three of them got up from their table and headed out. Na'naya parted ways heading down the street. Going in the opposite direction that Bellamy and Inara had taken from the inn. The Merchant's District was bustling with the sounds and conversations of the huge crowds of people going about their everyday lives. There were children running and playing around in the streets and small parks.

As their parents or nurses watched over them. Sounds of horns could be heard off in the distance, of the trains entering and leaving the central railway station hub. Vendors and merchants, at stalls and shops calling people passing by to come and look at the goods they had to offer. On the westside of the Merchant's district down a side road leading to a dead end stood a quaint two-story stone building with a wooden roof. Outside in front on the building attached to a signpost was the sign for the shop.

The sign read: *Dulhan's Workshop & Weaponry*. A bell rang as they walked into the weapon's shop.

Inside the shop the main floor area was lined with display cases and weapons racks running in five equally spaced-out aisles. The shop was filled with weapons and accessories of varying degrees of quality and material. From commonly found iron daggers to rarer Mithril swords, and everything between. With exotic options as well, that Bellamy had never seen before.

Each item in the store was exceptionally crafted by a master weapon's smith.

Through a keen eye for detail bringing out the weapon's true potential. At the back of the main floor area centered between the middle of the aisles was the check-out counter. Also a hallway with a door leading to the weapon's workshop beyond. The door to the workshop opened and a figured emerged walking down the hall to stand behind the counter.

He was an older Fae of the Dwarf variety, muscular and bulky in stature. He had long flowing auburn hair tied in a topknot and a bread just as long with three jeweled braids woven into it. Silver rimmed purple lens googles rested on his head above he somber green eyes. He looked over Bellamy with a stoic and calculating gaze. Then over at Inara and his gaze softened into a warm smile.

"Welcome, young one. It is a pleasure to see you again, after so long." He replied in a deep bellied voice, grizzled yet filled with care.

"It is good to see you too, Master Dulhan. The one standing next to me is a traveling companion of mine, his name is Bellamy. We came to your shop today to see if you would be able to repair and improve his bow for him."

Bellamy took the broken pieces of his bow out from his pack. Placing them on the counter, along with some of the material they harvested from the Tiger-Bear Behemoth. Master Dulhan examined the pieces of the bow carefully and looked at the material provided.

"Quality material. Quality material indeed, this will do. I can fix your recurve bow and improve it, making it better than it originally was. Come back in six days and you will have your new bow."

"Thank you, Master Dulhan. I am sure based on what I have seen in your shop that my new bow will be an exceptional piece. You have my gratitude."

"Consider yourself lucky young man. My wears and reputation are known far and wide. I don't sell, let alone do commissioned work, like repairs and such for just anyone. I am selective on who I choose to offer my services too. I have seen into your heart and can tell that Inara here believes in you, so I will work with you."

Master Dulhan picked up the items and turned to walk back down the hall to his workshop. Waving them off as he prepared to begin his work.

"Inara, make sure that you are taking care of that Warhammer of yours. It was one of my finest creations and you of all people know better than to misuse it my dear. And you boy, watch yourself with that one, she has a strong stubborn headedness to her."

Though only a short instant Bellamy swore he saw Inara lightly blush across her cheeks.

"Seriously master, when will you learn. We will see you in six days then, take care."

CHAPTER 9
RAINE ROLLO

After leaving the Songbird Inn, Raine didn't have a destination in mind, so he let his feet take him one foot at a time. It was late in the evening when the group had made it to the inn they would be staying at. He was tired from all the traveling so he wasn't able to take in the city the first night. Now that he was rested and it was early in the day, Raine planned on getting a better luck of the city he found himself in. The tales and gossip he had heard from travelers over the years, couldn't quite stand up to seeing Hoenheim in person with his own eyes.

The republic's capital was a city diverse in wonders. A melting pot of the many cultures and races that called the republic home or refuge from their homes.

The streets were crowed with all types of people, from the lowest classes of society, all the way up to the privileged upper classes. Expression of one's ideas and beliefs fueled by the will of the citizens was evident all throughout. Whether it was through writing, clothing, music, general interactions, etc. It was the heart of Hoenheim and its people. As he walked down the streets of the Merchant's District, Raine could see a carefree happiness in the eyes of the people going about their everyday lives.

It had been many years long ago since Raine last felt genuine carefree happiness in his life. His charismatic smile and flirtatious personality had been a mask that he had dawned. For a part to play that he had for a brief time thought was real. Though these short respites often abruptly end. Then he remembers the emotions and memories that were meant to stay buried deep within his conscience.

So, he would dawn his mask again and proceed to move forward. For he was one who told himself that the past should stay in the past.

After musing his way up and down the twisting streets and alleyways of the Merchant's District, at the end of one such street, Raine came upon a long steep staircase raising up to a platform area above. Walking and pondering random thoughts as he made his way up the steep staircase one step at a time. At the top of the staircase was a peaceful little park and flower garden. Surrounding an ancient Evening Star Tree at its center. Its long branches reaching out towards the heavens.

Cool pastel-colored leaves swayed in the warm mountain breeze. Raine walked over to the tree and sat beneath its cover, leaning his back against the tree's wide rugged trunk.

He reached into an inner pocket on his vest and pulled out an old ocarina. Delicately carved from the tusk of a mighty Oliphant. A somber and haunting melody filled the air and echoed off into the distance, as he played his ocarina. The song was the epic of the great huntress on her journey into the wilds. Setting out to retrieve her stolen child and avenge her slain lover.

It was a tale full of heartache, adventure, and the fear of what lies ahead of us all. The song was known by many different clans and tribes. Who had different interpretations when they played it. but for Raine and his clan it was a cautious tale on the consequences of misplaced trust.

"Umm…I don't mean to intrude, but that was a very beautiful song you played. Though also so full of sadness and longing. What is it called?" a sweet and gentle voice spoke out to him.

Raine opened his eyes as moved his ocarina away from his mouth and placed it back into his inner vest pocket. Standing a few feet away from him, was a young Human female maiden. Tanned of skin with long flowing raven-black hair and light purple eyes. She was wearing a long cloth and silk headscarf with jeweled beads tied around her forehead. She had a geometric patterned light long-sleeved blouse enclosed by a dark leather corset around her slender pro-portioned bodice, traveler's pants, and padded boots.

"It's an old song among my people called *The Huntress's Aria.* I'm glad you enjoyed the beauty of the song. Most people when they hear it are drawn into the sadness and longing. They miss the beauty that is hidden within its enchanting melody. What brings you here, young maiden?" Raine re-sponded with his charismatic smile.

"I was out for a stroll to clear my mind and come up with a solution to a problem. When I heard the song and followed the melody here. My apologies, let me introduce myself. My name is Sarai."

"Pleasure to meet you, miss. I am Raine Rollo. You said something about a problem that you have, if you don't mind telling me about it, I might be able to help you with it. I am an exceptionally skilled mercenary, so do not hesitate to ask."

At that moment Sarai's eyes lit up and a tension that was resting on her shoulders seemed to ease away. Perhaps this encounter had brought her to the solution she was seeking. It could bring an end to her troubles.

"I don't know where to start, so I guess I'll start from the beginning on how my family's troubles started. I come from a middle-class family born and raised in this city. My father is an inventor of sorts, and he is highly skilled, though he can be a bit eccentric when it comes to his work. Me and my younger sister are the only family he has left. As our mother passed away when we were younger from The Dreaming Sickness. It hasn't been easy on him, but he has done everything he could to take care of us..." Sarai paused, tears forming in her eyes.

"Recently my younger sister has become ill, and my father's age started to make it more difficult for him to do his work. I have done what I can to help by helping with his work and working at the library to cover some of the expenses. This proved to be a minor fix but our problems got worse when my father was killed. It was over a damaging deal he had made with some gangsters. They threatened to take me and my sister away to cover our father's debit if I didn't deliver on the deal. Please... help, I need to rescue my sister and leave this city for someplace else, far away from this nightmare."

Raine looked at the young maiden asking him for help. Her hands trembling and as she fought back to hold off the tears cascading down her cheeks. He pulled out a handkerchief from his pocket and handed it over to her, so that she could wipe the tears away. Standing up from his spot against the tree, He lifted his hand and patted the top of her head, while smiling back at her.

"There. There, wipe your tears away lovely miss. I am sorry for your loss and the heartache that you have felt. You should involve the proper authorities. But I can assume from your plea that it would not be in the best interest of you or your sister to get them involved. With that in mind, I will take the job and help you out. It is one thing to turn down a dangerous job. But it is entirely another to refuse the request of a lovely young maiden in need."

"Thank you, Raine. You have my gratitude and I promise you that I'll repay you for your service. Now if you would follow me, I can take you to where I am supposed to meet them. It's in the Industrial Complex, the district below the Low Summit District."

The Industrial Complex District was home to the city's factories, warehouses, and mines. It is the third largest of the city's six districts. Many lower-class citizens, criminals, those wanting to disappear, and those finding themselves on hard times would seek out work in the factories or mines of the city. Dangerous and difficult for even the most skilled workers, these jobs were not taken lightly or generally the first choice to be taken. With luck on your side and a strong will, there was fortune to be made in places like this, if you knew where to look.

It was at one such place that Raine had followed Sarai through the city to come to. In the older part of the district, lined with rundown and abandoned warehouses, they reached their destination. It was a grouping of four massive warehouses connected to a multi-story building by overhead walkways. Surrounded by an outer stone wall around the perimeter. Standing at the front gate were six, armed Human thugs. One of the thugs approached Raine and Sarai.

"Hold it right there. What brings you two here? You best be off if you don't have business here."

"I've come to see Carrigan, about squaring my father's debit and getting my sister back."

"Oh. If it isn't the older sister returning to pay her dead father's debit. You think that guy is going to be up to the challenge. Ha. Well missy, for your sake you better be right, because there won't be any more opportunities after this one. Open the gates!"

The thug stepped away and the others behind him, opened the gates to complex beyond. Sarai proceeded on forward, closely followed by Raine. The gates closing behind them as they pasted the threshold into the complex. The thug that had addressed them at the gate, escorted them onwards.

"Why didn't you tell me that, you had gotten others to help you out before."

"I didn't want to discourage you or risk you turn me down, if you knew that there were others before you that had failed. You have every right to be upset with me. I'm sorry to have lied to you."

"Though you may have omitted that part, you told me the truth about everything else. As far as I'm concerned that is all that matters in the end. So don't worry about a thing, it's going to be alright."

The raucous sound of a crowd cheering and the sounds of raging battle echoed in the distance. From the direction on the open warehouse door they were making their way towards. Inside the massive warehouse game tables were scattered around the outer area. In the center was rolls of wooden bleachers rising around a metal cage over a fighting arena below. The thug leads them through the warehouse over to a raised platform overlooking the center of the arena below.

He lifts his hand signaling for the two to wait at the base of the steps and proceeds up the stairs. On the platform is a large, cushioned couch, and a man with two women leaning against his broad shoulders, passing him a goblet of wine and a pipe.

The thug walks behind the couch, leans over the man's right shoulder and whispers into his ear. He claps his hands together and the women leaning on him move over, so that he can get up. He turned and walked down the steps of the platform to stand before Raine and Sarai.

"So, the prodigal daughter has returned, and with a challenger I see. Foolish or brave we will certainly find out soon enough."

Carrigan was an older human in his forties. He was tall with a lean muscular build, Burnette braids running down his head and a goatee around his stoic boxy chin. His eyes were a cold dark brown, hardened, and emotionless. He wore a silver chain adorned with fangs around his neck. A satin fur lined coat unbuttoned exposing his bare scarred muscular chest beneath. Satin trousers and laced sandals were on his legs and feet.

"I am Carrigan, master of the Thieves Guild in Hoenheim and proprietor of the Fighting Arena. If there are deals to be made or profits to be gained, I am the broker for business done in the underworld. Nothing is out of my reach. Nothing." His gaze peering deep into Sarai's frightened eyes.

Raine gently touched Sarai's hand to calm her fears before he spoke up.

"I have been asked by this young maiden here to help her and retrieve her sister, from their father's debit. Tell me what it is that I must do to settle the debt and I will."

Carrigan looked over at Raine with a wicked grin on his face. Knowing that he had him in the palm of his hand.

"Confident are you, young pup. You may soon regret that bravado of yours. Alright, you want to settle their debt, then all you must do is compete in the arena and beat the reigning champion in a no holds duel. Beat the champion, I will return the sister and consider their debt settled in full. Should you lose both sisters along with you little pup will be my property to do with as I so choose. Do you accept or will you walk away and leave the sisters to me."

"I accept the challenge." Raine responded defiantly.

CHAPTER 10

R aine stood in the circular arena looking at the area around him. The arena floor was paved stone and tightly packed dirt, making it a solid even surface to fight upon. Tall slick walls with small, spiked protrusion scattered intermittingly along its surface raised twelve feet up, encasing the arena. The metal gage overhead, ensuring no one was able to escape, if they managed to scale the walls somehow. The only way in and out where the two entrance gates on the far side and the one behind him, that he had entered through.

His weapons were left in the holding room, as he was instructed to leave them or forfeit the match. Carrigan stood up from his couch. He raised his hands into the air and addressed the gathering crowd on the wooden bleachers.

"Ladies and Gentlemen. My fellow patrons, I welcome you all to a special event this evening for your entertainment. A no holds match, where the match ends when the opponent falls unconscious, submits, or is killed. Tonight's opponent taking on the reigning champion is the newcomer Raine Rollo."

The enthralled masses booed and cheered on the challenger.

"Now entering the arena, I present to you the current reigning champion. With over two dozen wins, *the Nightmare of the deep mines, the Bane of Charlemagne, Draemond.*"

Roaring cheers echoed throughout and the stomping of feet Shaked the ground. The gates on the far side raised up and the champion Draemond walked out. He was a Demi-Human of the Dragonkin variety. With wise eyes of Sage and tanned skin, he was tall with a muscular athletic build. A pair of prominent horns and pointed ears upon his head poking through his long shaggy white hair.

He had red scaled clawed hands, feet, and a powerful tail swaying from his back. Upon his body was a long-sleeved leather and cloth vest coat over his bare chest. A decorative sash wrapped around his waist. It rested upon his leather and cloth trousers.

"No weapons will be allowed during the match. Just the fighter's bare hands and raw strength. Now with no further delay, let the match... begin!"

The two fighters stared at one another, as they slowly approached, sizing up their foe. A subtle motion here. A shift in balance there, the twitch of an ear. All were indicators a skilled fighter looked for to find signs of an opponent's potential move. Reyne had been in many fights throughout his life, both armed and un-armed. They had taught him to adapt. To refine his skills, when facing a variety of different opponents in battle. This battle was no different than the others, but he wasn't going to act rash or be overconfident.

Dragonkin were known to be fierce and skilled warriors in battle. Capable of breaking an opponent's back with the shear strength of their tails, if ensnared by it. Raine would have to be cautious with this opponent and do whatever he can to win the match. If the match lasted too long or became dragged out, there was no guarantee that his stamina would hold out.

Confident as he was, a Dragonkin's endurance was no joking matter to take likely.

He would have to knock him out, that was the only way. Raine didn't want to needlessly kill someone if it could be helped.

"Draemond, was it? I want you to know that I am going to win this match, but I will not kill you to do it. I do not want the young maiden up there to witness some needless bloodshed."

Draemond snarled a fanged grin towards Raine.

"Bold words, pup. You may try, but it is you that will be laying at the base of my feet. It is a lesson that I will beat into you, so that you understand your place."

Thrill and adrenaline pumped through the two challengers. They charged towards one another. Striking fast, with heavy blows, Draemond swing his tail in a whipping motion to Raine's right and then left. Bending and twisted his body in the opposite directions of the whipping strikes, he dodged his opponent's tail. In that instant when he dodged, two jabs struck firmly in his sides. Flinching from the hits, Raine answered with a kick of his own into Draemond's chest.

Knocking him backwards momentarily. Rebounding he charged forward and the two of them exchanged blows. As one would block, the other would counter with a strike of their own.

Block. punch to the face.

"Ughh." Draemond breathes an angered groan.

Jab to the center...punch to the side. Block.

Block. Jab... punch...Jab...Punch to the chest.

"Aaaahhh." Raine winces a pained breath.

Four strikes…. A quick jab…Block.

Backing away from each other, the fighter's chest rises and falls as they take long strained breaths. Sweat beads roll down the side of Raine's cheeks. He calms the raging beat of his heart, centering himself for what comes next. He has managed to keep up with his opponent, but the Dragonkin is proving to be a worthy challenge. Raine clasped his hands and cracks his knuckles, preparing for the next round of the match. Carefully watching closely for Draemond to make his move.

"As much as I hate to admit it, I can see why you are the reigning champion in the arena. You truly are a skilled fighter."

"Do not think your words will sway the outcome of this match. I will not lose to you."

"Oh. It was merely an observation is all. Now, I think this match has gone on long enough. Let's end it shall we."

Once again, the two fighters charged forward, with a burning desire to win gleaming in their eyes. Draemond extended his arms reaching out towards Raine, who grasped them in his hands. It was a match of shear strength. They grappled back and forth with their hands tightly gripped together. neither one giving ground. When it seemed like one was gaining the upper hand the other would take back control. Locking them in a perpetual stalemate. The fighters holding steadfast as they waited for the right moment to make their move. Turning the tides of the fight in their favor.

Raine felt a mere and minor wince in Draemond's grip, this was the moment he had been waiting for. He pushed upwards. Leaning forward allowing his momentum to create a space between him and his opponent. In that instant he dropped with a swift sliding motion. Scissor kicked Draemond's left leg and wrapped his body around his arm and neck. With this action Raine had dragged Draemond to the ground locking him in a restrained choke hold. His legs were firmly wrapped around his neck and upper arm, locking his opponent in place.

"It looks like I have the upper hand. Do you yield?"

Draemond huffed and stared with contempt at Raine.

"I told you once already, that I will not lose to you, pup. So, I will not yield!"

Draemond summoning what stamina he had left in him. Flexed his mighty muscles, and leveraged his tail to propel him back up onto his feet. Raine held on tight, not letting his grip on Draemond waver in the sudden movement. Draemond hadn't realized that when he stood up, he had sealed his outcome in the match, for he had fallen into Raine's trap. In that instant with the stage set.

Raine tightened his grip more around Draemond's neck and twisted his body. Using their combined weight to slam his body into the ground in a massive impact. The force of the impact knocking Draemond out cold. The crowd erupted in a roaring cheer, clapping, and chanting for the challenger.

"Raine...Raine...Raine...!"

"Bravo. Bravo. It seems you have defeated my champion. Impressive indeed. Very well, I will honor our deal, come to the gathering hall and we will finish up our business there."

Raine and Sarai were escorted from the arena. They headed to the central building of the complex, where the gathering hall was located. The gathering hall was a wide octangular room, with banners hung along the walls. Passageways leading to other parts of the building, and a raised dais in the center with a throne upon it. Carrigan was waiting for them, sitting on the throne as the made their ways towards him.

Standing off to the right of him was two guards, flanking a young girl in a blue and purple tunic dress. Sarai's eyes widened as she laid eyes on her sister and a sigh of relief passed her lips.

"Mari!"

"Sister. You came back for me."

"Of course, I came back for you. I would never leave you. I am sorry that you had to suffer because of me."

Mari's eyes filled with tears, happy to see her sister again, but also sad that she had caused her sister to worry. She wiped her tears away and put on a brave face for her sister, so she wouldn't have to worry anymore.

"Isn't it touching to see sisters reunited again. Though, I wonder for how long. We will have to wait and see." Carrigan spoke with a snug condescending remark.

"What do you mean by that, Carrigan. The deal was that I fight your champion, you would settle the debt and release the sisters."

Carrigan clapped his hands. A dozen of his men entered the gathering hall from the passageways surrounding Raine and Sarai. Draemond was amongst the group of thugs.

"Yes. That was the terms of the original deal, but you see I am very fond of the sisters and can't so easily part ways with them. So, the deal has changed."

"You can't do this. Raine did what you asked with no complaints. He risked his life to help me and my sister. Please, Carrigan honor the original deal." Sarai pleaded.

Carrigan raised his hand, and his men drew their weapons. Raine drew his daggers as well and prepared to fight.

"Damn you. You bastard! I will not let this go unpunished, you will come to regret crossing me, Carrigan. Those without honor deserve no peace in this life or the next."

"Get Him! Do not harm the girl, I want her untouched. Kill the pup."

Carrigan's men rushed towards Raine. Charging with a wild uncultured ferocity in their movements. Now, that Raine had his gear back, they would regret taking him lightly. With fluid and swift strikes, Raine cut down the first four men who haphazardly. Trying to overwhelm him. They were no match for his refined and skilled movements. Blocking strikes from blades and clubs, then countering right back with a slash and a strike of his own. From one opponent to the next, Raine would make quick work of his would-be challengers. Fighting them one at a time or in small groups.

The only one that Raine had cause to concern himself with was Draemond, who had fought in the arena not too long ago. He had seen him enter the room with the other members of Carrigan's gang. When they charged towards him, he was not a part of the foray. Raine kept an eye out for him but continued to focus his attention on the problem at hand. Dealing with the remaining thugs. At last, the battle was coming to its end.

Many of the men Carrigan had sent after him were down or dead, and only a few remained to challenge him.

"Ughh…"

The two guards that had been guarding Sarai's sister collapsed to the ground. Their necks snapped in an instant. In the commotion of all the fighting Sarai had made her way over to her sister. She embraced her with a tight hug, not wanting to be separated from her again. Appearing behind them, holding a massive Steel Claymore in hand, Draemond turned and pointed it at Carrigan's chest.

"Tell your men to stand down." Draemond commanded.

Carrigan stared him down in a quiet defiance, not so persuaded by bravado. Draemond with an inhuman quickness, thrusted the massive blade forward stopping mere inches from the base of Carrigan's chest.

"Stand down! Stand Down!"

The men stopped their fighting and back away from Raine and from encircling the sisters. Raine sheathed his daggers and ran over to the two sisters.

"What is the meaning of this, Draemond? Turning your back on our arrangement and threatening my life."

"I will not stand by and let you dishonor my fight and the deal that was agreed upon by both parties. My word is my bond, and you have no honor. As such our arrangement is no longer valid and I will do as I see fit. You three, go now and leave this place. I will keep anyone from interfering."

"Thank you, Draemond."

Raine picked up Sarai's younger sister and carried her in his arms. Sarai followed closely behind as they made their escape from the area.

CHAPTER II

A cool breeze filled the nighttime air. The lights of the city illuminated throughout the districts of Hoenheim. Creating a canvas of ethereal beauty. The bell of the clock tower in the square down the road from the central train station hub rung. Signaling the new hour.

Raine sat down on a bench next to Sarai, as Mari was laying down, resting her head in her sister's lap. People walked passing by as they made their way home or to a tavern for food and entertainment. The streets weren't as packed as they were during the day, so the area was peaceful.

"I am glad that I was able to help you with your problem and get your sister back . It seemed a little touch and go at times, but it worked out in the end."

Sarai smiled down at her sleeping sister, grateful to be back with her. Stroking the long curls of her brunette hair. Her heart raced and her nerves were starting to overtake her, as she took in a long calming breath. Inhaling long through her nose and exhaling slow through her mouth. Sarai repeated these motions. For a moment to muster the words she wanted to express to Raine.

"Thank you again for all your help Raine. I don't know what I would've done if I didn't come across you today or if you had turned me down. We only have each other now, and I won't let this sort of thing happen again. I swear it to the divine Night Mother, may she watch over us and guide us on our journey."

Raine reached in his pocket grabbed out a pouch of money and handed it to Sarai. She looked at it confused and speechless. It was the first time in a long time that somebody had showed her such kindness, without wanting and asking for anything in return. She was moved by his actions and knew that his gift was genuine.

"It's for you and your sister to start a new life away from this city and the threat of Carrigan and his men. I got it from the winnings I made in my match with Draemond. Consider it a gift from a friend, who only wants you to be safe and happy."

"I don't know what to say, Raine. It's more than I deserve for the trouble I caused you today. I promise that someday I will repay your kindness, somehow. This will help us out in more ways than I can count."

Raine got up from the bench and stretched his arms. Looking up at the stars and bright crescent moons overheard. Waving his hand to Sarai in farewell, he turned and walked off down the street, whistling an old tribal tune. Not taking a subtle glance back or turning to see Sarai's face. Raine pressed on feeling a sensation deep down that he had not felt for some time. It had brought a smile to his face.

"Goodbye, Raine. I hope we meet again. Take care of yourself." Sarai shouted in the distance.

Raine had no more reason to be concerned for Sarai and her sister, he knew that the two of them would be fine. The threat to them should no longer be a problem. He was certain that Carrigan would set his sights on the two fighters. Since they made him look like a fool and escaped from his grasp. He was not concerned with that, as he was confident, he could handle any situation that might come from it. It was past time for supper and Raine had worked up an appetite from all the fighting he had did earlier.

Raine wandered the streets and alleyways of the Merchant's District as he casually walked looking for a tavern to grab some food and drink. Off the beaten path and down an alleyway that appeared to be sparsely traveled. Raine spotted a sign hanging above a set of stairs leading down to an entrance below. The sign overhead read: *The Last Wish Tavern*. Raine walked down the stairs and through the oak and iron door leading into the tavern.

Inside the tavern was one large chamber. An octagonal dark oak bar lined with stools around it at the center. Booths and tables lined the outer areas surrounding the bar.

There was a hallway on the far side of the chamber leading back to the kitchen and storage area. A mixture of exotic fragrances, meals being cooked up in the kitchen. The chattering of the various patrons enjoying a drink or dining on delicious meals. Filled the ambient lit chamber with a sense of both a warm comfort and a strange loneliness. Raine made his way over to the octagonal bar and sat down at one of the empty stools.

He lifted his hand, signaling the bartender to come over and take his order. The bartender returned with a tankard of Wisteria Berry Ale and a plate of Chicken dumplings with wild rice. Finally able to relax, Raine took in the aroma of the warm food and the sweet taste of the ale before him.

"Well, I see you managed to make it out and get those sisters to somewhere safe. I knew that you would be able to do the job."

Raine turned at the sound of the voice and saw Draemond standing there next to him. Draemond nodded his head towards Raine and took a seat on the stool next to him. The bartender came over and handed him a tankard of beer.

"I take it, you must come here often?"

"This place is special and not easily found by the everyday people of the city. So, I've grown attached to it and come by every so often to enjoy a drink or meal. You know they say it takes a certain type of individual to find this place. I'm impressed you were able to find it, you are talented indeed."

Raine wasn't certain what Draemond meant by that or if he was jesting, but he sensed no ill intentions in his words.

"Thank you for aiding us back there, Draemond. Without your help, getting out of there with both sisters would have been difficult to pull off, even for me."

"There is no need to thank me, Carrigan had went back on his word and I couldn't let that slight go unchallenged. He was the fool to break a bond with a Dragonkin, a mistake that he won't make again, if he values his life."

It was evident to Raine that the stories and information that he had heard over the years about the Dragonkin were all but true and not mere rumors. Dragonkin were fierce loyal warriors whose bonds were like sacred vows. Not to be made lightly or dismissed carelessly. For their pride and honor would not tolerate such transgressions against them. Meaning the violator would certainly pay a high price. There was no escaping one's fate, when a bond with a Dragonkin is broken, least of all when done with ill intent.

"So, now that I find myself available and between jobs at the moment, I was wondering if I would be able to accompany you on your travels." Draemond inquired.

"Hmmm... that is an interesting proposition you have. I would have to talk it over with my traveling companions and see how they feel about it, first. Though I have no problems with it myself, as I have seen your character and know your skill."

"That is a reasonable point, and it makes sense as your friends do not know me. Then I will wait for you to get an answer from your friends on the matter. In the meantime, I have some business to take care of, I will come and find you at the end of the week. Until next we meet, so long for now Raine."

Draemond got up from the bar. He headed out down a hallway on the other side of the chamber. Through an iron door with strange intricate runic glyphs unknown to him that Raine had not noticed when he first entered the tavern.

CHAPTER 12
NA'NAYA ADINA

Na'naya had kind of hoped that one of the other's might have changed their mind. To come along with her on her sightseeing tour of the city. Or had asked her if she wanted to tag along with them, but she had no such luck this time. It wasn't that she disliked doing things on her own. It was that she felt livelier when she had others to go with her on her outings.

As an orphaned child it was tough on her living on her own. Having to find ways of adapting and surviving in the strenuous harsh environment of her desert homeland. She would get occasional support from passing caravans. Help from one of the local religious sects. Only ever given enough to get her through a few days on end.

Through that hardship and her sheer determination Na'naya was able to overcome the challenges that faced her. Until the day she met the traveling monk who would become her master and father figure.

She had learned much from him on the ways of the world. How to protect herself in the time she got to spend with him before the Dreaming Sickness took him. Grateful for what he had taught her, Na'naya decided to live her life the way her master had. by traveling and exploring the wide world around her. Through these travels that she had found her way to Aurontil and the Falling Star Mercenary Company.

Where she met Bellamy and Raine. They had become close friends and were the only other family she had ever known. So, she would do anything in her power to help them out, no matter the problem. They would do the same for her without hesitation.

Hoenheim was a majestic city to behold. There are many different cultural and famous sights to see within the capital of the Renata Republic. Several diverse cultures have come to call it home over the years. The city has been a beacon of refuge for expression of ideas. Beliefs and knowledge for people who had become oppressed in their homelands.

By embracing these other cultures. Hoenheim has flourished economically and politically in its influence with other nations. This was appealing to Na'naya's curiosity. Driving her to explore the city more and see what it had to offer her. Though she didn't forget the reason why she had come to the city in the first place with her companions.

So, she figured she would not only sightsee but also gather information on the workings of the city. To find out something useful that would help them out on their job.

Na'naya made her way through the city to the upper district of The Parliamentary Peak. The central location of the main governmental buildings and auxiliary offices running the republic. This district of the city was a wide area with densely packed groupings of buildings along evenly paced avenues running in crisscrossing directions of a compass's cardinal points. All the roads converging at a center focal point in the district where the Great Renatan Parliament Hall stood. The great hall was a marvel of artistic architecture constructed in the early years of the republic during its Renaissance period.

Crafted from the precious stones found deep within the mountains. It was comprised of a hexagonal multi-tiered spired tower. Connected by four covered bridge walkways in the center of a ring shaped outer three-story building.

The outer promenade leading to the main building was decorated with manicured greenery. Flanking obelisks along the walkway depicting the history of the republic and the different chancellors that have presided over it. Na'naya was awestruck by the building's beauty and grandeur. Something she hadn't seen since glimpsing the royal palace of Umbarah in her youth. As she made her way past the great hall, she noticed that only people who had proper credentials were admitted into the building.

The Parliamentary Guards standing at the entrance doorway and the side entrances for support staff would stop anyone without. Those who didn't were turned away or detained if considered a threat to those inside. She would have to let the others know about that. Perhaps the contact they were waiting for would have some information or help about getting access into the building.

"Excuse me miss, but you don't seem like you're from around here. Do you need help finding something or directions somewhere?" A calm and powerful voice spoke from behind Na'naya.

Na'naya turned around to see a tall middle-aged Human male with deep green eyes and long auburn hair tied into a ponytail. He was wearing a fedora with a Phantom Hawk feather laced into a greyish leather strap upon his hat. A long gambeson trench coat over a studded doublet, leather greaves and boots. The man had caught Na'naya off guard as she didn't feel like anyone was behind her or around her. There weren't many people around in the area, she was currently walking in.

She was a bit flustered that she had allowed herself to be distracted in her actions. She wasn't going to let this stranger notice.

"I appreciate your concern and the offer of help, sir. I recently arrived in the city and as this is my first time here, I wanted to explore and take in the wonderous sights. It is a wonderful city to behold."

The charming sentiment brought a subtle smile to the stranger's face and a gleam to his deep green eyes. Na'naya was drawn towards his magnetic presence. She was not a woman who was easily impressed or smitten by some man's charisma. At least that had been her general impression with the men in her life. There appeared to be something different about this man, that she couldn't place in the moment. She wasn't about to falter now, so she calmed her mind and focused on her friends instead.

"That it most certainly is. This city and its people are special. I have called this place home for most of my life and as such have done my best to serve her desires. She is my mistress, and I am one of her sworn protectors, here to keep the peace and enforce her laws no matter the cost. Pardon my ramblings miss, I am Andrias Charlemagne."

"Well, Andrias my name is Na'naya, and it was nice to meet you. There is something you could help me with. I heard that there is a sacred fountain of the Twilight Saint located at their temple here in Hoenheim. Do you know where to find it at?

Andrias raised his left hand, tilting his fedora down. He placed his hand on his chin, and brushed the side of his mouth with his thumb as he thought over her question. Na'naya noticed a white-gold signet ring with a crest etched into the precious stone adorning it on his ring finger. She couldn't make it out. The crest seemed somewhat familiar to her.

Like she had seen it somewhere before, though it escaped her. She didn't want to pry into his personal life, one of her friends might know or she might remember herself. It was best not to get too involved with this man, as she still had a job to complete with Bellamy and the others.

"Interesting. I know the place you speak of it is called the House of Twilight. It is a temple run by the Followers of the Twilight Saint, dedicated to them. It's located in the High Summit District. Keep following this current road north by northwest and you will find it."

Na'naya wondered about the first thing Andrias had said.

"Thank you for the information. Well, I will be heading off now, it was nice meeting you. Perhaps we will run into each again."

Andrias nodded his head and turned heading off down the road in the opposite direction. Na'naya proceeded to head to her destination at the House of Twilight. The High Summit district of Hoenheim was different form the other districts that made up the city. It was situated on the highest plateau of the mountains. A wide-open area of lush, majestic parks and fine manses.

Along with the Upper-Class, the Chancellor's estate, the High Summit District was also home to the temples of the four major faiths recognized in the republic and the other nations. These being: The Nox Pathos (Night's Pantheon), Nimhism, The Followers of The Twilight Saint, and The Followers of The Soul Flame.

Many other minor religions also have followers and temples located throughout the different nations. It is the major four that have risen to have the most power and influence in the world. An albeit teetering balance at best has been established. Between the major four religions. Along with the governmental bodies of the nations where they have followers.

In ensuring the balance exists, no one religion has completely dominated world politics for the last few centuries, for how much longer this will last remain to be seen. The House of Twilight laid beyond an outer wall. A great iron-clad gate closing the path to the inner courtyard was guarded by the temple priests. As Na'naya approached the gate was opened and one of the temple priests gestured for her to go inside.

She walked past him. Crossing the threshold of the gate and into the inner courtyard behind the outer wall. Inside the inner courtyard she followed a stone walkway past the main cathedral, gathering hall, and living annexes to a columned rotunda at the end of the path. Inside the rotunda at the center stood the sacred Twilight Fountain. The fountain was comprised of a lower pool at its base.

The duo-visage of the Twilight Saint rising from it, their hands outstretched. Two smaller upper pools resided in a disk that each of the visages of the saint held. Male on the left and female on the right.

Sunset lilies and Nightshade Roses floated in the pools of the fountain. Whose waters tranquil and serene glowed with an otherworldly beauty. Na'naya knelt before the fountain and closed her eyes while offering a prayer.

[*"You who embodies the duality of the soul. The light and the dark, the masculine and the Feminine. Sacred Wayfinder and traveler of both worlds. I ask for your guidance and protection as I continue down this path that I have chosen. In my brightest days and darkest nights, may twilight show me to what is right. In your name I pray."]*

Na'naya opened her eyes and stood back up, taking in the view of the fountain one my last time, before leaving. She was about to make her way from the rotunda when she noticed someone else on the other side of the fountain. Kneeling and crying into their hands. It wasn't her place to get involved with someone's problem, when they didn't ask for help. Na'naya couldn't bring herself to walk away.

From the looks of their clothing, they appeared to be a temple novice. Someone starting down the path of the Twilight Saint. Their dark blue robes and sky-blue sash around their waist, giving their position away.

"Excuse me, but are you alright? Would you like me to find one of the brothers or sisters to help you? I can leave you alone if you think I'm being a bother."

The novice wiped their tears away and stood up to face Na'naya. She was a young female Fae of the Gnome variety. With long Silver-Blonde hair, pointed ears, with a tanned skin tone and light Brown eyes. There were few Fae in the city. So she was surprised to see one, especially a Gnome as they tended to stay around their own kind more.

"I do not know you miss, but please stay and talk with me for a bit. You seem like a nice person, and I could use someone nice to talk to."

"Okay, I can do that. My name is Na'naya. What is your name?"

The novice smiled and appeared to be happy about having someone to talk to. Na'naya smiled back at her.

"You may call me Shae, a novice of the Followers of the Twilight Saint."

CHAPTER 13

S hae walked over to Na'naya, tapping her on the shoulder for her to come and follow her. The two of them left the rotunda and walked along the stone paths through the flower garden behind it. A symphony of dazzling colors and alluring fragrances filled the senses of the two women strolling through the flower garden. Filled with a wide assortment of flowers both foreign and native to the region. It was a rare pleasure to see some many beautiful and distinct flowers.

Some of which Na'naya had only ever seen in books or heard of from travelers chatting away in taverns. There was one small grouping of beautiful flowers that was separated from the other groupings of flowers. that Shae had stopped in front of, staring at it with a somberness in her eyes.

Na'naya had never seen the flowers before. They had blossoming petals that of a mix between roses and lilies that were blending colors of the sky at dusk or before sunset. Their stems were a dark brownish purple in color. Protruding with leaves of a deep crimson scarlet. She looked closer at the flowers. She saw that they weren't growing from the ground like a common everyday flower.

But from the decaying skull of a legendary Daemon known as a Chronosaur. It was a rare and legendary Daemon that had strange temporal abilities, causing it to shift between time and realities. A beast of such power that it was considered an unnatural natural phenomenon. That was best to avoid at all costs. Very few of the races have seen the Chronosaur in person. A vast majority of them were wiped out by a cataclysm brought on by the gods.

"This is an extremely rare and precious flower known as Twilight's Kiss. It only blooms twice every thousand years, and it gets its name from the coloring on the petals. The priests tell us that the flower is sacred and holds wonderous properties within it. How to harvest and use it is a closely guarded secret by the religion."

"That's amazing Shae. I had no idea such a rare and unique flower even existed, and That Followers of the Twilight Saint protected it. With such beauty and interesting marvels around you, why were you at the fountain crying?"

Shae placed her hands together. Tapping her fingers back and forth in a movement of hesitation. She wasn't sure of herself or what to do, was it proper for her to burden this woman she had met with her concerns. Had she done the right thing in opening to her at the fountain and bringing her to the sacred flowers. Shae had come this far already, what use would it be to back out now.

"I'm uneasy and afraid of what comes next. I was one of the chosen selected of the novices to undergo the sacred transition ritual tonight."

"What is this transition ritual, that you speak of?"

"It is a sacred honor that is bestowed upon gifted and devoted followers. It brings them closer to our god's enlightenment. This is accomplished by giving the chosen the ability to live as both genders. Switching between the masculine and feminine every three months as the seasons change for the rest of their lives. Though unlike our god, this gift comes with a heavy price. the chosen will not be able to shift between genders by time of day like our god. They will be baren unable to conceive or bare offspring."

Na'naya walked over to Shae and embraced her in her arms, providing her with some form of comfort that she could. It was a difficult decision placed upon someone still young and in her prime. Made even more harder by the fact that Fae in general live much longer lives than humans. What would she do, had she been put in this situation and given the chance for this sacred gift. Na'naya knew she would have to speak to Shae more about it.

If she was going to give her advice that would impact her future from here on. Now, it was about helping her come to the best solution for her.

"If I may ask, what brought you to join the faith. From what I can tell you don't seem to be much older than me and are intelligent, so why this life?"

Shae inhaled , taking in the fresh mountain air into her lungs and filling her body, before exhaling in a calm pulsing motion. Preparing herself to tell Na'naya her story and what led her to join the faith at her age.

"As you may know Fae have a longer lifespan than humans. For Dwarves, Gnomes, and Demi-Humans outer appearance changes more subtly and slowly before reflected in our ages. For my kind I am a young woman, but in Human terms I would be considered an old maid, for I celebrated my fiftieth year."

Na'naya looked down at her both surprised and impressed by her well-maintained youthful beauty.

"Well, I must say you look good for your age, Shae. You are blessed by the gods. I hope I can age as gracefully as you, later in my life."

"I appreciate your compliments; it fills me with joy. When I was younger the enclave, I grew up in was attacked and nearly wiped out by Savage Daemon attacks. We were forced to leave our homes and scatter into the winds. After traveling from region to region for a while I finally made my way to a coastal village here in the republic and called it home. It was there that I met a young trader who would become my husband. We were happy with our life together and wanted to grow our family. Having a child proved to be difficult for us, but we never gave up hope and after a few years then it finally happened..."

Shae's voice was filled with a sadness that seemed to be holding her back, as she continued with her story. An invisible force binding her to a long grief that stayed with her over the years.

"I gave birth to a beautiful and healthy baby girl; she was our world. As with such stories things took a drastic turn and our happy life was stolen from us. While on a trip traveling to gather new merchandise for our shop. We were caught in a monstrous storm that sunk the ship we were on. The waters raging as massive waves crashed relentlessly upon our lifeboat. Me and my daughter were thrown over into the depths of the ocean. The currents proved too powerful, and my husband drowned saving us from the depths.

Then it was only me and my little girl for a time, working to get by and live peacefully. Our problems seemed to be going away and we were happy again, then it came. The Sleeping Sickness spread like wildfire and my daughter was only six when it claimed her life. I was broken and all alone in the world,

I couldn't handle both of their loses. I isolated myself from the world.

Mourning my family, and locked myself away in an emotionless mundane haze of life for two decades. About three years ago, after my long-graduated recovery I went back out into the world. To try and live the life my family would have wanted for me..."

Na'naya continued to listen on to Shae's heartfelt story. Filled with empathy for the woman who had experienced strong happiness and sadness in her life. She was beginning to understand uncertainty with her decision about the transition ritual.

"It was during this time that I found the Followers of the Twilight Saint. I saw their efforts to bring a better world to the people, through their teachings and actions. Giving me a new purpose and the opportunity to help others who had suffered or continue to suffer. I joined the faith. Through its prominence I have been traveling again and helping others on their paths. But when I got the news that I was selected to undergo the transition, I was happy at first. But then filled with uncertainty at the fact that I wouldn't be able to bring new life into this world again. Not now, but in the future when the time is right, and I am in a better state of mind for it."

Na'naya stood in silence for a few minutes taking in everything Shae had told her and how best to respond to her. She wanted to choose her words carefully and with consideration. No matter what she said this woman's life was going to change.

"As I am only human myself. I can't understand the weight of what it means to be able to live for many centuries. Growing older at a slower pace than humans. Unlike yourself I haven't had the opportunity yet in my life to experience motherhood.

Though I hope one day the gods bless me with a child. The only advice that I would be able to impart on you is this: No one has the right to make choices about your body and livelihood, other than you. Whatever the circumstance you are loved and fine the way you are or choose to be. So, take your time and think it over, make the choice that rings true to your heart."

Shae rested her head on Na'naya's shoulders and embraced her back with a long caring hug. The warm embrace acknowledging her thanks. Showing gratitude for being there for her and listening to her story. Taking one last embrace, Shae let go of Na'naya and stepped back from her.

"Your words and you being here to listen to my story have been of much help to me. Thank you, Na'naya from the bottom of my heart. I will tell the priests that I am grateful for the honor. But will have to decline accepting the transition for the time being. As I am not ready to walk away from the path of motherhood."

"Good luck, Shae. I wish you the best and may your future prosper as you continue down the path between. "

The two women clasped their hands together with fingers interlocking and bowed their heads to one another. Shae then turned and left down a path on her right. Away from the garden heading in the direction of the cathedral and living annexes. Na'naya followed suit and left the garden in the opposite direction. Heading back towards the main gate leading into the grounds of the House of Twilight.

More time had passed than she realized. The sun was starting to set, and the streetlamps of the city were starting to come alive. The streets and buildings were illuminated creating its enchanting glow.

CHAPTER 14
INARA NOVIK

I nara was glad she was able to help Bellamy out in getting his bow repaired and for the chance to see an old friend again. Now that she was done with that, it was time for her to part ways with Bellamy for the time being. To fulfill some of the other matters that her mistress had entrusted her with. From the last reports her mistress had received there was no immediate concern or rush in dealing with them. She knew that it was best to check it out now and not let it linger for too long. Her mistress was a patient woman, but even so there was a limit to her patience that was not meant to be tested.

"Is there someplace that you would like to go to, Inara?"

"If I recall there should be a famous hot spring here that is said to have healing and restorative properties. I believe its located in the mountains just outside the Midway and High Summit Districts. We will have to check it out later, I'm afraid."

"Oh, that's right you did mention that you had other business as well to take care of today."

"I'm glad that it worked out for you. Now that it has been taken care of, there is somethings that I must go attend to for my mistress. I will see later back at the inn Bellamy."

"Alright. No problem at all, I will see you later then. Good luck to you."

When the two of them made their way from the shop back down the alley. Towards one of the main streets, Bellamy headed off down the street back towards the center of the Merchant's District. While Inara headed north towards the Midway District. The Midway District was located on the other side of the Parliamentary Peak District, where the main governmental offices of the republic resided. Unlike the other two residential districts of Hoenheim, The Midway was home to the Middle-class.

A wide area made up of a mixture of big private houses, luxury townhomes, and muti-story luxury apartments. It was a district where wealth and influence had high standards on the people who called it home. Those who had considerable wealth did all they could to keep their status and not loose what they had worked so hard to gain.

Down one of the calmer streets of the Midway lined with fine luxury townhomes made of stone, timber, and metal Inara had come upon her destination. The luxury townhome was of an older style constructed in the middle years of the republic. Intricate geometric patterns in the iron window frames, a darker shingled roof, and an ornate dragon head door knocker on its dark purple oak door. Inara walked up the six wide stone steps leading to the door. She grabbed the iron ring hanging in the ornate dragon head's mouth.

Three times she knocked the iron ring upon the purple oak door, each knock louder than the previous one. There she waited for someone to come and open the door.

Footsteps approached from the inside stopping before the door. Inara heard as the locking mechanism was being undone. The door opened. Standing on the other side was an elderly human male with blackish blue hair and a matching goatee mixed with streaks of grey dressed in a buttoned-up silk vest over a finely pressed tunic. A bowtie neatly rested at his collar, slacks, and polished shoes. He was wearing a sliver rimmed monocle over his left eye reflecting vibrantly the color of his pale blue eyes.

A fine sphinx handle cane of ebony and rosewood was in his right hand. Providing support for his aged body to lean upon. The warm gentle gaze in his eyes turned cold and emotionless, as he gazed upon Inara.

"Master Auron. I have come to see you at the request of Madame Rhea, she sends her apologies for not being able to come in person."

"So, she sent you in her stead it would seem. Come inside and we can talk in my study, more privately and away from preying eyes."

The elderly man turned and gestured for Inara to follow him inside. She walked into the townhouse and closed the door behind her. Following the man down a hallway with paintings from different masters upon its aging walls. The study was a modest sized rectangular room with bookshelves on one wall. Paintings hanging on the other, a star chart and world map on the third wall, and a fireplace on the last one.

In the center of the room was a seating area composed of five chairs situated around a round coffee table of cedar and purple oak at its center. The old man took a seat at one of the chairs and Inara sat in one across from him.

"Is there something you wish to say, Inara. I can see it in your eyes, so go ahead and say it."

"What is with the look? I know this version of you that is sitting across from me is not the true you. So, would you be so kind as to take off the façade and we can get down to why I am here."

"If you insist. [*Those three who weave the tapestry and guides man's fate. Turn back the hands of time, lift the veil that shrouds the truth and return my visage back to its proper form.*]"

The elderly man's hands began emanating a swirling mist of a purple blue haze. With the flick of his wrist the misty haze enveloped his body like a cocoon before vanishing in an instant bright glow. The man sitting across Inara was no longer the elderly gentleman she first met. He was now a younger mature Fae of the Elven variety who appeared to be in his thirties. Though his appearance was misleading as Elves are one of the longer lived of the races, near immortal as they did not die from natural causes.

"Now, what brings you to my home today, my dear Inara? So, tell me how is my wife doing these days? It has been some time since we last saw each other."

Inara reached into the pouch at her hips, she pulled out a sealed letter and small ornate metal music box. She placed them on the table for the Elven man. He picked up the letter and opened it, reading over the contents within. Warmth filled the cold look in his eyes, and he sighed, but one of happiness and not contempt. He picked up the small ornate metal music box and tapped it twice with his fingers. The top separated. Revealing the crystal figurine of a Djinn woman shrouded in a ceremonial dress and veil.

An angelic and captivating melody played. An enchanting voice sang in the ancient language of the Djinn. When the song stopped, the music box closed back up, and the room was quiet once more. The Elven man sat in his chair, looking off into the distance, lost in thought of times spent together with his wife. Inara sat patiently and waited before she addressed him.

"I do not presume to understand the complexities of your relationship with my mistress. I know she still loves you and speaks about you every so often, when not boggled down by business affairs. She would have been the one to come in my stead, had there been time, my lord Auron."

"You serve my wife well, and I appreciate the sentiment. Though, as you say our relationship is complicated to say the least, as it the case for ones who live long lives. She has always been one to get caught up in her business. Ever searching for knowledge in all matters on the functions and workings of society. One of the many reasons why I love her and do everything I can to support her endeavors. Have you heard anything from the contact in the parliament yet?"

"I received word from the innkeeper that the contact wants to meet up tomorrow when the parliament will be out of session for the day. They provided a meeting place and time to meet up, I need to let the others who came with me know about what's going on. We have gone through some challenges to get here. They have proven to be reliable and capable companions on this journey."

Auron let out a joyous laugh, that caused Inara to blush as it caught her off guard.

"What was that so suddenly? It seemed out of place coming from someone such as you."

"Careful now, that almost came off as insulting. I will let that go. I'm a little surprised is all that you speak so highly of your traveling companions. As you yourself are not so accepting of friendship from others, let alone a group of mercenaries at that. It must be difficult given your past, Though I suspected you haven't talked about it to them. Either way, your life is going to be an interesting one going down the path you chosen."

"There is one thing I wanted to ask you before I take my leave. Given your skills and powers, why do you hide your appearance from most others?"

Auron sat back in his chair looking over at Inara. His gaze watching the subtle shifts in her movements and the thoughts behind the question she asked. It had been ages since someone had the nerve or genuine curiosity about his disguised appearance. The question had piqued his interest and was evident to him by the one asking. His wife had a keen sense when it came to the people who served her.

"You think that I do it out of fear, or necessity, but that is not the case. It has proven to be helpful for my work and needs over the many ages I've been utilizing it. Though alas there is no great purpose to why I do it. I do it because for one who lives centuries being able to live different lives brings new excitement to the mundane passing of time. I have had the pleasure of being several varying types of people over the years. Each with their own triumphs and challenges. This current one developing in ways I didn't foresee, but still, I cherish it none the less."

Dong...Dong...Dong. The great antique grandfather clock, one the wall to the side of the fireplace signaled the top of the new hour. From the hallway outside of the study a Human maid, no more than sixteen came into the room. She kneeled before Auron and whispered a message into his ear, before rising and taking her leave.

"Is there a problem?"

"Nothing that needs to concern you. There was a bit of a commotion at an establishment in the Industrial Complex District. That was of a particular interest to me. Oh well, I will have to move on and look elsewhere for the time. A word of advice, not all solutions are suitable to certain problems. As not all problems have a suitable solution. Best to remember that."

"Thanks for the advice, I will be sure to keep it in mind. It goes to show that even cities that seem peaceful and safe, still have their fair share of troubles hidden out of sight. It is starting to get late, and I don't want to impose on you any longer, so I will be heading out."

Inara got up from her chair and Auron did as well. He led her out of the study and back down the hallway with the artwork on the walls to the front door. She had spent more time with the master than she had expected, as time passed her by as mere moments had become hours. The front door opened. Inara walked outside to the city beyond aglow by the illuminating light of the streetlamps and the stars overhead.

CHAPTER 15
BELLAMY LEONE

Now that Bellamy was on his own again, since Inara had to leave on an errand for her mistress. he was left free to his own devices for the rest of the day. Considering how big the city was and its importance to the republic as its official seat of power. There had to be some sort of popular places or entertainment to experience for people not local to the city. Unfortunately, Bellamy didn't know where to start, as this wasn't the sort of thing he would do.

It was the others who thought of the ideas. Places to experience when they traveled to cities or towns they haven't been before. Bellamy would tag along or stay at the inn if he wasn't feeling up to it that day.

He wouldn't admit it to his friends but he was certain that they knew. That he was more of an ambivert homebody with strong lone introverted tendencies. Being by himself never bothered him. It gave him the space to focus and think about what he needed to do to move forward in his life. Not letting the tragedy in his past consume him.

Bellamy would never forget what happened or forgive those who caused it. He decided to keep on living and taking a more diligent approach in finding his answers. He had no intentions to recklessly squander the gift his mother gave him by providing him with the chance to escape and live on.

So, with no clear destination in mind Bellamy decided to stroll through the city and see where it takes him. The more he saw of the city, the more he came to embrace the beauties and wonders of Hoenheim along with all it had to offer. Streets were packed with crowds of people from every reach of the southern continent and beyond. Going here and there, mingling with one another. From government officials of the Upper-class all the way down to the slaves of the Servant-class, called this city home and worked to keep it running.

He understood the value they provided in labor and manufacturing but was morally against the institution of slavery. Feeling that wages should be provided for work done.

If anything, he felt that if it must exist it should only be brought upon those who committed treasonous acts, war criminals, or heinous crimes. It should not fall upon someone because they were born into poverty or captured and sold into it. The Renata Republic in this regard has shown to have the same ideals. Implementing strict laws and protections when it comes to dealing with slavery within their borders. Other nations find themselves on multiples ends of the spectrum with how they choose to deal with it. In those nations it is best to stay on your heels or find yourself in unconditional servitude for the rest of your life.

Bellamy didn't know yet that it would be these ideals that would test him. Driving to his core, how strong and important his convictions were to his character. Only time would tell, for a matter of a different sort was about to fall into Bellamy's hands. In his wanderings through the streets of the city, Bellamy had found his way back to the Merchant's District. He came upon the outdoor trading marketplace.

It was a wide-open area lined with row upon row of booths and stalls. With wares from merchants, traders, and artisans from all over the republic and beyond. Browsing around the booths, Bellamy didn't hear the commotion going on in the distance or see the person who was about to run straight into him.

"Watch out! Move, move out of the way..."

Bellamy turned and side stepped out of the path of the person sprinting right past his eyes, mere moments later. The person was wearing a long-hooded cloak, obscuring their features below. Bellamy was able to get a brief glimpse of platinum blonde hair and honey brown eyes.

"This way! Hurry men, that filthy wretch headed down the row over there. Do not let them escape." A city watch guardsman shouted in the distance.

A small patrol of five city watch guardsmen came rushing down the row past Bellamy. Heading off in the same direction as the mysterious person. Bellamy thought to himself, ["I *wonder what all that was about? No. I should leave it alone and not get involved.*"] He reached down to grab his money bag from the pouch on his belt. but he didn't feel anything in the pouch. He couldn't believe the pouch was empty, he was certain the money bag was there. He had placed it back into his pouch when he left the weapon's shop, so it couldn't be empty.

"Fuck. How the hell did they pull that off. Looks like I'm going to be getting involved after all. There's no way the others will let me live this down, if I go back and tell them I got robbed in the blink of an eye. Damn it!"

Bellamy turned and headed off following in the direction the stranger and city watch guardsmen headed in. The marketplace was packed with customers. Making it difficult to navigate through the crowds, and keeping an eye out for his target. They had a bit of a head start on him. Bellamy wasn't about to give up, he had picked up some tracking skills on his jobs with the mercenary group.

He was confident that he would be able to find the stranger. He needed to get to them before the city watch did, as he preferred not to get involved with them. Heading up to a higher vantage point, Bellamy climbed up onto a nearby balcony to search the area around him.

He then spotted the city watch patrol making their way towards a secluded side alley. That the stranger headed down. Moments later it wasn't the guardsmen that emerged from the alley, but the lone figure of the stranger. The stranger casually walked through the crowds of the marketplace to blend in and not draw attention to them. Bellamy watched the stranger as they made their way to a street on the westside of the marketplace. He jumped down from the balcony and made his way towards the stranger, making sure not to follow too closely.

He followed the stranger for several blocks deeper into the city. Up and down the twisting streets of Hoenheim. They had come to the top of a staircase leading down to the lower Industrial Complex District of the city. When the stranger stopped and sat down on the steps. Bellamy paused a few feet away from the stranger, who lifted their hand and waved for him to come over and take a seat. He hesitated, not sure if he should accept the gesture.

"There's no need for hesitation, you can come and sit next to me. If I was going to do something, I would've done it from the moment you started tailing me. Don't believe me, here..."

The stranger tossed the small money bag that, they had lifted from Bellamy's pouch onto the ground next to his feet. He leaned down and picked up his money bag. Checking to see that it was all accounted for, before placing it back into his pouch. He walked over to the stranger and took a seat on the staircase next to them. The view of the district below from the staircase was captivating.

The silhouettes of the buildings contrasted against the backdrop of the mountains and trees beyond the outer walls. The stranger pulled down the hood from their cloak. Revealing the features of the person underneath.

The stranger was a Fae of the Nymph variety. Her long platinum blonde hair, honey brown eyes, and pointed ears only enhanced the ethereal beauty that was common amongst her race. Her skin was the tone of a light roasted coffee mixed with a sweet cream. It was the first time that Bellamy had seen a Nymph in person. As was common for Fae in general, they tended to rarely interact with the other races. So, encountering them outside their domain was few and far between, let alone in a predominantly human city.

"Sorry about that, old habits you see. It was nothing personal, I had to be sure about something first. You can call me Amiriss."

"I am Bellamy. I appreciate you giving me my money back, don't do that again if you mind. So, care to tell me what that whole commotion was back there in the marketplace with the city watch?"

"Ohhh. That was a little misunderstanding on their part, and they overreacted a bit much, if I'm honest. Still, it was fun, and they say a little excitement is good for the soul. I wished they put up more of a challenge, what a letdown...umph."

Something told Bellamy that he would have to watch himself around this woman. Whose disposition may end up causing him more trouble and headaches than he could manage. It was best that he takes it slow and see what he could find out about her, and talents she possessed. He could not deny the fact that she had exceptional skills. She was able to steal his money bag effortlessly and able to evade and detect him following her. She could be useful to the group on their journey. Though he would have to make sure before bringing it up with his companions.

"I see. So, you're saying if I were to go and take you to the guard station right now, they would hear your side of the story and not arrest you on the spot. Alright let's go see the city watch then."

Amiriss was fidgeting around a bit, as she looked at Bellamy and took in what he had told her.

"Now. Now…Hold on a second there, kid. You may think that doing that would be the right thing to do, but that would be a miscalculation on your part. For you see if you were to let it be, then we could come to a beneficial partnership. You help me out and in return I'll help you out."

"Okay. I'll take you up on that deal. Besides, I have a feeling that this is going to be the beginning of something interesting and exciting. Now, what is it that you need help with Amiriss?"

Amiriss gently brushed her manicured fingers through her long flowing hair. Twisting small curls caught between her fingertips. She was the very image of a calm and serene beauty. She contemplated the best way to address the matter, she needed help with. Amiriss didn't know how Bellamy would respond once she told him, or if he would even stay around. There would be no reason to be upset or mad if he decided to walk away. They had only met each other and were under no obligation to the other.

"As you may or may not know, my kind generally doesn't openly interact with Humans or the Demi-Human races on personal or political matters. It has been that way for many centuries. My kind are all female, and only look for outside companionship when we are seeking a mate. It is a rite of passage and a means of securing the future of my people. Nymphs undertake at four different times in our lives, since we have long lifespans. Be that as it may, these unions are not always fruitful, or tragedy strikes. That is why we are very careful and selective when searching out potential mates."

Bellamy couldn't say for certain what Amiriss meant by telling him all of this. But he had a feeling that she would provide an answer. He didn't see any harm in asking her to explain directly what she wanted.

"I can see how it must be difficult for you navigating through unknown lands. Carrying the responsibility of finding a mate that you deem worthy. So, what exactly are you asking of me, in this search of yours?"

" I want to join you and your companions on your journey. I see something in you, something that you yourself don't see yet and what to see it grow. You have the potential to be worthy of being my mate, I want to know for certain. Before you say anything, know that I do not tell you this or that I am some treasure to be taken. It is about a bond and connection that must take root and grow into something more."

When he got up this morning Bellamy wasn't expecting anything like this to happen to him. Even in his dreams he wouldn't have thought that he would find himself being involved in the romantic machinations of a Fae, a Nymph no less. What did the heavens above have in store for this life of his. All that he could do was to turn away and reject her offer, or embrace it head on and take on what may come. There was no lies or ill intent in Amiriss's words.

She was speaking of a possibility not a guarantee, so Bellamy couldn't see why he shouldn't take her up on the offer. One thing did bother him a bit though, it was that she knew he was traveling with others.

"Amiriss, I am humbled by your request and have no problem taking you up on it. But, before I can do that, I must know, how did you know that I was traveling with others and not on my own?"

A cool mountain breeze brushed past their bodies. The two of them stared at each other in an unnerving silence. Bellamy wanted to hear what she had to say about that, but he couldn't bring himself to push her farther. Whatever her reason, it took courage to do what she did and for that he respected her. If she wasn't going to answer him then he would have to get up and leave.

He wasn't going to put himself or his friends in danger. Bellamy got up to his feet and turned to walk away when Amiriss shot out her hand and grabbed the back of his tunic.

"Please wait."

CHAPTER 16

B ellamy stopped and turned back around to face Amiriss and hear what she had to say. Vigilant and cautious he watched her. Prepared to act at a moment's notice, should she try something. He was still optimistic that Amiriss had no ill intentions towards him or his companions.

"Bellamy, I have a special innate ability that gives me empathic powers. I can learn about a person from their feelings and emotions. A way of getting insight into who they are and their inner thoughts. That is how I know you are traveling with two others and not alone. I tend to keep this sort of thing guarded, so only a few close people know of my gift. So, I would appreciate it if you kept it between us for the time being."

"Yes, of course. It is your secret and I have no claim on who you decide to share it with."

Whatever lingering doubts he may have had about Amiriss left his mind. because it takes a certain character to tell a personal secret to someone you just met. A certain level of trust and faith in the person you are opening to is required on the person's part. Considering the implications something like that could impose upon both parties. He was grateful that she had considered him trustworthy of her secret.

That he was able to get an answer from her in the first place, without having to press. Bellamy was confident that the others would except her. Once they got to know her better and see the kind of person she was. Considering how Raine is with women. He was positive there would be no problem getting his approval. The two girls might be a little more difficult to come around.

Na'naya was generally easy going, going with the group's flow on most matters. She also had a strong-willed stubbornness to her that would overpower her easy-going mentality. Bellamy had been on the wrong side of it a few times since knowing her and has worked to avoid being in its crosshairs. Amiriss didn't come off as the type of person to intentionally provoke someone without reason. There wasn't any reason why those two shouldn't get along.

Inara was a bit of a wild card. He had not known her for as long as the others, but she had proven herself to be trustworthy and capable. She was a smart and calculated warrior. Who assessed the possibilities of the situations before she acted.

Acting calmly in the moment embracing her logic. Not letting her emotions cloud her judgment or take dangerous risk that might impede her quest. Bellamy respected and admired her for that, hoping to be capable of the same skills in the future. With that in mind they would have to appeal to her from a logical perspective. On how Amiriss would be an asset for their group by being able to provide an excellent diverse skillset.

He was positive that going forward, she would be of great help to them as their journey. It seemed it was only going to grow more challenging as they continued. The one thing that was clear to him was that no matter how capable the four of them currently were. They were going to need to expand their party by at least two other members.

Bellamy believed that she could be one of them, if given the chance to join them. She had stated her intentions to him in wanting to join him on his journey. So all that was left was talking it over with his friends.

"I cannot make any promises on how my companions will respond about you joining us, but I will talk it over with them. Give me some time and I should have an answer for you before the end of the week."

"Thank you. You've done more than what I expected a Human to do. It looks like my hunch about you has proved me right. I will wait to hear back from you on the decision that was made."

"Alright. How will I get in touch with you, to let you know of our decision?"

"Send a messenger to this spot with your decision. I will come and meet up with your group if that is what you decide. I enjoyed our conversation, but now I must be off. Take care Bellamy, until next we meet."

Amiriss stood up from her seat on the staircase steps. She walked away down the staircase to the district below. Bellamy looked on watching as her figured faded in the distance. As the sun began to set and twilight gave way to night. The street-lamps glowed illuminating the city in their dancing lights.

The hustle and bustle of the crowded day giving way to the serene and calm of the quiet night. The city was turning out to be an interesting place, with people as interesting if not more. Bellamy had accomplished a fair deal this day. He decided that it was time for him to head back to the inn and see if the others had returned.

It was strange to him how the atmosphere of the city changed between the daytime and the nighttime. He hadn't noticed it when they first arrived in the city because it was late at night. After experiencing the city today he had taken notice of the changes. During the daytime the streets, shops, and markets where busy and alive with people all over going about their day. At night, they city was both alive and eerily subdued at the same time.

As the establishments were packed with people enjoying conservation, libations, and entertainment. While the streets were empty with very few people passing by here and there.

Most people would be somewhat unnerved about the unusual quietness in such a big and lively city. It didn't bother Bellamy. He found comfort in it, calming his thoughts and being present in the moment. Taking in the view of the twin moons and stars above in the night sky. As he turned the corner bringing him back to the street the inn was on, the aromatic smell of a fresh brewing stew filled his nose and captured his senses.

The stew was calling to him, to come and eat his fill. Once he was back in the inn, Bellamy grabbed a seat at the closest table around him. he ordered the stew and a tankard of beer. He ate and he enjoyed his meal, while he awaited the arrival of his friends to return.

Raine was the first to return to the inn, He waved over at Bellamy as he entered. He went and stopped at the reception desk, before making his way to the table. Na'naya and Inara had strolled in at around the same time. They spotted Bellamy and Raine at the table and walked over to join them. Ordering food and drinks for themselves.

"So, how did everyone's day go? Anything exciting happen?"

The others looked at one another, to see who was going to speak first. Raine and Na'naya both opened their mouths at the same time to speak. He caught himself and let Na'naya proceed with her story first, on the events that occurred earlier today. The group listened on as she told them of her trip through Parliamentary Peak to check out the area. Her encounter with the novice at the House of Twilight in the High Summit District.

"I have heard tales about the Followers of the Twilight Saint. About the ritual that those chosen to become prominent authorities within its ranks must undertake. It is a life changing decision to make, and not one to take likely. She was lucky to have met you Na'naya. You are one of the only people, I know who can create a caring and empathetic connection. Providing them with comfort and understanding."

Na'naya blushed from the kind words that Raine had spoken to her. She was also a little surprised that he was capable of a genuine heartfelt compliment, and to express it to her. They were close friends. Their relationship was more teasing. Taunting, goofing around, and not one of complimenting or praising each other.

"Thank you, Raine. I didn't think I would hear that from you, but I appreciate it."

"What's that supposed to mean. I am capable of giving someone a compliment when they deserve one. Don't think that you'll get any others."

"It's good to hear that you were able to help her out on her decision, Na'naya. I'm sure if anything she was grateful to have someone that she could talk to about it. So, Raine I guess you are up next?"

Raine took a sip from his tankard of beer. Before he told his friends about the events that had transpired earlier in the day. He told them about how he was wandering through the city and while resting in a park, he had met Sarai. Who had asked for his help to rescue her sister Mari from the thief's guild master Carrigan. How he had fought in the fighting arena against the Dragonkin warrior Draemond.

How he had later helped him along with the two sisters to escape from Carrigan's clutches. Raine could see the look of concern on the other's faces as he was telling his story. Those looks quickly changed to excitement and gratitude.

"That must have been one though ordeal my friend, but in the end, you did the right thing in helping those girls out. A child shouldn't have to pay for the sins of the father or take on debt that was never theirs to begin with."

"Yeah, that good for nothing two-bit thief had no right going back on his deal, when you won the match fair and square. I despise people like that. It's good that… that dragonkin warrior Draemond you said was there to help you out."

Inara listened to the conversations go on, not saying a thing or providing any sort of input. She was focusing on the different events that occurred today and processing them one by one. From everything she heard so far. She could tell that their stay in Hoenheim was about to become more interesting, then she initially thought. It was almost a certainty that going forward they would have to be vigilant in their activities throughout the city. On not draw anymore unwanted attention to their mission.

"With keeping in mind everything that happened today, I want to know how you all feel about letting Draemond join our group. He is an exceptionally skilled and loyal warrior, and I'm sure him being Dragonkin will be helpful to us as well. What do you say?"

"I've haven't gotten the opportunity to get to know a Dragonkin warrior in my travels. He seems like a good person, and he helped you and those girls out of a tough situation. He has my vote."

Raine looked over to Bellamy and Na'naya for their answer on the matter. Inara nodded her head in agreement. Still processing everything and not ready to speak yet. Bellamy paused before he was about to speak, figuring out how he wanted to bring up his request as well.

"It would seem that we are on the same page my friend. There is someone, I must tell you all about as well, that wishes to join our group."

Bellamy proceeded to tell everyone about the events that unfolded after he had parted ways from Inara and the weapon's shop. He told them about his trip to the marketplace and about the mysterious stranger who caused a scene escaping from the city watch. How his money was seamlessly taken from him, and how he pursued them. Finding them and learning that it was a Nymph named Amiriss, who was on a journey of her own to find a potential mate. The girls stared at Bellamy, but Raine had a cheesy smirky grin on his face.

"Ah...Ha...Ah...Ha. Would you look at that, our Bellamy here has finally become a man. I don't know how you did it, but you did. You caught the eye of a Nymph, not an easy feat by far. You sly dog."

"Knock it off, Raine. It's not entirely like that or at least I don't think it is. Either way the thing to take away is that she would like to join us on our travels as well. I told Amiriss that I would bring it up with you all before deciding. So, how do you feel about her?"

Na'naya twirled her braids through her fingers as she thought about whether to accept Amiriss into the group. Raine merely smiled back at him. Bellamy could see that the thought of adding another beauty to their party was at the forefront of his mind. He wasn't sure how Inara would respond, as she had a calm stoic look on her face. She hadn't provided any input into their conversations yet. So it was difficult to figure out which way she would go. That changed however, when she finally spoke up.

"I'm sure that neither of you have forgotten the reason why we came to this city in the first place. Or about the job we need to do. Going forward it is most likely that we may find ourselves in difficult situations. Having extra help could make all the difference. With that in mind, I will accept Draemond and Amiriss into the group. But know that I will be keeping an eye on them for the time being to get a full understanding of their characters. I stand by your judgements and will give them the benefit of knowing you..."

Inara paused and took a drink from her tankard before continuing.

"Until we know them and their intentions, I ask that you only tell them certain things. Not anything that doesn't immediately concern them or our end goals. We must not forget that Madame Rhea mentioned that there were others, who are after the same thing we are. So, we must be careful, for now."

CHAPTER 17

After finishing up their meal and conversation, Bellamy left the others and headed upstairs to his room. It had been a long day exploring the city and he was ready to rest his body and prepare for the days ahead. He didn't know what tomorrow would bring for him and his friends. Only that he was going to face it head on and continue to experience life on this journey. The one thing Bellamy know for certain was that there was no better feeling than sleeping in a nice comfy bed.

It was a gift and one that he would not take for granted. Sleep came to him with ease, as he laid his head down. Closed his eyes and let his mind drift off, carrying with it his doubts and dreams.

The next morning Bellamy arose to the sunlight beaming through their window. The sound of Raine snoring, while sprawled out on top of his sheets. His face still lightly flushed. The aftereffects of spending the night drinking an excess of beer, ale, and wine. Raine was one to hold his liquor, so it wasn't too often that he could be found in such a state.

Bellamy knew that even in his present state, Raine was still a fearsome fighter. If threatened by attack. One of the perks of his Beastmen traits. One of the reasons Bellamy never questioned his friend's drinking habit.

"Hey, don't stay in bed too long. We have things to get done today. I'm going to finish getting ready and head downstairs."

"Yeah. Alright I hear you. I'll be down in a bit." Raine replied still half-asleep.

Bellamy finished changing and left the room, making his way down the hall to the stairs. On his way down the hall, he ran into Na'naya, who was coming out of her room. She spotted him coming down the hall and gave a gentle wave of her hand.

"Good morning, Bellamy. Did you sleep well last night, you left when the drinks were about to come."

"Good morning to you too, Na'naya. Yes, I feel well rested. I wasn't in a drinking mood last night, so I decided to catch up on some rest. It was a good enough time too, considering there is no telling how things are going to go from here."

"Yeah, I guess you do have a point. Inara is already downstairs, so we should head on and join her. Where's Raine. Is that bum still sleeping? I told him to take it easy on the booze, but he never listens to me."

"He has the tendency to do what he wants and whatever is beneficial to his goals. I wouldn't let it bother you, They, say you can't teach an old dog new tricks."

From out behind him, a hand suddenly came swiftly out and struck Bellamy on the back of his head.

"Oww...Ouch."

"Next time watch who you're calling an old dog, kid."

Raine stepped forward in front of the two of them. A smile on his face as he continued down the stairs with a casual swagger.

Bellamy and Na'naya followed behind, as they all made their way to the table to join Inara for breakfast. After they had eaten and gotten their fill, Inara explained what their next move would be on the job that lay before them.

"Yesterday morning, I received a note from the person we are to contact from the innkeeper. Its contents contained a location and time for the meeting. We are to meet with them after midday at the Celestial Observatory in the High Summit District. Past the Westgate from the Parliamentary Peak district."

Inara pulled out a folded piece of parchment from a pouch on her belt and laid it upon the tabletop. She unfolded it to reveal a map with a layout of the city. With details of the districts and the surrounding areas around them. Using her finger, she pointed out where they were currently located. Than destination that they would be making their ways towards.

At first Bellamy wasn't certain what he saw, but then it occurred again as before. He examined the map with a more focused glance. He could see that the writing on the map was alive with subtle fluid motions. As if created from a ripple in a pound disturb by an object on its surface.

The writing on the map would change based on were Inara was guiding her finger. Responding to her thoughts to bring up information on that area. The first time Inara pulled out the map, Bellamy had his suspicions about it, but he wasn't certain. There was no doubt in his mind this time that the map was an enchanted magic tool. That used specialized ink that reacted to the mana in the person using it.

Such items were not easy to come by. He had not seen one since the captain of the Falling Star Mercenaries procured one years ago. After he first joined them. Unfortunately, that was his only glance of it. That one had disappeared unexpectedly some time ago when they were on a dangerous quest in the Frozen Wilds.

"Inara, how did you manage to get your hands on such a rare item as a Wayfarer's Map? There are only two dozen that are said to be in existence. An enchanted magic tool that changes geography and information based on the user holding it. A world map that can provide a layout of any town, city, region, or country anywhere in the known world."

"Wow. That is amazing. I've never seen or heard of anything like that in my travels with my master or after he passed."

They looked at the map, as Inara laid out the information on the area that they would be heading off too. After making sure that everyone understood, she folded the map back up. Placed it back into her pouch. It was a relief to them to know that they had such a valuable and beneficial tool to aid them on their journey. The look in Inara's eyes told them everything they needed to know.

That it was of the upmost importance that they keep the map safe and always secured. There would be no escaping retribution if something where to happen to it. Bellamy nor the others wouldn't let that fate fall upon them.

"I'm not surprised as this sort of item tends to be guarded. Secretive amongst those who know of its existence. Mere rumor or myth to most all. The fact that you know about it Bellamy must mean that you have seen one before. As for this one, it was entrusted to me by Madame Rhea to use for the time being. There is a powerful protection placed on it, that will wipe away the memory of it to anyone who takes it without permission."

"Now, that is one interesting protection placed on it. But then again, I guess you can't be too careful when it comes to an item like that. That woman is clever and not one to be taken lightly, it is best that you remember that Na'naya and Bellamy."

Na'naya brushed Raine's words off, as she wasn't paying attention to them in the first place. She was enamored by the sweet, delectable yogurt and wild fruit parfait in front of her. Bellamy smiled and laughed at the excitement on her face. If there was anything capable of capturing Na'naya's attention in an instant, it was dessert. The irritation showed on Raine's face like an open book, there for all to see. Bellamy raised his hand towards Raine waving it in a shallow up and down motion, signaling him to take it easy and let her be.

"Don't worry we get what you were trying to explain to us. We are not so foolish about making unwanted enemies, so carelessly. Let her enjoy her dessert, as lax moments may not always be a luxury to us."

Inara stood up and looked at everyone seated at the table. Clear determination and conviction painted on her face.

"It's time we head out and make our way to the observatory, and finally meet the contact we were sent here to meet."

"Yeah." They all said in unison.

The others got up from the table and followed suit. Leaving the inn, and heading off in the direction of the Celestial Observatory in the High Summit District. Given the nature of the twisting and mazelike roads spread throughout the city. The districts that made it up, there were places located in the city that could be reached by several different routes. Some of the more important or strategic locations had two to three different routes.

While those that were more secluded only appeared to have one direct route. The Celestial Observatory was one such location as the later, secluded with only one route in and out. Past the Westgate of the High Summit District there was a long curving shallow road. Which ran through the tree covered outer reaches of the district, along the side of the mountain plateau. Where steep carved stone steps lead up to a wide overlook some two hundred feet above the ground.

As they cleared the trees to reach the steep stone steps, they took in the elegance and artistic craftmanship of the carved steps before their feet. From the age of the city's renaissance the beauty in the architecture of the buildings, streets, and walkways was not lost on the group. There are many beautiful places located throughout the world. but that kind that was evident in Hoenheim was far from the norm. Not seen outside of such places as those in the Zenith Imperium, The Umbarah Sultanate, and the Nimh Theocracy.

The beauty of the city's different districts could be seen as if on a large painter's canvas. The group climbed higher up the steps towards the top. As they came up to the top of the steps the fifty-meter-tall Celestial Observatory came into view. Nestled at the center of a manicured garden of wildflowers.

The Celestial Observatory was comprised of a rectangular base connected to a round spire that rose high up into the sky. The Celestial Observatory was divided into six floors. The ground floor in the rectangular base was a columned galley hall lined with rows of decorative columns, leading to the great spiral staircase at the center of the tower. On the second through fourth floors of the tower was the great spiral staircase heading up. With small landings indicating a new floor.

On the fifth floor of the tower was a library filled with shelves of tomes, parchments, books, and artifacts from all over the continent and beyond. Located at the very top of the tower on the six floor was the main celestial observatory. Star charts and a giant gyroscopic alchemical multiplanetary astrolade mechanism where located in the center of the room.

It was a visual representation of the world. Surrounded by the rotations of the planets that make up the galaxy and planes of existence that encompasses their reality. The Celestial observatory and the mechanism are some of the oldest artifacts in the city. Around since before the inception of the city itself. Dating back to the bygone Mythic Age of Heroes, a time in the world when Fae and Demi-human races where in their prime.

Humans were in their infancy as a race to the world. When Gods and Demons interacted more in the affairs of the mortal plane. Where *wild* Arts and Daemons permeated throughout the world in vast quantities. It was a time of great wonder and even greater chaos. A true testament to the will of those who survived its challenges.

"This is the place where we are supposed to meet our contact. We need to make our way up to the top floor, where the main observatory is located. Apparently, the place isn't open to the public. So there should only be a handful of researcher's and assistants inside the building on the fifth floor in the library."

"That's good to know, I still think that we should be careful and not let our guard down. We don't know the person we are meeting and for better or worse it could be a trap." Raine advised with a hint of jest and caution in his voice.

CHAPTER 18

"What do you want to do Bellamy? In the end you should make the final decision as this job is a favor towards getting the information that you seek."

They had been working as a group from the start of the journey. Inara was right in her words, that everything was for the benefit of getting Bellamy answers. He had to be certain about the actions he would take going forward. because it was not his own life that could potentially be put in danger but that of his friends as well. What mattered to him most was that he would not let the trust his friends put in him fail them.

Nor would he recklessly endanger their lives. Bellamy had made up his mind and decided on a course of action to take. What impact it would have on their lives only time would tell.

"Raine, your advice is as solid as ever and I agree. We've already came this far, so let's keep moving forward. So, keep your guard up and proceed with care. As it seems there is only one way in and out of the observatory. Which if I'm honest is not an ideal situation to be in, but we can handle whatever may come."

"Alright. Then lead the way."

The group made their way into the Celestial Observatory through its massive iron doors into the quite of the majestic columned gallery hall of the ground floor. The tall intricately carved marble columns ran ten meters high from the floor to the ceiling. Rows upon rows filled the gallery hall. Creating a cavernous effect and a vast lonely openness to the space. They were the only ones in the gallery hall.

Their footsteps echoing throughout as each step they took resonated in the distance. Bellamy and Na'naya looked in awe as they reached the grand spiral staircase in the center of the tower. Following its direction with their eyes up into the heights beyond.

It didn't cross their minds at first, but as they made their way up the grand spiral staircase. They came to understand that it was no easy task. The staircase appeared to be no ordinary staircase. With each landing they crossed the distance to the next one got twice as long as the previous one. Bellamy couldn't be the only one noticing, that the distance they were traveling was taking far more time than it should have.

Considering the tower was said to be fifty meters tall in total. The others didn't seem to notice anything strange, and he didn't want to cause an alarm if nothing was wrong. He continued walking on but made his way closer to Inara, to see if she had any insight into what was happening.

"Hey Inara, have you noticed anything strange going on? For some reason I feel like it is taking us longer to reach the top than what it would take."

Inara leaned closer towards Bellamy so that her voice wouldn't carry as far and spoke in a whispered voice.

"We need to be careful. It seems that something has caused our spacial perception to be misaligned with our reality. That is why the distance we are traveling seems to be doubling with each landing we cross. We must find the source of the problem and take it out before the effects become more dangerous."

Bellamy called the other two to come over to him and explained what was going on to them. Both Raine and Na'naya appeared to have an irritated look on their faces. They stayed calm as they tried to figure out what the source creating their predicament was. As they scanned the area around them trying to figure out what it could be. Raine noticed a faint exotic smell in the air, that he hadn't picked up on earlier. He closed his eyes and focused his senses on the faint exotic smell, homing in on where it was coming from.

"There!"

Raine dashed past the others, over to a decorative lantern hanging in one of the wall alcoves. He pulled off the lantern's casing and blew out the purplish flame inside. When the flame was extinguished, their vision shifted in an instant. The tower's height returned to normal. The others hurried over to Raine. Checking out the decorative lantern for themselves.

"I don't know what is going on. When the lanterns are lit their flame gives off a faint exotic smell that is nearly undetectable. It disorients your spacial perception in its area of effect. From the looks of it, they seem to be strategically located throughout the grand spiral staircase. Leading all the way up to the top of the observatory. Some form of defense in times past to protect the observatory and its artifacts. Though if they have been activated again, I cannot say."

"Whether it was meant for us or not. We have no choice but to extinguish the others if we are going to make it to the top of this observatory."

Now that they knew what they were looking for, the progress up the grand spiral staircase was proceeding much smoother. With each landing they crossed, they made quick work in locating the decorative lantern in the area. Extinguishing its purplish flame. Floor by floor they continued the same pattern. Until finally they had reached the fifth floor and the library located on it.

The library was filled with rows of shelves that rose from the floor to the ceiling covered in tomes. along with parchments, scrolls, and artifacts some far older than the city itself. As they made there way through the library, there was a few small groups of two to three robed scholars and assistants scattered about the tables entranced in their work.

Not giving their precious attention to the strangers walking about their sacred texts. Making their way to the stairway leading up to the top floor of the observatory. The rhythmic sound of the gears spinning and turning the giant gyroscopic alchemical multi-planispheric astrolabe mechanism filled the room with its enchanting melody. The star charts engraved into the walls ran the whole circumference of the room. The constellations and celestial bodies glowing in an ethereal light.

At the base of the mechanism a figure stood alone, covered in a hooded cloak watching the group as they made their way towards them. As the group stopped feet away from the cloaked figure, he removed his hood to reveal a middle-aged human male.

The man had long green hair tied into a ponytail and a matching groomed short beard. His eyes were an aquamarine clam as the sea on a summer night. He gave them a warm gentle smile, as he looked them over with excitement in his eyes.

"Greetings. It is good to see that you were able to solve the puzzle of the Celestial Observatory's defensive trick. had to make sure that the right people where the ones coming to meet me here. You may call me Niko."

"I am Bellamy. The others beside me are Inara, Raine, and Na'naya. We appreciate you meeting with us. Though that little stunt with the observatory's defensive trick was somewhat of a bother. You could have gone a different way about discerning who we were."

Niko clasped his hands together. The expression on his face shifted from his warm demeanor to cold and stoic. A sudden chill ran down Bellamy's spine.

"Oh. You are most right in that regard. You see a more direct approach was only needed if I had deemed your intentions to be hostile..." With the flip of a coin Niko's demeanor shifted back to his former warmness.

"Well, with that lets move on, shall we?"

"So, Niko what information do you have for us, to take back to Madame Rhea?"

Niko reached into his cloak and pulled out a wooden pipe and a lighter. He placed the pipe into his mouth and lit the contents inside the bowl of the pipe with his lighter. Before putting the lighter back into his cloak. Taking small puffs from his pipe, the bowl began to glow as the contents inside heated up. He took in a series of deeper puffs and exhaling the smoke through the side of his mouth.

"It's not as simple as that, there has been a situation which has caused a setback of sorts. The task you were given will no longer be possible, and other actions will have to be taken in its place."

Bellamy was puzzled by his words, [*how could this have happened? He was supposed to do a simple courier job and take it back to Madame Rhea for the information he needed. Now it seems that everything got turned upside down. He would have to do something else instead.*] He thought, trying to figure out what could be coming now that their plans where changing. He didn't know how to respond to that, he wasn't alone for he had his companions there to keep him grounded.

"It sounds like our job became more complicated and bothersome than intended. I expect to be compensated for the trouble." Raine responded dejectedly.

"Don't mind him. He doesn't like to put more effort that he feels necessary for a job, let alone changing it up halfway through." Na'naya interjected.

Bellamy was grateful for his friends' banter. He was able to reset his mind to focus on the things he could control. Not let himself get consumed by what was out of his hands. They would have to move forward and adapt to their new circumstance to get the job done that they set out to do. He looked over at Inara who had that same calm and calculated look on her face. She seemed to have whenever she was collecting her thoughts. It was subtle and quiet, but Bellamy was sure he heard her let out a sigh.

"Tell us Niko, what happened that caused everything to change from the original plan? I get the feeling that our job got more complicated."

Niko took another series of prolonged puffs from his pipe and exhaling the smoke from the side of his mouth. He then began his tale and the events that followed.

"Three weeks ago, when the new parliamentary session started to discuss the current situation in the republic, a report came in that had troubling implications. There had been an increase of sightings and encounters with Daemons along the boundary lands of the republic's territory. Normally this sort of situation would be taken care of by the Expeditionary Force. They would disperse and bring the number of Daemons back down to manageable levels. Yet, that wasn't the case this time around as the Daemon encounters appeared in many regions and the number of Daemons increased simultaneously. This has been an unprecedented event. To counter this and protect the populace, the Expeditionary Forces have been dispatched all over to help where they can.

Though that's not the troubling part about the situation. For you see recently there was reports that Daemons were not the only thing the Expeditionary Forces encountered. Mercenary bands and bandits fighting alongside the Daemons. The information is scarce, so we don't know how they are controlling the Daemons. They are somehow able to and to great effect against the republic's forces. So far, they have managed to keep the situation contained. To the boundary lands and outer regions of the republic. If the tides should turn, then the whole of the republic could be engulfed in a war."

The others looked at one another in disbelief at what Niko had told them. Unable to bring themselves to speak. It was troubling news that would rock the republic at its core. They had no idea how to stop it or if they should even get involved in it. They were under no obligation to fight some unknown enemy on the republic's behalf.

The only thing that they were responsible for was protecting their own self-interests and that of their client, Madame Rhea. In that moment Bellamy got an ache in his stomach as a question came to mind, that he didn't want to ask but knew he had to.

"You said that there was mercenary bands and bandits mixed in with the Daemons, controlling them?"

"Correct."

"If that is the case, then that means that someone is backing them and using them as some sort of preemptive strike. And the republic needs to find out who the mysterious benefactor is without blind accusations causing an international conflict between nations. So, to do that they need small independent teams to search for the answers. Let me guess Madame Rhea has already been apprised of the situation. She has told you to use our services in this matter. Considering an all-out conflict would be detrimental and bad for her businesses."

Niko merely smirked at Bellamy's words. Admiring the cleverness and insight the young man demonstrated.

"That is indeed the gist of the matter at hand. It may not be what you want to hear, but it's the only option available to you. As she stated that this job is of the utmost importance and cannot be rejected by any means. Sorry kid, that woman has a way with people and getting what she wants. But don't worry in exchange for your continued support you'll be fairly compensated for all the information you obtain. Now one last thing. After you have finished up your business in Hoenheim you're all to leave for the western boundary lands. Cross the border into the Nimh Theocracy."

"The Nimh Theocracy, Huh. Interesting place you have us going to. So why there?" Raine scoffed.

"There are others checking out the other nations as well. Considering their standing with the republic, we feel that there might be something there worth looking into. Your group just might be the right ones for the job. Oh, and do be sure to bring your new friends with you, you never know their skills might prove useful to you all."

"What's that supposed to mean and how in the world do you know about them? Who are you, Niko?"

Niko stood there in silence and replied with a smile.

"Well, our time is up. Until the next time and best of luck on your travels. Farewell."

As his last word fell silent, Niko jumped backwards and faded away until no sign was left of him. Everyone paused staring off in the distance at what occurred before snapping back into their senses, after realizing he was gone. Leaving them with more questions to ponder, than answers given to them. Who in the world was that man and what have they found themselves caught up in now. This day had brought with it unexpected encounters and new adventures ahead of them.

CHAPTER 19

After leaving the celestial Observatory Bellamy and the others made their way to the High Summit Hot Springs. A sacred hot spring that was said to have special spiritual and healing properties. One of Hoenheim's sacred landmarks. Travelers would come from far and wide to experience its effects. They had all agreed that this opportunity couldn't be passed up.

They deserved some relaxation before they left on their new quest. In truth Inara felt that the trip to the hot springs would help them recenter their resolve. Calm their minds from the troubles that were brewing in the outer boundary lands of the republic. Three days is all they had left of their stay in the city. Before they would have to leave and make their way to the border, and cross into the Nimh Theocracy.

The High Summit Hot Springs were located beyond a shrine dedicated to the Night Mother. At the top of a long steep stone staircase, rising high into the mountainside. Tall ancient trees lined the stone staircase. Creating a shadowy canopy that let small glimpses of sunlight through its leaves. The mountain breeze swirled through the air passing through the mighty branches of the tall ancient trees.

With each step they took up the staircase, the tension in their bodies slowly released as they made their way to the top. The hot springs were unlike anything Bellamy had seen before. They consisted of four circular tiered natural earthen pools each one diagonally across from the other. With waters of a deep aquamarine, steam rising from their surfaces.

To the side of the hot springs was a small cottage building. Travelers visiting would place their belongings and change to enter the hot springs. Thin cloth towels were provided to cover your bare body when entering the sacred hot springs. A partial form of modesty was expected. Considering it was a mixed bathing hot springs not separated by gender.

While you were in the sacred hot springs whether you wore the towel or not was entirely up to the individual. They were only required to wear it when entering and exiting the hot springs. After changing and placing their belongings in the cottage building, they made their way into the sacred hot springs. The hot springs had been calm this time of day, so the group had the place to themselves.

"Aww…This is what I needed. This water feels amazing on my body, I'm glad we were able to make a trip here to experience them." Na'naya expressed in a relaxed voice as she entered the hot springs.

"I couldn't have said it better myself. This was most definitely needed."

Inara, Raine, and Bellamy each followed in turn entering the hot springs. Feeling the waters wash over their fatigued bodies. Leaning back against the earthen walls of the pool, relaxing and taking in the serene view of the azure sky above. Taking the time to enjoy themselves before the reality of their mission came into full being. They sat in silence and let the waters of the hot springs soothe their souls and bodies.

"Inara. What is your opinion on that guy, Niko? It seemed to me that he knew more than he let on. I don't know yet if we can trust what he says or if he is merely playing us."

"I can understand your hesitation and If I'm right about him, then that makes this game more difficult. Considering how perceptive he seemed, and the information gathered about us, I would guess that he is an Aegis Agent. It is a bit troubling to think that my mistress would have dealings with them but knowing her I wouldn't put it past her."

That name seemed to affect Raine and Na'naya, but Bellamy wasn't sure why. It had been the first time he heard that name. Based off the reactions the other's had, he felt that he should have heard the name somewhere before. For all the time he had spent in the republic, the name Aegis never crossed his path. Whether it was fortunate or not Bellamy wouldn't know until he got information on what Aegis was.

"Tell me Inara, what is Aegis? Why does that name carry such weight with it, as to affect the actions of the people who hear it?

"It doesn't surprise me that you haven't heard of it before. Because that name is like an open secret, spoken only in myth and rumor. Aegis is a network of spies and informants whose members are shadows. Capable of being anyone and anywhere. Skilled agents in service of the Renatan Parliament and the Chancellor. Their exploits and power only mentioned as mere speculation amongst the general populace. Only certain members of senior leadership in the government know the truth about them."

"I've only heard of them through rumors that me and my former master heard from some traveling merchants. Who had visited the Umbar Sultanate."

Na'naya's response about her experience, gave Raine reason enough to provide his own encounter with Aegis as well. He waited to make sure that she was done talking so that he didn't interrupt her. What was important was that they got as much information as they could on the group. Whose interest have now become their own and the possible people they might have to deal with in the future. At this point any piece of information they gathered would be of some benefit. Even if it was only speculation or rumor.

"During a job in my younger days with the mercenary group before you joined. There was an elderly drunkard who had told the captain he had some information that would be useful to us. That if we valued our lives, we should hear it. At first the captain wasn't certain in trusting the drunkard. His information ended up being useful. We were able to escape an ambush that would have been devastating had we ignored it. Later, when the captain sent us to find the old drunkard, he was nowhere to be found. The people in the area had no recollection of there ever being anyone like the person we described when asking around."

"So, you believe that the old drunkard must have actually been a member of Aegis."

Raine looked on at the others. As if recounting the events had made the pieces to an unsolved puzzle, he had in his mind come together. A possibility that he would have not considered. Had it not been for their encounter with Niko and What Inara had told them.

"It's the only possible answer that makes the most sense now that I've thought over it again. The key point that brings me to this conclusion is the fact that the old drunkard knew information that he had no possible way of knowing. That his information was more than eighty-five percent accurate. Something like that wouldn't be possible for an old drunkard."

The first stars of the evening were starting to shine in the clear sky. The group departed the sacred hot springs and headed on their way back to the inn. Their long soak in the waters had relaxed their bodies and cleared their minds. It was what they needed before their next job started. All that was left was for Bellamy to wait for his new and improved bow to be delivered to him.

For the two new members of their group to join them. Both Bellamy and Raine had the innkeeper dispatch letters. Informing them of the groups decision for them to join. They decided to have everyone rendezvous at the Central Railway Station at the end of the week in the early morning.

There they would catch a train heading west to the border town of Star Cross. On the outer fringes of the boundary lands. Between the Renata Republic and the Nimh Theocracy. From there it would be another six days before they reach the border. Then figure out the best way to cross it into the theocracy.

Travel by train would be shorter for them. So they would reach the town in three days, as opposed to the seven days it would take by foot. In the uncertainty that lied ahead of them, it was best for them to save time were possible in their travels. There was no telling how the current events might change in the blink of an eye.

Over the next two days everyone went about checking their supplies and equipment. Making sure everything was in order before they departed the city. Raine spent his days making his way through the different taverns and pubs located in the Merchant's District. Getting his fill of booze and women, before returning to the inn before curfew. It was a sort of ritual cleansing that he would do to clear his mind.

Remembering to enjoy life before a major battle or when setting out on a long and dangerous journey. Na'naya was using her remaining time by visiting the city's other famous landmarks and destinations. Along with the occasional gambling dens. She didn't like to admit it, but when she got an itch to bet there no satisfying it until she did. This addiction of hers has gotten her into trouble more times than she could remember.

Though if it wasn't for that, she might not have ever run into the people who would eventually become like brothers to her. With their help and support she has gotten better at controlling her addiction. Inara spent her time gathering information on the locations they may travel to. Be it nation, region, city, or town and listening for any rumors that might be circulating around. On the current situation of the republic.

From working with Madame Rhea over the years, she had come to understand that information was neither good nor bad. Factual or conjecture until it was combined through intention and personal beliefs. She was fortunate to have learned the skills from her mistress on how to hone and use them to the best of her abilities.

On the day before they were to leave Hoenheim, Bellamy's new and improved bow was delivered to the inn. The bow was everything he had hoped for and more. It was sleek, well-balanced in his hands. The tinsel strength of the drawstring had been improved giving him more power in his shots. The bows durability had gone up tenfold.

Master Dulhan proved himself to be a truly gifted and exceptional weaponsmith worthy of his reputation. For that Bellamy was most grateful. He had learned over his years of training and actual combat experience. That it wasn't the quality of the weapon that mattered but the skill of the one wielding it as well. For even the most elegant quality of weapon proved to be useless if it wasn't wielded by someone of equal skill to use it.

In some cases could even be a liability to the wielder. It was for these reasons that Bellamy worked hard at continuously training with all the weapons that he utilized. So that his skills will match the quality of his weapons. Giving him the harmonious balance between weapon and wielder.

The sun had risen four hours ago. Its rays spreading throughout the city and bringing with it the clear mildly cloudy sky of a brand-new day. The group had gotten up early had breakfast. Setting off for the Central Railway Station to await the arrival of their newest members. While waiting outside the front of the station, sitting around a giant bronze statue commemorating the founders of Hoenheim, Raine spotted Draemond coming down the street towards them.

"Over here, my friend!" Raine shouted towards him.

The dragonkin warrior stopped in front of the group and bowed his head in greeting.

"Good morning. I am Draemond Ignis, Dragonkin warrior of the Southern Plains Tribes. It is most fortunate to be joining you all."

"Draemond these are my friends that I mentioned to you. The young man to my left is Bellamy, the two ladies on my right are Na'naya and Inara."

One by one they each waved to Draemond in turn and greeted him.

"Alright, so we are waiting on one more person, and we will be set to go. Speaking of which, here she comes now."

They all turned to look in the direction that Bellamy was looking in. Seeing the form of the beautiful Nymph coming towards them.

CHAPTER 20

“**W**ell, hello there, my name is Amiriss Inkheart. It is a pleasure to meet you all and I look forward to getting to know about you on our journey together.”

“It’s good to see you again, Amiriss. These are my friends Raine, Na’naya, and Inara. Along with our newest member like you, Draemond.”

Amiriss acknowledged each one of them with a simple cheerful smile. The others did the same with a nod, a wave, and a smile from some as well. Bellamy couldn’t seem to place it, but there seemed to be some tension between Amiriss and Draemond. He could be mistaken and its only in his head or it could be something, he figured he would ask them about that later.

“Good. Now that we are all together let’s head inside and catch our train to Southern Cross. It should be departing in the next hour or so. Since you two wanted to join us, I thought I’d let you know that we are making our way to the Nimh Theocracy. So if that is a problem or concern you are welcome to turn us down. We will not hold it against you.”

“It’s not a problem for me. I will continue with you.”

“And I as well.” Amiriss replied agreeingly.

The party left the founder’s statue. They headed into the Central Railway Station through the glass and metal doors. The station's architecture was as grand and majestic as the parliament building. Crafted in the same Hoenheim Renaissance style of the city's past. In its true artistic splendor, the station's main focal point was the great mural glass dome on the ceiling of the station. The images upon seemed to come alive with the sunshine emanating through them.

After purchasing their tickets, they made their way down to platform six where the alchemic train awaited. Bellamy and the others looked on in awe as they reached the train and saw it for the first time.

The train consisted of the alchemic locomotive in the front attached to three luxury cars. A dining car, five passenger cars, and four storage cars behind it. Standing at the entrance onto the train was the conductor. He was punching the tickets of the passengers one by one as he ushered them onboard. As the final passengers boarded the train, the whistle blew.

The doors were closed. With the gears turning the train moved forward leaving the platform and the station behind. As its engine picked up speed. Making their way through the passenger cars of the train, the group came to their private cabin. It was a medium sized cabin with bench couch seating on both sides capable of seating six people comfortable and overheard storage racks for their belongings. Everyone took a seat on the benches, after they put up their belongings in the overhead storage racks.

Bellamy, Amiriss, and Raine sat on the bench on the right, while Inara, Draemond, and Na'naya sat on the bench on the left. They came to this arrangement to use the space they had in the best possible way to still be comfortable. Since some of the members in their party were bigger than others. So, to make it fare, it would be two big members and one small member on each of the benches. No one seemed to object to the seating arrangement.

Though, there was a brief pout from Na'naya when she saw that Amiriss would be sitting next to Bellamy and Raine and not her. That went away when she noticed them staring at her. She changed it up and smiled, the two laughed and smiled back.

"Now's as good a time as any. Has anyone here ever been to the Nimh Theocracy? My travels have only been limited to the Umbar Sultanate and parts of the Renata Republic."

"No, I'm afraid not. My travels have taken me to the Free cities. Some of the Northern Continent, the Renata Republic, the Umbar Sultanate, and my homeland in the Dragonkin Tribal lands."

"I don't have much experience traveling. So, I've only been to a few places with most of it being in the Renata Republic. I made my way here from the Zenith Imperium when I was a young teen."

Inara, Raine, and Amiriss had not joined in on the conversation yet. Only sitting back and listening to what the others were saying. It didn't seem like they were going to respond to the question. It was something else that was making them hesitant to reply. There was a quite awkwardness in the cabin before Raine was the first of the three to speak up.

"I have been to the Nimh Theocracy, it was many years ago when I was still a young child. My mother and I were captured by slavers in our homeland and sold to a wealthy family in the theocracy. We worked for many years under the strict rules of our masters and the church's doctrine. Until the day my mother was able to earn my freedom. I had promised that I would free her from her bondage one day. Then three years after I was free, I had found out that my mother had been sold off. Slain by Daemons in transport to her new master."

Bellamy and the others grasped Raine's shoulder in a comforting gesture. Showing their support and sorrow to the hardships he experienced. Both him and Na'naya had known Raine for some time now and this was the first time that he had brought up his past with them. They wanted to say something to comfort their friend. They know that being there for him was the best course of action. Then offering hollow words to sympathize with a situation they couldn't understand. For now, this was the best they could do for him.

"It's a sad truth, but stories like your friend's are all too common in the theocracy. It is a nation governed by strict rules and doctrine enforced by the Nimh Religion. A questionable one that promises salvation through one of two paths: The Path of the Devout and The Path of the Pilgrim. The Path of the Devout is a lifetime of service to the religion. Through being clergy within the religion or a follower. and by living by its teachings and providing offerings. It grants you a privilege life if you obey. The Path of the Pilgrim on the other hand is one that promises a chance for salvation through hardship. Meant to cleanse the souls of heretics and non-believers converted into the religion. This I'm sure you guessed is by means of forced slavery."

Hearing those words from Inara, caused Bellamy to clench his fist in frustration. Knowing that one of the world's most influential religions was encouraging and built upon the practice of slavery and so-called salvation through it. It was another reminder to him that good and evil is a matter of perception. Capable of being twisted by the power of the ones with the most influence. That morality and sin were merely opposite sides of a single coin, and that one's blessing could be another's curse.

Why the Gods would allow such things he could not say. The only thing he could do was to continue to live by his convictions. Doing what he could to help make the world a better place, any way he could.

"With all that in mind there is something else that we must all be aware of. The theocracy is not as welcoming to outsiders as other nations. As such we must tread carefully when dealing with its citizens. One serious misstep and we could find ourselves locked up in prison or worse forced into slavery. If I'm not mistaken runaway slaves lose a limb on a first offense, crippled on a second and executed on a third. I don't know about you, but neither option sounds appealing to me, so let's be careful, for all our sakes." Amiriss cautioned.

The conversation had turned into a heavier topic than Na'naya and the others had expected it to. But they were still grateful to express their concerns and get to know one another's view. The sound of the steam bellowing from the engine stack and the rhythmic nuances of the wheels gliding along the tracks gently echoed in the background. As the train passed through the final stretch of mountains and into the countryside. Throughout the day the members of the party would come and go from their cabin.

To stroll through the train cars, grab some food or drink from the dining car, and rest in the cabin. For their first day of travel on the train this was their routine. As they settled into this form of travel, which for everyone except for Inara and Amiriss had been new to them. On the second day of their train ride something unexpected happened that everyone on board had no means of predicting. A knock-up tempest had appeared in the region the train was traveling through.

Throughout the world and in different regions from densely crowded lands to vast open vistas strange unnatural mana-imbued weather phenomenon would occur unexpectedly. In the wake of these events, the regions affected would experience great geographic and climatic changes. That would alter the landscape for many years if not centuries at a time. Because such events were sudden, rare, and infrequent there was no accurate way of predicting when one might occur. The only thing one could do was try to ride it out and work through the aftermath. A knock-up tempest was one such event and a very dangerous one at that.

"Hey, come and look at this!"

The others dropped what they were doing to look out the cabin window and see what Bellamy was talking about. Shock and surprise were painted on their faces as they looked on.

"Wh..Wha...What in the seven hells is that?"

Swirling dark miasmic clouds filled the clear sky. Blocking out the sun's lights and casting a dull blackness over the land. Mighty howling gales, a torrential downpour, thunder, and flashing lighting strikes where the overture of the lethal symphony brought on by the knock-up tempest. The turbulent force Shaked and swayed the train cars with such ferocity. As it struggled to move along the tracks.

Passengers were advised to stay in the seats or cabins, and to not move about for their safety. The train had no other option but to keep moving forward. It meant certain destruction to stay in one location in such unpredictable and dangerous weather.

Bellamy and the others embraced their benches with firm grips. They watched the storm rage on outside their cabin window. They witnessed the ground tremble. Being torn asunder as large chunks of rocks and trees were violently flung into the gale winds up into the sky. Some crashing back into the landscape like meteors falling from the sky.

As the train made its way across a bridge, the raucous sounds stopped. There was a dead silence, in that brief eerie quiet. Everyone stared at one another with concern in their eyes. Then a sudden explosive boom of geothermal mana pressure burst beneath the train knocking it off the tracks and up into the air all in an instant.

CHAPTER 21

In the wake of the knock up tempest, the land in the surrounding area was ravaged. Altered from the peaceful and tranquil countryside it had once been. It was transformed into A jagged spiderweb fissure that spread throughout. Creating a deep canyon with twisted perverse trees in a barren hellish wasteland. The train cars had separated from the powerful force.

They came crashing down into different locations with a fearsome impact. Smoke stacks and fires signaled like a beacon in a stormy night. The locations of the train wreckage, while haunting screams of suffering and dying passengers filled the air with their voices. A soft thumping rain was all that remained of the malicious storm. Rain drops pinging as they contacted the steel frames of the overturned train cars.

A throbbing internal pain echoed up and down every inch of his body. A dazed concussion pounded at the forefront of Bellamy's head. Muffled sounds filled his ears, as he opened his eyes trying to focus in on his surroundings. The fuzzy visage of a female standing over him mouthing something he couldn't make out, started to clear up. After a few moments, he was able to concentrate and see that Inara was standing over him. Small drops of blood were running down the side of her head and left arm.

"Bellamy...Bellamy..."

"It's alright Inara, I'm okay. How are you and the other's doing? What happened?"

"A massive geothermal mana pressure knocked the train off the tracks and into the sky. Before it came crashing down. Everyone is alright. A couple of cuts and bruises but no serious injuries. We were lucky because Draemond quickly softened our impact somewhat with a protective aura. As it only lasted a few seconds since it was hastily casted."

Bellamy carefully got back up on his feet, as Inara grabbed his arm to help him keep his balance and not fall over. His feet were wobbly as he was gaining a firm foothold on what appeared to be the cabin's ceiling. Looking around the cabin, he saw that the whole train car had been turned upside down. All their belongs had been thrown all over the place. As Bellamy looked around the cabin, he saw the others collecting their things.

Checking over themselves to make sure there was no wounds they were unaware of on them. Bellamy walked over towards Amiriss and grabbed his pack that was lying by her feet.

"I bet you didn't think something like this would happen to you, two days after leaving the city."

"This was a surprise to me indeed. One, if I'm honest I wouldn't want to experience again if I can help it. Though, if anything I suspect my life will be filled with both excitement and danger if I continue to follow you and your friends."

Bellamy smiled at Amiriss's words. Feeling calm that she could be lighthearted and collected even in a dangerous situation.

"You make an interesting point. I hope we don't disappoint, and you enjoy your travels with us, wherever they may lead."

He then made his way over to the broken cabin window where Raine and Draemond were standing looking out the area beyond. Watching for any signs of danger or the other passengers. As Bellamy approached, they turned their heads towards him and nodded, seeing that he was up on his feet and okay. Draemond gestured for him to come closer and stand next to him by the broken cabin window. Bellamy walked over and stood on his right side.

"I'm glad that you are doing better. Unfortunately, you struck the side of the bench harder than I expected when my protective aura dropped around us. For that I apologize."

"There is nothing to apologize for. If it wasn't for your quick thinking, then we would've suffered from much serious injuries. So, thank you for your quick action and help."

They clasped one another's forearm and hand as a sign of gratitude and mutual respect. Both demonstrating that they could count on each other in a time of need. Raine had been quiet. Looking off into the distance and assessing the situation with his keen sight. He turned around to face everyone. Then he addressed them of their current situation.

"Listen closely, as I think I have a firm grasp of our current predicament. It appears the Knock Up Tempest created a giant fissure altering the landscape for miles in all directions. The train has been wrecked beyond repair. Its passengers and cars have been scattered throughout this canyon. Are best course of action would be to make our way west along the canyon. Until we can find a suitable place to climb out and proceed to our destination. I understand you may feel an urge to seek out any survivors and try to help them. We most forego that urge and press on as it is for our continued safety."

Bellamy could see in some of their eyes, that it didn't sit right to move on and not try to help any of the other survivors. Considering their circumstance, he could see the reasoning behind Raine's words. But it still bothered him a little knowing that he couldn't do anything for them now. That as hard as it might be they had to keep moving on time, as there was no telling how much time they had. Bellamy walked over to his pack and put it on his back, as he collected his belongings.

"The right thing to do isn't always the easiest or the morally conscious thing to do. But a matter of the given situation and the possible outcomes from it. We were given a mission that could potentially affect thousands of lives and many nations. So the needs of the many must be more pressing than the needs of the few that are here. Let's move out and balance our scales one day through the future actions we take."

Everyone followed Bellamy's example and grabbed their belongings. They exited the train wreckage making their way west along the canyon's tall, jagged walls. The sky changed from its clear deep blue into the orange and purple hues of twilight, as the sun began to set. With the fading light of the last rays of sun, the shadows grew as they ensnared the rocky faces of the canyon's walls. A ominous mist flooded over the top of the canyon.

Snaking down the jagged walls to the ground below making visibility difficult. As everything became shrouded in the mist. Reaching into their packs, everyone pulled out a small crystalline orb lantern attached to a metal rod.

With three taps to the base of the lantern the crystalline orbs inside began to glow emitting a light aura around the lantern. This aura provided them with enough light so that they could see ten feet in front of them. It wasn't much but it was enough to watch out for each other and show them the path ahead or behind them. They proceeded on through the canyon. watching their steps as they made their way over the uneven ground of the canyon floor. To avoid being separated they walked in a single formation of two people side by side with the other pair behind the one in front.

Bellamy and Inara where at the front of the pack leading the way. Na'naya and Amiriss where in the middle, then Raine and Draemond brought up the rear. Based on their member's ability, this formation was the best to use their skills. Allowing them the flexibility to change up based on the situation. It was late in the evening when the mist had cleared out.

The stars of the night sky shined on the depths of the canyon below, with their ethereal light. They had finally reached the end of the canyon wall where they would ascend and make their way out. After what had been hours of trekking through the jagged twist and uneven ground of the canyon. The canyon's walls ran sixty feet upwards at a slanted incline. Protruding formations and tricky edges, making the climb up difficult and dangerous.

"Hey everyone, we should rest here for a little while before we try to scale the canyon wall. We have been walking non-stop through here for hours with no rest. It would be dangerous to rush this in our current condition."

"I agree with Amiriss. She makes a valid point; we should rest up some while we can. Besides, climbing up the canyon wall this late at night with low visibility would be a much more dangerous risk. Let's wait to scale in the early hours of the day."

Inara and Bellamy set their packs down next to some boulders. They looked around the area before speaking. They looked at one another and came to an agreement, nodding in support of the decision.

"Alright we will take the time to get some rest and recover before making our way up the canyon wall in the morning. Draemond and Na'naya will take the first watch. While Amiriss and I take the second, followed by Inara and Raine who will take the last watch. So, do try to get what rest you can because we have a long day ahead of us tomorrow."

The others went about in finding a place to lay down and rest. Though finding a comfortable one was hard pressed, as the ground was uneven and bumpy. This didn't stop them in the least, they were going to rest one way or another. It required little work arounds on their parts. Bellamy leaned his head against his pack that was propped on a boulder as his pillow.

Looking up gazing at the stars in the night sky, until he drifted off into sleep. It wasn't the most comfortable sleep as he was accustomed to recently. It was restful enough for his fatigue to dissipate and for his stamina to recover. He felt a small tap on his shoulder and the sound of his name being called. He opened his eyes and awakened from his sleep.

"Bellamy, it's time for your watch. Get up, so that I may go and rest my head to dream of the comfy bed and warm baths we left behind."

"Alright, Na'naya I am getting up. Go on and get your rest. You know there is more to life than simple comforts."

Na'naya smiled as she thought about those simple comforts as Bellamy called them. She extended her hand and Helped Bellamy to his feet.

"Certainly, there is but you don't get it. I'm afraid such things are beyond a male's understanding it would seem. Well goodnight."

Na'naya turned and headed off to the spot she had claimed for herself, to lie down and dream of her simple comforts. Bellamy made his way over to a small rock formation where Amiriss had taken up the watch. Scanning the area around them for any signs of trouble. Amiriss waved as she saw Bellamy approach. Taking spot on a boulder elevated above where she was standing.

As, he got up onto the boulder, he was able to get a clear look for the first time of the weapon in spun leather and metal scabbard strapped to Amira's back. It was a falchion, a long-curved blade sword made from a Unicorn horn with a dark aquamarine leather and gemstone studded hilt.

"That's a unique and beautiful sword you have there. It a suitable weapon that compliments its owner's own beauty."

"Aww. Thank you for the lovely remark, Bellamy. I didn't take you for a flirt when I first met you, it's a welcomed surprise. So, tell me what is it that you hope to do on this journey of yours? Something tells me its more than mere financial gain. There are other ways if not as lucrative of earning serious coin."

Bellamy reached into his pouch and pulled out a small ancient looking circular medallion coin. Engraved with the visage of a goddess on one side and a great mythic wolf howling to the twin moons on the other. He tossed the coin into the air, catching it in his hand and rolled it through his fingers back and forth. Lowering his hand, He handed the coin of to Amiriss who looked it over with care before she handed back up to Bellamy. She could sense that the coin was precious to him, by the way he was handling it and keeping it close to his person.

"That medallion of yours, is a masterfully crafted work of art. It must be made from rare materials because I don't think I have seen any of its like on my travels. Where did you get it from?"

"It was my mother's and she had given it to me for my eighth birthday. She told me that it was forged long ago in the Age of Heroes by mystics from a lost civilization. It and my memories are all I have left of my mother. She was killed seven years ago, and I have been searching for information on why and by whom. I need to do this so I can do something this time and not be helpless like I was that day."

Amiriss gently rubbed the side of Bellamy's leg to offer some comfort. She could hear the pain in his words brought by the memory of his mother. The pain of losing a loved one or someone close is never an easy thing to bear. It proves exceptionally harder when the loss is not of natural causes. It is in these hardships that a person's true character is tested.

By how they deal with it whether it be positive or negative. She had seen before how such feelings could drive someone to do something completely different from what you would expect of them. See it consume them until they drowned in their grief. The only thing that she could do that she had learned was to be there for the person. Be willing to listen if that's all they wanted from you in that moment.

"I don't know if it's my place to say this as I haven't known you for long. You have companions who care about you and would do anything for you. Know that you are not alone in this and that we are here for you, you only need to ask."

CHAPTER 22

T he night sky had been calm and all had been relatively quiet for the remainder of Bellamy and Amiriss's watch. There had been no signs of Daemons or people to speak of in the general area around them. It wasn't wise to let their guard down and relax, for the canyon was new ground to them and they hadn't made it out of its clutches just yet. The twin moons were at their zenith in the night sky shining brightly with their ethereal glow when Bellamy felt a rumbling in the ground. He quickly stood up on the boulder and knocked an arrow into his recurve bow, Amiriss responded by going to draw her falchion, but Bellamy signaled her to wait.

"Amiriss, hold off and go and wake the others. Quickly! There is something heading our way."

Amiriss jolted off towards the direction the others were in sleeping to wake them up. The rumbling beneath Bellamy's feet slowly grew in intensity as the footsteps of whatever was heading their way moved closer. He scanned the branching paths that lead to them, but even with the moonlight from the twin moons, the visibility on the canyon floor was still in poor conditions. So, he wasn't going to get a clear view of what was coming their way until it was much closer that he would have liked. There was nothing to be done about it, he would have to rely on his skills and knowledge to respond in a timely manner with his actions.

"Bellamy. Tell us what you need, we are here to help."

Amiriss and the others had come up and spread-out surrounding Bellamy, with their weapons drawn and at the ready. Each one of them facing down the different branching paths that lead to their location. Draemond was a fearsome sight to behold, the dragonkin warrior was wielding a Behemoth and Basilisk bone war club, with a dark leather handle and oval primal stone head in one hand and a Prism buckler shield on the other. They were traditional weapons wielded by only the most skilled and veteran of dragonkin warriors, as they were unnaturally heavy and cumbersome to use in battle without the proper conditioning. The rumbling on the ground grew louder as the footsteps were drawing closer and the raucous screeches echoed on the canyon walls as the Daemons came into view.

Approaching down the connecting paths in their direction was a horde of Darkling Spore Imps, low mid-level fiends four feet tall, that had been corrupted and twisted into vicious, mindless zombie-like husk by the Darkling spores infecting their bodies. Normally in small numbers they are not much of a threat and can be easily managed, but when encountered in larger numbers it can be lethal if you're not cautious. The group had to proceed carefully as they had two major handicaps to deal with in this battle, the terrain, and the number of enemies at hand. Bellamy thought [*if they were able to buy some time and hold them off long enough, then perhaps they could scale the canyon wall and escape.*] It could work but it would mean holding them off until the sun's rays reach the canyon floor, as the Darkling Spore Imps where nocturnal and vulnerable to sunlight.

"Listen closely as I have a plan. We need to do everything we can to hold them off until the sunlight hits the canyon floor, then we take the opportunity to scale the canyon wall and escape. They have us outnumbered about six to one and the terrain is tight, but we must do this. So, stay vigilant and fight with all you got."

"Aaaahhhh...." The others echoed fiercely in unison.

With the plan set and their minds focused on the task at hand the group prepared to engage the approaching enemy. In a swift succession of one arrow after the other, Bellamy let loose a volley of three arrows with mere seconds between each volley. The arrows flew and hit their targets, striking down the Charging Darkling Spore Imps square between the eyes. As one imp fell another quickly popped up in its place charging head on towards the group, while Bellamy pressed on with his volley of arrows to thin down their ranks. Down a path on the right side of Bellamy, Raine had advanced forward to engage the enemy head on.

Utilizing his keen flexibility along with his strength, Raine countered the wild and primal slashing strikes of the imps surrounding him, as he strikes them down one by one. Keeping his distance well calculated between him and his targets so that they don't gain the upper hand over him. He knew that with each fatal blow he landed with his daggers, meant that there would be one less enemy that his companions would have to worry about dealing with. It was no easy feat he continued to press on with his attacks to thin the enemy, while carefully monitoring his stamina. On an interconnected path to the left of Bellamy, Na'naya and Amiriss were aiding each other to handle the advancing group of imps they faced.

Their two fighting styles where the complete opposites of one another, Na'naya's focused on deflection with powerful counter strikes, While Amiriss's was more of a dance made up of elegant, swift slashing strikes. They were masters of their chosen weapons and wielded them with exceptional skill, the enemies were no match for their combined prowess. Yet there were no signs of the enemy letting up, as another imp was there to take the place of one that had fallen. Their numbers alone were proving to be the most difficult part of the challenge facing them. Along another path to the left of the girls north of Bellamy, Inara was engaged in an overwhelming battle outnumbered by the enemy.

Odds likes these didn't affect Inara's fortitude in her clashes as they might have someone else who wasn't as adapt at fighting large numbers, but she and her twin brothers were accustomed to such hardships from their earlier years growing up. The Frozen Wilds are a dangerous place to live and as such the Daemons there tend to always hunt in big packs to outnumber their prey or fight off threats. Meaning you had to learn to adapt and fight against many enemies at a time if you hoped to survive in the wilds or live long enough to make it out. Still, she powered through striking down her enemies one by one, as they continued to hopelessly advance on her.

Down the last path on the left of the girls south of Bellamy, Draemond ferociously held back the advancing imps with his shear unadulterated force, crushing them beneath his powerful war club and mighty tail. The dragonkin warrior fought with a blend of skill and raw brutal savagery in his strikes against the imps attacking him. His eyes glowed with deadly intent, as he embraced the frenzied berserker trance his kind would experience when locked in combat with large number of enemies or an extremely deadly threat. Though considered a powerful ability, in truth it was a double-edged sword capable of harming both the wielder and their targets if not in balance. For this reason, many dragonkin warriors avoided using the technique without the proper training and mindset to use it effectively, because it could without a doubt cost them their lives.

As the battle raged on for what seemed like hours, Bellamy and his companions began to feel the effects of the strain and fatigue put on their bodies from the prolonged fighting. The enemy numbers appeared to be finally dwindling down but that was only a false hope, as more imps appeared to come onto the battlefield, like a malicious plague infecting everything around them. Bellamy thought, [*it shouldn't be much longer, we just need to keep pressing and hold out. The sun should be rising soon, now.*] Just as he was shooting another volley of arrows towards the advancing imps, Bellamy glimpsed up at the sky and noticed the hues beginning to change as the sun had stated to rise.

"Everyone, it is almost time. The sun has started to rise in the distance, so fight on and hold fast!" Bellamy shouted through the commotion of the battle towards his companions.

With his words echoing throughout the battlefield, his companions felt a second wind course through them, as their effort doubled to hold the enemy back. With each step they managed to push the enemies, they would find themselves moving two steps forward only to take another step back. Each and every strike was proving more difficult to land than the previous one, as the battle prolonged the imps gradually start to adapt, more than likely an after effect of the Darkling Spore's hive memory. That was going to cause them serious trouble if they didn't escape as soon as possible. It seemed they still had some luck on their side, as the sun's rays cascaded through parts of the canyon's floor at long last.

As the sunlight started to wash over the canyon floor, the masses of imps started to break away and retreat into the shadows. The imps that were hit with the sunlight wailed and screamed in agony as their bodies erupted into flames engulfing them, till only ash remained. Seizing their chance, everyone carefully made their way towards the canyon wall, fighting off any imps still advancing towards them through the pockets of shadow that remained. With the sun's light protecting them, one by one they began their arduous climb up the canyon wall. Allowing the others to climb up ahead of them, Bellamy and Draemond where the last two to climb up.

Advancing methodically up the canyon wall from makeshift foothold to foothold, Bellamy cling closely to the wall making sure his hands and feet were firmly in place. Progressing slowly but still moving in an upward direction, everyone was getting closer towards the top of the canyon, When Bellamy heard a voice call out to him from above.

"Watch out!"

Bellamy looked up and saw the loose rocks of the canyon wall give way, breaking off and falling towards him. There was nothing he could do but try to side jump out of the way of the debris and hopefully grab hold of the wall before he found himself falling. Just as the rocks came plummeting towards him, Bellamy pushed off the wall and side jumped out of the way of the debris reaching for a new place to grab. His reach barely fell short of his mark, and he fell backwards from the canyon wall down towards the floor below.

"Aaaahhh!"

"Bellamy!" Amiriss wailed.

Non coherent thoughts were racing through his mind as he was trying to think of something he could do and lessen the impact of his fall. It all happened so quickly, but in that instant, it felt like an eternity. Bellamy jerked and came to a sudden halt mid fall as Draemond's tail wrapped around his body catching him just as he pasted right next to him.

"That was close. For a moment there I wasn't sure if I was going to catch you. You are certainly a lucky one, the gods must have plans for you."

Bellamy sighed in relief.

"Thank you. I wasn't sure what was going to happen there."

"Is everything alright down there?" Amiriss called down in concern.

"There's no need to worry, we are okay and heading up towards you now."

Pulling him back up towards the canyon wall, Bellamy firmly grabbed hold and they continued their climb up to the top of the canyon. The chaotic sounds on the canyon floor below had faded in the distance, as they climbed higher and higher. As Bellamy and Draemond reached the top of the canyon, Amiriss rushed over and jumped into Bellamy's arms giving him a big embrace. Small tear droplets were running down the sides of her cheeks, but she had a joyous smile on her face.

"You scared me back there, you insensitive oof. Try to be more careful in the future. I'm not ready to lose you."

"I'm sorry I worried you. I can't make any promises, but I will do my best to be more careful."

CHAPTER 23

With their ordeal in the canyon behind them, Bellamy and the others continued their journey. Using the day to make progress towards their destination. The outlying countryside and vistas of the republic were wide and vast open regions for miles in all directions. Even with the Renata Republic being a populous nation. Many of the population centers were spread sparsely throughout its territory.

Far to one another. For this reason, vast expanses of open land were commonplace in the republic. Other nations as well had a similar style. This came about to both protect them from outside threats and a way of control over the nation's populace.

From what Bellamy had learned in his studies, these methodologies came about in ages past. The world was a more much wild and chaotic place. Separated remote havens were a pivotal part for people to survive and prosper in their world. So, over the centuries these havens grew and expanded. Beholden to their founding methodologies in a different world than the one of their past.

Over time small frontier towns and villages sprang up. Providing waypoints for travelers. The vast expanses of open wilderness separating the different cities. Though this didn't ease the burden or dangers of travel. so long distance travel was undertaken by those who sought adventure.

Fame, money, or the opportunity to live their lives the way they wanted to. Since leaving the canyon the group had been making up lost time. Trekking through the countryside nonstop for the whole day, traveling miles upon miles.

The sun was staring to set, when they finally decided to stop and set up camp for the night. Satisfied that they had covered a good distance. They had found a small grove of trees running along the edge of hilly grassland plains to rest. The location was what they needed as it provide cover and a clear view in many directions. Bellamy set his pack on the ground and rolled out his sleeping mat. The others did the same as well before gathering firewood and preparing their meal. Gathered around the warmth of the fire, everyone sat around enjoying the delicious stew that Inara had prepared for them. It was a broth of wild greens, herbs, potatoes, and horned rabbit meat.

"How far out would you say we are from reaching Southern Cross?"

"Taking into account where the train wrecked. How far we traveled today, I would say still about half a day away from the town." Inara responded directly.

"Ughh...So you're telling me we are still about a week away from reaching the boarder and crossing into the Nimh Theocracy. That and unless we get some form of transportation, we are going to be walking an absurd number of miles to get there. Don't get me wrong I have done my fair share of traveling by foot over the years. This is starting to be seen like some cruel joke being played at our expense." Na'naya sternly vented.

That was one hard truth that everyone knew but didn't want to accept. Unless you had the means or foresight, you were uncouthly forced to travel by foot to your destinations. Na'naya understood this all too well. She wanted to catch a break for once and not have to tough it out like she always had to. As much of an inconvenience it was becoming, Na'naya welcomed traveling through the republic as a more pleasing experience. Better than traversing the harsh climate of her homeland. This didn't change how she felt about the current situation. She wasn't about to let it set her back, after all she was doing this to support her friends and see more of the world.

"What is the plan when we get to Southern Cross? Are we going to stay there for a bit then head out. Or were you thinking about getting some mounts and leaving right afterwards?" Raine inquired.

"I've been going over the options and trying to figure out which course of action would be most prudent. Our best bet would be to stay in town for two days and secure some mounts, then head out for the border. That shouldn't pose a problem or put too much of a delay on things."

"It works for me, Bellamy. How about the rest of you?" Inara replied.

"Yeah." The others responded in unison.

At the rising of the sun on the next day, everyone had gathered their belongings and cleared out from the camp. The temperate mild warm days of mid-autumn were ending. The cold winds of winter and the first signs of snow appeared in a light blanket nestled on the changing leaves sprinkled on the ground. With winter coming up upon them. Traveling through the open vastness of countryside was going to become more strenuous in the coming weeks. Bellamy and the others were prepared for the coming cold winter weather. They would need to stock up on some extra supplies because with the cold comes an unnatural darkness. During this time travel is exceedingly dangerous for the Daemons that appear are lethal to the inexperienced and foolish.

Hunting and trapping jobs were big business during the winter months. Providing an opportunity to make ample coin for those brave enough to take up the jobs. Bellamy had taken up such jobs with the mercenary group the last few winters. He improved his skills because of them. If it wasn't for Raine's guidance in the early winter jobs, he wouldn't have been where he was now.

He had his fair share of close calls more than he cared to admit. He was grateful that he had reliable and capable friends with him on his travels. Their presence gave Bellamy the push he needed to keep moving forward. Not let his past regrets anchor him down. There were days were that was easier said than done, and he would be out of sorts, these days were far and few between. On those days, Bellamy would be closed off to people and unavailable emotionally. His friends would give him the space he needed to cope and process.

He appreciated that his friends could understand that he needed that space. So he could fortify his mind and strengthen his mental health. A balance between the mind, the body, and spirit was essential in honing his skills. To unlocking any latent *Arts* ability he might possess. Bellamy thought, [*When the time is right, one of my new companion's might be capable of teaching me how to finally unlock latent Arts within me.*]

It was worth the try of asking since he still haven't had any luck in finding a teacher yet. His companions have showed that they possess *Arts* abilities. Now, whether they would be open to training him was a different matter.

"Amiriss, considering you're a Fae and a Nymph at that, would you be open to training me in how to use any latent *Arts* ability I might possess? I have been searching for someone to teach me, but I haven't had much luck. As I'm sure your aware of, most *Artist* tend to keep their knowledge close to them and not very open about teaching others."

"I will have to see what potential you may have and from there we can see if I'd be willing to train you. I cannot make you any promises, but I will consider it. For now, let's focus on getting to Southern Cross and the border."

"That's all I ask. Thank you, Amiriss."

After walking several more miles throughout most of the day, the group reached the top of a hill overlooking a lowland plain below. Down in the lowland plain south of their current location, the frontier town of Southern Cross finally came into view. It was a medium sized settlement. Surrounded by an outer fortified wall comprised of wood and stone. With Southern Cross being a frontier town, it had only the essentials needed for the settlement to survive and prosper.

That being: a temple, a blacksmith, a bank, merchant shops, taverns and inns. A butchery, stables, a doctor, resident homes, a city watch garrison, minor guildhalls, and some brothels. Also in this instance a train station since it was one of the stops on the railway.

Medium sized frontier towns like Southern Cross and farm villages where commonplace along the borderland regions of the republic. Used as waystations in the vast wilderness regions. When they passed through the town's main gate, they saw that the town was scarcely alive with commotion and people. The streets were barren and quiet as there was hardly anyone on them. An unnerving tension filled the air with a heavy invisible weight on the back of their shoulders.

They headed towards a tavern to gather some information. The liveliness and conversations going on inside the tavern went silent for an instant, when Bellamy and the others walked through the door. The eyes of everyone inside turned towards them.

"Hey. What's going on with all the looks?" Na'naya whispered towards Inara.

"Best to leave it be and don't overthink it. We're not here to cause any problems." She whispered back.

The look in their eyes, was not of hate or distrust, but what one could only call contempt. After the group had walked by and headed towards a table to grab a seat. The tavern patron's eyes turned back. The conversations resumed like nothing happened. Before taking his seat with the group at the table, Raine walked over to the bar. He struck a conversation with one of the lovely young bar maidens.

Then returned to the table with drinks in hand. He handed everyone a drink and sat down next to Draemond. He raised his tankard taking a long refreshing swig of his sweet ale. Relaxing his nerves before telling them what he had gathered from the bar maiden and their conversation.

"So, from what I could gather from the bar maiden about the reason for the looks we received coming in and the way the town appears to be connected. It seems the town is on edge and in a state of high alert. There are reports of skirmishes occurring in the region. Sightings of hordes of Daemons. Unknown mercenaries and bandits causing trouble for the people and towns. The local city watch garrisons and the republic's frontier regiments are engaged in battles all over the outlying regions. Travel has become extremely dangerous and banned outright in most areas."

"So, it makes sense that people would be weary of outsiders traveling at a time like this. Securing the mounts and extra provisions might become a bit of an ordeal because of the current events. We'll have to see and adjust if that proves to be out of our hands." Inara stated her observation.

The others sat around the table in silence. They were contemplating the best options for them given the information they heard and how to act on it. Bellamy smiled as he looked over at Na'naya and Amiriss who seemed to have been lost in thought. The looks on their faces were that of someone distracted by something else entirely.

"Hey, you two, what's got you distracted?"

"Huh. What, its nothing." The two girls replied in unison blushing.

"Ha...Haa...Ha...Ha."

Draemond and Raine burst out laughing from their reaction. The others joined in caught in the euphoria. The mood had changed in an instant. Everyone was cheerful enjoying the drinks. Not being consumed by the seriousness of the situation they would have to deal with later. Together with the others Bellamy filled his stomach with ale and food. They enjoyed each other's company partying late into the evening.

CHAPTER 24

The next morning when Bellamy awoke, he let out a long yawn and stretched out his body. Refreshing his energy and thinning out the small constant throbbing he felt in his head. [*Never again, that is the last time I let Raine goad me into drinking so much. Damn, this accursed hangover.*], Bellamy thought over as he changed and collected his belongings.

He left the room he had shared with Raine and Draemond. They had already changed and headed out before him, to meet the girls. Everyone was waiting outside the tavern. They had decided to stay there last night after they finished partying. It had some rooms available for them upstairs. Raine smiled as he saw Bellamy come out the door and head over to them.

"Good morning, nice of you to come and join us. In case it might have slipped your mind last night. We must secure some mounts and extra provisions before we leave today."

"Don't give me that, I know. It's all your fault I'm a little out of sorts this morning, I have told you that I'm not a crazy lush like you. There are limits to how much I can drink, yet you keep pushing."

"You don't see the beauty in it kid, limits are meant to be pushed and surpassed. One day you might finally understand."

"I'll be fine in a bit. Let's go and get what we need. We still have more distance to cover and it's only going to get harder as this weather changes."

They headed towards the town's western gate, where the stables were located. Making stops at a few of the merchants along the way to buy the extra provisions they would need for their journey. It was no surprise to them given the current situation that the prices on some of the provisions they brought were higher than normal. About three times the normal rate. There was nothing they could do about it. Except for not buying the supplies, but that wouldn't be a wise course of action for them.

If they didn't get the extra provisions now, there was no telling when they would be able to stock up again. It was too much of a risk to continue with what they currently had. At best it would last them one maybe two weeks, and they needed enough to last them closer to a month at the most.

With their extra provisions purchased and packed, the group made their way to the stables. In a more peaceful time, the stables would have been packed with a nice variety of different mounts available to buy. The ones they saw today were on the average and aged side of mounts remaining in the town. Given what was available to them, they had to consider what would be of greater benefit to them. Individual mounts, shared mounts, a mount-drawn carriage with a single strong mount or a combination.

There was pros and cons with whatever choice they decided on. The key thing was to remember that they had to work with what was currently available to them. Bellamy and the others walked through the stables. Looking over the mounts to see if any would fit their needs.

"So, does anyone have any suggestions on what we should buy or any preferences?"

Inara was the first to provide her thoughts to Bellamy's question.

"We should consider getting a mount-drawn carriage and two shared mounts. That way we can travel lightly and effectively."

"I agree with Inara's suggestion. It would make sense, considering we are on the more statuesque side. A carriage would provide more room to travel with comfort for the number in our group." Draemond responded in agreement.

Amiriss was the next to offer up her suggestion to the group.

"Though I completely see the benefit of the mount-drawn carriage. I think it would be best to buy three shared mounts considering the nature of our journey. This would provide us with more flexibility to act if somethings were to change unexpectedly."

Raine and Na'naya looked at each other and nodded in agreement with what Amiriss had proposed.

"Very well, it seems we have come to a majority decision. I will go with Amiriss's suggestion of getting three shared mounts." Bellamy replied.

With the decision made the group continued looking over the mounts in the stables, now that they knew what they were going to need. It took some time to find the mounts. In the end for the three shared mounts they went with three Dire Fangs. A beast that was a combination of a Dire Wolf and Sabretooth with characteristics of a Wolverine. They are smart, fearsome, and loyal mounts that stand at about half the size of a stallion but twice as strong.

Dire Fangs were also known to be stubborn beast that took a strong-minded spirit to tame them. Making them a more costly mount to find and acquire. The fact that they came across them in a frontier town was even more reason to buy them for their aide.

After purchasing their mounts they loaded their bags into the travel cases attached to the mount's saddles. They split up into three groups of two per mount. On the Lead Dire Fang who was the oldest of the three. She had dark bluish black and white silver accents in her fur rode Inara and Bellamy. The second Dire Fang the first of the two pups with bluish black fur like his mother rode Na'naya and Amiriss.

The last Dire Fang and the second of the two pups with grey fur and bluish black accents the opposite of his mother rode Raine and Draemond. With everything set they left the stables. Heading out of town through the western gate. Making their way towards the boundary lands and border.

Riding the Dire Fangs was making it easier for the group to traverse more miles through the open countryside in a day, than they would have done on foot. Though progress was being made, they made sure to travel at a steady pace. So that their mounts wouldn't become fatigued from the journey so soon. It was important that they conserved as much energy as they could. The terrain and weather was only going to get more challenging with the coming winter.

The sun was at its zenith in the overcast sky when the group decided to stop for a moment. Giving their mounts some rest before they traveled through some cascading foothills.

A region covered in a sea of tall waving multi-colored grass changing with the coming winter weather. Inara jumped off the Dire Fang grabbed some horned rabbit meat from a pack and tossed it into its gapping mouth.

"We will stop here for a bit to let the Dire Fang's rest before we continue. We still have a good distance to travel but we are making good progress."

"The overcast is a bit of a concern. As long as the weather stays steady, we should reach the boundary lands next to the border in about four days. With the Dire Fangs we were able to cut off two days from our travel time."

With the Dire Fangs eating and resting to restore their energy, Bellamy and the others took the time to check over their supplies. Taking a little afternoon nap, or grabbing a bite to eat themselves. Bellamy was laying on his back staring up into the sky when Na'naya walked over. She learned over casting a shadow upon his body. Her eyes were bright, and she had a smile on her face as she gazed down into Bellamy's eyes. Bellamy looked at her with suspicion in his gaze, contemplating what she was up to?

"Na'naya, do tell what you are up to?"

"Why must I be up to something. Couldn't I just want to come over and talk to my friend. There doesn't have to be a reason other than that."

"Because I know you and how you tend to act whenever you feel like me or Raine don't give you enough attention. More so me than Raine at times, and then you pull some childish prank."

Na'naya was taken aback for a moment, but quickly regained her composure. Her smile still visible on her face.

"Bellamy, I can't believe you would accuse me of something like that. That may have been true of me in the past, but I am a changed woman. But then again, some habits are hard to break."

With those last words, Na'naya moved her arms from behind her back. She dropped a hand full of snow that she had collected onto Bellamy's face. The sudden chill from the snow as it hit his face caused him to jump up from the ground. Na'naya fell to the ground laughing at the look on Bellamy's face and the reaction he had to the snow she dropped on him. She wiped away the tears that came to her eyes from laughing so hard and returned to a more casual tone.

"Thank you for that Bellamy, I needed that laugh. I feel relaxed now. As the for the reason, I came over, Amiriss said she wanted to talk to you."

"Why didn't she come over and talk to me herself."

"She had to prepare something first and asked me If I could tell you. So, I agreed and came over, but I found some fresh snow on the ground and couldn't help myself. Well with that I'll be off to see if I can pull the same trick on Raine, now."

Na'naya walked off heading towards Raine to bother him. Bellamy headed over towards Amiriss to see what she wanted to talk about. Amiriss was sitting on the ground at the top of a nearby hill with a small ceramic bowl at her feet. Inside the bowl was a surreal viscous liquid. Reminiscent of a clear night sky adorned with the light of countless stars. Bellamy sat down next to Amiriss, looking at the ceramic bowl by her feet. Amiriss grabbed the bowl and placed it by Bellamy's feet.

"Pick up the ceramic bowl and drink the contents inside. It will not taste like what you believe it does, but you must finish every drop. The bowl must be empty for the potion to take full effect."

Bellamy gazed down at the ceramic bowl at his feet and leaned over to pick it up, bringing to the edge of his mouth. He could smell an interesting aroma coming from the potion in the bowl. He couldn't quite place it as it smelled sweet yet bitter, with a floral scent or was it berries and nuts. Whatever the case, the potion was playing with his senses creating a sense of euphoria and fear laced anxiety within him. Bellamy went for it and he took a calming breath. He then drank the contents of the ceramic bowl in one long continuous gulp until it was completely empty. He then handed the bowl back to Amiriss.

"What was that potion that you had me drink?"

"One would call it a catalyst of sorts. It is used to unlock potential mana flow that may lay dormant inside of a person. This is the first test that you must past if I'm going to consider training you."

"So, now what?"

"We wait for the potion to run its course and take effect."

Bellamy was about to speak when he felt a beating pulse circulating throughout his entire body. Gradually the beating of the pulse increased in intensity. Until only the sound of the pulse was all he could hear echoing deep into his mind. Amiriss stood by watching Bellamy, as his body was frozen in place. The only movement coming from his eyes as they darted back and forth in a rapid motion locked in a trance.

Amiriss counted slowly in her mind, then snapped her fingers. The rapid movement in Bellamy's eyes stopped. His eyes glowed for an instant, then began to close as his body became limp. Amiriss caught him in her arms and gently rested his head in her lap.

CHAPTER 25

B ellamy felt lightheaded as he opened his eyes to see an unfamiliar landscape around him. It was a vast hazy emptiness spreading in all directions for as far as he could see, nothing in front of him or behind him. There was no landmarks or visible indictors to give him an idea of where he was at or in what direction he should head in. Bellamy didn't realize it at first because he was disoriented. Now that he was able to recover, he noticed that everything had a muted greyish blue hue to it. Even his normally tanned skin. The last thing he remembered was drinking down that strange potion that Amiriss had given him.

"Amiriss! Anyone. Is anybody out there?" Bellamy's voice echoed in the vast emptiness as he called out.

There was no reply or sign of anyone around as the echo from Bellamy's words faded away. He didn't know what to do or how to move forward, Amiriss hadn't explained to him what was going to happen next. [*After all this had to be the work of the potion he drank, right it had to be.*] he thought wondering if uncertain. There was no other explanation that he could think of that would account for the strange unfamiliar environment he found himself in. The physical change of his appearance. Whatever the case he was going to have to figure out what to do if he hoped to past the test and return to everyone.

Figuring it would do him no good to stand around and do nothing. Bellamy picked a direction and started walking. So, he walked onward through the vast hazy empty landscape not knowing where he was headed. For what seemed like ages, when the haze around him cleared up. He found himself on a dark sand beach at the edge of a great lake with unnaturally still waters.

A strange and beautiful muted night sky loomed overhead. Filled with stars that glowed but did not sparkle. Bellamy dropped down and sat in the sand, staring off into the distance at the great still lake before him.

"Bellamy...Bellamy...Bellamy..."

"Who's calling for me? Show yourself!"

"Bellamy...Bellamy...Bellamy..."

Bellamy jumped to his feet. Searching around looking for signs of where the voice calling him was coming from. He searched around the area looking for where the mysterious voice was. No matter where he looked, he couldn't find any trace. There was a sudden unnatural breeze that passed over him.

Sending a chill down his spine causing him to turn around and face the great lake again. That is when Bellamy saw it, at silhouette off in the distance in the lake. He felt an undeniable pull to head towards the silhouette out in the lake, though he didn't understand why.

"This way Bellamy...This way Bellamy...Bellamy..."

Before he even realized what was going on, Bellamy had started walking towards the silhouette in the distance. He didn't know how but leading with one step after another, he was walking on the surface of the lake. As if it was the ground beneath his feet. Small ripples spread from each of the steps he took. That did not stop Bellamy from moving towards his destination.

As he approached closer the silhouette came into focus. Bellamy dropped to his knees in disbelief at the sight that stood before him. Words failed to leave his lips as he couldn't find the words to say to the spirit of his mother.

"What is going on? How are you here, mother!"

"My precious boy, look how you have grown. It appears that the time has come for you to unlock the power that lays dormant within you. Be warned, that all power comes with a cost and that no matter the outcome that price will be paid. If this is what you desire, then take my hand and your power will be awakened."

Bellamy slowly extended his hand out towards the outstretched hand of his mother. He stopped midway and lowered his hand back down, in frustration as he couldn't bring himself to take the offer. Something didn't seem right to him about the events unfolding before him. Now, was not the time for him to act hastily because of stirred up emotions. He needed to be certain before he acted and did something he could not take back.

"Tell me mother, on the day that you were killed, who was it that killed you and why didn't you try to escape with me?"

A cold and distant silence filled the air around them. They looked at one another with solemn looks in their eyes. Bellamy wanted the woman before him to truly be his mother. Providing him with something to ease the pain that has been weighing on him. After all these years or even a little hint of understanding so that he might find closure.

He wanted to be capable of doing more but felt trapped in wondering if he was making the right choice to begin with. The longer he stood there waiting for her reply, the more challenging Bellamy found it to keep his resolve. To continue to move forward. Whatever happened next was out of his hands. All that he could do was wait and see how she would respond to his questions.

"I'm afraid I don't have the answer you seek my son. All I do know is that, if it meant protecting you so that you may live, I knew that I couldn't go with you. There was no other way."

Bellamy stood back up on his feet. He looked on with both happiness and a bitter sadness at the woman he had once called mother. He took in a deep breath, then slowly exhaled out as he regained his composure.

"Do you not trust what I have told you to be true? The dead are bound to their words. They can't withhold the truth of what they know and what they have learned in their death. This is an undeniable pact that cannot be easily broken."

"As I know it to be true, it pains me, but I am still grateful for the chance to look upon her again. Now, if you would be so kind and reveal your true self to me. As you yourself said the dead cannot lie about truths they know or knew, but you are not dead, nor my mother."

"Clever boy, very well I will show you my true form."

The form of his mother began to glow as swirls of water raised up from the lake spiraling around her body. As the glow of her body faded and the spiraling column dispersed falling back into the lake like raindrops. The form of the woman standing in front of Bellamy had completely changed. What had once been his mother was now a tall voluptuous beauty with an hourglass figure. She was wearing a loose silk robe of deep aquamarine draped around her body.

Four elegant arms, pale skin of the whitest sand. Long flowing hair with the celestial cosmos in its strands, with eyes and lips of lilac. Bellamy could not believe what he was seeing, for he knew the woman standing before him. He had seen statues of her at temples. Depictions of her in books, paintings, and sacred manuscripts. Why of all people would she show herself to him. He couldn't figure it out, so he did the only thing he could think of and bowed to honor the goddess.

"I am humbled by your presence, revered Matron of the Deceased and Goddess of Creation. It is an honor to meet you Night Mother."

With the gesture of her hands, Bellamy raised his head. He looked upon the divine radiance of the Night Mother. Though she wore a calm and stoic expression on her face, there was no denying that she was a beauty beyond measure. Ageless and eternal. Bellamy could feel her aura emanating from her body. A powerful raging current that could drown him in its fathomless depths were he not careful.

The Night Mother was the living embodiment of a mana storm, both its calm eye at the center and the storm itself. The pure duality of what all mothers strive to be. Absolute protector and enduring caregiver, ever watchful over her precious children.

"Forgive me Night Mother, I do not mean to be rude or ungrateful, but why have you chosen to appear before me? It has been many years since I've last prayed to you. I'm not the most devote of followers if I'm being honest, for I would not dare to lie in your presence."

"Curious are we boy? My reasons are mine own. Though I will leave you with this: In a dying mother's aria her dreams and wishes are known for the child she loved most dear. For in his eyes hold the truth of the secrets and sins of the father, he never knew."

With the goddess's last words, she stepped forward. Gently embracing Bellamy's face in her hands and kissed him upon his forehead. He was caught off guard by the unexpected warmness of her lips and blushed. The next moment the Night Mother faded away in front of his eyes. He was alone once again standing upon the still motionless lake. The mysterious haze returned and enveloped everything in sight. Until the only thing Bellamy could see was his hands in front of him. He suddenly couldn't fell anything below his feet, and he fell into the void.

"Aaaahhhh..."

As he fell deeper and deeper into the dark endless expanse of the void. A bright ethereal light flashed from the center of his being. In that instant Bellamy vanished body and all.

CHAPTER 26
RAINE ROLLO

The group had stopped to give their Dire Fangs a chance to eat and recover some stamina from their prolonged travel. So Raine figured it would be a good opportunity for him to do the same as well. He walked by the others as they were checking their gear and found a quite spot on a hill a few yards away. Where there was a nice gentle breeze blowing through the grass. He set his pack down on the ground and opened it up to check its contents one last time.

He pulled out some wild jerky to snack upon. The wild jerky was a delicacy made from Bison-Ox that are only found to graze in the plains of Beastmen Territories. Their meat was valuable and hard to find outside of those areas. Raine was lucky to still have some left from the last shipment he got. He was going to have to find a way to get some more in the future. Though that was going to prove more challenging with how things currently stand.

The merchant back in Southern Cross had told him when he was getting more supplies. That the import and export of foreign goods to the smaller settlements were experiencing supply shortages and delays. The increase in dangerous activity has caused merchants to take their goods to more stable areas. Demanding higher prices because of the supply troubles and higher risk involved for them. The Renatan Parliament has been taking actions to counteract these concerns.

So their actions have caused problems of their own between the Guilds and the Government. Such matters would die down or be acted upon according to importance and relevance to the current situation. for some reason that has not been the case this time and an uncertainty clouded everything. The point the merchant was making to Raine was that he best be prepared and adaptable to the changing circumstances.

After he had finished his snack. He put his belongings away back into his pack, as he used it as a pillow to take a short nap in the gentle breeze. Though he was resting, with his other keen senses he was still aware of what was going on in the general area of his surroundings. A little practical ability he had picked up in his travels over the years from being a mercenary. It was especially useful whenever one found themselves in unfamiliar places or hostile areas traveling.

So, he was ready for Na'naya when she slowly and stealthily walked over to him and tried to drop snow onto his face. Right when she was standing over him, Raine caught Na'naya by surprise. Using his tail to knock her backwards onto her butt with the snow falling onto her in the process.

"Hmph. No fair, you cheated. Look at me, I'm covered in snow now because of that cheap trick you pulled." Na'naya whined.

Raine opened his eyes and looked over at Na'naya, who was wiping the snow off her body. She had an unamused expression on her face and pouted her lips at him. He nonchalantly smirked backed at her, before closing his eyes again.

"I did not cheat; I took the opportunity to turn your little prank back onto you. You still haven't learned to not play pranks on me when I'm taking a nap. Why don't you go and play your prank somewhere else, perhaps on Bellamy."

"I already did and that's beside the point, Amiriss wanted to talk to him, so he's busy right now and not able to talk with me."

"So, that's what brought you over here to me. I see. I'm not surprised, this sort a thing tends to be a habit of yours. You may not want to hear this, but you may want to sort your feelings out sooner rather than later. Or you'll find the decision made for you and it might not be the one you want. Some friendly advice to do with it what you will. Men aren't always aware of what's in front of them when it comes noticing someone's emotions. They often need a little nudge sometimes."

Na'naya blushed in embarrassment from Raine's words, not knowing how to respond to them. She got back up off the ground, turned away from him and walked off in the other direction away from his sight. It wasn't his intention to get under her skin. but he knew that she needed to hear those words and sort out her feelings. It was only going to get difficult where they were going.

The reality of the situation they were getting themselves into wouldn't do anyone any good if they weren't in the right mindset to deal with it. He was helping Na'naya realize that in his own way. She may be upset with him for now, but in time she would come to understand what he was trying to do for her.

Raine closed his eyes. He continued with his short afternoon nap that had been interrupted moments earlier. The sun had moved its position in the sky away from its zenith. It was in the third hour of the afternoon when Raine awoke from his nap. Though he would have preferred to take a longer one.

It was important to make up time traveling where they could and not get delayed any more than need be. He got up, took his pack from the ground, and headed back towards the others. After placing his pack back in the travel packs on the Dire Fangs, he noticed that everyone seemed to be gathered around Amiriss.

"What's going on over here?"

Draemond turned towards Raine. He pointed down at the ground where Bellamy was lying unconscious. his head resting on Amiriss's lap.

"He seems to be under the effects of the Unbinding Tea still. Amiriss had prepared some for Bellamy to help him unlock his *Arts* potential, but he hasn't awakened yet. Amiriss isn't certain about why he hasn't but believes it shouldn't be too much longer before he does."

Raine tapped the top of his forehead in concern over how this incident is going to change things up yet again. The groups dynamics would have to take these new factors into account. When it came to dealing with their fighting strategies and how they take on enemies. The way he saw it was that it would give then more options when dealing with challenging enemies. Even give them an advantage in certain situations if Bellamy gets a handle of his new abilities.

Which at the same time could be as dangerous if he is unable to use his abilities properly or at all. Even those who have *Arts* aren't always capable of using them forthright or conveniently much of the time. So proper training is crucial to hone and master one's abilities. Assuming your able to find someone willing to teach you. That or your crazy enough to except the risk and train yourself.

"What was he thinking? Attempting to unlock his abilities at a time like this, that fool. Unfortunately, there is nothing we can do about it now, but to wait. It could be dangerous to move him in that state."

Draemond lifted his hand and patted the Raine's shoulder in a gesture of comfort. To ease the sense of tension he felt coming from him.

"We are not always given the luxury of choosing when we get to do the things, we have control over. We must be willing to take the opportunity whenever it may present itself. Bellamy may not have understood what he was getting himself into. But he felt that now was his chance to do something that would eventually not only help his friends but him as well. In times like these the only thing one can do is to have faith in your companion and trust in their choices."

"I appreciate your words, Draemond. However foolish it was, you're right in that I must have faith and trust in Bellamy and choice he has made."

The timing of everything wasn't ideal. The longer the stayed in the area the greater the chance of running into Daemons. The weather was also about to be against them as well. for with his keen eyes Raine saw the forming of a snowstorm on the horizon. It would not be wise to camp outside this evening, they needed to move and find a cave to shelter in for the night. They didn't have much time to debate over their next course of action. So Raine did what he considered would be best for the group and addressed them.

"Everyone listen to what I have to say. There is a snowstorm forming on the horizon that is going to hit in the evening. We need to pack up and find a cave to take shelter in for the night. It would be too dangerous to camp outside, and we are miles away from any village or homestead. Unfortunately, we do not have the time to wait for Bellamy to wake up. We will have to carry him in his current condition."

"I wouldn't recommend moving him like this. Are you sure that will be alright? Isn't there anything else we could do?" Amiriss replied looking down at Bellamy still unconscious in her lap.

"If we had more time, we could have come up with a better solution but I'm afraid we don't. It is already going to take us some time to find a cave nearby before the snow starts to fall. We need to move out now, there is no time to waste."

Understanding what they needed to do. Everyone gathered up their belongings and packed them back into the Dire Fang's travel packs. With everything loaded up, Draemond picked up Bellamy. He carried him over to the Dire Fang him and Inara had been riding. He handed him up into her arms and she wrapped her arms around him in a tight embrace.

Draemond secured them both together with some rope. When he was safely secured around her, Inara grabbed firmly on their mount. She headed onward with the others following close behind. They made their way through the cascading tall grass hills at a slower pace than they would have preferred. Into the deep woods of a wild forest as the finals moments of day were disappearing behind the tree line.

When the darkness of night came upon then, so too did the cold of snow fall from the snowstorm overhead. The chilling wind swept past their faces and down their bodies. They traveled through the deep woods of the wild forest. Weighted branches creaked and groaned from the snow falling onto their ancient limbs. Spreading from wide sturdy trunks that have been growing since ages past. As they made their way along makeshift paths through the dense woods the snowstorm grew stronger. Narrowing their visibility of the surrounding area.

"We need to find a cave as soon as possible. It's getting rather difficult to see what's around us. Keep an eye out and be careful, we don't want to get separated not in this weather." Inara called back to the others.

"Got it."

Raine had Draemond moved their Dire Fang up from the rear of the group. Checking out a strange shadow he spotted in the distance. The snowstorm was affecting how far and clearly, he could make things out with his keen eyes. He was able to compensate for the shortcoming. Lowering the distance a little between him and what he was looking at.

As they approached closer in the general direction of the shadow. Raine was able to make out what he had spotted. He called out to everyone with a loud steady voice, so his words would reach them and not be impaired by the snowstorm.

"Everyone, we must go this way. I have found us a cave to take shelter in."

The other's turned to follow Raine's and Draemond's Dire Fang towards the cave he spotted several yards in the distance.

CHAPTER 27
BELLAMY LEONE

The aroma of a delicious warm stew filled the air of the cave. The stew continued to warm upon the fire. Draemond, and the others had made once they were safely settled into the cave. They had made their camp within the cave's mouth to seek shelter and wait for Bellamy to wake up. Raine, Inara, and Draemond headed farther into the cave to make sure it was safe.

To get a sense of how far it expanded into the earth. Na'naya and Amiriss stayed behind to prepare the food and watch over Bellamy. Protecting him and their camp. The two of them took turns alternating between cooking the food and watching Bellamy while the others were gone.

"Amiriss, how much longer do you think it will be? He has already been out for some time now and I'm starting to get worried about him."

"I understand how you feel, Na'naya but he should wake up soon. The process doesn't normally take this long, though it's not a set length to begin with and tends to vary person to person. We must be patient and believe in him."

"I know. It bothers me not being able to do anything to help. I don't like that feeling of powerlessness. It is a feeling I have done my best to avoid feeling again. Training both my mind and my body past their normal limits to survive."

An unfamiliar sight came into focus as Bellamy opened his eyes adjusting to the area around him. He had awoken inside of a cave and was no longer on the cascading hills he had drank the potion on. As he looked around the cave, he saw the Dire Fangs off in a corner cuddled up around one another. A fire was burning in the center area and there was no sign of the others. Amiriss was laying down a couple of feet away from him.

Then he spotted Na'naya standing watch towards the mouth of the cave. Looking out into the raging snowstorm. Bellamy got up to his feet and walked over to join her. A big smile lit across her face, when she saw him coming towards her happy that he was now awake.

"Bellamy."

"How long have I been out and where are Raine and the others? The last thing I remember was drinking that strange potion Amiriss gave me on the cascading hills."

"I'm glad that you're finally awake, it's been about twelve hours. We had to find a place to take shelter in because of the snow-storm. The others went deeper into the cave to check it out and should be returning anytime now. What happened to you?"

Bellamy looked out into the snowstorm with Na'naya. He re-counted the events of the dream he had and his meeting with the Goddess of Creation. She was captivated by the story he had told her and the feelings she felt in every word spoken of the encounter. Between Na'naya and Inara, Bellamy knew that they were the more religiously devoted of his friends. They would appreciate the significance of what happened to him and what it could possibly mean.

Even for Bellamy the whole experience was surreal, and he was still processing it all. He was grateful that he had someone he could talk about it to. Not worry about them not believing him or being judgmental.

"It's hard to believe. I know and I still find it hard to believe myself. It's hard to describe but I know it happened and I feel like I can still feel a sign of her presence on me."

"That is beyond belief, you met a goddess and not any goddess but the Goddess of Creation herself. To think that the divine still grace our presence by interacting with mortals. Something that is said to not have happened since ages past long ago. I wonder what this all means, because if this is all true then Bellamy, you have been blessed by the Night Mother."

Bellamy paced back and forth in the mouth of the cave. Na'naya stood and watched, keeping her eyes peeled to the surrounding area around them. The snow was still falling heavy and steady with no signs of it letting up anytime soon. They would have to wait it out before they could travel again. Or they could find an alternate route, through the cave perhaps.

"I'm still trying to figure that out myself, what it all could mean for myself and the group going forward. Now, I am left with more questions than answers in my head. For now the best thing I can do is to figure out how to use my newfound abilities and go from there. How long have the others been gone exactly?"

"About three hours since they went off to check out the cave. We told them when they left not to be gone for too long. To come back if there were signs of trouble or something of interest to see."

"Okay, that's good to know. I am starving. It feels like it's been so long since I last ate, so I'm going to go get some of that delicious stew I smelled earlier."

"When you're done, wake up Amiriss and let her know that it's almost time for her to take watch."

"Yeah, I'll let her know."

Bellamy had faith in his companions being able to handle themselves if something came up. They hadn't been gone too long yet for the task they set out to do. It was best to be patient and wait for the time being, the others were bound to be making their way back to them shortly. Afterall, it was no easy task navigating through some unknown cave that you had never been in before. He left Na'naya at the cave entrance and headed back inside towards the fire and the cooking stew. Bellamy poured himself a bowl of the stew and sat down eating it. He felt each spoonful, he ate warm the inside of his body and fill his empty stomach.

The stew was a hearty. With a creamy broth made up fresh vegetables, wild herbs, and dried meats. They had procured from the merchants in town. Slowly cooked over the fire long enough for the ingredients to mix and the juices to marinate. Providing the most nutrients to provide their bodies with the energy they needed to perform at their best.

Meals like this were especially important for travels on long journeys. As there was no guarantee that the situation would allow them the time, they need to get proper rest or a decent meal. To compensate for the inconsistencies travelers would make nutrient rich stews to offset the lack of meals. To recover as much energy as they possible could before their next decent full meal. Bellamy was well versed in this practice before he joined the mercenary group. While he was traveling solo in his earlier teen years trying to survive and searching for answers.

When he finished eating, he cleaned his bowl and went over to wake up Amiriss from her sleep. The stories Bellamy had heard in his youth about the enchanting beauty of Nymphs were all too true. He gazed upon Amiriss sleeping. She rolled from the side of her sleeping mat to lay on her back as her blanket slipped off her shoulder. Amiriss opened her eyes and saw Bellamy looking at her, she pursed her lips in a coy smile.

"Well, hello there. It's rude you know to stare at someone sleeping. You could at least buy a girl a drink if you're going to stare like that." Amiriss replied with a tease.

Bellamy cheeks turned a light rose color as he was overcome with embarrassment. He turned his gave away in another direction to recover, before speaking to her.

"I didn't mean to stare; your beauty was unimaginably enchanting while you slept it captured me for a moment. I came to tell you that Na'naya said that it was almost time for you to take watch."

"Thank you. I'm glad to see that you're awake, you had me worried for a moment as I didn't expect you to be out for so long. I guess it must have been a success considering everything and now you need to learn how to channel your *Arts*."

"Yeah, about that something unexpected happened to me while I was in that dream state. I was met by the Goddess of Creation, and she gave me her blessing."

Amiriss's eyes widened in excitement and disbelief at Bellamy's word. Taking in everything that they meant. When the excitement left her face another emotion took its place. One of trepidation over the scale of weight placed upon his fate. Gifts of blessings from the divine are a rare occurrence in themselves.

They are said to alter the fates and events of those that bare them with great grandeur or turmoil in their life. Whatever the outcome may be only time would tell and the histories written of their deeds. The di has been cast and all Bellamy could do now was go forth and play with the hand that was dealt.

"In all my travels I have never known for someone to receive a divine blessing in this age. Though not confirmed there have be rumors of such things occurring in different parts of the world. What it means I can't say but I promise to do what I can to train you to use your newfound gifts. It won't be easy, and you may find yourself wanting to quit. But you must continue and pull through to unlock your potential."

"Your help and tutelage are much appreciated Amiriss, and I promise you that I'll do my best to fulfill my potential."

Amiriss got up from her sleeping mat. She folded her blanket up placing it on her pillow and headed to switch off with Na'naya in keeping watch. With Amiriss taking over for her, Na'naya came back inside the cave and grabbed herself a bowl of stew to eat. Before laying down on her sleeping mat and getting some rest. Bellamy guessed from what Na'naya had told him earlier that it must be a little after the Mother's Hour.

The twelfth hour of the night halfway before the dawn of a new day. He was finding it hard to rest himself, most likely the cause of being in that dream state for so long. His body wasn't feeling as tired as it should have been. He didn't want to be a hinderance in battle or any other unexpected situation. He laid back down on his sleeping mat staring up at the ceiling. Recounting important historical dates until he drifted off to sleep.

CHAPTER 28
INARA NOVIK

The snowstorm had made traveling more difficult given everything they had to deal with, along with Bellamy in his current state. Inara was relieved when Raine had found them a cave to take shelter in and get out of the snowstorm. Now, that the group had found shelter, they had to make sure that the place was safe enough for them stay in. Everyone settled inside the cave. Inara laid Bellamy down on his sleeping mat and decided on what would be their next course of action. She went over to speak with the others on her plans.

"Now, that we have a place to shelter from the snowstorm, we need a group to go deeper into the cave and check it out. We must make sure it's safe. If there is another way through or something that might be beneficial for us. Would any of you care to volunteer?"

Raine and Draemond looked at each other and then towards Inara.

"We volunteer to go and explore the cave." Draemond replied for them both.

"Alright then us three will go and explore the cave, while you two stays back and keep an eye on Bellamy and our camp."

"You can count on the us." The two said in unison.

With the groups decided, Inara and the others grabbed their packs. They made their way deeper into the cave to explore what lies within. From the main entrance from where the group had entered the cave and sat up their camp. The antechamber was long and wide running straight back deeper into the earth. It ran for several meters before splitting off into a series of narrow passages.

The narrow passages snaked and turned heading off in one direction before shifting into another. All the while changing between narrow and widened areas. As they followed each of the passages one by one to see where they led. Inara marked a stone indicating which ones they checked, so that they didn't get lost or lose their way back. Traversing one of the passages they hadn't checked yet required the group to go at a slower pace. They maneuvered around rock formations jetting up from the ground and overhead on the ceiling.

Unlike the other passages which led to dead ends or connected to a previous passage. This one proved different and opened into a massive underground cavern. The cavern seemed to run for miles in every direction. The ceiling was many meters above them and a great chasm ran down the middle appeared bottomless. They could not see any sign of one from where they stood, separated one side of the cavern from the other.

Floating rock masses drifted in the air above the great chasm. A mana natural phenomenon that caused unusual gravitational effects on landmasses causing them to float in midair. This occurrence was on a minor scale. Inara had heard tales of much bigger landmasses. Affected in the same way creating floating islands or varies sizes. Both Daemons and innovative groups have used such places as personal territories or safe havens from enemies for their difficulty to reach by normal means.

"Inara, we have been gone for some time now. It would be wise for us to head back to the camp now. If we are going to proceed on any further, it would be best to do so with the whole group."

"Draemond makes a valid point. We might find ourselves unable to come back this way the farther we go. We need to let the others know what we found, and I want to know if Bellamy finally woke up."

Inara turned to the side of a wall and marked it like she did the other ones. Taking in one last look of the cavern, she faced Raine and Draemond walking back towards them.

"Alright. Let's make our way back to camp. We can see how they feel and decide what to do next."

The way back to the entrance of the cave where they had made camp, wasn't as close as they thought it was. As they retraced their steps the route became unexpectedly longer. For the passage that should have led them back to the main one led them down to a dead end. They turned around and headed back through the passage. They did not come out at the cavern again, but instead in another connecting passage. Not turning around this time, they proceeded on down the passage following its path. Then it opened back into the massive cavern again.

"Huh. What in the seven hells is going on? I thought you marked the passages, so why didn't we end up back in the main passage but here again instead."

"That doesn't make any sense. I know I marked the passages. We must have taken a wrong turn somewhere. Come, follow me."

Inara led the others through the passage again. Following the marking she had left when they first entered the massive cavern. This time the passage that should have led them back to the main one led them down to a connecting passage. They turned around and headed back through the passage. They did not come out at the cavern again, but instead at a dead end. They turned around this time and proceeded on down the passage following its path. This time it opened back in the massive cavern again.

"Damn. I know we all saw what happened. We ended up doing almost the same thing as last time only slightly different in order. That should not have been possible. What is going on here?" Raine expressed barely covering up his frustration.

"I don't know, there could be any number of reasons why this is happening. The only thing for certain is that none of them bode well for us if we can't figure out the reason. Given the current situation it doesn't appear that we are going to be able to get back to the others. What do you think, Inara?"

Inara looked around the area surrounding them, to see if she could figure out what was going on. Both Raine and Draemond had made valid points. Something was causing this unnatural state of displacement to occur. She needed to figure out what. Nothing appeared to be out of the ordinary from when they entered the massive cavern and left the first time. To when they ended up back in the same area the second time.

Yet, the paths that got them there changed up positions somehow. Inara ran her hand through her hair. She racked her brain for some clue. A situation that she or her mistress might have mentioned before of a similar event.

"Ugh…What to do, what to do. The way I see it, we have two options currently available to us. Option one: We wait here for the others to come and find us, then figure out how to procced with all of us together. Option two: We figure out how to solve this ourselves and hope to make our way back to the others. Before they come searching for us and getting caught up in our predicament anyway."

"One option has our companions get involved and the other option they may get involved. It's not ideal but I would rather not get the others involved if we could help it. I vote for option two, it may be selfish, but it's the right thing to do."

Inara looked over to Draemond who was thinking things over, waiting to hear his answer. She knew where she stood on the options she presented. She wanted to hear from them both. To understand their opinions and how they responded to situations. Raine's response didn't come as a surprise to her, as she has gotten to know his character during their travels.

He wasn't one to put his friends in danger carelessly. He would do all that was within his power to do so to keep them out of it if he could. Draemond on the other hand she didn't know all that well, other than what's she seen so far.

With that in mind she has seen that he is a strong and honorable warrior, who fights with a code. It is that code that drives his actions in and out of battle whatever it may bring. Living one's life such a way is no easy feat. Requiring an amount of discipline that isn't common for most people. Who care more for their personal being then that of others. Inara was confident in what option Draemond was going to pick. She wanted to hear him say it, to see that they were on the same page.

"There is only one clear option in my mind and that is option two. Let's solve this problem and head back to our companions, so that we may all leave this place together."

"Then it's time we head out and end this farce, once and for all."

With all of them in agreement and the decision made, they headed off further into the massive cavern searching for the source of the problem. They searched high and low for any sign of the source. While being careful to watch their footing when they got too close the edge of the great chasm. It had seemed like time was going at a slower pace in their search. The minutes seamlessly dragged on becoming hours and still no sign of their prize.

The ongoing search was taxing their bodies and draining their fortitude. It was becoming harder to remember where they had last checked. It was with the onset of the disorientation that the situation started to change.

The ground beneath Inara's and the other's feet rumbled and quaked. Causing them stumble back losing their footing. When the mouth of a giant Daemon emerged from the ground, as if it were water preparing to catch them in a single bite. They jumped back out of the way mere moments before the creature's mouth snapped closed. Then submerged back into the ground. In that instant, they drew their weapons. Taking up a defensive position with their backs to one another. Their weapons pointed outwards.

"Was anyone able to get a good look at the Daemon that attacked us?"

Inara took in a calm steady breath before responding to Raine's question.

"Just a brief glimpse, but I'm certain it's a Soul Eater Boa. A Daemon phantasm snakelike creature. Thats capable of moving through solid ground as if it was swimming through water. One of the rarer and more dangerous Daemons. We need to be cautious when dealing this threat, or it will cost us our lives."

"That would help to explain what was going on with this place. The Soul Eater Boa is said to have an ability that affects the spatial perception of intruders who enter its domain. Appearing to alter the surroundings and cause disorientation. Which means if we want to get out of here and back to our companions, we are going to have to defeat the Daemon."

"Easier said than done I'm afraid. It won't be easy, even with our skills, this is going to be a challenging fight."

Emerging from the shadows overhead, the Soul Eater Boa's tail came striking down like a whip lightning fast and lethal. Using his buckler shield Draemond blocked the first strike. He deflected the second strike an instant later. Inara and Raine grounding themselves firmly to support Draemond from getting knocked backed from the force of the impacts. Three other times the Daemon attacked the group with the power of its lightning-fast whiplike tail. Each time from a different direction from the previous strike. Each time the group blocked the strike, all the while standing their ground unwilling to budge from their spot.

Their defenses were holding up. With each strike the blows became harder to block and harder to read where they were coming from. Draemond was holding firm blocking each strike that came his way. A testament to the Dragonkin warrior's natural durability. But given their situation he didn't know how much longer would he be firm before his stamina gave out.

When he blocked a tail strike, Inara and Raine would use the opportunity to strike at the Soul Eater Boa's body and head with quick multi-strikes. The Daemon was swift as it was powerful. Their strikes that landed would shallowly cut it minimizing the damaged it received. while their other strikes would just miss the Daemon. Forcing them to continue their unrelenting dance of blocking, dodging, striking repeatedly.

"We need to come up with a plan. Our current strategy is barely affecting the boa. If we continue this way, our stamina is most certainly going to give before the Daemon does."

Raine expressed his thoughts, while taking what moment he could to catch his breath before the next attack came and the dance continued.

"I have a plan that could work, but I'm only going to get one shot at it. I need you to buy me some time to prepare. If this doesn't work, we had best come up with something else quick, because I won't be of much help afterwards."

"Alright Inara, do what you have to do, and we'll buy you as much time as we can."

This time when the Soul Eater Boa struck and Draemond deflected the blow. He and Raine charged forward with their attacks driving the beast back. Providing Inara with the opening she needed to move into position on the other side of the conflict. Slowing her breathing and calming her mind, Inara began the invocation for her spell.

["*All knowing and powerful Mother beyond. Imbue in my hammer your divine power, so that I may smite the threat before me. In your name I offer you my essence as proof of my devotion and love for your blessing.*"]

The air swirled around her body and enveloped her Warhammer. Charged ethereal energy sparking and glowing with bright blue light, became visible as the spell started to take effect. It created a manifestation of a small maelstrom. Howling winds and torrential rains were imbued into the Uru Metal wide-bodied sledgehammer head of Inara's Warhammer. Inara spun the Warhammer around and around, building up momentum for her strike.

"Now, back away from the Soul Eater Boa!" Inara commanded.

The others jumped back as they heard her words. Inara pivoted and charged forward. She jumped into the air. With a downward overhead blow, she struck the Soul Eater Boa on the head with her Warhammer. A loud thunderclap and concussive explosion echoed throughout the area. The blow impacted on the Daemon's head. When the smoke from the impact cleared, the Soul Eater Boa laid sprawled on the ground. Inara stood next to it leaning on her Warhammer for support. Tiring exhaustion aching throughout her body, as she tried to keep her balance and stand.

"Inara, move out of there. Hurry!" Draemond yelled with urgency.

The Soul Eater Boa twitched as it raised up behind her, still recovering from the impact of her spell. Its mouth wide open let out an agonizing screeching hiss. It pounded on their ears mercilessly. It was poised and ready to strike down on Inara, blinded by rage and bloodlust to kill the one who injured it so gravely. With bated breath and his keen eyes locked on his target, his twin rondel daggers drawn, Raine charged towards the Soul Eater Boa. Focused, he chanted the invocation to cast his spell.

["*Twin Moon Goddesses of Wisdom and the Hunt, bestow my daggers with your divine power. So that I may strike down this evil before me. In your names I offer you my essence as proof of my devotion and love for your blessing.*"]

The air swirled around his body and enveloped his daggers. Charged ethereal energy sparking and glowing with bright white light, became visible as the spell started to take effect. It created a manifestation of a swirling sea. Crashing waves were imbued into the Alchemic steel blades of Raine's Twin Rondel daggers. Then in a swift swirling motion, Raine slashed through the Soul Eater Boa's neck like a crashing tsunami.

The creature's severed head came tumbling to the ground. Its body spasmed violently before sliding off the edge. Falling into the depths of the great chasm below. Panting heavily Raine collapsed to his knees next to Inara. They both dealt with their spell's recoil on their bodies.

"Thanks for the assist back there. We would not have been able to achieve victory without working together. You Raine and Draemond are exceptional warriors, it is my honor to call you friend."

"The same goes for me. You two had shown great skill and courage in the battle. The key skills I look for in my companions as a Dragonkin warrior. We have been here far too long, lets collect our materials from the Daemon and get back to the rest of our group."

"Yeah."

CHAPTER 29
BELLAMY LEONE

It was midday on their second day in the cave. The snow-storm outside had finally died down. The sun was shining again, though hidden by lingering clouds. Inara and the others had returned late last night from their exploration of the cave. They told the group about what they had found deeper in the cave.

The fierce battle with the Soul Eater Boa, that took a hard hit to their stamina and gear. Everyone agreed that it would be best to stay in the cave for one more day. So that the others could regain their strength. So everyone could be well rested before they headed out. It was the best thing to do for them. As it would have been dangerous and reckless to leave right away in their current conditions.

Bellamy was on guard duty at the entrance to the cave taking in the quietness of the surrounding area. Watching the little specks of snow falling from the sky. After being caught up in everything that has happened since he set out from Aurontil on this journey. He had forgotten how peaceful it is to be in the calmness of the vast wilderness. He may have grown used to the hustle and busyness of the bigger cities, but he had grown up in the wilderness and small villages.

It was places like these that reminded him of his youthful days. The happy times he had with his mother, before it was all taken away from him. They were happy always together; it had been the two of them for as long as he could remember.

He didn't have any memories of his father that he could recall, for he had died when Bellamy was still very young. He had asked his mother about him on different occasions. She never told him much about who he was or what he was like. It seemed to be painful for her to talk about filling her with a deep sadness. She would only say that he had loved them both.

That they were his most precious treasure in this troubling world. So, Bellamy would not press the issue more with her and stayed close to his mother's side to make her happy. Now after all these years of not thinking about it, the last cryptic words the goddess had spoken to him had him wondering again. Who was his father and what sins of his could have led to the events that Bellamy found himself facing.

"What's on your mind? You seem to be lost in thought, considering you didn't notice me come up behind you. No matter what you must always try to stay focused and present in the moment. It could cost you your life if you're not aware of your surroundings."

Bellamy snapped back to the present and looked at Inara leaning up against the side of the cave entrance.

"Sorry, you're right and I appreciate the advice. I haven't got the chance to tell you yet. When I was in that dream state to unlock my *Arts* abilities, I met the Night Mother and received her blessing. I was thinking on something she had told me before our encounter ended."

"By the goddess, you are a lucky man to have seen her and been bestowed with a blessing. Bellamy, that is something rare and precious to be sure. You must do all in your power to live up to and honor the expectations she has of you."

Bellamy walked over to the wall of the cave entrance and leaned up against it next to Inara. He sighed and stayed there not saying a thing for a few moments of silence. Inara could sense the uneasiness over the situation that he was feeling. The new pressures that it would undoubtedly put on him. So, she stayed by his side in silence. Offering him her continued support on their journey together.

"With all of this, I find myself caught up. Trying to put the pieces together to a complex puzzle, only to find that it is a part of a much bigger one. I can understand the implications of what receiving the goddess's blessing implies. The responsibility that comes from it. It's a lot to process and feels overwhelming at times."

"Bellamy, your feelings are justified. Its normal to feel overwhelmed by something you don't understand. Remember that you are not alone in this and that you can always lean on any one of us for help, we are here for you."

Bellamy and Inara headed back into the cave to gather up their belongings. They discussed with the others their next course of action. After breaking down their makeshift camp. Then loading their belongings back into the Dire Fang's travel bags, they gathered around Inara and her wayfarer's map. She laid out to show everyone their current location.

Based on their position on the map, the cave they've been sheltering in was only a day and a half out from their destination, the border between The Renata Republic and The Nimh Theocracy. According to the map there was three paths available to them for crossing the border in their area. They looked over and examined their paths, as they figured out which would serve them best.

The first and most direct of the three paths was to cross the border at the theocracy's Eastern Bridge Checkpoint. Given the current situation going on in the borderlands the bridge checkpoint may be closed off to foreigners. Or travelers without a proper merchant license. For the time being, to prevent attacks on their populace. There was no concrete evidence that the theocracy was behind the ongoing attacks. Restricting travel between the border as a safety precaution isn't an admission of guilt.

Merely circumstantial. That was why they were sent on their mission to gather intelligence. To find evidence of theocracy's innocence or guilt in the conflict. Then reporting back their findings, so that the Renatan Parliament can make their decision on the matter.

The second path available to them was to cross the border by going through the Shattered Marshes. A labyrinthine swamp region covered by a perpetual fog. One making it extremely difficult to navigate. It was for this reason that area acted as a natural defensive barrier for the theocracy's outer territory. The dangers of the area made it one that was avoided by travelers.

Worthwhile risk for the enterprising smuggler or fool hardy adventurer looking for fame. Not ideal the path would be helpful in keeping their mission from drawing unwanted attention. and provide less governmental interaction with the theocracy's military. Choosing this path was worth considering the pros and cons involved in it.

The third and final path available also had the most risk involved out of all of them. The cave the group had been taking shelter in the last two days was one of the ancient entrances to The Undermore. A subterranean parallel realm below the surface. Outside their physical realm that laid across the veil between realms. It was a place that was neither here nor there and yet at the same time everywhere.

One that is only capable of being accessed by a series of gates located in different caves throughout the world. Their cave was one such place. This path was the most dangerous. Once they crossed over, they would have to search for another way back to their realm. They could end up hundreds of miles away from their destination.

There was that uncertainty combined with the unknown dangers they could find themselves facing, that was a hard truth to swallow when considering that path. Bellamy knew even with the path available to them, given their current situation and mission it wouldn't be worth the risk at the present. So, it would have to come down to one of the other two paths to crossover the border into the theocracy. The Undermore would have to wait for another time to explore. A decision needed to be made and quickly so they could move on, for they had lingered for too long.

"It would be a waste of time to head to the checkpoint bridge and find out that they have restricted travel. Then having to take marsh path anyway. So, let's save ourselves some time and go through the Shattered Mashes."

"Raine makes a valid point. We need to get to the theocracy anyway we can. I would prefer not to cause an incident at the checkpoint bridge, by fighting our way through." Amiriss chimed in.

"I agree with them both."

"So, do I."

There was more than enough votes and the decision had been made. Inara folded back up the map and put it away into her pouch, ready to set out for their next destination.

"Then the decision is made. We will crossover the border into the Nimh Theocracy by going through the Shattered Marshes. Let's head out."

Fresh fallen snow lingered in several areas throughout the forest. Making the groups traversal slower than they would have liked. The Dire Fangs' thick fur and powerful paws made them excellent mounts for traveling in the coldest of environments, or challenging terrains. As the last light of day faded from the sky, the group took out their lanterns. They continued traveling through the deep woods all through the night.

When the sun had risen to bring about the new day, they had made their way out and reached the edge of the deep woods. On the other side spreading out for many miles going north, south, and out towards the west was the misty labyrinthine swamplands of the Shattered Marshes before them.

"Everyone, listen. From here on out we are going to be traveling by foot through the marshes. We will guide the Dire Fangs by their reigns and proceed close behind one another. We do not want to get separated in there, so pay close attention to the person in front of you and be careful."

"Inara, why must we go through the marshes on foot and not ride the Dire Fangs through?" Na'naya asked with bated breath.

"The marshes are said to be unpredictable. The terrain can be troublesome to trudge through in places, so its best if we travel on foot."

Everyone dismounted from their Dire Fangs. Grabbed their packs from the travel bags to lighten the weight on the Dire Fangs. Giving them more maneuverability in their movements. Proceeding on following behind Inara at the head of the group. Bellamy and the others headed down the slope and into the Shattered Marshes.

The perpetual misty fog of the mashes made the area appear as if it was locked it an everlasting state of a hazy twilight. With each step they took, the murky mud and swamp pulled at their feet. Grasping to hold on to the boots trudging forward. Bellamy looked around at the long grass around the base of the tangled roots of the twisted mangroves growing throughout the marshes. Making sure to keep an eye on the direction Inara was heading and their Dire Fang that she was leading.

As they continued through the marshes, Bellamy would look back to check on the others. Seeing how they were holding up. Everyone seemed to be fine. The looks he saw on Na'naya and Amiriss's faces told him that they weren't too happy about trudging through the knee-deep swamp their path had brought them to. The depths of the marshes would change from area to area.

With it ranging from being solid ground all the way to swamp many feet deep. They would do their best to avoid such areas when possible. Causing them to shift directions and back track at times to find a better path forward. In truth it was not easy keeping track of the direction they were heading in. As it was rather easy to lose one's way in the labyrinthine marshes.

Bellamy was certain that if Inara hadn't been leading them with her exceptional abilities, they would have been lost in the marshes. Over their travels he had come to admire not just her combat and practical skills. But her ability to keep her mind calm and focused even under the most stressful of situations. He had grown to respect and care for her like anyone of his precious friends, that were close to him. It had been sometime since Bellamy had developed these kinds of feelings towards someone.

He had always kept his distance from such romantic feelings. Never letting himself get to close when interest sparked in him or the other person. Starting a conversation and getting to know them was never really his problem. It was more a sense of being emotionally available and not guarded in the follow through.

As much as he hated to admit it, his past traumas had played a key impact in his emotional openness. His willingness to trust someone intimately with all his being. It was for this reason that throughout his life, he has had sporadic occasional bedmates. Nothing ever lasting more than a few days to a few weeks. So, he lived a bachelor life focusing more on his work with the mercenary company.

Training, his friends, and searching for answers to his mother's murder. With these things taking up most of his time, Bellamy didn't have to focus on the emotional walls guarding his feelings. His lack of intimate connections with women. Though why such thoughts where populating his mind in this moment he could not say. Only that this long journey has given him time to examine them more thoroughly.

CHAPTER 30

"Hold!" Inara called out to everyone.

Everyone stopped in their tracks and looked around to see what was going on. To figure out why they had stopped. There didn't appear to by signs of anyone or anything in the distance, other than the twisted mangroves native to the marshes.

"Inara, why have we stopped?"

"The marshes have become dense and thicker, than in previous areas. It's becoming harder to move through, and I can't explain it, but my body feels heavier than what's normal for me. Don't you feel it too?"

The thought hadn't crossed their minds at first. Now that they had stopped walking, they could feel that something was different about them. There was a heavier pressure exerted on their bodies that wasn't there before. It was affecting them both mentally and physically draining them of energy. It was like something was trying to pull them down into the depths.

Drowning them in the weight of their emotional burdens. Bellamy looked around at the others standing around waiting to see what their next move would be. Then he saw the Dire Fangs sinking into the marshes. They let out a haunting howl, as they thrashed around trying to get free from the marshes' embrace.

"Grab their reigns and pull. We must try and help them. Hurry!" Na'naya called with fear in her voice.

Bellamy and the others worked to grab the reigns of their Dire Fangs as quickly as they could despite the difficulty in their movements. Grabbing hold of the reigns, they pulled and pulled with all their strength. Trying to free the Dire fangs from their imprisonment, but their efforts were in vain.

"Nooooo!" Amiriss and Na'naya cried, as tears dropped from their eyes.

They were overcome with emotion. The realization came that there was nothing they could do for their trusting mounts. Unable to set them free, they watched on in pain as the Dire Fangs howled. Struggling over the next few minutes before being swallowed by the marshes. Bellamy walked over and embraced Amiriss in his arms. Holding her tight until the tears in her eyes were gone and she was calm.

Raine went over to check on Na'naya, who seemed to have a better handle on her emotions. She was still struggling with what had happened. It had hurt them the most because they had cared for and bonded with the Dire Fangs more than the others had in the time they were around.

"Though it pains me, I was reminded on why they call this place the Shattered Marshes. It is a place that is emanating with a mana phenomenon that weighs on one's spirit and emotions. The overwhelming pressure shatters your will and drowns you in the depths of the marshes. So, few can overcome its effects and make their way out, it's not a place that one enters lightly." Draemond replied with a heavy heart.

"I can see how you are feeling, but it's alright there is no need blame yourself. Even if we had known before hand, it would not have stopped us coming here. This was the only path available to us that made to most sense for our plans." Na'naya said reassuringly.

The loss of the Dire Fangs was a painful blow to their morale that would linger for a time. But they would have to find another time to process, as staying too long in the marshes was not advised. Slowly and meticulously, they trudged on through making their way across the region to the other side. It was becoming more and more difficult to tell if they were making any significant progress. Their time in the marshes seemed to drag on for hours, one exhausting minute after another.

The haze of mist that blanketed the area was lighter. The pressure that had been plaguing their bodies was being washed away. The group had finally reached the other end and made it out of the Shattered Marshes. Bellamy was relived to be able to see the azure sky and clouds again. The perpetual hazy mist of the marshes had clouded his mood long enough.

From what they could tell, without realizing it the group had spent a straight nonstop two days traveling through the marshes. As their sense of time and the exhaustion they felt returned to them the minute they were clear of the marshes' effects. In that moment everyone dropped their belongings. They sat on the ground to rest and recover their stamina.

"Ughh. I don't know how but we did it, we made it out of those godforsaken marshes. Let's not do that again anytime soon."

"I agree with Na'naya. That was one place I'd rather not have to travel through again in my life. So, now that we've made it into the Nimh Theocracy proper, what's our destination."

Bellamy was curious about Amiriss's question as well. They were told to check out the Nimh Theocracy, but they were never given a specific location to go to once they got there. That opened several different possibilities and potential destinations to investigate. He suspected Inara had some thoughts of her own on the matter.

"Inara, what are your thoughts on what our next move should be?"

"If we want to find the information we're seeking, then our best bet would be to make our way to the capital of the Nimh Theocracy, the Holy City of Larounge. It is the spiritual center of the Nimh Religion and the seat of power for the High Pontifex. If the theocracy is behind the skirmishes against the republic, then it would be on the orders of someone within the church or government. Albeit here they are not mutually exclusive from one another. From our current location it should takes us eight days to reach Larounge."

"Eight days, huh. Alright then, let's get some rest and recover our energy. We'll set out first thing in the morning."

With the first rays of sunshine falling upon the land, the group was early to rise. They packed up their belongings and teared down their camp. Rested and their energy restored, they set off through the lowland plains and open wilderness of the Nimh Theocracy's outer frontier. As was quite common with most of the nations on the Northern and Southern continents, the frontier regions along with about seventy-five percent of the nation's lands where sparsely populated. The populations were focused in hub regions around major cities and towns.

Followed by the intermittent villages or homesteads. In truth Bellamy enjoyed the vast openness between population centers. It gave him a sense of freedom and a longing to experience the wonders of the world.

They had missed the pace they were able to travel when they had the Dire Fangs. They did not let their loss slow them down and pushed on. Three times a day, Inara would pull out her map to check their progress. Seeing what might be in the local area, after they stopped to rest or grab a bite to eat. During these times Draemond and Raine would often spar with one another.

Having a chat over a pipe of Sylven Herb. A narcotic weed that grows in the Fae Commonwealth with a variety of different effects depending on how its prepared. The most common being a state of calmness and euphoria when smoked. The herb was often hard to come by in the republic. Making it rather expensive to buy, so Bellamy rarely partook in its use.

Na'naya would spend most of her time with her head in one of her precious books that she loved so much. Filled with legends and tales of long ago. When she wasn't reading, she could be found talking with Inara. Trying to mess with Raine and Draemond on their sparing sessions. As for Bellamy, he would use the time to practice. Learning to control and hone his abilities with Amiriss's guidance.

He knew that it would be a challenge, but he wasn't expecting how difficult it was going to be. Understanding the principles and concepts behind them was one thing. Utilizing them in a practical sense was a different thing entirely.

"I don't get it. I understand what you told me about the tenets of *The Arts* and channeling one's mana. I can't seem to manifest these connections."

Amiriss walked over to Bellamy and placed her palm on the center of his back. Tapping it three times, Bellamy straightened his posture. He inhaled slow controlled breaths before exhaling to the rhythm of her taps. Closing his eyes, clearing his vision of distractions, and focusing on Amiriss's voice.

"Channeling your mana and manifesting your *Arts* abilities is not about the thoughts or the words used to invoke it. It is about the flow of energy and emotion. That is expressed through your will to bring about the manifestation into physical form. The balance in harmony of both order and chaos intertwined, in a way that one does not overpower the other. Too much of one can cause adverse effects or nothing at all, same goes for the reverse with too little of one. When you come to embrace and understand this tenet then you will be able to manifest your *Arts* abilities."

Letting go and clearing his mind, Bellamy let the mana in the air, the ground, and his body flow around him. He concentrated focusing the flow to a main focal point. Maintaing the order while adjusting the chaos of the energies created by the mana's flow.

"Bellamy, cast your invocation."

[*"In the light of the Cardinal Stars I pray With the North star to seek your guidance. That with the East Star I may gain your knowledge. That with the West Star I gain your forgiveness. So, with the South star you pass judgment, upon my enemies. In your name I offer you my essence as proof of my devotion and love for your blessing."*]

The mana concentrated into three luminous orbs. Miniature stars of swirling energy caught in a gravitational orbit around the center of Bellamy's opened palms. He could sense the power coursing through the orbs. It was unlike anything he ever experienced before, wild, and untamed with a mind of its own. Bellamy could feel it push back against his will wanting to be released from his restraints.

"Now, you must focus and let go or the power will become unstable or diminished, Bellamy. There. That's it, now move the orbs and show them the target you want to strike."

Bellamy envisioned the location of the targets Amiriss had set up. Twenty feet away in different spots and elevations. The luminous orbs rotated faster around his opened palms. In an instant one by one they shot off into three different directions towards their targets. Three explosive bursts followed afterwards.

Each of the targets were impacted one after the other. Bellamy opened his eyes and breathed heavily as his was mana drained. The exhaustion of the aftereffects hitting his body like a massive blow to his chest. He looked over and saw Amiriss smile at him with a bright look in her eyes.

"Well done. Your skill has started to increase and with continued training you'll learn to master your multi-shot mana missile ability. Increasing both the number and range of your projectiles. It will also help you manage the effects of the blowback so that you're not as exhausted afterwards. You'll still be capable of fighting if need be. For now, though I would recommend that you only use the ability as a trump card or only if you can take out your enemy in a surprise attack. Any other time would be dangerous and reckless at your current state."

"Thank you, Amiriss for all your help and training. I would've never made it this far without your guidance. I will take to heart what you have taught me. Keeping your recommendations in mind, though in actuality I don't know if it will be that easy. Still, I will try."

CHAPTER 31

Over the next few days, the group continued traveling through the lowland wilderness. Rolling hills, and grassland plains as they made their way to the Holy City of Larounge. Their routine had started to become second nature to them; travel for a few hours. Then stop to eat and train, followed by traveling again, until nightfall. Then make camp to rest for the night before heading out the next day to repeat the routine.

It was a bit unsettling how quiet and peaceful the outlying wilderness was. There was hardly any signs of wildlife or people anywhere to be found in the areas they were traveling through. Other than the occasional small animal they came across or the flock of birds passing by. Though Bellamy wasn't all that surprised about it. Inara had been guiding them in a way that would avoid populated areas.

Bringing them to the very outskirts of villages or homesteads that they might pass. They had thought it over and decided that it was best not to get involved in populated areas until they needed to. As a way of protecting themselves and traveling faster to their destination.

It was on the sixth day of travel that the group had to make their way back towards the main highways. For the rest of the journey to reach the holy city. At the center crossroads where the highways interconnected leading to different parts of the theocracy was the fortified merchant city of Nocturne. A place known of commerce and contradiction. By those traveling throughout the theocracy or making pilgrimages to the holy city.

One must be careful when roaming the streets and districts of the city. Beneath the vibrance of grandeur lies the grim darkness of sins and shadows. That corrupt the hearts of the faithful. Where the true moral ambiguity of the Nimh religion's commandments is tested to their limits.

"So, there it is Nocturne. We will have to cross through the city to continue to the Holy City of Larounge. Will we be resting here for the night or heading straight on?" Raine inquired with distaste. "Though, I would rather not be lingering here any longer than needed to."

"It must stir up some horrible memories for you, my friend. As I would not want to cause you anymore pain. I'm afraid we are going to have to spend some time here before we press on to the holy city."

Bellamy saw the disappointment in Raine's eyes from his words. He knew that he would bare it for the time being if it meant helping the mission. He would find ways to distract himself and take out his frustrations in more creative ways. Inara clarified Bellamy's words and intent in his decision to stay in Nocturne.

"Taking this time to re-center from our long travel will help us for what's to come. Providing us with time to gather information on the region and the theocracy itself. It's important to understand and be careful in that matter. The theocracy is not the safest or very open to outsiders. We must stay watchful of the people and places that we interact with while we are here."

"Not a problem." The others said together.

The fortified merchant city of Nocturne was unlike any city Bellamy and the others came across in the republic. It was spread across both banks of the river than ran through the city. An island in the center connected each of the four districts through a series of wide two-storied bridges. Tall multi-storied buildings were encompassing every area of the city. Spreading across the top floor of the two-storied bridges.

Making the widespread city feel enclosed and sealed off at the same time. It was a strange feeling that stayed ever prevalent on the edges of one's conscience. A city covered in shadows brought on by its own fruition and desire to continuously grow into something grander. But such progress doesn't come without a price for not all gain glory and riches. Most fall into the trappings of poverty and despair. Bringing out the inevitable appearance of slums.

Though in truth no city is immune to such areas. Being more of a matter on how they are handled. Determining whether they are a major hinderance to a city or merely an afterthought. Nocturne was an outlier of the two, as it was a combination of both types. The slums of Nocturne were like an open secret that everyone knew existed.

Acting as nothing happened there that concerned the general population. Though that was not entirely true and far from the reality of it. It was in the slums that hardships and the cruel reality of those who do not believe in or follow the Nimh Religion. Plain to see on the faces of its inhabitants. People from all walks of life and races, none were immune to this fate.

With Inara leading the way, Bellamy and the others entered the city. Going through the South Gate into the South End Merchant's District. This was the district that most travelers passing through Nocturne would enter first. Before making their way to Northern Gate leading to the holy city. As such the South End was the largest and busiest of the four districts.

Making it the location of many inns. Taverns, shops, marketplaces, low-end brothels, gambling houses and resident apartments in the city. After wandering around the district for some time. The group looked around to get familiar with their surroundings. They found a quaint little three-story inn to stay in called *The Painted Lady*.

The proprietress of the inn was a middle-aged Demi-Human of the Ogre variety. Long flowing bluish-black hair, pale blue eyes, and a slightly thicker body than the normal athletic-slender build of her kind. She had tanned Almond skin, pointed ears, and three horns protruding from her forehead. Which was not common as most ogres tended to have one or two typically.

"Greetings travelers, I welcome you to Nocturne and my inn. My name is Kesh, how may I be of service to you?"

"We would like two rooms for the next few days."

Kesh opened the leatherbound ledger on the counter. She turned a few pages to check her availability, before writing in the book and closing it. She then turned to grab two room keys hanging on the wall hooks and placed them on the counter in front of Inara.

"The rooms will be on the second floor down the hall on the left. Breakfast and dinner are served daily, so feel free to partake. Also, there is a public bath house down the street about two blocks away if you wish to bathe. There are lavatories located on the second and third floors that you are welcomed to use. I will collect your payment at the end of your stay, feel free to ask if you have any questions about the city."

"Thank you, ma'am."

Inara grabbed the keys from the counter. She handed one to Bellamy, before they headed upstairs to their rooms. Inside the room was a widow looking out to the alley behind the inn. A small square table with two stools, a writing desk with a chair, and three single beds along the wall. Bellamy set the room key on the square table, before dropping his pack in front of one of the beds.

He took the one closest to the window. Raine and Draemond took the other two beds and dropped their packs as well. As Draemond laid down on the old bed, he felt it creak beneath the weight of his body.

"You'd best be careful there. I don't think the bed was built for the stature of one such as yourself, my friend." Raine told him in jest.

"Very funny, young pup. I assure you I have slept on beds of a more questionable nature than this one here. It will be fine."

With those last words, Draemond tapped the back of his bed, which began to shake and wobble. A loud crack followed, and the bedpost fell. The mattress slammed into the ground taking Draemond with it. Raine busted out laughing at the sight of Draemond on the ground and confusion on his face. Bellamy walked over and offered him his hand to help him up off the ground.

"Are you alright, are you hurt anywhere?"

"I'm fine. Just my pride is all."

"Ha. I told you to be careful and take it easy, but you didn't listen and now the bed has fallen apart. Well, nothing can be done about it now, we'll have to let the proprietress knew and see if it can be fixed or replaced."

Draemond left the room heading downstairs to find Kesh. To inform her about the condition of his broken bed. Moments later Raine collected his pipe and pouch from his pack. Before leaving the room to check on Draemond and see if a little smoke might change his mood. Finding himself alone for the time being.

Bellamy decided to train channeling his mana. Through meditation like Amiriss had showed him. He found an open area on the floor and sat down crossing his legs beneath him. Keeping his posture as straight as possible. Closing his eyes, he focused on inhaling and exhaling slow, deep, and steady breaths.

Sensing the mana as it flowed around him. Moving throughout his body following the natural flow of his circulating blood. As if they were one and the same and not two separate entities. Bellamy stayed in this state for about a half hour when he heard a knock at his door. He opened his eyes and got up off the ground to go and check it out. When he opened the door, Na'naya was standing there with a small bottle of Blood wine and two glasses in her hands.

"Are you busy, right now?"

"No. I just finished up with my meditation. Here, come on in and have a seat."

He stepped to the side, and she came inside the room taking a seat at the small table. Bellamy closed the door behind her, before going over to join her at the table.

Na'naya opened the bottle of Blood wine and poured some into the two glasses, then handed one to Bellamy. They raised the glasses in the air tapping the brims together. They swirled the glass around before taking a drink. It was called Blood wine because the liquor had a dark crimson and amber hue to it. Daemon blood was mixed into it during the refining process.

This gave the wine its strange blended sweet spice flavor. It proved surprising tasteful by all accounts. It was well advised not to be fooled by it. As it had a very high potency that would sneak up on you if you weren't careful with the number of drinks you had.

"How long has it been, since we last had the chance to talk and share some Blood wine together?"

"It's been a while. If I recall, the last time was the night we got back from that expedition mission we went on with the Vice-Captain. Checking out some ruins the Adventurer's Guild wanted investigated."

"Do you remember the look on the Vic-Captain's face when you showed her the stone tablets that you found. They ended up breaking into pieces by accident when you were removing them from an altar. She was so furious and upset with you because of your carelessness."

"Did you forget? The only reason I ended up breaking those tablets was because you distracted me by screaming. That Slime Snake slithered across your back, and you jumped into my arms."

Na'naya's blushed and her cheeks turned red from embarrassment. She downed what was left in her glass and poured herself another drink.

"You fool. I only did that because it caught me off-guard with its weird cold sticky mucus and I didn't know what it was. I went and explained to the Vice-Captain later that it was my fault that you dropped the stone tablets."

Bellamy was a little surprised by Na'naya's words. He never knew that she had went back and explained to the Vice-Captain what had happened. Since he had known her, Na'naya had always been there to have his back and support him. She had been like a sister to him and a close friend. He suspected that there might have been more to her feelings, though he wasn't sure he felt the same.

Bellamy and Na'naya drank some more and laughed. They recalled past adventures they had together. One glass after another, they continued into the late hours of the night talking and drinking.

CHAPTER 32

The early morning rays of sunlight shined through the bedroom window. Lingering on Bellamy's face waking him up from a deep hazy sleep. His head was experiencing a mild throbbing as he raised it from his pillow. Not recalling ever going to sleep in his bed. [*Ugh. Never again. I have got to take it easy with the Blood wine.*]

He thought as he remembered that he and Na'naya had spent the evening drinking and talking. He figured by the looks of things, he most likely got hammered and Na'naya helped him get into bed. She was always much better at holding her liquor and not one to get easily drunk. Bellamy was no lightweight when it came to drinking. Some liquors were more than he could handle if he got carried away.

Today the group had things to discuss and what their next steps would be while they stayed in the city. Bellamy changed and headed downstairs to find his companions. Everyone was gathered around a table in the common room. They were eating a delicious smelling breakfast that the proprietress Kesh had prepared for them. Bellamy took a seat at the table next to Raine and Inara. He grabbed a bowl of the wolfberry porridge and herb potatoes along with a glass of fresh squeezed juice.

"Good morning, everyone. It seems I am the last one down to the table again."

"Good morning, sleep well? You were a bit out of sorts my friend. It seems you'll never learn to moderate yourself when it comes to Blood Wine."

"I did, thank you. Trust me I know all too well that I need to moderate my intake more. It's one lesson that's a bit harder for my mind to follow through with."

Raine smiled and laughed at his words, though he could not blame Bellamy for a lack of trying. He himself was powerless when it came to his vices as well. As Bellamy looked around the table, he saw that everyone had appeared to be in good spirits. Enjoying themselves by being present in the moment together. Not letting their thoughts be clouded by what lies ahead.

After their stomachs were full. Their breakfast gone and the dishes cleared away, they stayed at the table to discuss what comes next. Inara pulled out her Wayfarer's map from her pouch and laid it out on the table. When she did so in that moment the power of the map did its trick. Changing to reflect the overview layout of the city of Nocturne.

"As you can see on the map, we are currently located in the South End Merchant's District. The largest and most populated of the city's four districts. The next of the four is the Narrows District. It is spread out across the upper and lower levels of the different bridges connecting one side of the city to the others. The third and smallest of the four districts is the Central District. Located on the island in the middle of the river. Where the church, university, and governmental buildings are located. Then we come to the last of the four districts which is the second largest. Also the location of the North Gate leading to the holy city, the North Shore District. In this district you will find the Governor's manse, upper-class residences, and one of the theocracy's garrisons located there."

"That information on the city will be useful to know. Thank you for the insight on the general layout of Nocturne, Inara." Amiriss replied with praise.

Everyone looked over the map of the city and the locations that Inara had told them about. Seeing which ones they would be checking out. They had a wide area to cover and search to gather the information they were seeking. So it would certainly take some time on their part. What seemed to be the more pressing matter was gathering information without drawing suspicion. That and any unwanted attention on to them and finding reliable sources. For now, it seemed the best thing they could do was to split up their search and go from there.

"So, here's the plan; we will split off into groups. Each check out a different district of the city to gather the information we're searching for. Then meet back up here at the inn at the end of each day to discuss anything we might have found. Na'naya and Amiriss will check out the South End Merchant's District. Raine, you and Draemond will check out the Narrows District. Then Inara and I will check out the Central and North Shore Districts."

Bellamy looked around at his companions and saw that everyone seemed to agree with his plan. He figured the plan was solid enough that they had no objections to it. He was still figuring out how to best pair up his companions. Better compliment their strengths and balance out any weaknesses. It would be a matter of trying different formations out, but it was proving to work so far. So, he proceeded to explain the rest of it and express some concerns he had as well.

"Once we have what we need, we will then make our way to the holy city. That or head back to the republic strictly based on the outcome of the information we are able to gather. I know we are all capable fighters. My only concern is that if we find ourselves in trouble it may prove far more troublesome to handle. Consider we are in a different nation with different laws than where we came from. I ask that you all be careful out there and use your best judgement when it comes down to it."

"Will do. Alright Raine, it's time we head out while the day is beginning. It will give us more time to search." Draemond advised.

Raine and Draemond got up from the table and turned to head out for the Narrows District. On his way out he placed a hand on Bellamy's shoulder and offered him some advice.

"I expect the same from you, my friend. Inara I can count on you to watch his back out there, the kid doesn't always know when to back away and leave things be. I will say that you've gotten better albeit slowly, but nobody is perfect, except I do come damn close."

"Enough with the bravado Raine. I'm sure Bellamy gets it. You should be the one listening to your own advice as well. You tend to get distracted by a pretty face and a tight waist. But don't worry Bellamy we will be fine out there."

With those last words, Na'naya, and Amiriss where the next ones to get up. They set out into the South End Merchant's District. Inara folded up the map and put it away back into her pouch. They sat around the table to talk a little longer about where their first stop should be when they got to the Central District. After deciding on a location, the two got up from the table and headed out on their way.

CHAPTER 33
NA'NAYA ADINA

When the two ladies left the inn, they weren't sure where to start their search for the information they were seeking. They decided to wander around the district and see what the city had to offer. As Na'naya and Amiriss walked down the crowded streets observing the citizens. Going about their daily lives and interact with one another. They began to realize that Nocturne was not like other cities they've been to.

It had a strange feeling of both closeness and isolation. The people would only seem to interact with people of similar status or those of authority. Outside of that they would not bother to acknowledge the others unless there was some sort of absolute need to. Those without status or authority were no more than mere shadows. Treated as such, a second-class citizen with no voice of their own.

The city was made up of a diverse population of races. The majority with status and authority being Humans. It was the case with the theocracy. In its entirety the Nimh Religion has been Human centric in its beliefs and practices.

These views have caused a widespread xenophobic ideology to indoctrinate its followers. Caused its growth to be practically non-existent outside of human territories. Giving raise to foolish notions of human superiority. The belief that the other races are not the true testaments of the Gods. Only circum-stantial experiments on their search to creating perfection.

Through dangerous thoughts as these the religion has found itself at an impasse. With the other religions and more moderate factions growing within. The Nimh religion has been slow on the uptake of adapting to the changing times. Locked in a past that doesn't suit the ever-changing world. If nothing is done to change their path, then Nimh religion will fracture. To fall apart in the years to come as a relic of the past.

"Amiriss, do you know anything about the different colored sashes and pins? I see some of the people wearing and what they mean?"

Na'naya pointed over at group of middle-aged human men. Standing around the outside terrace of a restaurant at the end of the street they were walking down.

"If I recall correctly, they are meant as a sign of rank and status used within the Nimh religion and the theocracy. Brown was for commoners. Orange was for merchants and artisans. Green was for scholars. Red was for military. Blue was for *Artists*. Purple for nobility and aristocracy. Finally white for priests. Then in turn each color is governed by a hierarchy within it. Based on a star rating of zero a Novice to seven stars a Grand Master. The more stars one has the more authority and status one has over others in and outside one's color to an extent. As the authority goes from: White, Purple, Red, Blue, Green, Orange, and then Brown."

"I see, I appreciate the explanation. I had no idea about how the structure of the Nimh Religion was set up or how they operated. Though, considering you're not human I am a bit surprised that you knew anything about it given their stance on other races."

Amiriss looked at Na'naya with a strong sense of determination. Resolve gleaming in her eyes, as she gave her a smile that was equally as gentle and kind as if from a loving parent.

"Your sentiment is understandable. It is for those reasons that I make sure to gain as much information as I can on potential threats. Along with subjects of interest that spark my curiosity. Its best to be prepared for the many possibilities one may come across in this dangerous and unforgiving world of ours. Especially for those of different races and the feminine gender."

The ladies left the street the restaurant was on. They made their way strolling down the different streets of the district. As they made their way up and down the streets, they would investigate the windows of shops here and there. Seeing what wares they had inside to sell. Stepping inside to take a quick look around at merchandise. Ranging all the way from artwork to weapons, and rare curiosities.

The merchants and people that they managed to talk to, would only seem to keep the conversations vary casual or straight business. Not bothering to mention gossip or rumors they might have heard from a friend or on the streets. It was a strange sight for them to see when it happened. They always seemed a little hesitant to talk. Suddenly change subjects when asked questions about the current affairs within the theocracy or about their foreign policy actions.

They had a feeling that something was going on. That the citizens were fearful to comment about to outsiders. The girls knew better than to press too hard to get the information from them. Arousing unwanted attention on themselves or the others was the last thing they wanted to do. They cut back on asking the merchants anymore questions.

They considered taking another approach to get the information. Na'naya had an idea about where they could go to try and find information. Given the diverse population and size of the city, she was positive that she would find one of those places here. A special kind of place where one could go to lose themselves. Forget about their worries, troubles, concerns and even their dreams and desires. A place that on accounts originated in her homeland. quickly spreading whether openly or in secret to other nations throughout the world.

Na'naya had seen Raine and Draemond partake in smoking Sylven Herb. The place she was thinking about revolved around a potent and more dangerous strain. The herb known as Stardust. It was in one of these Stardust dens that Na'naya was positive they would find a lead. It always sent a chill down her spine whenever she had to go to such a place.

When her master was still around, she would find him there when he was at his lowest. Searching for any means he could to forget the pain that burdened him. Since, he would try to hide from Na'naya, she became keen on finding him. Tracking down the locations of Stardust dens. As their locations tend to be well hidden, you had to seek out the subtle signs that led the way to a location.

"Hey Amiriss, I have an idea about where we can search next. I'm going to need you to trust me and follow my lead. The place we are going to can quicky ensnare you in its environment if you're not careful."

"No problem. lead the way and I will do as you say, Na'naya."

"Alright. Then, let's go."

The girls continued down the streets and alleyways of the district. Examining any signs or artwork that they came across on posters or painted on walls. Na'naya had told Amiriss that they were looking for a marker. One represented by a glyph of an open hand with a blue lotus embedded in its palm. The sun had reached its highest peak in the sky and was waning into the afternoon hours.

They searched and searched but still found no signs of the marker. Amiriss decided to take a little break. They had been searching for hours with no luck. Then she spotted a local message board. The guilds would use to post announcements.

Jobs, wanted posters, and any other local information relevant to the citizens of the city. While she was looking over the message board she noticed something hidden beneath one of the announcements. She lifted it up to find a worn painted glyph of the marker she had been searching for.

Amiriss called over to Na'naya to check out the glyph, to make sure that it was the real thing. After looking it over Na'naya smiles. She heads down the alley to the west of the message board, grabbing Amiriss's hand. At the end of the long alleyway the girls come to a dead end in front of a brick wall. Na'naya stops and scans the wall up and down when she spots the glyph marker on six different bricks. All protruding from the wall barely visible from a distance. One by one, Na'naya pushed in each of the bricks into the wall, locking them in place.

There was a subtle low rumbling as the brick wall in front of them started to shift. Moving in different directions. Forming an archway leading to a descending staircase. The girls passed through the archway making their way to the staircase. They heard the subtle rumble of the shifting brick wall close behind them.

Shaded lanterns hanging on the wall illuminated the staircase. The girls descended towards the bottom. At the bottom they came to wooden door with the glyph marker engraved into it. Na'naya knocked on the door three times, when the glyph marker began to glow. The door swung open to a massive chamber that laid beyond.

Waiting on the other side of the door was a tall tanned older human male with a long salt and pepper beard in robes native to Nanaya's homeland. He bowed and gave the girls a wide grinning smile, that appeared welcoming and off putting at the same time.

"Greetings, honored guest. I welcome you to the Dreamer's Palace, a place to ease your burdens and release your desires. Feel free to have a look around, grab a drink, or eat some delectable food. Partake in games or in Stardust, and enjoy the entertainment. Whatever you may find yourself wanting or need, here your wishes will become reality."

"We appreciate the hospitality and look forward to enjoying this place."

Inside the Dreamer's Palace the air was filled with a sweet and intoxicating aroma. It spread throughout the many chambers. The main chamber was a massive two-storied room with a long bar towards the back center of the room. Booths scattered around three different stages, and the second floor was a casino with a variety of different gambling games. A Demi-Human band and singer were playing on the main centered stage.

On the other two side stages were exotic tribal belly dancers locked in a ritual dance of sensual passion and ecstasy. Along the walls were hallways down which were lined with private nooks on each side. Draped by fine curtains covering rooms withs plush bedding pillows on decorated carpets. A place to smoke in private drifting off into fantasy, have private conversations over drinks and food. Enjoy the company of a bed slave or all the above, it was a place for any wish you wanted to become reality.

The music was enchanting. The conversations and attitudes of the patrons were all consuming. The euphoric environment captivated the senses of all around. A never-ending party where the concerns of everyday life didn't seem to exist. Only the undeniable urge to keep the party going.

Time alluded them. They listened to the enchanting melodies of the band, drank the wine, and ate the food. gambled at the tables trying to get information from the euphoric patrons. Not noticing that all this time their thoughts became clouded. Everything blurred into a frenzied dream. They got entangled into the spell of the Dreamer's Palace.

"Na'naya, how did we get here and how long has it been? I can't seem to remember, and I suddenly feel tired." Amiriss said with a drowsy yawn.

Na'naya turned and rushed over to Amiriss catching her in her arms, as fell back fast asleep. Supporting her on her shoulders, Na'naya carried Amiriss to one of the private nooks. She laid her down on the plush bedding pillow.

"Hey, come on and wake up. Amiriss. Amiriss!" Na'naya shouted.

Na'naya tapped on Amiriss as she tried to get her to wake, while slowly becoming overwhelmed with sleep as well. Until her eyes closed and fell to the bedding pillow fast asleep next to Amiriss.

CHAPTER 34

Na'naya was the first to wake. Still groggy from the sudden and unexpected sleep, she and Amiriss experienced. She took a deep breath to re-center herself and help her focus. As her senses became clear, and she could take in the scene in front of her. The two of them were not the only ones in the private nook anymore. They had been bound by restraints and collars around their necks. Amiriss woke up afterward startled and puzzled as she realized what was happening. Four hooded and cloaked figures stood behind them wearing dark leathered armor.

"Na'naya, what's going on here? Who are these people?" Amiriss whispered quietly, barely audible to anyone else around them.

"I'm not sure, but the one sitting on the chair in front of us, seems to be in command." Na'naya responded as calmly as she could, biting down on her lip to hold off her frustration.

"You need to hold your composure and stay calm. If we are going to get out of here or find anything out, we need to be focused. I believe in you, Na'naya. We can do this."

Sitting in front of them leaning back into a chair was a man in black robes. Wearing a metal and leather strapped cuirass, a crimson red sash around his waist, and a Harlequin mask on his face. His emerald eyes pierced through the mask staring with an eerie calm at the two girls bound before him. Defiant looks gleamed in their eyes. In that instant, he knew he was going to enjoy breaking these two lovely ladies. It was in times like these that the true character of one's spirit was tested. Revealing the type of person one truly was when their freedom was taken away from them.

"Good day ladies, it's nice to see that you're awake and well. I know you must have questions about why your restrained and collared. Don't worry I will be getting to that shortly, but first I would like you to answer a few questions for me. Be warned it would be in your best interest to answer me honestly. Now, do I have your cooperation?"

Na'naya stared straight at the masked man with a vehement distaste and an expression that could kill.

"Ohhh. You're a spirited one, little miss. Though I do wonder how long you will be able to keep that bravado of yours."

She wasn't always able to hide her frustration and anger. Especially in situations where she found herself outmaneuvered by a potential enemy. Amiriss on the other hand, was calm and deliberate in her moves and expression. Not giving them any openings to exploit.

"You seem to have us at a disadvantage here, sir given that you seem to have some sort of idea of who we are. Though, we don't have any idea of who you might be and why you bound us."

The masked man leaned in closer so that the ladies could understand what he was about to tell them. That there would be no doubt in their minds about what was going on.

"I am no more than a devout follower of the one true god, Nimh. I protect the faithful, seek out and punish those who violate or doubt his will, and all forms of heresy. I am *The Jack of Clubs*, High Inquisitor Tearyn of the Nimh Theocracy's Inquisition. About why you're bound, it's because you are suspected of committing heresy. Sedition against the theocracy and I am here to judge your guilt or innocence."

Na'naya and Amiriss were speechless as they looked to one another. Trying to figure out where they went wrong and how this could have happened. Na'naya thought [*there's no possible way that this man had any significant evidence of proof to the claims. They had been careful. Hadn't done anything that could have drawn attention.*] The high inquisitor sat back against the chair. He gave them some time to reflect. To think on their responses before, he started questioning them.

"Now, let's start with a relatively easy and simple question. Are you and your companion the only ones traveling together. Did you enter the theocracy's territory outside of normal entry? Either one of you may answer my questions."

Na'naya and Amiriss stayed silent for the moment. Not wanting to betray the trust of their companions, or put them in danger. They were resolved to answer the High Inquisitor's questions. Only to see what information they could gain from him, so it would be half-truths. Whether this ploy of theirs would work or not was about to be tested. Amiriss spoke up first for the two of them.

"It is only me and my friend here, who have traveled here to this place. As for entering the theocracy's territory we came by crossing the border. Are you perhaps implying that there are other ways of entering the theocracy that are outside of the government's control. That seems to me like that could pose a potential concern to your nation's security."

The High Inquisitor's eyes gleamed beneath his mask, as if to give the impression of a sly and calculated smile.

"I see. Oh, dear it seems you weren't listening to me when I told you that it wouldn't be wise to lie to me. Though, I do applaud your audacity. Thinking that you would get away by telling me half-truths. That gamble of yours will not pay off to your benefit."

The High Inquisitor raised one hand. He signaled with two fingers to the one of the hooded figures behind the girls. The hooded figure touched a gemstone centered on a metal gauntlet he was wearing. The restraints and collars around the girls vibrated with an intense force. It shocked their bodies, sending pulses all throughout.

"Ahh...Ahh...Aaaahhh...Ah.!" The girls moaned and screamed in an absurdly twisted agonizing pain. That was almost on the brink of being pleasurable.

The High Inquisitor signaled again. The hooded figure moved touching the gemstone again, stopping the intense vibrations. The girl's bodies were trembling. They were breathing hard panting as they slowly recovered.

"You damn, sadistic bastard! What in the seven hells was that? What right do you have to inflict that perversion of pain and yet pleasure upon someone?" Na'naya yelled in frustration.

"Let's say I have found it to be rather effective in breaking the wills of my prisoners. Making them more agreeable to my questions. It doesn't matter to me what you think, but either way in the end I will get the answers I seek, one way or another."

The High Inquisitor signaled to the hooded figure again and again.

"Ahh...Ahh...Aaaahhh...Ah.!"

The girls were forced to endure the different sessions for what seemed like hours. As each one was never the same in duration. Fighting to stay strong and not give in to the twisted sadism of the High Inquisitor. Na'naya and Amiriss refused to give their captors the satisfaction of seeing them express pain or pleasure. They endured the vibrations pulsing through their bodies. Focusing as best they could on one another and ignoring everything else around them.

"Ahh...Ahh...Aaaahhh...Ah.!"

The High Inquisitor signaled once again. The hooded figure moved touching the gemstone again, stopping the intense vibrations. The girl's bodies still trembled. They continued breathing hard panting as they slowly recovered.

"Si...six. Six of us traveled into the theocracy's territory. Crossing the border through the Shattered Marshes." Na'naya answered dejectedly. Tears running down her cheeks as she was struggling to stay conscious.

"Well, my dear that was the first truthful thing you've told me. You see in the end I always get the truth. That will be enough for now, grab the prisoners and prepare to move out. We'll be transporting them to Nalran Prison."

"You can't do this to us. Our companions will come for us when we don't return to them." Amiriss said with what little strength she could muster.

"Oh. I'm counting on it. I have no doubt in my mind that they will come for you... You, there come in here."

The tall tanned older man that had greeted the two girls at the entrance stepped into the room. From behind the curtains he walked over to the High Inquisitor. He bowed his head, and the High Inquisitor handed him a sealed letter.

"Take the letter and see that it makes its way to the Painted Lady Inn."

"As you wish High Inquisitor. It will be done."

The tall tanned older man made his way out of the room and hurried off to complete the task given to him. Signaling his men, the High Inquisitor stood up from his chair and walked out of the room. Following behind him the hooded figures lifted the two weakened females from the ground. They carried them out of the room. Na'naya and Amiriss were powerless to do much of anything. They were barely able to stay conscious before everything started to fade to black.

CHAPTER 35
RAINE ROLLO

The Narrows District was not what Raine and Draemond expected. When they first crossed onto one of the many bridges that made up the district. Coming from the South End Merchant's District. The buildings were tall, slender, and oddly shaped constructs. That were stacked exceedingly close to one another.

Spread through the twists and turns of the narrow streets. Walkways and ladders connected many of the buildings together. Creating a series of passages for the residents to interact with their community. Lower-Class citizens, refugees, servants. Slaves and criminals made up the residents of the city slums, That was the Narrows District.

It was a dangerous place plagued by violence and thievery. Sickness and a desire for the self-preservation of one's livelihood. Through whatever morally ambiguous way possible.

In this regard the district was its own self-contained and governed world. Within the confines of the larger city enclosing it. The laws of the city and nation still held sway over the residents of the district. More so loosely enforced by the whims of city watch guards often bribed by local gangs to look the other way. It was by no means a lawless free for all.

There was always the ever-watchful presence of the Nimh Theocracy's Inquisition. Judge, jury, and executioners of divine retribution. Against heresy and sedition within the theocracy and its territories. They above all were the one thing to be genuinely afraid of in the power that made the theocracy's military and religious strength. It was best to pay respect and stay out of their way, not to get involved in matters dealing with them.

"Raine, do you have any ideas on where we should search next. It looks like this section of the Narrows is going to be a bust as well. That makes three of the upper sections we've checked so far and no luck on finding anything useful. What if we take the advice of that drunkard from the tavern and check out the lower sections?"

Raine tapped his foot on the ground as he thought about Draemond's suggestion. A little cautious of the drunkard's advice, for a good reason. The lower sections of the Narrows District was the locations of the Slaver's Marketplace and Auction House. A place that Raine didn't think he would ever see again in his lifetime. Though, for reasons he didn't understand. It appeared that the threads of fate were drawing him back towards his past.

"I would prefer to avoid those areas if we could help it. But I have a feeling that going there is the only option if we want to complete our task. Let's head to the lower sections then. Keep a watchful eye, for we are going to be around people who would rather profit from us than help us."

At the end of the street, they turned down a side walkway passing behind some of the other buildings. They made their way to the stairway descending to the lower sections of the Narrows District. The lower sections of the Narrows District proved to be different from the upper sections. Apart from being located on the bottom floor of the two-storied bridges, it was also spread out on elevated platforms. Connecting the areas to one another one through various interconnected walkways.

Creating a massive web below the many bridges making up the district. The elevated platforms varied in size and some even went as low as the river shore. Making the area ideal for shipments of contraband. Along with ambiguous merchandise by boats and river barges. The only other docks located in the city, were those in the North Shore District. Where the more legal shipments arrived. The Slaver's Market and Auction House was located on one of the massive lower elevated platforms closer to the river shore.

Animal pins and broad iron cages aligned around stalls. Decorated with fine fabrics and furs filled the open area in spaced lanes. Creating the sprawling grandeur of the Slaver's Market. While surrounding the main theater building of the Auction House in the middle. People of Middle-Class status and proxies of wealthier clients were all around.

Browsing the stalls looking over the different merchandise. Bound for auction or available for private sale. Raine and Draemond walked about as they were forced to hold back their feelings. Growing frustrations over the scenes they saw within the market. Men, Women, and Children of varying races and different physical conditions were bound in the cages.

Put on display for peering eyes and ill smiles to gawk over like playthings. The conditions of some slaves were significantly better than others. There were physical beauties dolled up and stripped nearly bare. Showcasing their assets. The life of a personal maid, bed-slave, harem courtesan, or high-end prostitute awaited the lucky ones.

Others depending on their physique and intelligence would be made into servants. Personal attendants. Fieldworkers. Miners. Foot soldiers.

Gladiators, or any other profession deemed necessary by their future masters. What pained them the most as they were walking towards the Auction house was the empty and blank emotionless looks, they saw on many of the slave's faces. Seeing it on children was a horrible sight.

"Raine, this is an unforgivable sight. Though something of greater concern, I've noticed that many of the slaves here are Demi-Humans and even astoundingly some Fae. What could be the reasoning behind this atrocity?"

"This is the dark reality brought about by the dangerous xenophobic ideologies of the Nimh Religion. Its views of Humans as being the true successor of their almighty god. That the other races are failed afterthoughts. So, in return they offer salvation and redemption through servitude as a so-called great honor. To me it is a lie they use to justify their unwarranted cruelty towards races. They never bothered to understand as people like themselves."

Draemond stood in silence. Looking around with pity towards those misguided in their limiting ways and thoughts.

"However, we may view the institution of slavery whether it be justified or not. There must be a better way forward. I fear that only dark times will lay ahead for our world and the people who make it what it is. This senseless cruelty and violence will only breed more cruelty and violence." Draemond preached adamantly.

Raine understood the sentiment behind his friend's words. He knew all too well the horrors one was put through when forced into slavery, for whatever reason. It pained him not being able to act. If he were to act, he would more than likely cause more harm for the slaves, than any good he might have brought to a few slaves at best. The risk was too great for him to jeopardize not just his life and freedom but that of Draemond as well. For the slim chance of rescuing any of the slaves here.

"I know how you feel my friend. We unfortunately cannot act and do something that would cause problems. For better or worse it is legal in this country, and we don't have the authority to do anything about it. We must move on and proceed with our task. We can't do anything now, but we can help to prevent others from becoming victims of it in the future."

"Very well. I will do my best to let it be." Draemond responded with clear irritation in his voice.

As Raine and Draemond walked through the Slaver's Market he stopped in his tracks. He spotted an older Demi-Human woman of the Wolf-Beastmen variety with long flowing white hair, blackish fur ears and tail. Though, a slave collar was around her neck she was wearing the garments of a seamstress. A simple fabric cotton tunic blouse and layered skirt. Overlayed with a canvas apron and leather sandals on her feet.

Time and circumstance had barely left a mark on the elegant beauty with the deep cherry brown eyes. They reminded him of the amber sap of the Sacred trees that grew in his homeland. Always there to provide love and comfort to the wild and carefree boy he used to be in his youth, before they were separated. Raine felt tears in his eyes as he couldn't believe what he saw in front of him, she was still alive and here of all places.

Draemond walked over to reach out to Raine after noticing the look on his face. Before he could reach him, Raine sprinted off in the direction of the woman without any hesitation. Raine caught up to the woman. She was about to walk up the stairs towards the Auction House, when he stopped behind her and called out to her.

"Mo…mother!" Raine trembled as the words left his mouth.

The woman stopped as she was about to place her foot on the steps and turned around to see who had called out to her. A warm smile came across her face and tears rolled down her cheeks. She collapsed to her knees seeing her son for the first time after so many years. Raine rushed over to his mother's side and gave her a big embrace. His tough composure melting away in that moment.

He was not the battle-hardened mercenary he had become. But that lost boy that had been separated from his mother long ago. Remembering why he was there in the first place; he centered his emotions and helped his mother back onto her feet.

"Raine, my precious boy, I am so happy to see the fine man you've become. I've prayed to the ancestors that you were safe and that I would see you again someday."

"Mother, I don't understand how are you here? After we were separated and I escaped, I heard that you were killed in an attack when I was finally able to search for you."

Raine saw sadness and anger in his mother's eyes, as she was thinking on those painful memories from the past.

"When I was sold and being transported to my new master, the caravan I was in was attacked by Daemons. I was injured in the altercation. After I had woken up, I found myself being taken care of. At one of the church's monasteries for a time, till

I regained my strength. Then when they found out that I was a slave, I was bound back into servitude for the theocracy. I'm so sorry that I couldn't be there for you. I tried my best to get information on your whereabouts and contact you. My efforts were always stopped by the theocracy. They value their order and secrecy above all else, so I had no choice if I wanted to keep you safe and out of their sights."

Raine clenched his fist at his mother's words. Hearing how the theocracy had stopped her from getting in contact with her own son. He took slow and steady breaths as he calmed his growing anger towards the ones responsible for his mother's pain. Raine didn't know how he would do it, but he would find a way to free his mother from her bondage. Draemond was standing of in the distance leaning against a poll, when Raine signaled him to come over.

"Draemond, I would like you to meet my mother Aveline Rollo. I mentioned how we were separated when I was younger. It turns out that she had survived her attack and ended up in bondage to the theocracy."

Draemond bowed his head in greeting towards Aveline, she smiled at him in response.

"Ma'am. It is a pleasure to meet such a lovely beauty. Your son has been an exceptional traveling companion on our journey here."

"I thank you for the compliment and it's nice to meet you as well. I am glad that my son has a strong companion as yourself by his side."

"I am grateful to him and the others who are traveling with us as well. Two of them, Bellamy and Na'naya belong to the same mercenary group I've been a part of the last few years are my closest friends. I hope I get the chance to introduce you to them."

"I hope so too, my boy."

At the top of the Auction House the central hand of the clock hit the top of the hour and the bell rang three times. Aveline looked up at the clock noticing the time and realized she was going to be late. She turned to head back up the stairs in a hurry, waving back towards Raine and Draemond.

"I must go now. I'm sorry but there isn't any more time, they will not tolerate me being late. Raine stay safe and know that I love you, my son now and always. I hope we meet again, so I will say farewell for now."

Aveline hurried up the stairs making her way into the Auction House and out of sight. Raine stood in silence. He watched his mother disappear from his sight again, powerless to do anything about it.

CHAPTER 36

Draemond walked over to Raine and put his hand on his shoulder to reassure him that there was no need to worry. He would see his mother again someday. Raine glanced back at his companion acknowledging his support. Bringing him back into the present moment and their task at hand. The two of them proceeded up the stairs making their way to the Auction House.

At the top of the stairs across the platform outside the front doors to the Auction House, there was a big crowd of finely dressed patrons. Covered by dark cloaks talking to one another as they were standing by waiting for the doors to open. The conversations began to die down as the patrons stood in silence. The sound of a horn was blown and the doors to the Auction House opened.

Everyone began to make their way into the Auction House's interior. Raine and Draemond followed in behind after the last few patrons went inside. A grand gilded ornate foyer, decorated in fine tapestries and fine art spread out before them. Leading to many hallways and a grand split staircase in the middle that went to the upper floors. The two of them took in the sight of the opulent grandeur that laid hidden in the depths of the Narrows District.

They followed the patrons down the halls and into the massive theatre where the auctions would take place. Finding a spot along the back of the main floor, Raine and Draemond sat down in a pair of seats. When everyone was seated the lights slowly dimmed in the theatre. A tall slender man with long black hair and goatee, wearing a dark crimson trench coat and top hat, carrying a cane in his left hand walked onto the stage.

"Greetings one and all, welcome. Today's auction will be a special one indeed. We have special merchandise and artifacts up for auction. That have come from all corners of our world. I can promise you that they will not disappoint, so prepare yourselves as we are about to begin!"

The sound of the horn they heard outside was blown again and the auction was underway. Strange and ancient artifacts, along with artistic masterpieces from some of the old masters where in the first few lots that went up for auction. Raine and Draemond watched. Patrons would bid against one another for the chance to claim their coveted prize. It was a sight to see as they would spend what most commoners would consider a small fortune.

Capable of changing their lives. Their children's children lives in an instant on items as small as a music box to giant pieces as big as a small Daemon. It was a grand spectacle as they were caught up in the atmosphere of the menagerie of wonders.

"Bravo. Bravo. Today's auction has been wonderful so far, wouldn't you agree? It is a pleasure to see that many of you dear patrons will be leaving with marvelous prizes in hand. Now, let us move on to what I'm sure you've all been waiting for."

There was a subtle shift in mood as the auction went on. The lots switched up to the real reason most of the patrons were there, to bid on the living merchandise. Starting with rare animals and exotic beasts, the auction continued. The bids became even higher than previous ones with each of the different lots brought forth. But Raine and Draemond weren't ready for what they experienced.

At long last they brought out the Demi-Human and Human slaves for auction. They saw families being torn apart. As children were separated from their mothers. husbands from their wives, and siblings from one another. For those not a part of families that were captured or grow-up in bondage it was a much different affair.

Men from children to adulthood were the first to be presented on the stage. Sold off in groups or by the individual. For labor, slave solider, or gladiatorial servitude. Once they finished off auctioning the men or taking away the ones that didn't sell, they began to auction off the women. Unlike the men, the women were not auctioned off in groups but individually and by age-range.

It was hard for them to witness these people treated as nothing more than possessions or livestock. Seeing what the more attractive adult maidans had to go through was difficult for the two of them. For those ones were paraded on stage in no more than a thin silk cover-up. That they would have to remove once their lot was called. So that the patrons could see their exposed naked bodies. Exposing yourself because you were with a lover or in the heat of an exotic dance out of free will was one thing. Being forced to outside of your control for others to gawk at was a different beast all together.

"Raine. I understand that we are searching for information. How much longer are we going to have to put up with this terrible farce? I don't think I'll be able to reframe myself from doing something outside my control if this keeps up."

"You're right, we should go elsewhere to search for information. I don't blame you; I might have done something foolish as well had we stayed any longer."

Draemond got up from his seat, making his way back towards the aisle and the exit of the theatre. Raine got up as well and followed him shortly after. On the upper mezzanine level in one of the private boxes to the left of the stage, a shadowed figured raised their hand. The lights in the theatre dimmed completely all at once. A moment later the lights came back on.

There on the stage was Raine's mother bound in chains standing next to the auction announcer. Raine stopped before he exited the theatre, staring frozen at his mother up on the stage.

"One and all, I give you the final item of the auction. This lovely specimen of a female Wolf-Beastmen with long flowing hair as white as snow. A rare trait amongst her kind and not to mention she is an exceptionally skilled seamstress with an intelligent mind. If you happen to be of a more refined and discerning taste. Though a little past her prime, she still has a figure on her that would rival even beauties half her age. Keeping that in mind, let's start the bid for this gem."

The voices around the room became raucous and rowdy as the patrons began bidding on Raine's mother. Each one more expressive than the previous one, as they tried to have the winning bid. Raine's bottled up feelings burst through the dam keeping them at bay. He was lost in a fevered haze as the scene around him turned into a blur. Patrons were screaming and running in panic, rushing their way out of the theatre.

When Raine's senses returned to him, he was standing on the stage with his daggers drawn dripping in blood. The auction announcer's body laid sprawled out beneath him. His mother's chains had been severed and she was standing next to him with both sadness and joy in her eyes.

Draemond came rushing up towards the stage, calling out to Raine. He was still processing what was happening when he finally heard his friend's words.

"Come. We need to get out of here, the commotion will have drawn the attention of the guards. Hurry!"

Aveline grabbed her son's hand and pulled him towards her as they made their way off the stage. She led the way for the two others to follow behind her. They made their way to a back hallway and through a series of servant passages. exiting at the back of the Auction House. They moved with a swift urgency through the backstreets behind buildings.

Down stairwells, and across bridges staying hidden in the shadows. The sounds of whistles and hounds echoed in the distance. Throughout the lower section of the Narrows District. Slave soldiers and guards were searching for the missing slave and assailant. The three of them had found an abandoned warehouse on one of the lower docks to hideout in and catch their breaths.

"My foolish boy, what were you thinking? You've should have let them sell me and prevented yourself from being hunted down."

"It may have been foolish of me, but I would rather deal with them, than see you stuck in bondage any longer. I will get you out of here and protect you this time, mother."

Aveline smiled and embraced her son in a deep caring hug. Overflowing with emotions she had locked away long ago. Draemond stood watch peering out the window for any sign of pursuers after them. Letting his friend take in the new moments he had with his mother. The sky was darkening as the last light of day faded and the night fell upon the city.

They had managed to evade the pursuers for the time being. Raine knew that they would have to come up with a plan sooner rather than later. as time would only be on their side for so long. The cover of night would provide them with some breathing room. But not much to where they could afford to let their guard down.

"What should we do? I don't want to leave you again, after getting you back. Though, if I'm honest it is the only way right now that would keep you safe and out of harm's way. I won't let them take you back and punish you for my actions, mother."

"I can see that questioning whether your actions are the right ones to take or not. Know that seeing you again and being here has filled my heart with joy. So, I will do whatever I can to ease your troubles, Afterall any mother would do that for their child."

Raine was taken aback by the warmth he felt from her words. The joy she expressed in her smile, not letting the uncertain future of the situation grip her in fear. She had always been a strong woman with fierce determination for as long as he could remember. He was grateful that through everything his mother had been through, she was still that capable person when she needed to be. Draemond left his spot at the window and went over to where Raine and Aveline were talking, to see what the plan was going to be.

"So, I assume you have a plan for what our next course of action will be?"

"Now that she escaped, it will be too dangerous from my mother to stay in the city any longer. My plan is to get her passage on one of the barges leaving the city and out of this country in general. Then once she's safe and on her way, we'll split up and make our way back to the South End Merchant's District and head back to the inn. They don't know who we are and haven't seen our faces, so we should be fine for the time being."

"Alright. Sounds like a decent plan, let's go and get your mother out of this godforsaken city."

After making sure the area was clear around them one last time, they left the abandoned warehouse. They searched the docks for a barge to take Raine's mother away from the city. Even though it was nighttime, the docks were buzzing with people and merchants. Who were in the line of taking care of business after normal daytime hours. It was the kind that normal citizens avoided getting involved with.

A business of black-market deals, smuggling, piracy, illegal gambling. Unsanctioned gladiatorial fights, and other manners of business they wanted to keep from sight of the authorities. They still had to be careful and watch their backs. Money had a way of influencing people against their interest. So they only went to a few different barges to find passage. It took them a little longer than Raine would have liked given the situation. But they were able to find a barge that was departing shortly for Aurontil.

"You are finally going to be free from this life, mother. Remember, head to the Falling Star Mercenary Group, they will help you get settled and taken care of. They're good people, that I've been working with for a while now. Take care and I promise that I will see you again."

"Until we meet again, my dear boy. Know that I love you and always will. Stay safe out there and rely on your friends when you need help. Be free."

The captain was rescued by The Falling Star Mercenary Group a few years back. He was looking forward to paying back the debt he owed to them. Raine watched as his mother boarded the barge turning to wave back to him. The anchor raised, and the barge departed from the dock. Draemond left a few minutes afterwards. While Raine stayed watching the barge move down the river until it was finally out of his sight. He looked off into the starry night. He prayed for his mother's safe travels, before turning and heading off back towards the inn.

CHAPTER 37
BELLAMY LEONE

After the others left the inn to check out their assigned districts. Bellamy and Inara followed suit heading off to the Central District. The streets leading to the bridge that crossed over to the Central District were not as crowded as most of the other streets. Because of the different checkpoints' setup along the way. Access to the Central District was limited to citizens and travelers coming from the South End Merchant's District.

There were strict times when they would be allowed to pass. Either early morning or before sunset. It was said to be a means of providing the best possible protection against outside threats. Though in reality, it was that and more importantly a stopgap. Separating those without means from those with means. A blatant and obvious form of segregation. That the theocracy openly acknowledges through their antiquated beliefs.

Unlike the other connecting bridges in the city, the one connecting the South End Merchant District to the Central District was wider than normal. With enough room for six people to walk abreast. Lined with miniature obelisks along the sides of the stone bridge. Bellamy and Inara made it through the final checkpoint with barely moments to spare. Before it was closed off for the morning.

They had gotten lost along the way. Going down the wrong side street, getting turned around and had to double back. With Inara's help they found their way and made it to the checkpoints in time.

"Sorry about that. You were right in your directions from the start. I thought we could have saved some time by going down that street, but it was the wrong one." Bellamy replied slowly catching his breath.

"Mistakes can happen, but we made it in time. Follow my lead next time and then we won't have to turn around and rush to where we are going."

Bellamy let Inara take the lead as they walked down the bridge. Crossing over the river and into the Central District on the other side ten minutes later. When they stepped off the bridge it was like entering another world. The atmosphere of the Central District was completely different from the South End Merchant's District. Though smaller in size, it felt wide open and spacious.

The buildings were more spaced out from one another. The air seemed fresher. There was more greenery present than in the claustrophobic confines of the South End Merchant's District. It was a sort of hidden paradise. Concealed between the false facade of the sprawling metropolis covered in shadows.

As they walked along the quite tree-lined avenues of the Central District. Bellamy realized that more and more of the people they crossed were higher ranked members of the theocracy. There were only handfuls of people around that weren't directly or appeared connected to the theocracy. He wasn't certain, but the area for all its pleasantness gave him an uneasy feeling. Liked their actions were being watched.

[*I should let Inara know, but I don't want to jump to any conclusions. For now, I'll keep an eye out and see how it goes. I'll make sure to mention it if it comes to that.*] Bellamy thought as they made their way to the university.

"If there is something bothering you, you know you can talk to me about it."

Bellamy was not surprised that Inara had said something. He figured she must have sensed something or saw something in his expression. They had been traveling for some time and have gotten to know each other. So it would only make sense to pick up when something was bothering them.

"I don't know, it feels like we've been watched ever since we crossed the bridge and came into this district. It's a little unnerving is all."

"Well, I see your senses have been improving with your training, that's good. Those skills will help you survive as challenges become more difficult. You're not wrong in your assumption, we are being watched."

Inara looked at him with calm eyes and waved her hand towards him to signal to him to not react. Bellamy saw and continued to walk, listening closely to what Inara was telling him.

"Keep acting normal and don't give off any sign that we know. We'll act if the time comes, but until then let's stay focused on why we're here. It could be people suspicious of outsiders and nothing more than that." Inara said in a whispered voice.

"If you think so, then alright. I will try to not let it distract me; I trust you."

Given that they were outsiders the places they could gain access to within the Central District was limited. So the university was the more logical choice for them to check out. The university in Nocturne was one of the oldest and most prestigious institutions in all the theocracy, outside of the Holy City of Larounge. Applicants from all over the theocracy and even some of the different nations would apply to be admitted to the great university. The university was a bit of a paradox in this regard.

It educated a variety of different people who would both go on to serve the theocracy and its beliefs. But also those who would go down other paths not in line with the theocracy. Thus, it contributed to the theocracy's survival. Along with its possible downfall in the same instant.

The university was surrounded by a high stone wall all the way around its perimeter. There was two entrances at the south and west ends of campus. Seven different colleges of concentration, four dorm houses, an administration building. Library, dining hall, chapel, and training arena made up the school's campus. The seven colleges of concentration were: Alchemical Studies, Business Administration.

Combative Warfare, Geo-Political Studies. Literature & Creative Studies, Daemons & World Phenomenon Studies, and World & Cultural Histories. Once admitted into the university students would undergo six years of study. Earning a Master's title in their chosen concentration. Be expelled if they failed to meet the college's requirements. Or were unable to defend their final dissertation. A fate however cruel that was unfortunately common for about eighty percent of students who enrolled into the prestigious university.

It was not a place for the faint of heart and as such was highly sot after despite its low passing rates. Honor and status were awarded to those few who are brave enough to take on the challenge of graduating from the university. Opening many opportunities not accessible if you came from a lower social class. Bellamy knew of the university and its reputation. He didn't see it aligning with his priorities in those earlier years.

Before he joined the Falling Star Mercenary Group. Though brief, seeing it now in person did make him wonder. In the back of his mind if it would have been worth considering. The manner in the way the students interacted with one another and the staff, reassured him that he had made the right decision in not applying to the university.

"For a place of learning and advancement, the students seem somewhat haunted. It's like they're present and not here at the same time. Consumed in only what is presently in front of them, not involved in the world around them. I especially see that in the older students. The younger ones still show a little gleam of expressiveness in them. This place would not have worked out for me. I enjoy my freedom and desire to explore too much for me to be confined in a place like this."

"This kind of environment is not the right sort for most people in general. I do understand how such places can be valuable to improving one's life or their communities. My mistress is one such individual who has benefitted from a place like this. She as such has used the knowledge she gained to grow to unimaginable heights. But I am not her and as such I have used life experiences and my mistress's teachings to gain my knowledge. Which I wouldn't have had it any other way."

After walking through the campus for some time. To get a general layout of the area and to lose their watcher's interest, they finally arrived at their destination. The School for Daemons & World Phenomenon Studies. The college was housed in a multi-storied stone and wood manor of Nocturne's Classical Gothic Era style. Prevalent during the theocracy's Middle Ages.

An architectural style that utilized characteristics as pointed arches, stained-glass windows, flying buttresses. Ribbed vaults, and spires in its design. This college was amongst the oldest of the seven colleges that made up the university. Playing a critical role in the research and understanding of Daemons. The various Mana World Phenomenon that affected different parts of the world. Inara figured they might find clues here. Something related to the incidents going on in the Renata Republic.

They made their way into the building through the massive doors beneath a circular stained-glass window depicting a fight between two Daemons. Students in black and emerald robes gathered around in the common area beyond the entrance a great hall. High ribbed vaults created a wide cavernous feeling in the room as they were talking. Studying in small groups, and making their way to another lecture. Bellamy watched and stood by as Inara walked over to one of the students, striking up a conversation.

After a few minutes, she waved him over to follow her. The student walked down a hallway and up a few flights of stairs with Inara and Bellamy following behind him. At the top of the stairs the student pointed to a door at the end of the hall. Before turning and heading off down the other hallway towards his next lecture.

"So, what was all that about?"

"I asked that student if he would be kind enough to show us the way to a professor who specialized in Daemons. That should be their office right over there. Let's go see if they will have a little chat with us."

They walked to the end of the hall and Inara knocked on the door the student had pointed at. There was no response at first, so she knocked again. This time a voice came from inside.

"It's open. You may come in."

Inara opened the door walking into the office. Bellamy came in afterwards closing the door behind him. The professor's office was a circular room with a curved bookcase along the wall. A large desk was at its center covered in tomes and parchments. Two chairs in front of it and one behind the desk as well as a window looking out to the courtyard below.

The professor was an older female human of rather striking beauty. In the scholarly robes of the faculty with long amber hair wearing thin framed glasses over her dark blue eyes sat at the desk drinking a cup of herbal tea. After setting her tea down, she gestured for Inara and Bellamy to take a seat. They made their way over to the chairs and sat down.

"Hello, I am Professor Ophelia. Lead researcher on all things Daemons and Mana World Phenomenon. I haven't seen your faces around here before. Are you new students, or are you here because you need my advice on something?"

"Greetings professor it is an honor to meet you. No, we aren't new students here, but we would like your advice on some interesting rumors that we've heard.?" Inara responded.

The professor picked up her teacup and took another sip of her herbal tea. Glancing over at Inara and Bellamy as she looked over her guests.

"Very well, what is it that makes these rumors you heard so interesting? Try not to waste my time if you will, I have my research and upcoming lecture that I need to finish preparing."

"We have no intention of taking up too much of your time. Have an open mind and I'm sure you'll find what my friend here has to say of interest." Bellamy chimed in to reassure the professor.

"I've heard that there have been sightings of Daemons of varying variety being used as weapons and pack animals against opponents. That the ones using them where somehow able to control and tame the Daemons to follow their orders. I was wondering if and how such a thing could be even possible, given their chaotic nature in all."

The professor sat back in her chair as she thought about what Inara had told her. She seemed to be intrigued by the idea and all the possible implications such a thing would mean for the future. Of not the theocracy but the whole world. Bellamy couldn't get a clear read on the professor. She was careful in what emotions her thoughts expressed on her face or through her body language.

This professor had a way about her that one would only expect to find in that of a skilled high-stakes card player. Who's fate was locked into how well they could read their opponent's and conceal their intentions. It was going to be important for Bellamy and Inara to listen in how the professor chooses her words. In the answers she gives them.

CHAPTER 38

"That's an interesting story that you have there miss, but I'm afraid it's just that, a story. It has been brought up in discussion amongst my colleagues in the past. Though there was no practical way of implementing the theory into actual use. There were too many unaccountable variables to consider. Let alone the life-threatening risk involved in even securing the proper test subjects. It was for these reasons that the idea was discarded by the institution. Deemed unauthorized to pursue."

"But professor, what if hypothetically speaking, someone had managed to find a means of utilizing a combination of Alchemical Engineering and *Arts* Abilities. Counteracting the chaotic nature of a Daemon's mind to subdue it to their will. Say through the means of an augmented Sealing Collar. Like the one that is supposedly used on slaves and prisoners with *Arts* abilities to keep them in check. Then wouldn't such a thing become more possible into making it a reality?"

Bellamy noticed a subtle smile on Inara's face, as her words seemed to have caught the professor off guard. The calm expression she had on her face, shifted to an uneasy irritation for a moment. When Inara had brought up the Sealing Collar. The professor was quick to hide her reaction. She grabbed her herbal tea and took another sip, composing herself once again. This didn't stop Inara from continuing with her questions.

"Now, if what I said was possible, then it would have to make you wonder. Where would someone come up with the means and backing to support such a dangerous endeavor? The only possible explanation would be that the person found a backer with significant power. Influence to support their work and keep it out of the public's view. So perhaps a private benefactor in the government or an upper-class noble. Even a foreign power who agreed with their views?"

The calmness in the professor's face had faded away completely. Replaced by visible anger and frustration in her eyes.

"I don't know who you think you are. I will not sit here and listen to baseless accusations that you are implying about me or one of my colleagues! Get out of my office this very instant, or I'll be forced to call the guards on you two!" She yelled out vehemently.

Bellamy and Inara raised from their seats, heading out of the professor's office. As Bellamy was closing the door behind him, he turned looking back at the professor. She threw her teacup towards his head. The teacup shattered into pieces as it hit the back of the door, Bellamy quickly closed behind him. Muffled sounds of the professor pacing and irritated thinking out loud echoed through the hallway. Bellamy hurried to catch up with Inara. Inara was at the other end of the hallway making her way back down the stairs when Bellamy caught up to her.

"Don't you think you might have been a bit too forward with your questions to the professor? You pretty much accused her of lying and being involved with the incidents."

"You're not wrong, but you saw the reaction she had at my questions. She all but confirmed that it was some form of augmented Sealing Collar. That the mercenaries were using to control their Daemons in the attacks. That and the theocracy is somehow involved along with another nation backing their interest. I have a feeling that there is more to this than that alone. Come, we need to get out of here before we find ourselves dealing with the guards."

Bellamy followed Inara as they headed down the stairs. Making their way through hallways and passages. Looking for another way out of the school building. They exited the building through a door leading out to the back courtyard that was visible from the window in the professor's office. They made their way through the groups of students gathering about.

Walking slowly but with purpose to not draw the attention of anyone around them. The crowds of students were starting to die down and disperse. They left the perimeter of the school building back towards the open campus grounds. They walked through the campus grounds towards the West End entrance. Heading back out into the district, Bellamy and Inara found themselves walking alone in a area with no students or faculty around them.

A chill ran down Bellamy's back and an icy breath left his mouth, as a cold unnatural mist filled the air. Everything around them become shrouded in the mist. They could hardly see anything beyond their fingertips. Bellamy and Inara both stopped where they were, not wanting to get separated in the mist from each other. He reached out and grabbed the shoulder in front of him, which he thought was Inara's. It belonged to a woman, but she was not Inara.

Bellamy didn't understand what was going on, he and Inara had been standing relatively close together. [So, *who was this woman that he had grabbed on to. Where did Inara go?*] he thought as the woman turned around to look at Bellamy. He took a sudden step away from her. He saw the woman in black robes, wearing a metal and leather strapped cuirass, a crimson red sash around her waist, and a Harlequin mask on her face. With sultry Lavender eyes she looked deep into the depths of Bellamy's soul from beneath her mask.

"Who are you, and what is going on?" Bellamy asked unsettled.

"I am no more than a devout follower of the one true god, Nimh. I protect the faithful, seek out and punish those who violate or doubt his will, and all forms of heresy. I am *The Queen of Diamonds*, High Inquisitor Althea of the Nimh Theocracy's Inquisition. I have some questions I would like to ask you if you don't mind."

Bellamy didn't know what was going on, only that he needed to be careful around this woman. He had to figure out where Inara went and how to get back to her. He wasn't going to be able to do that with this High Inquisitor standing next to him. The only thing he could do for the time being was to see what she wanted and find a way to get her to leave. Whether that would work out that way or even be possible, Bellamy had no other ideas before him.

"I'm not sure if I'll be of any help to you, ma'am. You see this is my first time here and I don't know my way all that well around the city yet."

"Now. Now. There's no need to be nervous. I promise not to take up too much of your time, Bellamy..." The High Inquisitor paused. She watched the subtle twitch in his body language and look in his eyes from her words.

"You are Bellamy, right? Or I have you mistaken with someone else. But no, you are indeed Bellamy Leone of the Falling Star Mercenary Group. The one that operates out of Aurontil in the Renata Republic. You are a long way from home, and what brought you all the way to Nocturne?" She spoke with a chill seductive charm that struck like daggers with every word.

"No, ma'am you are right. I am indeed that Bellamy that you speak of. I have done nothing wrong as to warrant the interest of the Nimh Theocracy's Inquisition. I was only taking some personal time to travel around with some companions. Visiting different places we haven't been before and explore the sights." Bellamy responded with a calm and even tone. Not to seem suspicious or lie about being someone else when she knew who he was.

"I see. Hmm...Then you might be able to help me out with this?"

The High Inquisitor pulled out a wanted poster from within her robes and showed it to Bellamy. On the wanted poster was the following: [*Wanted Dead or Alive. The Ogre Pirate Caspian for charges of piracy. Smuggling. Sedition against the theocracy, and the killing of inquisitors. A reward was being offered for information or the capture of the fugitive and his whereabouts. It was noted that he was armed and dangerous, that he shouldn't be taken likely if encountered.*]

"Sorry, but I have no idea of who that person is and haven't even heard of him until you showed me that wanted poster."

The High Inquisitor folded up the wanted poster and put it back into her robes. She turned and started to walk away, but not before leaving Bellamy with some parting advice.

"I would be careful in who you call friend. That very friend that you value could just as easily be the one to bring you to your downfall. Learn it well or you'll be in for more hurt in this unforgiving world. Until the next time."

Her words echoed in Bellamy's ears, as she walked away disappearing into the mist. The mist covering the area began to fade away. Bellamy was standing next to Inara again, who looked at him with a puzzled look in her eyes.

"Are you alright? The last thing I remember was that you stopped and had a dazed look on your face. I called out to you and even shuck you, but there was no response. Then a strange mist surrounded us, until now when it cleared, and you moved again. What happened?"

Bellamy recalled what transpired. He told Inara about his encounter and conversation with the High Inquisitor Althea. The wanted poster she showed him. He could see that Inara was bothered by the events, and that she had failed to notice her presence watching them. It wasn't an easy task to escape Inara's notice. Only demonstrating that they needed to take caution with dealing with the Inquisitors. They would have to warn the others when they got back to the inn. Their mission was hit with an unexpected complication.

"I would rather not cross her path again if it can be helped. Its best if we try to stay out of the sights of the Inquisition for as long as possible. Once, we hear what the others have found out, it would be best to make our way out of Nocturne as soon as possible."

"The Inquisition is a complication that we should avoid for the time being. Getting the information, we came for and getting it back to Hoenheim is of the utmost importance. So let's focus on that and not become their target." Inara replied agreeingly.

"Good. Sounds like a plan. Let's head back to the inn now, that was enough excitement for one day."

The two of them left the campus grounds, making their way back through the Central District. To the bridge that would take them back towards the South End Merchant's District. As the day went on the streets of the city became less crowded. As people were making their ways back home or to cafes and taverns for a bite to eat. The breathtaking aromas of different dishes filled the air and taunted Bellamy's nose.

They passed by cafes on the street and taverns down another. He could feel his stomach grumble, pleading to be filled with some of the tasty food he passed along the way to the inn. Soon, they would be back, and Bellamy would be able to have his fill and sooth his hunger.

Bellamy and Inara seemed to be the first to get back to the Inn. They took the opportunity to fill their stomachs and get something to eat. After, their supper, Bellamy and Inara sat around the table having a few drinks. While they continued to wait for their companions to return. The last hours of day had come and gone when the door to the inn opened and Draemond came through.

Bellamy didn't know what happened to him and Raine, but he could see exhaustion in his eyes. The way he carried himself as he made his way over to them. When he sat down, Inara handed him a tankard of ale. He grabbed and took long sips of the sweet ambrosia colored liquid inside.

The exhaustion on his face faded away. He was finally able to release the tension from simultaneously keeping his guard up and walking. Not to draw attention as he headed back to the inn.

"Are you alright? Where is Raine? You both left for the Narrows District this morning, and you came back looking all exhausted. What happened to you guys?"

"So, Raine hasn't made it back yet? I see…" Draemond paused as he took another sip of his ale before continuing.

Draemond told Bellamy and Inara of the excursion he had in the Narrows District with Raine earlier in the day. About how Raine had found out that his mother was still alive and in this city. The Slaver's auction they attended and how it was brought to a sudden end. How Raine killed the announcer and rescued his mother. Then how they escaped to hide in an abandoned warehouse for some time.

Until they were able to get passage on a ship for Raine's mother out of the city and back to Aurontil. Finally, Draemond told how they then split-up to not draw attention and find their own ways back to the inn.

CHAPTER 39

"That is crazy to think, That Raine would find his mother alive and well. Not to mention everything that you all went through afterwards. I'm glad that you made it out and back safely. I'm sure Raine will be popping up any moment now. He tends to have a habit of making people worry about him, but he still always comes back."

"Aww. Was the kid, worried about me?" Raine's familiar voice sounded off behind Bellamy.

Bellamy and the others turned. Seeing Raine walking over from the reception counter with a note in hand to join the group at the table. He sat down and grabbed one of the other tankards of ale that was on the table, helping himself to a drink.

"You, bastard. How long have you been back?" Bellamy replied with a slight irritation.

"Not too long, I walked in when I heard you talking about me. It's good to see that you made it back Draemond."

"You, as well my friend. I wasn't sure how you would be, after the emotional whirlwind you've been through today."

Raine leaned back in his chair, as he sipped his ale. He had that same charismatic smile on his face, the mask he wore to keep his emotions in check and his mind clear.

"I'll be fine, I needed a little fresh air to sort my thoughts. But that aside, I see that the girls haven't returned yet. Should we be concerned by that?"

"I know the girls can take care of themselves, but it does seem a little odd that we haven't heard from them. Considering we did agree to meet back here tonight. They would have left a note or something if they were going to be late."

Raine handed Bellamy the note he had gotten from the front desk.

"Perhaps, that is what the note's about. The Proprietress at the front desk said that a note was dropped off earlier today addressed to you."

Bellamy opened the note and read it over. He was speechless as the note fell from his hand to land on the table. Inara reached over and picked up the note and read its contents out loud for everyone in the group to hear.

"[*Greetings,*

You and your companions have crossed into the Theocracy's territory illegally. As such are guilty of conspiracy against the Theocracy. Your friends have been taken prisoner to be questioned. They will be held at Nalran Prison until their judgement has been passed. You are more than welcome to come and try to take them back if you can that is. Come rescue them or flee and run, it doesn't matter to me what you do. Our judgement will be swift and final for all those who defy the Theocracy.

High Inquisitor Tearyn, Jack of Clubs]"

Everyone looked around the table at one another. Silent as they processed what Inara read to them in the note. It was hard to believe that the girls had been captured by the Inquisition and were being held in a prison. Both Draemond and Raine grabbed the note from Inara's hand and read it over again. They themselves checking to see that what she read was true.

They knew she had no reason to lie or play a cruel joke on them. But knowing that the contents of the note were genuine was a truth that was hard to accept. After some time, Bellamy finally spoke up and expressed his thoughts on the matter.

"I know this may not be the best course of action to take, but I can't sit by and abandon them. Without any doubt it is likely a trap, still I want to go and rescue them. I cannot make you come and risk your lives, so I am only asking if you would continue to support me and offer your aide."

"That my friend was a question not worth even asking. Whether it was the girls or not, we don't abandon those who need our help. Besides, that brat will owe me one for saving her ass again."

"We're not going anywhere, so you can count on us as well." Inara and Draemond said in agreement.

Inara got up from the table and walked over to the front desk to have a conversation with the proprietress. Their conversation lasted for a while. Bellamy noticed the shocked and concerned look on the woman's face. Inara asked her about anything she might know about Nalran Prison and its location. When Inara finished up, she headed back to the table.

Sitting down and discussing the information she found out with the others. Before she began talking, she pulled out her Wayfarer's Map from her pouch and unfolded it on the table. As she concentrated the map shifted from its current city view to a general regional view. Showing the area around Nocturne and the surrounding areas.

"According to the proprietress, Nalran Prison was built into the cliffside of a valley. Located about four to five days Southwest of Nocturne. There is a river that flows close to the valley. The only access into the valley is through a land pass. The mountain range surrounding the valley is dangerous and unstable for travelers to cross. She said that in ages past Nalran was a Dwarven Mining settlement. Before a catastrophe wiped it out and the Dwarves were forced to abandon it. Then many years later, the Theocracy found it and transformed it into the prison it is today. She also mentioned that it's a terrible and cursed place. That many unfortunate souls never leave who are sentenced to be confined there."

"Sounds like a lovely place..." Raine replied with a hint of sarcasm.

"Well, jokes aside this a going to be a difficult undertaking no matter how you look at it. The main concern is whether we travel there by a land route or the more direct route of the river to the land pass. Each option has its own challenges and benefits. But which would be the most beneficial to us is the real question."

Inara, Raine, and Draemond where thinking over the options Bellamy pointed out. They couldn't afford to make a rash decision. Whatever option they ended up choosing, they would have to live with that choice. However the outcome turns out. Time was a factor in their decisions as well.

The longer they took the more their friends would have to endure until they got there. Making it to the prison was one thing. They would have to figure out where their friends are being held and a way to escape from there afterwards. assuming they're able to rescue them in the first place. It is never a good ideal to dwell on negative possibilities or what ifs. It was important to understand the reality of a given situation. Bellamy and the others were aware of the risks involved in the choices they make.

"It might take us longer to get to the prison, but I think the land route is the best option to take. Though faster, the direct route by the river comes with more complications, than the four of us want to deal with. That being the river patrols and the three checkpoints along the river."

Inara was the first to offer her opinion in the discussion. Draemond decided that he would follow whatever decision was made. He hadn't known the girls for as long as the others and felt it was best to let the others decide on the matter. Raine was next to give his thoughts.

"I understand the risk involved, but we should take the more direct route. Given the situation there is a albeit small chance that the enemy wouldn't expect us to take a bold action like that. So, the security should be at normal levels and not at a heightened state. I know it's not full proof, but it would be the option that saves us more time. Well, Bellamy what do you think given that the final decision is up to you, as we stand at a tie."

Bellamy understood the responsibility of being the deciding vote. How he would have to deal with the aftermath of his decision, but he always tried to avoid it whenever possible. Lately he wasn't so lucky and had to accept the responsibility even if he never asked for it. This decision was pulling at him from all directions. Knowing that whatever he chose his friends were still going to suffer.

There wasn't anything he could do about it. Bellamy did something he hadn't done for some time. He prayed silently thinking, [*please watch over Na'naya and Amiriss. Divine Night Mother. Protect your children with your grace so that they may stay strong and endure until we are able to rescue them.*]

"I've heard both sides and thought about it. I want to rescue the girls as soon as possible, but we can't risk being overconfident and bold. We will take the longer land route to the prison. The girls are strong and with luck they should be capable of holding out till we get there. We need to believe in them and believe in ourselves to make up time whenever possible on our way there."

"Alright, you can count on us." The others responded in agreement.

"Then let's prepare and head out first thing in the morning."

Inara folded up her map and put it back into her pouch. They stayed at the table discussing their plans, before heading back to their rooms. Getting their last night of rest in Nocturne. The streets were empty and the people still asleep in their beds. The first rays of light hit the top of the buildings and the early morning mist of the river slowly faded away.

Bellamy and the others were already outside the city gates. Heading down the road leading South from the city. They decided to follow the road for the first couple of days of their journey. Before going off the trail into the wilderness and Southwest towards the prison. The main roads and highways of the Nimh Theocracy were well maintained cobblestone and packed earth roads. They provided easier travel for traveling caravans and merchants between cities and regions within the theocracy.

People on mounts as well as traveling on foot were not an uncommon sight to see on the main roads and highways. Bellamy and the others only ever interacted with travelers they passed on the roads in circumstantial encounters. Preferring not to get involved in the affairs of others. In return, the other travelers would generally do the same but that wasn't always the case. They would have to interact as to not draw suspicion.

It was during one such encounter that Bellamy and the others came across some unexpected information. On the afternoon of their second day of travel down the highway. The group encountered a traveling merchant heading back north.

The traveling merchant was an older Fae male of the Gnome variety with Honey-Brown eyes, pointed ears long grey dreadlocks and bread tied in a braid. Wearing a casual travel tunic, quilted vest and woven trousers, gear which all had seen better days. It was worn and tattered but had finely woven patchwork on his sleeves and trousers. On his back was an enormous backpack unbelievably big for one his size. It was stuffed to the brim with his assortment of merchandise.

From trinkets to medicine and everything in-between. If there was something exotic or unexpected that was hard to find or common everyday goods, this merchant was the person to seek. As he approached Bellamy and the others, he stopped and waved over to them.

"Greetings, fellow travelers. Allow me to introduce myself. My name is Pip, *Purveyor of Provisions, Merchant of many things. Curator of Curios,* and a favorite of mine *Weaver of Wonders.* Could I interest you in some of my wares?"

The others didn't seem to be interested in amusing the traveling merchant to see what he had to offer. But Bellamy was curious to see what he had.

CHAPTER 40

"Alright, Pip. I would like to see what you have to offer."

The traveling merchant smiled as he took off his backpack and placed it between him and Bellamy. The moment the backpack touched the ground, something that Bellamy could not understand happened. It was as if time itself had stopped all around him. His friends seemed motionless as statues and off in the close distance two birds appeared to be frozen in mid-air. The only ones that were moving was Bellamy and the traveling merchant.

"What is the meaning of this?... How is this even possible...What did you do, Pip?"

There was an uneasiness to the traveling merchant's smile. Something about it troubled Bellamy but he didn't seem to mean him or his friends any harm.

"Don't worry my friend, everything will be as it was soon. When we are done, all this will feel like no more than a fleeting dream. So, tell me Bellamy, what has caused your group to head away from Nocturne and head towards Nalran Prison?"

Bellamy was feeling a bit unsettled. Running into yet another person who already knew who he was. Even though it was their first time meeting each other. Though, from the moment Pip first introduced himself, he suspected that there was more to this traveling merchant than what his eyes could see before him.

"My friends Na'naya and Amiriss have been captured by the Inquisition. We are heading to Nalran Prison to rescue them. I know that it's going to be near impossible to do on our own, but we can't leave them there. We need to find a way to give ourselves a better chance at succeeding even if only a small one."

"I see. Well, you're in luck for I might have something of interest to you and your endeavors." Pip replied with a sly smile.

He opened the top of his backpack and leaned inside. Searching, and rummaging through his wares. The backpack was no doubt much larger on the inside than it looked. Pip's whole upper body went into the backpack as he was reaching for the item he was searching for. When he emerged, he had in his hand a small Obsidian Ore spinning top enclosed in a starry metallic binding. Engraved with strange runic glyphs on the surfaces. A faint luminous glow emanated from within the spinning top. Bellamy couldn't take his eyes off the mysterious item in Pip's hand.

"What is it?"

"Aww, This. This my friend is a rare and ancient Mana tool known as a *Chrono Trigger*. It has the unique ability of being able to break the world's natural laws. Sending the user five minutes back in time. It is capable of being used only three times, then it will be erased from existence. But such power doesn't come without a price to be paid and the price for this is no feeble matter."

Pip could see the look of determination in Bellamy's eyes. That he wasn't afraid to accept the risk and pay the price for the power.

"Four years... Four years off your lifespan every time you use the tool. Be warned if someone else uses the tool, nothing will happen. But it will still count as one of the three uses and the toll will be taken from you. So, knowing what you know now do you still want the mana tool?"

Bellamy reached out his hand and grabbed the spinning top from Pip's hand into his own.

"Then we have a deal. Before I leave you, let me offer you some information. Instead of heading straight to Nalran prison. Continue down this road for three more days until you reach the port city of Kor'Jarin. There is a person who is rumored to have escape Nalran Prison and may prove valuable to your cause."

Pip then clapped his hands and in a blink of an eye, everything was as it was. But there was no sign of the traveling merchant Bellamy had been talking to. Bellamy walked back over to his companions. Telling them about his strange encounter with the traveling merchant and the information he gave him. He decided that he would keep the part about the mana tool he acquired to himself for the time being.

Somethings where better off being left unsaid. Bellamy could tell that the others were having some doubts about his story. They barely recalled seeing such a traveling merchant on the road. Even so, they listened to what their friend had to tell them.

"I don't know, how I feel about taking a detour and traveling farther away from our friends to find some help. There is no telling if we'll even be able to find the person, let alone how long it might even take to do so." Raine responded with concern.

"I understand where you're coming from, but I think it's worth taking the traveling merchant's advice. We likely are only going to have one shot in rescuing our friends from that prison. So it would be beneficial for us to find any advantage we can to succeed. I am open to other options but this one seems to be our best choice."

"You're right as usual my friend. Don't let it go to that head of yours, there is still a lot you need to learn about the world, kid."

The group proceeded to make their way down the highway following it South for three more days. On the third day as the sun was rising in the distance, Bellamy saw on the horizon a sight he hadn't seen for a while. The vast wide openness of the Sapphire colored waters of the Evening Star Sea. Walking to top of a hill Bellamy and the others looked down the road. They saw on the coast, nestled in the cape just past the lighthouse was the port city of Kor'Jarin, their next destination.

The port city was divided into three districts: The New Town, The Old Town, and The Merchant's Port. Many of the Nimh Theocracy's imports and exports came through Kor'Jarin before making their way to other parts of the theocracy.

The port city's strategic and economic location made it one of the nation's prosperous strongholds. Giving it special authoritative powers not common in the theocracy's other cities. As such the city has experienced unparalleled autonomy when it comes to dealing with both foreign and domestic policies. Such policies over the years have given rise to the unofficial moniker that Kor'Jarin has become known by. By those of more ambiguous alignments as *The City of Thieves*.

For wherever there is a prosperous economy. Little to no outside interference, and opportunity for those willing to take it. A haven for those who operate outside the law following their own desires emerges. Law and Order may rule over the city. But it is the cunning ones who have found a way to operate under their righteous stuck-up noses. Hiding in plain sight.

"So, did that traveling merchant happen to tell you who it is that we should be looking for?"

"About that. All he mentioned was that the person was said to be in Kor'Jarin and that they managed to escape from Nalran Prison. That's all, sorry."

Raine tapped his foot on the ground. Feeling annoyed that they didn't have anything to go on to conduct their search. Other than the vague description. Draemond took his pipe from his pack and lit the contents inside, before handing it to Raine. Raine took a couple of puffs, slowly beginning to calm his nerves and clear his annoyance. He then passed it back to Draemond who took some puffs as well. Right before providing some input into the conversation.

"So, if we want to find this mystery person, then we should check out the local taverns in the Old Town District. It would give us a feel for the city and helps us find some information on the person, whether its rumor or not. Anything now could prove useful in our search."

"I agree. That plan of yours is solid and could work out in our favor. Let's make our way into the city and find a place to stay first before we start our search."

Inara placed a hand on Draemond's shoulder, showing support for his plan. She then walked past them heading down the hill along the road towards the city. Bellamy turned towards

Draemond and Raine. Nodding his agreement as well before following Inara. The two of them followed behind the others, making their way down the road to Kor'Jarin. As they passed through the city gates, Bellamy noticed wanted posters hanging along the walls.

One of the wanted posters, Bellamy remembered seeing before. It was the one the High Inquisitor had asked him about. It could be a mere coincidence or happenstance. Bellamy was starting to think that the man from the wanted poster was the one that Pip had mentioned for him to find. The streets of the port city were bustling with life.

Crowds of people from regions and lands all over mingled here. Unlike Nocturne, though present the theocracy's doctrine was not all consuming. Meaning there were more non-human races around. It was somewhat out of place and otherworldly to see, within the theocracy's domain.

Given the city's location and wider autonomy. It made sense to the locals that their city was an outlier. One the theocracy allowed for as long as it benefitted them. They understood the freedoms they enjoyed would be much more restricted in other cities. That it could all be taken away from them if they went against the theocracy's authority.

So, the ones who chose to live their lives in such a place knew it was a false paradise that was best left the way it was. After wandering the streets, Bellamy and the others finally found a small inn on the edge of the New Town District. It had rooms available for them to stay in. The inn was an old two-story carriage house, that was called *The Weeping Widow*. It was run by a young married couple who had inherited the place from the husband's mother-in-law.

"Greetings travelers, welcome to our lovely little inn. I am Dawn, and the man over there in the kitchen preparing meals is my husband, Marco. How may we be of service to you?"

"We are in need of two rooms for a few days?" Bellamy replied.

Dawn looked over Bellamy and his friends with a glance. It seemed to come from a place of curiosity, more than uncertainty. Her eyes were fixated on Inara and Draemond.

"Pardon my staring, I do not mean to be rude. It's just that we don't see your kind around here very often. A Half-Giant is one thing, but I couldn't tell you the last time I've seen a Dragonkin. You have some interesting members in your party and must have traveled a long way to come here."

"Yes, my friends and I have traveled a long way indeed. That is why we are hoping that you have some rooms available for us? I was also wondering if you happen to know where we might find a guide."

"Here you go. You may use two rooms on the second floor, up the stairs and at the end of the hall on the right. As for a guide, I can't say for certain but the Hunter's Guild in the New Town District might be of help. If that's not quite what you're looking for, then in the Old Town District near the docks is a tavern and gambling hall called *The Siren's Song*. Just be careful if you head there, it's not the sort of crowd one would want to be around."

Bellamy took the keys to the rooms from Dawn and handed one to Inara. They left the front desk and headed up to their rooms to drop off their belongings. Afterwards, they met back downstairs and headed out.

CHAPTER 41

After giving it some thought. Bellamy and the others decided that The Siren's Song should be the first place they check. Given the type of people who go there. For the person they were looking for, the Old Town district made the most sense if you were trying to hide from the authorities and still wanted control over your actions. Compared to the New Town District, the streets in the Old Town District were twisted and narrow.

A reminder of older times when such layouts were a necessary defensive measure against outside attacks. The buildings appeared in more rugged and rundown conditions. With worn paint, loose bricks, missing roof tiles, and broken or boarded windows. It was clear to see that the older district was neglected and left to deal with their own troubles. A shell of its former self that could barely be seen on the surface if you looked close enough.

The city's ruling authority and utter abandonment of the Old Town District was the very cause of its eventual fall. Into the corruption and lawlessness present there now. During the day the district was like any other. Filled with crowds of people traveling and shopping albeit in a smaller capacity because of the area. The locals came to an understanding that the streets where no place to wandering around after sunset in the Old Town District.

When the dimly lit lanterns started to glow. At night however, the district was a hauntingly empty place. Except for the few pockets of rowdy, dangerous, and raucous commotions that filled the taverns, gambling halls, and brothels. Bellamy and the others were wandering through the twisted streets of the district. Draemond spotted a sign hanging over an archway leading up staircase to an establishment above them.

"We have found the place the innkeeper mentioned, *The Siren's Song*. So, what's the plan?"

"Let's go inside and get a feel for the place. Observe what goes on and see if we can find some information on the person we are looking for. We don't want to draw too much attention on us, so try being subtle in your approaches." Bellamy explained with a calm even tone.

"Sounds good."

The Siren's Song was one of those types of places where if you didn't see it with your own eyes, you wouldn't believe it. Outside the building was like any other one in the Old Town District in disrepair and abandon looking. Inside it was like a scene taken out of a fairytale. Elegant silk drapes and intricately crafted metal lanterns hanged from the ceiling. Finely carved wooden booths with cushioned pillows spread across the main floor.

Surrounding the marvel of crafted stone and oak round bar. A massive stage in the center of it all. Holding the attention of the patrons captive. An alluring songstress sang a haunting soulful ballad. She was accompanied by a bard troupe behind her.

["*Far away. Far away.*

Across the seas of time, in ages past long ago.

Great heroes arose in epic battles against threats Divine.

Scattered across the shattered realms, they journeyed to restore what was lost.

Far away. Far away.

They never considered what it would be the true cost.

For with their victory came a time of peace and prosperity.

As the heroes were cursed to be haunted by those who perished.

Far away. Far away.

Forever locked in an endless battle.

May this sound carry their hopes and free their dreams.

Rest great heroes and be at peace.

Far away. Far away."]

The boisterous sounds of the patrons at the gambling tables echoed from the floor below. were bets and games were being played.

Bellamy and Inara grabbed a tankard from the bar. Before finding a booth to sit at, while Raine and Draemond went off to check the gambling tables. Though, as those two went off they became separated as a beautiful young serving wench caught Raine's eye. He proceeded to strike up a conversation, she smiled and laughed as she was drawn in by his roguish charm. Draemond then headed down to the gambling tables alone, leaving Raine to his own devices.

However unorthodox it may come off as, Raine had a way. Always finding out information from such interactions. That was one trick of Raine's that Bellamy couldn't seems to pick up. Despite Raine showing him how to do it on a few different occasions. it never felt natural to him and that was the most important part, making it come off as naturally as possible.

"You know, I'm surprised this place is rather lively, given where its located and all. Though, people have said that some of the best things can be found in the most unexpected of places. It doesn't disappoint."

"Bellamy you think the person the traveling merchant told you about is that Ogre Pirate from the wanted poster outside the city?"

Bellamy took a drink of his ale from the tankard and leaned in closer to Inara, so that he could talk in a quieter tone. The tavern was bursting with conversations, but he didn't want his being heard. They were in an unfamiliar city and place. With no certainty that people would be willing to help them or even trust them. It was best to stay optimistically cautious.

"I don't think it was a coincidence that the traveling merchant sent us here. That I end up seeing the same wanted poster the High Inquisitor asked me about. The Ogre Pirate Caspian must be the one we're looking for; he has to be."

"You know you can count on me. If we take our time and feel this place out, I'm sure we are bound to find him. There are only so many places one can go in a city such as this if you're trying to stay out of the authority's sight."

They sat at the booth and drank tankard after tankard of ale. Watching the patrons as they came and left throughout the night. As the night went on and the minutes turned to hours. Bellamy had slowed down on his consumption of alcohol. He couldn't keep up with Inara's Half-Giant stamina and needed to get some fresh air.

He got up from the booth and made his way out onto the balcony past the bar. The balcony was attached to the backside of the tavern, with a serene view. Looking out over the lower parts of the port and the dazzling sea beyond. Both twin moons were visible on the mildly cloudy and star filled night.

Bellamy wasn't the only one taking in the fresh air of the calm night. In a corner off to the right of him was a figure leaning back in a chair smoking a pipe and staring out to sea. A long dark rugged cloak covered the stranger's body. Bellamy couldn't make out his features from where he was standing. As the clouds parted and moonlight illuminated the balcony more, he saw the stranger for who he was.

He was a middle-aged Demi-Human of the Ogre variety. Wearing a Burgundy patterned bandana covering long wavy dreads of Silver and Purple. Pointed ears with two small piercings in each ear and a long pendant earing hanging from the left ear. He had two-horns centered on his forehead with one slightly more prominent than the other. Calm sapphire eyes deep in color as the Evening Star Sea.

Beneath the long dark rugged cloak, he wore a layered canvas tunic with a padded quarter vest over it. Strapped across his chest and over the silk sash around his waist was a unique sword with a strange handle in a scabbard. Also a leather bandolier with many pouches. Dark canvas trousers and knee-high boots adorned his legs and feet. He had looked as fierce and elegant as his wanted poster described him.

Bellamy was grateful for whatever luck had led him to the Ogre Pirate Caspian. He stood there in silence looking at him, as he searched for the words to say to him. There was no time to waste by standing there and doing nothing. Bellamy walked over to Caspian and sat down in a chair across from him.

"You know it can be dangerous for one's health, to intrude on a person's personal space, boy. So, I would suggest you leave me be and I will let this little indiscretion go."

"I meant no offense, it's when I saw you, I had to come over and see for myself. You are him aren't you, the Ogre Pirate Caspian?"

"And who might you be, boy?"

"My apologies. I am Bellamy."

Caspian took a long puff from his pipe. He blew out a trail of smoke that drifted off into the night sky, carried on the cool breeze. His aloft glaze shifted locking on to Bellamy like prey marked by a hunter's sight.

"What business do you have, that you would seek out the likes of me and my kind?"

"My companions and I came searching for a guide to help us with a rather challenging endeavor. We heard rumors that you might be the person we're looking for."

The semblance of a faint smile crossed his face. Caspian took another long puff from his pipe as he blew the smoke into the air.

"You don't say and just what is this job that you require my assistance as a guide is? Deep sea exploration, treasure hunting in some ancient ruins. Leading a caravan through uncharted territories. Perhaps retrieving something precious that was taken from you. Whatever the job may be, there is no one better than me."

"That's exactly what we need, the best. We need you to guide us into Nalran Prison, so we can rescue our friends who have been taken captive and sent there. What do you say, can you help us?"

Caspian stared off into the distance, the look on his face was solemn as he took in another puff of his pipe. He exhaled the smoke slowly, passing through his lips and out into the night sky. The mood between them had changed as the ebbing tide. Bellamy sensed that his words had brought up complicated emotions within. Breaking the tranquil calmness that Caspian had given off.

"Give up and go home. If you want to rescue your friends, then the best thing you can do is leave them be. They are on their own now and must learn to accept that and adapt or become swallowed up as a forgotten one to that place. It is a place that will break you down mentally and physically until there is nothing left but a numb husk. No more than a shadow of the person you once were. Only isolation and despair await those condemned to that accursed place. There is no escape from there."

Bellamy felt his frustration and anger tense up in his body. He was unwilling to accept what Caspian had told him. He slammed his fist into the wall behind his chair. The impact caused his hand to tremble as he tried to re-center his emotions.

"I don't want to hear that crap! I'm not about to give up and abandon my friends, because you say that there is no hope. That's not true and you know that you've obviously been there before and somehow found a way to escape. So, it's not impossible to do but I need your help if I'm going to succeed."

"Ah...Ha...You're a fool, but you most certainly got spirit. I'll give you that much, but we'll see if you're up to the task. Alright, if you want my help then you'll have to do something for me first."

"Tell me what it is, and I'll get it done."

"Good, no hesitation, I like that. My vessel is currently undergoing some critical repairs and upgrades, so it won't be ready for a few more months. But before it can be completed there is a component that I need you to retrieve for me. Its located inside of an alchemic research lab beneath the Kor'Jarin Lighthouse."

Caspian reached into his cloak pulling out a folded piece of parchment and handed it to Bellamy.

"Everything you need to know about the component and the lab is on that parchment. I'll leave the rest up to you. If your able to get the component bring it to me. Three miles northwest of the city, there is an old stone quarry where I'll be waiting. You have six months, that is all the time I can give you. Succeed or fail, in six months I'm leaving this place with or without you."

"Got it. We'll get the job done for you, so make sure you keep up on your end of the deal. Though, what is with the time frame?"

Caspian blew one last puff from his pipe, putting it away into one of his pouches, before he got up from his chair. He walked over to the edge of the balcony and stood up on the rail, turning his body to face Bellamy.

"Oh, trust me. You'll be welcoming the time I've given you. See you around, Bellamy."

With those last words, Caspian jumped back off the ledge and vanished into the night. Bellamy sat in the chair for a little longer. Enjoying the night air before making his way back inside to rejoin the others.

CHAPTER 42

The next morning Bellamy awoke to the rhythmic sound of rain drops tapping against the roof tiles. Trickling down the bedroom window. A light spring shower had come with the rising sun. After his conversation with Caspian, Bellamy had returned to the others. He told them what had transpired.

They stayed at the Siren's Song into the late hours of the night. Enjoying themselves before making their way back to the inn. Draemond had some uncanny luck that night. Winning a decent prize from a high-stakes game of Sojuko. It was a strategic tarot card game of two to six players. Where wagers are placed and the player with the higher hand combination would win the round.

The different combinations of cards, along with intricate rules of play made the game popular amongst the Middle and Upper classes. They could appreciate the strategic thinking and subtlety that went into the game. A simpler version of the game much like a game known as poker, was more embraced by the masses. Making Sojuko a widespread game that could be found in gambling halls and casinos throughout the civilized world. Raine was lucky in another way that night.

His charm gained him an admirer and he left with the young serving wench. He had returned to the inn an hour ago, making his way up to the room to change and wash up. Bellamy knew that his friend was bothered by the events and still processing. He would only tend to have a random tryst with women when he needed another way to distract his thoughts and clear his mind.

It didn't happen all that often. By the end of however long the affair may last, it usually involved the woman either wanting to see him again. Whenever he was back in that town or her heartbroken and wanting nothing to do with him ever again. His actions where ultimately an extremely fine double-edged sword. That would cut those involved with him emotionally one way or the other.

After he had finished cleaning up, Raine headed back downstairs to join Bellamy and the others for breakfast. He sat down at the table, while Bellamy passed him a cup of coffee and a bowl of porridge with fruit and mixed nuts.

"Long night with that young maiden I see. Well, I hope you managed to get some rest because it looks like we are going to have some long days ahead of us." Draemond responded with a stoic tease in his voice.

"One of many I suspect, but that is a tale for another time. What did Draemond mean by long days ahead, Bellamy?"

Bellamy pulled out the parchment Caspian had given him the other night. He handed it to Raine, while he explained everything. Raine unfolded the parchment and read it over, glancing over its contents.

"As I was telling the others, Caspian gave us a job to do if we want his help on our mission to rescue our friends. There is a component that he wants us to retrieve for him and we have six months max to do so. The component in question is in an alchemic research lab hidden beneath the lighthouse. It's some sort of ancient tech power source according to what the parchment says. Why Caspian wants it I can't say for sure, other than that he needed it for his vessel."

"So, what are your thoughts?"

Bellamy sat back in his chair. Thinking for a moment about what their next steps should be, before giving his response to the others. Inara watched him to see how he would handle the situation. She had been pleased with the growth he has been showing over their time traveling together. She would provide her advice or input if Bellamy couldn't figure out what to do. But that wasn't necessary this time around.

"Given that we don't know the area and are going in blind minus what little information we do have. It would be best for us to take are time and scout out the area. We need to gather as much information as we can and then come up with a plan to complete the job."

"Sounds good. Though there is a complication that you all should be aware of. I head last night from one of the patrons at the Siren's Song that the High Inquisitor known as the Ten of Spades is rumored to be here in the city. We should try to avoid encountering them if possible."

"It doesn't make this any easier. We will continue with the current plan and adjust accordingly should the need arises to do so."

Raine folded up the parchment and handed it back to Bellamy. Then finished up his breakfast before heading out into the city to gather information. Inara got up afterwards and followed Raine out. Choosing to tag along with him this time around, leaving Bellamy and Draemond to team up. Bellamy was excited for the chance to team up with the Dragonkin warrior.

They hadn't had the opportunity yet to work together as just the two of them. This would give them the chance to get a better understanding of one another and their unique skills. The two of them got up from the table and headed out into the city to gather information as well.

When Bellamy and Draemond left the inn, they followed the narrow twisting streets. Down the edge of the district leading to the wider avenues of the New Town District. The people living in this part of the city were lively and carefree. Enjoying the prosperity the city provided for them. Everything from houses to the different shops around were clean and in solid conditions.

As the avenues experienced non-stop movement through-out the day. It was a painting of tranquility and happiness that spanned from one end of the district to the other end. A perfect mask hiding the sickness beneath its pristine surface. From the outside looking in travelers would never know that crime and corruption where main benefactors behind the city's prosperity. That for the right price you could get about any type of information you needed on current events effecting the local area. Bellamy and Draemond experienced this firsthand when they made a stop at a small newspaper stand on the corner of a street.

"Come one, come all and read all about it. [*Dangerous storm off the coast decimates trading barge. Sending entire cargo into the watery depths.*] [*Mysterious fever plagues local villages in the East.*] [*Escaped fugitives still on the loose. Authorities raise bounty for information on whereabouts or capture.*][*Discovery of ancient ruins may hold proof of a lost civilization from the Age of Heroes.*]"

Draemond walked up to the newspaper stand looking over the assortment of different newspapers. Some from the local area and others from different regions and nations as well. After browsing the different offering, he approached the newspaper vendor. The vendor was a Demi-Human of the of the Beastmen variety. She was a younger looking Cat-Beastmen with long braided Chestnut hair, tannish fur ears and tail. Silver-rimmed glasses rested on the brim of her nose. Reflecting the beauty of the orangish-red hue of her eyes, the same color of the setting sun.

"Welcome, sir. Where you able to find what you were looking for? I have a variety from regions fall and wide, so if there is something you seek, you've come to the right place." She replied with a caring smile.

"I wanted to know if you have any information on the Kor'Jarin Lighthouse and the area surrounding it?"

"Well, officially the city authorities have closed off access to the lighthouse for citizens and travelers alike. On account of poisonous natural fumes emanating from breaches in the ground and foundation."

"What about, unofficially?"

The newspaper stand vendor put out her hand towards Draemond. Signaling to him that if he wanted that kind of information, it would cost him. Draemond pulled out a few Silver Stags from his pouch and placed them in the vendor's hand. She counted the coins in her hands and leaned closer towards Draemond.

"The poisonous fumes were a cover story. To hide the existence of the Alchemic lab and the experiments conducted there from the public's eye. They want to keep it a secret about what's going on in that place. Also, it might be of interest to you that a High Inquisitor is in the city and the one running the Alchemic lab."

"Thank you. Your help was much appreciated."

Draemond moved away from the newspaper stand making his way back over to Bellamy. Who had been leaning against the side of a building. Watching the crowds of people move about the city streets. They left the area and continued through the city streets. Past the marketplace and outlining shops towards the hill where the lighthouse stood overlooking the city and the sea beyond.

The streets grew emptier the closer they got to the hill. The buildings and shops in the area were vacant or boarded up with signs posted on the windows. Warnings of poisonous fumes and dangerous hazards in the quarantine zone ahead. At the base of the hill on the street leading up to the lighthouse Bellamy and Draemond had come to the end of the road. A massive stone wall and gate blocked their way forward. Preventing any entry into the area from the city streets.

They walked up and down the length of the massive wall a few times from end to end. They examined it for any possible signs on how they would cross it. The wall ran along the majority length of the district before curving inward. Enclosing the hill with the surrounding area. One end of the wall went all the way intersecting at a junction point.

Connecting to one of the outer guard towers spaced along the city's outer wall. The other end of the wall ran all the way towards the steep cliffside edge of the hill. Where the district came to an end and the sea began. Given the layout of the area it was clear to them both. They would have to take their time and go over their options. Any sort of misstep would prove to be fatal.

"By the current look of things, we have three options presently open to us. One: is to access the area by going through the main gate. Two: access the area by going over the wall and through the guard tower. Three: we access the area by scaling the steep cliffside." Draemond mentioned methodically taking in their most viable options, before adding.

"Given the circumstances, we should scope out each of the options every day for the next two months. So we can see and learn any guard routines and occurrences."

Bellamy stood looking out towards the calm sea. Watching the boats coming and leaving the port from distant lands. Their excursion through the city had caused the time to slip by them. The rich blues of the morning skies turned into the red, orange, and purple hues of late afternoon. The gentle breeze flowing past his face and slightly unkempt hair that hand grown into a tangled mess on his journey. With Draemond's words sinking in. Reassuring him that coming to Kor'Jarin was the right choice, if they wanted to rescue their friends.

"Yes, each will prove to be difficult, it's a matter of picking the best one that will suit our purposes. For now, we will do as you suggested before we make the final decision."

"Sounds good to me. We should let the others know what we have found out and the plan moving forward."

CHAPTER 43
INARA NOVIK

After stepping out the door from the inn, Inara had caught up to Raine walking down the street. Instead of going directly to the lighthouse. Raine and Inara walked through the streets of the New Town District. Heading in the direction of city's records hall and library. They knew that it could provide them with more information about the lighthouse.

Possibly some blueprints on its construction and layout. The records hall and library were responsible of keeping detailed records. Documents. Any knowledge on all buildings found within the city or within the regions surrounding it. Such places where a valuable resource and treasure trove of knowledge about other topics as well. Making them key locations for those who knew how to use them.

Neither Raine nor Inara were the type of person who would frequent such establishments in their day to day lives. But knew their value when it came to gathering insight on an unfamiliar subject or needed a more concrete source. The records hall and library of Kor'Jarin was one of the older buildings within the New Town District. Constructed after the city's distinct boundaries were established. It was a three-storied pentagonal stone building that had a botanical garden in the central courtyard.

A statue at its center dedicated to the Founders of the city. The two of them admired the beauty of the multi-season flowers planted in the botanical garden. The intricate and detailed craftmanship that went into the carving of the statue of the city founders before making their way back inside the building. The main lobby and administrative offices were all located on the ground floor.

The second floor was the location of the library. Study rooms, and research rooms that were open to the local citizens and foreign travelers. On the third floor was the records hall and it was closed off to the public and non-governmental staff. Making access to it challenging without the proper credentials. There was only two ways to access the third-floor records hall.

One was on the first floor via a guarded private lift in the back of the administrative offices. Or the second floor in the library's enclosed restricted area. Where a staircase would take you to the third floor. So, Raine and Inara headed upstairs to the library on the second floor. To browse the books and get a closer look at the enclosed restricted area.

In the library they each grabbed a few books a piece. Then went and sat down at one of the open tables, with the closest view to the restricted area.

"It looks like your intuition paid off, Inara. The entrance to the records hall through the restricted area doesn't appear to be as guarded as the one on the main floor. Though, I'm certain we could have handled the guards without too much of a hassle."

"That may have been the case, but the idea here is to get in and out without anyone knowing that we were here. It goes without saying that what we are going to do isn't above board. The last thing we want is to get caught by the authorities."

Raine gave Inara a carefree smug smile as he opened one of the books he got from the shelves and flipped through its pages. Quickly skimming through its contents while keeping his attention on the conversation. Simultaneously looking for useful information about the city and surrounding region.

"I am aware of that. But are we certain that blueprints to the lighthouse are still going to be located within the records hall. Given the information that we got, they may have been moved or destroyed to keep out of outsider's hands like ourselves."

"That could very well be the case likely. Even so, it could still be of use to us to see what we may find. We won't ever know if we do nothing and walk away. Look over there..."

Inara pointed across the way over to a man in long clerical robes making his way to the enclosed restricted area. When the man reached the bared gate sealing off the area. He stopped in front of it and pulled out a small jewel embedded key. Placing it into a keyhole on the gate. As he turned the key the sealed gate glowed with glyphs that had previously been concealed. The bars separated opening the gate. The man took the key out of the keyhole and walked through the opening. Closing mere moments after he passed through the threshold.

"That's our ticket inside. When the cleric comes back from the restricted area, we get the key from his person. Using it to access the restricted area and the records hall beyond. So, for now we wait."

Raine and Inara searched book shelfs. Browsing through different books on an assortment of varied subjects as they waited for the cleric to return. Time seemed to past as minutes turned to hours and the sun made its way across the sky. Inara hadn't noticed at first, but sometime ago while they were waiting Raine had fallen asleep. His head in a giant leatherbound tome of ancient lore and lost civilizations.

When, at last as the sun was starting to set and the number of people in the library was dying down. the sealed gate opened, and the cleric came through. Inara nudged Raine waking him from his nap.

"I'm up. I'm up."

"It's time, the cleric is walking this way."

Inara stood up from the table carrying a giant stack of books. She clumsily walked in the same direction as if to not notice him. In that moment to avoid colliding into her, the cleric stepped out of the way down one of the aisles of bookshelves. Before he could even realize what was happening the cleric's eyes closed. As he was struck in the back of the neck with a quick swift subtle blow.

He fell back in Raine's arms. Raine laid the unconscious cleric on the ground. Then grabbed the small jewel embedded key from his robes. Then headed over to the sealed gate where Inara was waiting for him.

"Smooth work as always, I see."

"I aim to please. We should be in and out of there before he wakes up and realizes what happened."

Raine placed the key into the keyhole and turned the key. The sealed gate glowed with the concealed glyphs and the bars separated opening the gate. He removed the key and the two of them made their way into the restricted area. As they walked through the restricted area making their way towards the staircase leading up to the records hall. Inara noticed that all the tomes and books on the bookshelves were connected to them.

Bound by linked chains. Making it clear that none of the items were allowed to leave to vicinity of the shelves they were located on. Beyond the podiums spaced between each section of bookshelf. Or the long narrow tables in the middle of the aisles. The books and tomes located in the restricted area were of great value.

Forbidden knowledge that was deemed too dangerous for the public to handle. Making access to the materials limited.

As strong as the temptation was pulling at their curiosity to look at the pages within those books, Inara and Raine stayed focused on their mission to find the lighthouse blueprints. The records hall on the third floor was thought to be set up the same way as the library below. Except for the fact that rows upon rows of bookshelves were organized in such a way that the whole floor was one complex maze. Finding what they were looking for was going to be more difficult than they thought. They would have to find their way around.

Searching for the section that held the blueprints without getting caught by any patrolling guards. They made their way through the maze. Up, down and around the aisles past sections they previously passed. Starting to get a feel for the layout of the maze. When they finally came upon the section they were searching for. The shelves were staked high with multiple pull-out trays containing numerous parchments.

"What we are looking for should be in this section, somewhere amongst the shelves. You take one side and I'll take the other."

"Sounds good."

They took a different side of the aisle pulling out trays one by one as they shifted through the parchments. In the different trays Raine came across everything from fine art. Invention schematics, family histories and trees, to city planning blueprints. He couldn't seem to find the blueprints for the lighthouse though, as he continued his search. Inara seemed to be having the same troubles as Raine, as everything she came across was not what they needed.

On the last tray she pulled out, Inara came across something unexpected. Possibly more valuable than the blueprints they were looking for. She took the parchment from the tray and folded it up before placing it in her pouch.

"Hey Inara, come over here. I think I found what we are looking for."

Inara pushed in the tray and made her way over to Raine. He moved out of the way, and she looked over the pieces of parchment that he had pulled out. Examining the blueprint pages, she made out the floor plans and foundation make-up of the Kor'Jarin lighthouse. Along with the Alchemic lab located beneath it. She opened her pouch and pulled out some blank pieces of parchment.

Carefully laid them over the blueprints. With her other hand she reached down into another pouch. Pulling out a small vial with bioluminescent liquid. Which she sprinkled a couple of drops onto the blank pieces of parchment.

"What are you doing?'

"Watch and see. It's a clever little trick for retrieving information. For when you can't afford to take the original documents. My mistress taught me, a few years ago on a job."

As the drops seeped into the parchment it glowed with a faint light. As the light faded away the blueprints below begin materializing on the blank pieces of parchment. Exact copies of the blueprints had been created. Inara took the copies and folded them up to place back inside her pouch. She then pushed the tray back into place.

As the sound of footsteps and the reflection of light from a lantern were heading in their direction. Inara and Raine turned around and made their way back through the maze quietly. Being careful not to get caught by the patrolling guards. Finding their way back to the staircase was intense and a little unnerving at first. They had to back track or change their route a few times. They had come close to running into a patrolling guard that was too close for comfort.

"We need to get out of here. This game of cat and mouse with the guards does not suit me. I prefer a more direct and subtle approach in situations like this."

"I agree with you on that matter, but this time it wouldn't be in our best interest to do that. It shouldn't be much longer; the staircase should be around the next bend."

They knew this was not the place they could afford getting into a confrontation in. Any misstep and the alarm would sound. Sealing them in the records hall until the city guards came and arrested them. It didn't make it any easier on them to hold back. They continued onward down the aisles and around the bend reaching the staircase.

The sealed gate opened, as the two of them left the restricted area. Making their way back into the library general area that was now closed for the night. Raine placed the key back into the unconscious cleric's robes. As they passed by him heading to an open window at the edge of the hall. The hour was late, and the twin moons were shining bright in the night sky. Inara and Raine climbed out the window making their way back onto the empty streets below.

CHAPTER 44
BELLAMY LEONE

After Bellamy and Draemond returned to the inn, they grabbed a bite to eat and some ale to drink. While they waited for Inara and Raine to return. It was in the late hours of the night, when the few other guest staying at the inn had already turned in heading off to bed. When Inara and Raine stepped through the front door to see Bellamy and Draemond sitting by the fireplace. They made their way over to them and sat down.

A tired looked clearly expressed on their faces evidence of the long day the two had. Bellamy handed them a bowl of warm chowder and a tankard of ale, to feed their tired bodies. They sat around relaxing in the gentle warmth of the fire. As their friends ate their meal, before discussing the day's events.

Bellamy told them as they finished eating about how him and Draemond explored the area around the lighthouse. How they had found three possible ways to enter the area. He was clear that they would need to take some time watching the possible entrances. Seeing which would be the most viable for them. Afterwards, Inara told them about the records hall.

The blueprint copies they were able to retrieve of the lighthouse and alchemic lab below. She pulled them out of her pouch and showed them to Bellamy. He looked over each of the pieces of parchment. Searching for possible access points that they could exploit to ensure their mission was a success.

"These blueprints were an incredible find. What we need to help us in our plans for finding a way in and out of the lab. See this area right here on the blueprint, looks like it might be promising."

Bellamy pointed to an area on the blueprint which appeared to be some sort of ventilation tunnel that ran through the structure. With exit points at different locations throughout the facility. Taking note and emphasizing an exit point about halfway up the cliffside. One opening out into the sea below. From the scale of the blueprint the ventilation tunnel was about five feet high by five feet wide.

They wouldn't be able to walk through it but there should be enough space for them to crawl through. Well, Him and Raine at least, but Inara and Draemond would be another thing. Bellamy kept that in mind as he continued to look over the blueprints for other possible options.

"It looks to me that we will have to split up when we enter the lab, by taking two separate approaches and them exiting from one main spot."

"So, what do you have in mind, Bellamy?" Inara asked intrigued by his idea.

"Raine and I will scale the cliffside. Entering the lab through the ventilation tunnel located there. Unfortunately, it won't be big enough to accommodate you or Draemond. You two instead will climb to the top of the cliff. Entering the lab through an entrance located at the back of the lighthouse. Where we'll meet up and proceed on together. We don't know what might happen down there, so its best that we take it on as a group."

"Sounds like a solid plan. Well let's get to work and prepare everything we are going to need and in two months we hit it."

With their plan set in motion Bellamy and the other spent their days gathering supplies. Mending their equipment. Exploring the city, and training to prepare for the day of the mission. As the days went by the thought of his friends having to suffer in Nalran for longer than he had hoped, weighed on Bellamy's mind. There was nothing he could do in his present circumstances.

Only believe in his friend's strength and will to keep them safe. Until they could finally get to them. That thought kept Bellamy's motivation high on succeeding with the mission. Getting what he needed. So that he could make the reality of rescuing his friends come true.

At last, the time had come. The group gathered around the fireplace the night before their mission. Reveling as they prepared themselves for the morning ahead.

The sun was slowly rising on the horizon, appearing to emerge from the depths of the sea. The sound of crashing waves echoed in the early hours of the morning along the cliffside. The dark silhouettes of Bellamy and the others pressed against it as they made the ascent. They made their way up the cliff moving from one foothold to the next, following the path of the person in front of them. He was a little over halfway up the cliff, when Bellamy spotted the exit point of the ventilation tunnel.

Carved into the cliff a few more feet above where he was at. When he reached the opening, Bellamy signaled down to the others that he was heading in. He climbed inside the ventilation tunnel. Crawling forward on his hands and knees. The blueprints had been accurate on the spacing available inside the tunnel.

A few moments later, he heard Raine enter the tunnel behind him. Inara and Draemond continued their climb to the top of the cliff. The ventilation tunnel itself was a series of interconnected passages that ran in several directions that changed in elevation and size. Bellamy made sure that he memorized the route that they would have to take days before. Even though he knew where to go, getting through the ventilation tunnel was no easy task.

Maneuvering his body through some of the narrower passages involved slow uncomfortable progression. Bellamy could hear Raine behind him grumbling from time to time. He would move the wrong way and smack a part of his body into the tunnel walls.

"You okay back there? I thought you liked tight enclosed spaces."

"I'm not a feline and you know very well the kind I prefer. This my friend is not it."

"Well, you just have to put up with it for a little longer, we are almost to our exit point."

After crawling down a few more passages and making one final turn, the vent cover Bellamy was searching for was in his sights. Listening for signs of movement outside. He waited patiently until he was certain it was clear before pushing out the vent cover slowly. He placed the vent cover on the ground and crawled out of the ventilation tunnel. Into a long empty stone and timber hallway.

Alit with lanterns embedded along the walls carved into the cliff. Raine made his way out a few moments after Bellamy, stretching out his body in the wide-open space. The two of them headed down the hallway. Following its path through the underground complex.

They made their way down hallway after hallway. Heading in a Northeast direction passing through a few vast columned chambers with branching passages. Leading to areas where a storage room, holding cells, a dining hall, solider barracks, training rooms, and a couple of workshops were located. Bellamy was navigating them through the hallways that bypassed those locations. As to avoid encounters with any guards before they were able to meet up with the others.

After turning down another hallway, he had found what he was looking for. The main stairwell that would lead them up to the surface entrance behind the lighthouse. Given the time it took them to reach the stairwell, he was certain that Inara and Draemond had reached the top of the cliff. Waiting for them to open the surface entrance. At the top of the stairwell at the end of the raised platform landing stood the massive iron forged door leading out to the surface beyond its threshold.

On either side of the door in recessed access points on the walls, Bellamy and Raine grabbed the levers located within and pulled them together. The ground rumbled beneath their feet as the massive iron forged door began to rise out of the ground. Stopping about halfway up. Providing enough room for people to enter and exit without any issues. Bellamy called out with a birdcall to signal the others that it was safe to enter.

A few moments passed. Then Inara and Draemond walked through the entrance to join Bellamy and Raine. The massive iron forged door lowered and closed behind them. Sealing the surface entrance once more.

"I take it that there haven't been any problems on your end, Bellamy."

"So far everything has been going according to plan. We were able to make it here without running into or alerting any of the guards. Did you run into any complications on your climb up. Or with the guards patrolling the lighthouse, Inara?"

Inara walked over to Bellamy, wiping off dirt and dust that had covered her cloak.

"The climb up was fine, but there was a small group of guards that we had to quickly take care of. We were able to incapacitate them before any could raise the alarm. Honestly, it was a mere accident that we even ran into them in the first place. They had gotten off their shift later than usual and were heading out, when one had to relive themself. He wandered over to the cliffside. Draemond caught him off guard and knocked him out. I took care of the other two who had come to see what was taking their buddy so long. Needless to say, we acted accordingly given the unsanitary outcome that would have happened if we didn't."

"You were right in your judgement. There is no way I would've let something like that slide. Some people just don't learn, and it becomes our job to set them straight." Raine said agreeing.

"Now, that we are all here, lets proceed on and find the device we came for."

Following Bellamy's lead, the others followed him down the staircase. Back into the heart of the underground complex. Down the hallways and through various corridors the group made their way deeper into the alchemic lab. Clearing floor after floor with minimal encounters with any guards or research personnel. Except, for the occasional patrol of guards they were able to evade without notice.

The whole situation didn't sit right with Bellamy. [*There should be more guards patrolling given the secrecy of this lab. It doesn't make any sense; this has been too easy. There must be something else going on here.*]his thoughts raced through his mind.

Whatever the feeling was, Bellamy had in the back of his mind. He knew there was nothing to do but keep pressing forward, they couldn't afford to back down now. According to the blueprints for the layout of the alchemic lab, the device they were searching for would most likely be located on the sixth sublevel in the isolation vault. A location for artifacts of ancient or unknown origin. Studied and secured as potential dangers if deemed unstable.

Though larger than the previous sublevels. They noticed that after making their way to the third sublevel, there were fewer chambers on the remaining sublevels. After going through one last hallway down a steep spiral staircase they had arrived at the sixth sublevel. To find their way into the chamber known as the isolation vault.

The isolation vault was a circular chamber that had a sixty-foot diameter with forty-foot-high walls that arched into a dome ceiling. Artifacts of varying sizes and designs were stored in alcoves along the walls. Sealed behind translucent crystal prism cases. Allowing someone to see what was located inside but unable to touch it. In the center of the room four pillars surrounded an intricate alchemical mechanism with an assortment of tubes and pipes branching off it.

Connecting into the pillars like roots, radiating mana-energy flowing through them. At the heart of the mechanism enclosed in a translucent crystal globe was a smaller ancient artifact powering the mechanism. Bellamy and the others walked over to the mechanism. Looking it over for ways to detach the crystal globe at its heart.

CHAPTER 45

"It seems that what we came looking for is sealed within the crystal globe at the heart of this mechanism. The only thing left is to figure out how to take it out and not raise the alarm."

"That shouldn't be a problem, Raine. Caspian provided me with the information I would need to retrieve the artifact."

Bellamy pulled out the piece of parchment he had got from Caspian. Following the instructions written on it. He deactivated the mechanism by turning a few nobs. pulling three levers, and pressing the proper glyph tiles in the correct sequence. The hum of the mechanism slowly died down as the pressure from mana-energy depleted.

The locking points holding the crystal globe released. Allowing him to open the crystal globe and retrieve the ancient artifact inside. Outside of the crystal globe the artifact was as big as a human heart. Heavier yet more complex and elegant in design. In all his travels Bellamy had never seen anything like it before, and by the looks of the others, they hadn't either. He opened his pack and carefully placed the artifact in a secured pouch meant to safeguard precious items.

"Seems like the pirate knew what he was talking about. You might want to ask him about that and how he even knew about the artifact in the first place." Inara replied with a hint of skepticism in her voice.

"It's time we go. We've been here too long, and I don't know how much longer our luck will hold out." Draemond urged the others.

The group turned and made their way out of the isolation vault. Heading back up towards the higher sublevels. When they made it back up to the fourth sublevel, the previous passages they had used to make their way down were unavailable to them. The hallways had been sealed off forcing them to travel down only certain hallways and passages. Unable to head down the sealed ways they followed the only path open to them.

Until they reached the testing ground arena at the center of the fourth sublevel. It was a massive open space octagonal arena. There was three other entrances besides the one Bellamy and the others had come through. The moment everyone crossed the threshold of the arena entrance, all the entrance's sealing gates closed trapping them inside.

"So, you've come at last." A disembodied voice sounded all around them.

Bellamy and the others drew their weapons while taking up defensive stances by one another. Preparing themselves to respond to any threat that was about to come their way. On the other side of the arena one of the sealed gates opened. A lone figured flanked by four Clockwork-Golems entered the arena. They made their way towards the center of the arena.

They stopped awaiting to receive orders from the lone figure. Who Bellamy and the others were now able to see more clearly. They saw a woman in black robes, wearing a metal and leather strapped cuirass. A crimson red sash around her waist, and a

Harlequin mask on her face. Her ice-cold grey eyes stared deep daggers at the intruders from beneath her mask.

"I am no more than a devout follower of the one true god, Nimh. I protect the faithful, seek out and punish those who violate or doubt his will, and all forms of heresy. I am *The Ten of Spades*, High Inquisitor Eris of the Nimh Theocracy's Inquisition. You got here a bit quicker than expected. But still within the margin of error I calculated for this prediction."

"What is going on here. How!... How, are you here? You shouldn't be here; we were positive that you would be away from the city today." Bellamy responded momentarily puzzled by the turn of events.

Eris raised her hand. In that instant her Clockwork-Golems spread out to surround Bellamy and the others on all sides. Blocking any means of escape for them. The Clockwork-Golems moved with a precision and accuracy not normally seen in artificial constructs of semi-humanoid design. Their movement was that of what one would expect of Daemons of similar stature. Not of a construct that was artificially created. They would have to be careful dealing with these opponents. It was evident to them that they were no ordinary constructs.

"That was a miscalculation on your part. Oh, well it can't be helped, you had no chance of outsmarting my predictions. Now, if you would be so kind as to hand over the artifact you stole, I might be willing to let one of you go. Refuse and none of you will leave this place alive." Eris commanded in a cold unemotional venomous voice.

"I wouldn't be so quick to underestimate me or my companions here, that mistake may very well cost you. We aren't looking for a fight, but we will not back down when challenged either. As for the artifact, I'm afraid I cannot give it to you, we need it for our friends' sake."

"So, call off these toys of yours and move aside, little girl." Raine replied in jest. He noticed that the High Inquisitor was short in stature and appeared rather young.

"You should learn to keep your dog on a leash..." she affixed her glaze onto Raine. "Watch your tongue or I will show you what this little girl is capable of. This has gone on long enough, if you will not surrender then you leave me with no choice."

Eris raised her hand into the air signaling the Clockwork-Golems to advance towards Bellamy and the others. They sprang into action taking on each member of the group in single combat. Spreading the battle out across the wide-open arena. Eris stayed in her spot as she observed the battles. Calculating the possible outcomes in her head. All the while prepared to strike. Should any of the foolish intruders get the idea, that attacking her would immobilize the constructs and bring them a better chance of winning. Though sound in thought, achieving such a plan would be near impossible in execution.

Inara was the first to engage with her opponent. The Clockwork-Golem came charging at her with quick long reaching slashing strikes. Keeping her guard up, she blocked each powerful strike as each impact nudged her back. The two of them appeared to be evenly matched at first as they exchanged blow for blow. Blocking and countering in turn.

Inara watched her opponent's movement closely. Gaging its reach and timing the intervals between attacks. As she waited for her opening to strike. That's when she spotted it, the subtle shift in her opponent's stance. Indicating that it was getting ready to strike at her again.

In that instant, Inara sprinted driving the shaft of her Warhammer into the ground. She vaulted forward in a high arching motion. Once in midair she grabbed the Warhammer swinging it forward in an overhead cartwheel. Slamming it down with incredible force and speed into the Clockwork-Golem. The impact shattered the construct into many pieces as it cratered into the arena floor.

Inara was content knowing that the journey and her training was paying off. She could feel that her skills had improved a great deal from where they were at. She looked over at the others engaged in battle watching and ready to assist if they needed her help.

Raine and Draemond were doing fine against their opponents. They were getting closer to finishing them off. Even as the Clockwork-Golems were capable of quick and powerful movements. They were not able to match Raine's versatile agility. Draemond's overwhelming primal strength.

Assured of their victory, the two of them finished off their opponent's moments apart. The arena echoed from the impact of the two Clockwork-Golems shattering into pieces. At the center of the arena Eris observed, with no signs of reacting to the destruction of her constructs. Bellamy looked out of the corner of his eyes and saw that his friends had won their battles, and now he had to finish up his.

"My friends have already taken out their opponents. So, it looks like it's time for me to put an end to our little dance. Let's finish this, after you."

The Clockwork-Golem charged at Bellamy. Striking with more fierce and powerful blows, than it had earlier in their fight. When it came to strength and combat experience, Bellamy knew that his friends were in a whole different league compared to his current abilities. That didn't stop him from training hard. Finding creative solutions to narrow the gap in his abilities when it came to dealing with challenging opponents. Positioning himself off-center from the Clockwork-Golem's right shoulder, Bellamy lounged forward.

As if to strike with an overhead slash. The golem moved to counter his slash. In that instant, when its arm was raising upwards, Bellamy pivoted on his left foot switching up the motion of his slash.

Striking the golem's exposed joints. Severing the connection to each of its limbs in one sweeping successive motion. It faltered to a stop before crashing down into the arena floor. Bellamy delivered the final blow through the Clockwork-Golem's back straight into its power core. He then headed towards the center of the arena with the others to regroup.

Preparing for their next opponent. Though her creations laid destroyed in pieces. Scattered throughout the arena, Eris stayed as motionless as a statue. Observing the scenes around her not making any move to intervene. The high inquisitor was still a mystery to them.

They still couldn't be sure of the extent of her powers. As they approached her while keeping a good amount of space between them.

CHAPTER 46

"Your toys have all been destroyed and as you can see, they weren't up to the task of stopping us. Do you still believe this will end with us losing to you?" Raine said with a mocking bravado.

"Wrong. That statement of yours was incorrect. My golems were never meant to stop you, they were meant to gage your abilities. For whether you defeated them or were defeated by them, I would understand what you are capable of. Who knows, you lot might be able to put up a decent fight against me, we will find out. You should have surrendered to me when you had the chance."

"Do not underestimate us. You are going to wish you had let us go in the beginning of all this. We won't lose to you, Eris!" Bellamy responded adamantly.

Eris shifted her body into a fighting stance. Raising her arms slightly as four chain whips moving like serpents emerged from her sleeves to rest at the base of her feet. Bellamy and the others held their position, waiting for Eris to make her move and strike. The air around her was electrified. The pulsating mana coursing through each of her four chain whips.

Ready to act on their master's will. In that moment, Eris shifted her hands and chain whips surged like a crashing tidal wave. Moving with both random movements and incredible force.

The chain whips struck multiple points of impact in a wide area of effect. Surrounding Bellamy and the others. Conducted under the rhythmic movement of Eris's hands.

The wide area made it difficult to attack from a close range without getting knocked back by one of the chains. Nimble and light in weight by their movement, the chain whips were unquestionably denser. As the group experienced firsthand when they parried back an attack. Eris's offensive and defensive capabilities where machine-like. She executed the transitions with minimal effort making no minimal careless motions. Each moved they attempted to make had to be precise. Or it would quickly be countered and redirected towards them. They found themselves in a dangerous game, as the battle shifted between both sides.

"We have to do something about those chain whips of hers, if we are going to have a chance of landing an attack on her."

"There must be some way of damaging those chains. If physical attacks aren't working, then we need to use more powerful *Arts* attacks on them." Inara suggested.

They gathered their thoughts, as a series of strikes came down around them. Bellamy and the others evaded strikes. Blocked others as they tried to figure out a plan to bring the battle in their favor.

"What about your spell, Bellamy? It might work to take out the chains and give us the upper hand over her."

"I haven't used my power on moving objects in combat yet, so I can't be certain. It's going to be a gamble, but if you guys can buy me the time, I'm willing to try."

"Alright. Then wait for my signal and give it everything you got, because there won't be another shot if this doesn't work. May your aim be true."

Inara and the others moved away from Bellamy and spread-out surrounding Eris on all sides. They charged her one by one in a continuous alternating attack. Keeping her attention locked solely on them. Inara swung her Warhammer in a wide sweeping circular motion. Drawing in dust and debris from the arena floor creating a dusty haze smokescreen momentarily obscuring Eris's view. Bellamy spring into action upon seeing Inara's signal and began his spell invocation.

["*In the light of the Cardinal Stars I pray With the North star to seek your guidance. That with the East Star I may gain your knowledge. That with the West Star I gain your forgiveness. So, with the South star you pass judgment, upon my enemies. In your name I offer you my essence as proof of my devotion and love for your blessing.*"]

The mana concentrated into four luminous orbs like miniature stars of swirling energy. Caught in a gravitational orbit around the center of Bellamy's opened palms. His continued training had paid off as he was now able to conjure four projectiles. Which gave him better odds if his shots hit their marks. There was no time for doubt.

He would only get one shot at this spell and had to act quickly while he still had to brief element of surprise. Picturing the chain whips in his mind while holding the images firm, Bellamy acted. Firing off his magic missile multi-shot. The glowing orbs zoomed out of the palm of his hand. Seeking out the snake-like chain whips moving rapidly about striking towards his friends.

SWOOSSSHH.

VMMMM... SWISSSHHHH...

BOMPH...BOOMPHHH......BOOMMPHHH...BOOOMPHHH...

The semi-simultaneous impacts of the spell sent out a powerful concussive wave throughout the arena. Knocking everyone back from the momentary explosions. The landscape of the arena had changed. The ground beneath their feet fractured along its foundation. Columns crashed to the ground crumbling. As the smoke started to clear, Bellamy and the others stood back up on their feet catching their breath. Getting a better look at his companions, Bellamy could see that the prolonged battle had taken a toll on them. Exhaustion and various injuries were present on them. Though nothing looked to be life-threatening or critical.

"Nice shot, Bellamy."

"That was close. I'm glad it worked out, but we can't let our guard down. I don't think that alone will be enough to stop her."

Pieces of the arena floor hurtled through the air flying towards Bellamy and the others. Forcing them to jump out of their path. From the shadows of the flying debris, Eris emerged her robes torn. Cuts and bruises over her body as droplets of blood fell from her. The harlequin mask covering her face was cracked revealing a twisted smile beneath.

Her precious chain whips laid on the ground shattered and broken. It was as if she had become unshackled. She moved at inhuman speeds striking at them with unrelenting strikes. Her calm cold demeanor nowhere to be seen, she was a feral beast hunting its prey. They countered and blocked her onslaught the best they could manage. Barely holding back her attacks.

"Clever trick boy, but foolish in your target. Now, that there is nothing to restrain my power, its time I brought an end to this little game of ours."

Eris jumped back away from the group. Chanting an invocation below her breath that Bellamy couldn't make out. A sudden chill fell on the arena. An ominous fog raised from the ground. Freezing everything it touched as it rushed over the arena in a thunderous wave.

They tried to dodge its area of effect. Bellamy watched as his friends were sealed in an icy prison as the cold crept up their bodies. They fought back with everything they had; the icy embrace overpowered their efforts. Frozen statues were all that remained in place of the people he had called his friends. Sealed away in an icy prison stuck in a state of neither living nor dead, a perpetual purgatory of stillness.

Bellamy had to figure out something quick as he was running out of time. The ominous fog had reached him and was creeping up his body. He could feel every inch of his body starting to freeze solid. With no other option left to him, Bellamy using the last bit of movement he could muster had reached into his pouch. Placing his hand on the Chrono Trigger. He uttered a single word, as his body succumbed to the icy embrace.